GROWING PAINS

Sabatino stumbled back, nearly knocking Finn down. A bright burst of energy seared Finn's eyes, tugged at his flesh, tore at his bones. Sabatino cried out, but Finn couldn't hear. The Great Horror shrieked, thundered and roared, clattered and howled, twisted and tangled in tortured convolutions, as if it might rip itself apart. . . .

. . . and, once more Finn was frightfully aware of the foul, obscure distortions, the sluggish bits of darkness that wound their fearsome way through the vile crusted entrails of Calabus' hellish machine. Even this close, he could not tell what those shapeless forms might be. And, he was more than thankful he could not.

He and Julia had guessed that Calabus' strange device was, indeed, prodding, pushing, thrusting itself blindly through the Nucci mansion as it grew.

And where might it go after that, he wondered. What might it want to do . . . ?

❧ The ❧
Prophecy
Machine

Neal Barrett Jr.

BANTAM BOOKS
NEW YORK TORONTO LONDON SYDNEY AUCKLAND

THE PROPHECY MACHINE
A Bantam Spectra Book / December 2000

ISBN 0-553-58195-3

Published simultaneously in the United States and Canada

This book is for
William Browning Spencer,
An Absolutely Awesome Writer,
My Very Dear Friend,
and Comrade in Arms against
The Wretched Foes. . . .

∽ The ∽
Prophecy
Machine

One . . .

Master Finn filled his lungs with the clean salt air, with the heady ocean breeze. The *Madeline Rose* raced atop a gentle swell, then plunged once more into the briny deep.

"Great Socks and Shoes," Finn said aloud, dizzy with the sweet intoxication of the sea, "Why, a man could bottle this wondrous stuff and sell it in every foul alley, every dank and smoky town. There's a fortune to be had in pure, uncontaminated air!"

"What's that now, lad? Were you speakin' to me, Master Finn?"

Finn looked up to find Captain Magreet in his path, boots spread wide, poised upon the deck with perfect ease. The ship might roll, the ship might sway, might turn upon its back for a while. Nothing, Finn was sure, would trouble good Captain Magreet.

"Just muttering, sir," Finn said, "taking in the air. And a lovely fine day it is, too."

"Might be, might not," the captain said. "Might be heading for a squall."

Finn raised a brow at that. "A—squall, sir? We're headed for a squall?"

"Of course not, a day like this? Not a chance of that at all."

"That's good to hear."

"Never been to sea before. I'll bet I'm safe in sayin' that."

"No, sir. My very first time."

"Aye, then you've never heard the wind shrieking in the shrouds, never seen a fifty-foot wave comin' at you in the night."

"My heavens, no."

"Neither have I. Hope to hell I never do."

The captain, lost in some frightful image of his own, gripped the rail and stared out to sea.

Finn, clad in ordinary clothing—putty-colored trousers, gray flaxen shirt, broad belt and ankle boots—felt much like a common sparrow next to the dapper Magreet. The captain was a colorful sight indeed, dressed in the customary garb of an officer at sea—ruffled crimson shirt, harlequin knickers and a fancy plumed hat.

Finn, without meaning to criticize, felt that this radiant attire was somewhat out of sorts on a short stub of a man like Magreet, a globular fellow with stumpy legs and scarcely any neck at all. Tanned, parched, seared by the weather and the years, his skin was dark and furrowed as a nut. His nose was a great inflammation, a monstrous knob that looked as if tiny red spiders had spun their webs there. Finn guessed, with little hesitation, that the captain was wed to Madame Rum, the curse of many a man who went to sea.

"And how fares your, uh—whatever it be, Master Finn," said Magreet, studying the deck for a moment, then facing Finn again. "I hope you don't take offense, sir. I don't mean to pry."

"Certainly not, none taken," Finn said. He was, in fact,

greatly surprised Magreet had kept his silence this long, as they'd been asail for half a week.

"What I thought is," the captain said, rubbing a sleeve across his nose, "I thought, with the salt air and all, the ah—object on your shoulder there, that's the thing I mean, might be prone to oxidation, to rust as it's commonly called."

"Indeed."

"I've been some curious, as others have as well, just what it might be. Now don't feel we're trying to intrude . . ."

"Of course not, sir." Finn smiled, taking some pleasure in finding the captain ill at ease. "What you speak of is a lizard. I design and craft lizards of every sort. Lizards for work, lizards for play. Lizards for the rich and poor alike. I make them of metal, base and precious too, sometimes with finery, sometimes with gems. The one you see here is made of copper, tin, iron, and bits of brass."

The captain closed one squinty eye, looked at Finn's shoulder, then looked away again.

"And these—lizards, what exactly do they *do*, Master Finn?"

"Oh, a great number of things," Finn said. "When we have some time I'd be pleased to explain. It might be I can make one for you."

"Yes, well . . ."

"This one, now, this one is somewhat unique. This one is strictly ornamental. It really does nothing at all."

"Ornamental, you say." Judging by the captain's expression, he had little use for ornamental things of any sort. "Well then, I wish you a good day, sir. Enjoy your voyage aboard the *Madeline Rose*."

"I surely will," Finn said.

The captain turned, then stopped, as if a thought had flicked like a moth about his head.

"Your servant," he said, "I hope she's some better today."

"Sadly no, sir. I fear she finds little comfort in the sea."

"I'm sorry this is so. Please tell her again, I view that ah—incident with regret. Assure her she is perfectly safe aboard my ship. No harm of any sort will come to her here."

"I've had no success in quieting her fears thus far, Captain. I am most uncertain that I will."

"Nonsense," said the captain, waving Finn's words away. "I'm sure she'll come around. And when she gets on her feet, you are welcome to bring her to table. You will find us more casual than dry-leggers, lad. Close quarters, you know."

"I've no complaints, sir."

"Quite—pleasant in appearance, as I recall," Magreet added. "Most attractive for her kind."

The captain seemed to pause, a vessel poised to brave the sea. Finn, however, showed no sign of answering at all.

"So. Indeed, sir . . ." the captain said finally. "A pleasure to see you, Master Finn."

He turned, then and walked aft, ducked in a passageway and disappeared below.

Finn felt the heat rise to his face. He had not missed the spark, the sooty little thought, the foul, damp anticipation that danced for an instant in the captain's tiny eyes.

He took a deep breath and shook the seeds of anger away. Anger, even displeasure, were not emotions he dared display. Not here, or anywhere, not in a world where bigotry still held sway. One might wink, as the captain implied, at what went on between a man and a maid of lesser kind. Still, he did not speak about it to a stranger, or scarcely even to a friend . . .

"Ornament, am I? Doesn't do anything at all?" said a

voice like a croak, like a rattle, like a saw cutting tin. "A fine thing that is, Finn."

"Shut up," Finn said. "There are ears everywhere. You can't *talk*, Julia. Try and remember that."

"Oh, I'll remember, all right. Next time you need Julia Jessica Slagg to save your neck from some terrible assault, to drag your bony flanks out of the fire, to—"

With nary a glance, Finn tapped a copper scale at the tip of a brassy tail. Julia gave a hiss and a *sckruk!* and went silent at once.

"There are times," Finn sighed to himself, "when a man takes pride in his work, when he knows he is master of his craft. Then there are times when he wonders why he didn't choose an ordinary trade, like magic or the law, some dreary task that takes scarcely any skill at all . . ."

Two . . .

THE *MADELINE ROSE* RACED ACROSS A TRANQUIL
sea with a song in her rigging, the wester-wind full behind
her sails. The morning sky was bright, the sea as green as a
wicked maiden's eyes.

The particular maid that came to mind brought a smile
to the face of Master Finn, a smile so full of pleasure past of
a lady he'd not forget, that Finn turned at once from the rail
to be sure no other was about.

With great relief, he thanked whatever gods held sway
upon the sea that Letitia Louise was down below and out of
sight. Granted, she was sick, weary, greatly out of sorts, and
most likely cursing the day she gave her love to Master
Lizard-Maker Finn. Still, all in all, bless her, she was there,
not *here*. . . .

If fair Letitia had seen that smile, he knew he would be
in deeper trouble than he was. Letitia had an uncanny talent for guessing what—or who—might be in his head. It
was no sort of magic, nor any kind of spell—every Newlie
born, every number of the Nine, carried both the burdens
and the gifts of the animals they'd been.

For Letitia's folk, it was caution, quickness, a shifting of the eyes, habits born of a bone-cold fear of the creatures who'd preyed upon her kind, stalked them, tracked them, hunted them down, ages before they'd both taken on a higher form. That fear was with Letitia's people still, for in many ways, their ancient foes had scarcely changed from what they'd been.

Now, standing on the foredeck of the *Madeline Rose* watching the beauty of the foam-flecked sea, Finn was shaken once again by utter disbelief, by the cruelty of the joke that Fate had seen to cast their way.

"How, in all creation," he said aloud, "could things go so awry? How could I have possibly gotten poor Letitia into *this*?"

It was difficult to stay on deck at all; only Letitia's tears and the heat down below had driven him up into the day. Once there, he found it near impossible to peer into the vessel's very peak, through the maze and the tangle of the headsails and halyards, the beckets and the blocks, the mainsails, foresails and who knows what. Still, as if this action might purge him, as if he might atone, he made himself lift his eyes again.

And there, in the dizzy heights above, leaping from the shrouds, scrambling up the masts, was the very source of Letitia's nightmares—screeching, howling, loathsome creatures with pointy tufted ears, flat pink noses and pumpkin-seed eyes: striped, spotted, ginger, black and white. They all wore mulberry, plum, or lilac pantaloons, and little else at all.

Here then, the crew of the *Madeline Rose*, likely a hundred of the dreaded Yowlie folk, maybe more than that. And somehow, with no great effort, Finn had managed to pay a small fortune to set Letitia down in their midst.

He could tell himself there was nothing else for it, that it wasn't his fault. They had boarded in the night, gone to their cabin and awakened with the land far out of sight. How was *he* to know these agile, evil-eyed devils were prized the world over for their prowess in those shaky heights above the sea?

"What did I know?" he said aloud. "I was born and raised a landsman, and I ply a landsman's trade. What am I supposed to know about anything that floats?"

He had learned a great deal that very first morning when Letitia's screams brought him quickly out of sleep. There, in a porthole, caught in the early dawn light, was a flat-nosed creature with grinning opal eyes. Her screams had brought another, then another after that, until there were half a dozen horrid faces pressed against the glass. Only the appearance of the captain himself had finally chased the brutes away. All this was but a single day gone, but it seemed an eternity to Finn . . .

"I always say," said a voice as soothing as hail on a roof of rusty tin, "I always say there's trouble enough come tomorrow without all this moaning about the past. One takes what comes, one shakes away sorrow and trods on ahead. One—"

"By damn," Finn said, "I turned you off, now you're blathering again."

"Don't build a bleeding wonder if you don't expect her to act like one," Julia said. "I'm more than you imagined, less than what I'll be."

"That makes no sense at all. Are you aware of that? You're a braggart's what you are, a pompous, puffed-up bag of tin. I can't imagine how you turned out like you did. I must have put something in backwards somewhere."

"There's no use blaming yourself for this grievous turn of events. It *is* your fault, of course, but there's little you can do about that. Wisdom comes easily to the man who's waiting for the axeman's blade to fall. For the first time in his life, he knows exactly where he's going next."

"Am I mistaken? I don't think I asked your opinion. I don't think I asked you anything at all."

"As a matter of fact, I don't suppose you did. Still—"

"Julia, another sound, any sound at all, and I swear you go into the sea. Where, as the good captain put it, you'll learn what rust is all about."

"Finn—"

"I warned you, I vow I won't again."

"Quiet," Julia hissed softly in his ear, "now it's you that's rambling, Finn!"

Julia saw them first over Finn's shoulder, coming from the maindeck to the bow. An instant later Finn heard them too, turning hastily as Julia became ornamental once again.

Finn had glimpsed the pair before, a pinch-nosed lawyer and his unlovely spouse, each the very image of the other— gaunt, spare, stiff as winter reeds, each wrapped tight in heavy robes, as if the fair sun might burn their pale visages away.

"A good morning to you," Finn said, though neither deigned to look his way. Instead, they paused well away from the rail and muttered darkly to each other, careful not to look at the blue and churning sea.

"That woman's face would curdle lead," Julia croaked in Finn's ear, "and *he's* no great prize himself . . ."

"Quiet," Finn said, "I don't believe I asked."

The man looked back just then as if he might have heard the two. His frown, though, was not for the lizard or Finn.

"*You.* Stop dawdling around back there," he shouted, "Get your useless carcass up here, Gyrd!"

With a whimper and a whine, the Newlie lad appeared, stumbling along the larboard deck balancing a silver tray of goblets, oat-bread, goat-bread, two-pepper cheese, and a dark red beaker of ale.

This, in the right hand, flailing for a hold with the left. The lawyer scowled, the woman shook her bony chin. The Newlie slipped, caught himself again. Far overhead, a gaggle of crewmen screeched and laughed aloud.

Startled, beset on every side, Gyrd's pointy nose twitched, his ears perked up and his red eyes sparked with sudden fear.

"By damn, watch what you're doing," the counselor warned, "I'll thrash you good and proper if you drop that, boy!"

Like all of his kind, Gyrd was a lean and graceful creature on the land, yet plainly uncertain out to sea. Just as those harsh words rent the air, the ship plunged her oaken bow into the deep, leaped up again, burying the foc'sle in a veil of foamy white.

Finn grabbed a rail and held his breath. Ahead and to his left, the Newlie took one good step and then the next, fought the wall of water, coughed, spat out the sea, and never gave way.

"Good lad," Finn shouted aloud, "You've done it, boy!"

Gyrd turned to face him, started to grin—

—and that was the moment a burly, pock-faced, mean-eyed man with a shock of red hair lurched out of nowhere, bursting up from a passageway with no sort of warning at all.

Gyrd cried out as the man struck him soundly, lifting him off his feet, sending him sprawling, nearly sweeping him into the sea. His legs hit the railing, bringing him to his knees. Tray, tidbits, goblets and bottle went whirling into the deep.

The lad shook himself, tried to stand, then fell back again.

"Onions and Leeks!" Finn swore, "Stay down, don't move, you've likely broken something, boy!"

Finn raced quickly across the deck. The boy gave a plaintive little bark, stared at Finn and thrashed about. The bow dipped again, hurling tons of water from the sea. Finn choked, wiped his eyes, opened them again. The big brute stood there blocking his way.

"Watch yourself, sir," Finn began, "You've no right to just—*whuuf*!"

The man didn't bother to look. His palm struck Finn in the chest, knocking him roughly aside.

Finn swore, caught himself, and turned in time to see the fellow clutch the boy's jacket in his fist and jerk him off his feet. He shook the poor lad like a rag, then slapped him hard across the face.

The boy howled in pain. His head snapped back, his feet kicking feebly in the air.

"Stinking beast!" The man held the lad close to his face. "I'll teach you to lay hands on your betters. By *damn*, the day's coming for your kind!"

He took a step toward the railing, raised the Newlie high, held him there screaming, thrashing above his head.

Finn knew, saw how it would happen, saw it as clearly as if it were happening then. He moved in a blur, not even looking at the man, his eyes locked only on the boy. He leaped, grabbed the Newlie's skinny legs and hung on. The man stumbled back and hit the deck hard. He yelled at Finn, but Finn couldn't stop. He walked right over the brute, flailing for balance, much like moving on slippery stones across a creek—stepping on the groin, then the belly, then the head.

Folding the lad between his shoulder and his chest, he ran across the foc's'le past the big foremast to the maindeck below.

"Stay here," he said, setting the lad down, "Right here. Don't move. No, that's wrong. *Don't* stay here—go. Go anywhere. Hide."

"S—sir—"

Finn didn't have to look. He heard the heavy boots, heard the deep and throaty roar. He turned, then saw the man coming, decided he couldn't be *that* big, nobody could . . .

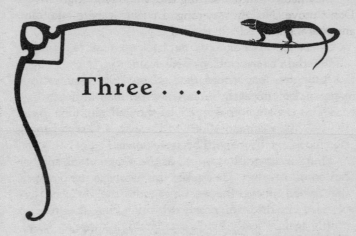

Three . . .

HE GLANCED ABOUT THE DECK, SEARCHING FOR A weapon, anything at all. Thought, for a second, that he might use Julia, swing her like a club, knew she wouldn't care for that. Besides, he noted, Julia wasn't there. Somewhere in the melee, Julia had disappeared. Fallen, jumped, leapt down a hole. Whatever, she was nowhere in sight. There was no one there but Finn himself, Finn and the Newlie, a wailing, barking, quivering lad behind him, and the ugly, flame-headed lout with murder in his eyes.

"Look, there is simply no reason to behave like this," Finn said, backing off a step, then backing off again. "I'm sure you were—distraught; simply out of sorts back there. I'm certain you meant no harm to the lad. If you'd just apologize now, I'm sure we can—*Pickles and Pots, man, don't do that!*"

The short silver blade flicked out of the man's long sleeves, sang a nasty song as it whipped in a swift and killing arc, clipping a brass button from Finn's favorite shirt and sending it rattling 'cross the deck.

Finn sucked in a breath. Before he could get his wits together, the fellow was at him again, leaping, slashing, cutting wicked circles in the air.

There was nothing to do but back up, feint to the right, shift to the left. Back off, do it all again.

And how long could *that* go on? One man with a weapon, frothing at the mouth, another man without.

"This is a stupid pastime," he shouted, shuffling to the right as the madman sliced to the left. "This is simply ridiculous, totally inane. This is—*Huuuuk!*"

Finn's heart nearly stopped as the weapon took another button off his shirt. He backed up, nearly to the bowsprit that arched out over the sea. Once more, the *Madeline Rose* plunged into the foam, nearly drowning Finn, then rose up swiftly again. Clearly Finn's assailant didn't care for water. He growled in anger, tried to slap the stuff away.

Finn took a moment to catch his breath.

Maybe this lout will break for lunch, he muttered to himself, *and while he's filling his belly, I'll run down and get my blade, see how the bugger likes that . . .*

"*Rawwwk!*" the bully yelled, or words to that effect.

Spilling pools of water, water splashing out his boots, out his pockets, out his nose, he sprang at Finn, forcing him back against the rail. Finn tried to leap aside, but the man was quick for his size. Twice, the blade slashed across his chest, venting his shirt and nearly kissing his skin.

Finn stepped away, hard against the rail with nowhere to go except the churning sea below. He felt the rough touch of the tangled lines at his back. His foe slashed out again. Finn sucked in his belly, grabbed the rail with both hands, and kicked the brute soundly in the head.

The man howled and staggered back. Finn grabbed a line and pulled himself up into the shrouds. Red Hair was on him in a second, climbing up behind, the knife clutched in his teeth.

"Come on, you overgrown lout," Finn shouted, "get at it or take a nap!"

Bushes and Trees, he said to himself, now why did I have to say that?

He risked a look down, and almost lost his hold. The deck already seemed a mile or so below. The ship yawed to port, jerked him backwards, then shoved him to starboard again, the bully still right on his heels.

Worse yet, the crewmen were all around him now, yowling and howling, hissing and leaping about, sometimes swinging so close he could smell their vile and fishy breath.

"No more of this nonsense," Finn said aloud, "I'm damned if I haven't had enough!"

He didn't take time to weigh his odds. He jumped, caught a line and pulled himself aft, hand over hand, to the thick mainmast. There, several lines ran straight down to the deck. The big man cursed him, but he didn't look back. He closed his eyes until his boots touched wood again. The trip nearly burned his hand raw, but he was down, and—

—so was the double-ugly lout. Finn could scarcely believe his eyes. The monster had taken the longer way down, climbing back the way he'd come. Still, he hit the deck running and raced after Finn.

"Tomatoes and Toads," Finn groaned. He took one look at the fellow, then turned and sprinted aft. Almost at once, a figure blurred to his right, a figure with a great plumed hat atop his head.

Finn stopped and turned back. His foe was sinking to his knees. His mouth dropped open and his hands hung loose along his sides. Captain Magreet, in glorious regalia, stood over the man with a wooden belaying pin gripped in his hand.

"A nasty customer," Magreet said, looking up at Finn. "I hate like the devil to sap a payin' passenger, but this isn't the first time, I'll tell you that."

Finn kept a cautious distance from the fellow on the deck. He was still on his knees, eyes rolled back in his head.

"I'd say he's lost his senses. Either that, or someone's got him in a spell."

"No magic to it," Magreet said, leaning over to spit into the sea. "This fellow's plain mean. He's one of the Nucci clan, they're all a nasty lot. You hurt, are you, lad? If you are, why, I've got a potion below that'll fix you up fine." He cast a wink at Finn. "Take the pain away, clean out your liver and everything besides."

"Thank you, Captain, I'm fine." He'd never heard of the Nuccis and didn't care to ask. "That boy, now, he could use some help."

"Ah, now I expect he'll be fine." He glanced at the boy who still sat cringing by the mast. "Those Newlie folk are tougher than you think. I guess that's likely enough, seeing what they were before . . ."

The captain paused and grinned at Finn. "Now why am I telling you for, sir? You'd know better than me, seeing as you got one yourself."

Finn was seething inside, but he'd learned to keep his feelings off his face.

"If you'd seen what happened, sir, you wouldn't dismiss it so lightly. This—this lunatic here committed wanton assault on the lad. Tried to kill him, quite frankly."

Magreet frowned. "Now that's strong talk you're layin' on me, Master Finn."

"I was here, Captain. He damn near killed *me*." Finn took a breath. "Look at him, sir. Tell me he's *fine*."

Magreet cleared his throat. "Well, I suppose not entirely fine. Slightly beaten, possibly bruised you might say."

Finn ignored him, walking quickly to the lad.

"Can you stand up, boy? Do you feel as if a limb is broken, or some other vital part?"

All the boy could do was whimper. He shrank from

Finn's touch, moaning, and his slight form trembled from head to foot.

"I'll do what I can," Finn said, "and that's not a great deal. There is surely someone aboard acquainted with the physical arts . . ."

"You needn't bother," said a voice behind Finn. "We'll take care of its damage now."

It?

Finn stood. In all the trouble and strife, he'd completely forgotten the black-clad lawyer and his wife. Clearly, they had managed to vanish when the mayhem and bother began.

"If I may, I'd suggest you get some medical help for the lad. I'm sure there's some kind physician aboard. Just ask the captain to—"

"Gyrd, get up," the man shouted, "Get up or by damn you'll regret it!"

The man kicked out viciously at the boy, aiming at his head.

"Here, now." Finn stopped him with an open palm to the chest. The man staggered back, nearly going to the deck.

"You interfere with my goods, and I'll have the captain put you in irons!"

"He will, too," his wife put in.

"I shall interfere if it's the proper thing to do," Finn said, "and if I catch you abusing this lad again . . ."

"Gyrd is not a *lad*," the man said, glaring at Finn, pulling himself to his feet. "An IT is what it is, and nothing more than that. Now step aside, Master whoever you are, and I'll take my property below."

"Call him what you like. Just don't hurt him again. He has the same rights as you."

The counselor rolled his eyes at that. Still, he clearly saw something in Finn he didn't like. Turning away, he nodded at his wife, then walked off with his head in the air as if he'd just astonished the judge, the jury and everyone in court.

His wife squatted down and lifted the Newlie to his feet. The boy gasped, swayed and nearly fell, but the woman had a firm, bony grip on the boy's slender arm.

"You'll think twice afore you spill your Master's precious tray again," the woman said, in a voice like iron striking tin.

Dragging the whimpering lad away, she turned and stomped after her husband. First though, she stopped, drew a small blood-red stone from under her robes, kissed it twice, held it beneath her left eye, then pointed it at Finn.

At once, Finn felt a sharp prickling chill, as if the woman's amulet had burrowed its way into his heart.

It was not a big spell, but it hurt all the same. Finn took a breath to shake it off. Almost at once, the pain disappeared. As had the black-clad woman and her miserable charge, gone back below.

He felt a great sorrow for the boy. He wanted desperately to chuck the skinny bastard and his wife into the deep, but that wouldn't help, really wouldn't do at all.

"Master Finn . . ."

Finn turned to face Magreet. The burly oaf at the captain's feet was off his knees now. He leaned against the mainmast, rubbing the back of his head. He was still the same enormous lout who'd tried to make sausage out of Finn. Yet, Finn thought, something was not the same. He was still large and ugly, his hair was still red. Now, however, whatever demon drove him seemed to be at rest.

"I must officially warn you," the captain said, "that I will brook no more of this violence and poor attitude aboard my vessel. If you have any further quarrel with one another, you will cease hostile action until you get ashore."

Finn stared. "Does *he* know that? By damn, sir, it was he who tried to stick a blade in me, not the other way around."

"I have informed Mr. Nucci as well."

Nucci frowned at Finn. "I need to know your name, and your family history as well, sir—if indeed you did not spring from common folk. Honor demands that I meet you again and battle until one of us is dead."

Finn had to laugh. "Do I get a blade this time, or just you?"

"Whatever you wish." The bully waved him off. "I assure you, though, a weapon will do you little good against me."

"You think not?"

"Oh, I am certain of it, sir."

The man's ugly face split into a joyous grin. "I hope you will join me for supper tonight. I do not wish you to think ill of Sabatino Nucci, in spite of our little quarrel."

"Thank you for the invitation," Finn said. "But I don't believe I will."

Sabatino shrugged. "As you wish, then. Captain, if you ever strike me again, I shall consider it extremely annoying. Good day to you both."

Sabatino Nucci strolled away. Finn watched him until he was well out of sight.

"Feathers and Birds, what in bloody hell is the matter with him? Why, he would've fair *skinned* that lad if I hadn't come along. And he nearly skinned me."

"I told you," Magreet said. "He is a Nucci. The Nuccis are vicious, every one."

"But not all the time."

"No, not all the time. And the trouble with a Nucci, Master Finn, is he will never tell you *when* . . ."

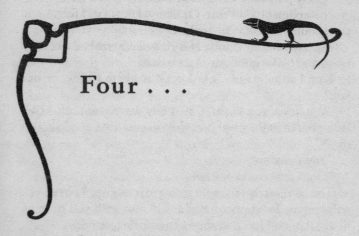

Four . . .

"HE NEVER EVEN ASKED ABOUT THE LAD. WAS HE hurt? Was he maimed? Was the poor boy alive or was he dead? I tell you, Letitia, I am not even certain this Sabatino fellow remembered what he'd done."

"Why, how could he not?" Letitia pressed a delicate finger to her chin, a gesture Finn always found enchanting. "Of course he did. The boy was a Newlie, so the man didn't care."

"Maybe," Finn said, pacing the small cabin from one end to the next. "I'm not too sure of that. When it was over, he was rude, pompous, nasty, terribly overbearing, but quite a different fellow from the frothing lunatic he'd been. . . ."

"Lunatic or not, he's a *human* person, and that's the way they think." Letitia wrinkled her nose and smiled. "Not you, of course, dear Finn. Sometimes I think you're simply too nice to be a person at all."

"I appreciate the thought."

"Well, it's true, my dear."

"Nicely put," said Julia Jessica Slagg. "You'll never get a finer compliment than that. Or likely deserve it, I fear."

"Be quiet," Finn said, "nobody asked."

Julia gave a rusty cackle and clawed up the bed to Letitia's lap. "If this poor lizard had to wait for someone to *ask*, she would never get to speak at all."

"I'm grateful you reminded me of that," Finn said. "That switch is not working as it should. If the ship would hold still for a moment, I could remedy that at once. Of course, with all this rolling and such, vital cogs and gears could spill out and roll about . . ."

"Stop it, both of you," Letitia said. "I have to spend our vacation in this—tiny, stuffy room, but I do not have to listen to you two bicker all the time."

She sighed then, and reached out to touch Finn's hand, as she nearly always did when a single cross word had passed between the two. And when Finn looked into those enormous, glossy black eyes that swirled with iridescent color like opals drowned in warm and fragrant oil, his heart near swelled with joy.

Granted, her ears were perhaps a bit long, but they came to a soft and lovely curve, peeking like furry pink secrets through her long ashen hair. Her lips were small and shapely, and, while her nose was somewhat pointy, Finn found it to be a very nice nose indeed. Her form was quite slender in all the proper places, and not too slender where slender wouldn't do at all.

How, he wondered, could he not love Letitia Louise? What she had been was not what she was now. An animal was one thing, a Newlie something else again. Many, of course, couldn't see the truth of that. Many, he knew, likely never would.

And who, in the end, was blessed with more kindness and love? Fair Letitia, or Sabatino Nucci and that vile and scrawny pair with little but stone in their hearts? All three were human through and through, and what did that gain them but cold and empty lives?

The world was full of questions, and Finn, Master Lizard-Maker, knew the answers to very few at all . . .

He brought their supper from the galley, a meal Letitia hardly touched—watery oyster soup, oat-bread and fish. Letitia nibbled on the bread, but, as ever, wouldn't touch the soup or fish. Meat was meat, whether it came from land or sea. Her kind had never been predators, they'd always been the prey.

"Did you see anyone?" she asked, her precious pink tongue finding crumbs at the corners of her lips. "Does everyone go and eat there? I mean, it must be interesting, meeting new people at sea . . ."

"Not especially," Finn told her. "There were quite a few diners, but no one of note, as I recall."

"Passengers, you mean. But not the crew."

"Oh, no, not the crew. They have their own quarters forward, quite a distance from here."

He couldn't miss the little shudder at the mention of the Yowlies. That encounter had shaken her to the core.

"And the man who attacked you wasn't there? Truly, Finn?"

"Truly, Letitia. I didn't see the man."

"You could have been killed. A man like that has no love for humans, either. He only cares for himself."

"I should say that's true. But you needn't worry. He'll not bother me again."

Finn was glad he'd slightly edited his adventure with Sabatino Nucci. He hadn't mentioned that the loony had challenged him to a duel, and asked him to supper as well.

He could scarcely fathom the man's bizarre behavior, and saw no reason to share it with Letitia Louise.

"I think," Julia put in, scratching herself with sharp iron claws, though, as Finn knew, there was no way she could possibly itch, "as the captain suggested, I could use some lubrication. This salty air is not beneficial to creatures of the metal persuasion. You might, while you're at it, oil that sword in your pack, Master Finn. I expect it's been affected too."

"Thank you for the advice," Finn said, tossing the lizard a frosty look that Letitia couldn't see. She flicked her brass tongue and pretended she'd dropped off to sleep— which, like itching, was a talent reserved for creatures of skin and bone, not those of copper, iron and scraps of tin.

"I almost wish we hadn't come," Letitia said, taking up her thoughts again. "I miss our house and my kitchen. I even miss the smells of Garpenny Street. They are odors less than sweet, to be sure, but they are *our* odors, Finn."

"Yes, well, you'll like Antoline Island when we get there," Finn assured her quickly. "I understand the hotel is practically new, and the beach is quite grand . . ."

"That boy," she said, as if he hadn't spoken at all, "he was injured, you said. And no one, certainly not his—his *masters,* or the captain of this horrible vessel, seem to care. I feel so sorry for the lad. The Foxers are very nice folk. Several of them clerked at Counters Hall, you'll recall. I'm sure you've seen them there."

"I have indeed," Finn said.

"Before the Change, they were as hungry for my kind as the Yowlies were, Finn. But that's not their way now. They're different, but the Yowlies are the same . . ."

She paused, and held him with her magnificent dark eyes.

"We remember sometimes, all the Newlies do. It's there

in our heads from those who came before. Sometimes I'm running through a burrow, squeezing through a musty hole running for my life. It isn't me, Finn, but it is. It's there, and it doesn't go away just because you want it to."

"I'm sorry," she said, shaking her fears away once more. "I can't help being what I am."

"There is nothing else I want you to be," he told her. "Nothing but what you are."

"Yes, I know. And I thank you, Finn."

He wanted desperately to take her in his arms, hold her, and assure her the world would surely change, that all that was wrong would then be set aright. He knew, though, that this wasn't so, that Letitia knew it as well as he.

Newlies had the same rights as humans, but laws are only as good as people want them to be. The Foxer boy was a servant in name, but in truth, little more than a slave. The counselor couple had "hired" him from someone who dealt in such things, and the boy could never get away.

Things should change, and they would, Finn knew, but not today or tomorrow, not when Letitia wanted them to . . .

"I should have stayed to help," Julia said, when Letitia had dropped off to sleep, and a candle made shadows on the walls. "I could have bitten that lout's hand off and saved you a little time."

"For once," Finn said, "you did exactly what you should have done. If you had joined the fray, they'd all know now you are neither an ornament nor a toy. We've been through this before. Many people are not quite ready for talking hunks of tin."

"Hunks of tin, is it?"

"So to speak. I suppose one could word it another way."

"Surely one could."

"Do not be quick to take offense, Julia. I am not in the mood for this."

"Don't be quick to give it, then. I've got feelings too, you know."

"Yes, I do know," Finn said with a sigh of resignation, not far in truth from a sigh of regret. "Whatever came over me to fill you with emotions, like a baker squeezing custard into a tart? I must have been reeling drunk to do such a fool thing as that."

"You were quite sober, as a fact," Julia said. "A glorious moment, a brilliant achievement, the high point of your life, the—"

"That's quite enough. Be still, now, I'm taking a nap."

"Then I will too."

"We are both aware that you can't do that."

"Sleep well," Julia yawned. "I shall wake up promptly at six . . ."

Five . . .

WITH THE SETTING OF THE SUN, THE SEA HAD changed from a very pleasant blue to a most unseemly green. The wind was up, having its way, blowing from the south for a moment, then shifting to the west. Crossways, sideways, this way and that. All this mischief played havoc with the *Madeline Rose*. The crew would get the sails set properly, the wind would swiftly change, and howling, hissing, knocking one another about, they'd swarm into the rigging once again.

Captain Magreet stood on his quarterdeck shaking his fists, cursing the crew as the crew cursed him, shouting out orders that changed from one moment to the next.

"In for bit of a blow, are we, Captain?" Finn asked. "Smells like rain to me."

"Ah, does it now?" Magreet sent him a withering look. "So you're a master of gizzards, and a master of storms as well?"

"Lizards, it is. And I meant no disrespect, sir. It was merely an effort to be polite."

Magreet spat a gobbet at the deck. "Well, take your bloody manners somewhere else. I've no use for them here."

"Indeed," Finn said, "I can see, at the moment, you're somewhat distracted. I appreciate that."

The captain turned and stomped away, mumbling to himself. Finn walked forward past the great mainmast, which was thick as an ancient tree.

There was no one else on deck, no passengers, at least. That suited Finn fine. He didn't need company, especially the unfriendly Nucci, and the pair of scarecrows. And, to be honest, he didn't want to be with Letitia for a spell.

As ever, he chided himself for such a thought. Though he knew it wasn't so, he could not abide the idea that he might, as so many others did, harbor some small intolerance for what Letitia's folk had been.

It was not the wisest thing a man could do, falling in love with his Newlie housekeeper, taking her for a wife. Not in legal terms, of course, for what he'd done was a felony, a criminal act, one that could cause a careless man to lose his head. Everyone knew there were men—and very likely women too—who had quite intimate relations with one of the Newlie kind. No one *said* anything about it, of course; one simply looked the other way.

On the whole, Finn had to admit, beasts should never have been changed into men. It was no great favor to the world, and a tragedy to the creatures themselves. He thought of the sad, sometimes hopeless look in Letitia's dark eyes: a look that held the sorrows and the fears all her kind brought with them from the past.

Letitia was mostly a woman, and a breathtaking woman at that, but she would always be a part of what she'd been. Her kind were not animals now, but they would never, ever be human.

Shar and Dankermain, the great seers who'd cast that unholy spell three hundred years past, had paid very dearly for their crime, for the sin of creating the Nine. Why they did such a deed went with them to the grave, but the spawn of their magic was left behind.

And why, the thought came to Finn, as it often did at such a time, *why did you do the same? What's your reason, Master Finn?*

He had asked himself the question a hundred times past, for he, like the two mad seers, had broken a law of nature himself, giving life and reason to a thing of brass and tin. Given his creation the brain of a ferret, a poor creature caught in a trap and nearly dead.

And why? For much the same reason, he supposed, that the rebel magicians had crossed the line themselves. Though his was no act of magic, he, like the seers, had done what he did because he had the art—because he had the talent, because he had the flair. He had dared the act of creation simply because he could.

The wind was high now, snapping, cracking in the sails, whining through the shrouds, scattering foam atop enormous dark waves. The sailors, Finn noted, had set cheap weather amulets and charms in the rigging—a rattle of bones, strings of shiny stones, pots, pans, bundles of colored sticks, bloodwood dolls and dead leather toads.

And even above the shriek of the wind, the captain, legs set as solidly against the deck as if they'd sprouted there, could be heard yelling and cursing at his horrid crew.

"Set the headsails!"

"Man the halliards!"

"Keelhaul the bos'n!"

"Get aloft there!"

"Let fly the jib!"

That, Finn imagined, or something wholly different, he couldn't say for sure. It all sounded quite the same to him.

By the time he reached his quarters, the storm was full upon them—a gale, a blow, a raging hurricane, a loud and frightful thing that tossed the ship about like a stick of rotten wood.

Still, Letitia stayed fast asleep. Fear and exhaustion had finally brought her down. And, in a corner of the cabin he could see Julia there, two ruby flares of light, crimson points of fire in the night.

Slipping off his clothes, he slid in gently beside Letitia and took her in his arms. She made little sounds in her sleep, and curled into him like a spoon. Her warmth, her touch, the satin feel of flesh next to his nearly set him afire. He desperately wanted her then, to fully share their love, to light the passion between them.

Instead he held her, let her sleep, touched the tiny pulse in her breasts, listened to her breathe. He was certain he couldn't sleep, sure he'd have to stare at the ceiling all night, listening to the shriek of the storm. All of which he did for a minute—or a minute and a half.

Something brought him up out of sleep, he couldn't say what. The storm was weaker now, but the *Madeline Rose* still bobbed about.

Voices. Out in the passageway. Two or three people, maybe four. He pulled on his trousers and opened the door. Three men stood there, two short and one tall, passengers he might have seen before.

"What is it," he asked, "what's going on here?"

"Someone's come up missing, can't find him anywhere," the short man said, squinting past Finn to see if he kept the pretty Newlie in his bed.

"Who? What are you talking about?" He blocked the man's way, came out and shut the door. "Missing from where?"

"That young Foxer," one of the others said. "The one that got hurt up there."

Finn felt a chill in his heart. *No. Make it not so . . .*

"Aren't you the one makes blizzards? The fellow got the tar beat out of him today? Say, weren't you—"

Finn was already gone. He took the steps topside four at a time. Suddenly, the captain was there at the top of the hatchway, his bulky figure in the way.

"I'm not needing your help here, Master Finn," Magreet said, "Get on back where you belong."

"Who did it?" Finn demanded. "Those skinny lawyers or that devil Sabatino, which?"

"Damn you, mister, you're not listening to me!"

"Get out of my way, Captain."

"Or what, sir? If I do not, sir, what might you do then?"

In a flash of faraway lightning, Finn saw the captain's eyes. No rage, no fury, no feeling at all, only cold determination and will. More than that, he was suddenly aware that there was a pistol, a nasty-looking weapon with a bell-shaped muzzle, clutched in Magreet's heavy hand.

"Now, Master Finn, if you'd go back down as I said . . ."

"Don't go any further with this," Finn said. "Don't point a weapon at me."

Magreet, showing no expression at all, raised his pistol and pressed the muzzle against Finn's chest. Finn heard the cold, distinct sound of a metal hammer drawing back. He knew, in that instant, that under that ridiculous hat there was still a pompous fool, but one who would just as soon kill a man as swat a bothersome fly.

"I don't feel I can reason with you," Finn said. "I don't think you're in a rational state of mind."

"I think you'd be right on both counts, Master Finn," the captain said. "I'm near certain that you are . . ."

He sat in the dark in a chair against the cabin's outer bulkhead, near the sound of the churning sea. He was certain he wouldn't sleep now. He felt no anger, no shame in backing down from Magreet. The man was an elemental force, like the very storm itself. The sea and the wind didn't think, they simply did. And that, Finn reasoned, was how the captain stayed alive, how he kept his crew of nasties from killing him in his sleep.

The fury, the rage, the sorrow in Finn's heart was for the death of the Foxer boy. Whoever had done the deed had simply tossed the lad away, like a thing no longer useful, a tool, a device, a thing that didn't *work* anymore. What a thoughtless, chilling thing to do! And, in the world Finn lived in, not a shocking act at all.

After giving the matter thought, Finn believed the couple who'd held the boy had brought about his death. They were the ones who'd worked him until he was useful no more. Sabatino Nucci would toss a Newlie away without a blink, but he had no reason to do so.

It didn't matter who'd done the deed, it was done. For an instant, Letitia's face replaced the image of the boy in Finn's mind. With a shudder, he quickly swept the terrible picture away . . .

He could not recall how long he'd been sitting there, whether he'd been awake, whether he'd slept or dreamt. He couldn't say what compelled him to stand, pull himself up and peer through the small porthole in the cabin wall.

It was there, or it was not, he couldn't truly tell—a great, black vessel, a vessel so big, so dark, it swallowed the very sea and sky itself. Yet for all its size, it made no sound at all. And even though it seemed a massive thing, it was clear to Finn that it had no bulk, no weight of any kind. It was plainly a spectral craft, a vessel of shadows, a ship with skeletal masts and tattered sails, a chill and hollow vessel, as cold as death itself.

And if Finn needed further assurance that no living creature sailed upon this craft, a dead man raised a wispy arm from that cold quarterdeck, and sent a ghostly greeting across the dark sea . . .

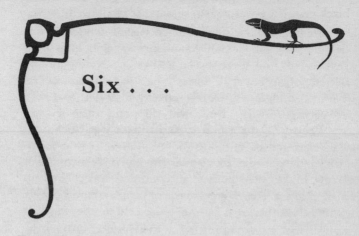

Six . . .

FINN DREAMED.

He dreamed about a lot of things he didn't ever want to dream again. He dreamed he was sizzling, broiling, frying in a pan. Someone was having him for lunch. Someone was hungry, someone who didn't care to wait till he was done.

He woke up flailing, thrashing, and kicking about in a pool of salty sweat. He sat up with a start to find a lizard patiently gnawing on his leg.

"Custard and Clams," Finn exclaimed, kicking out at Julia, sending her skidding across the room. "What in holy hell's wrong with you?"

"You break it, you fix it," Julia said. She flicked her scaly tail, shook her tinny head. Everything seemed to be in place.

"You snore like a storm, and sleep like the dead. If it wasn't for me—Custard and Clams, indeed. Get your big feet on the floor. Look out that porthole and tell me what you see."

"Why would I want to do that?"

"Don't, then. Lie there and roast in the heat."

Finn muttered to himself, then padded across the floor and squinted out the small, salt-encrusted window at the hot and brassy sea. He blinked and looked again. Unless his eyes deceived him, there was no sea in sight. Neither brassy nor hot, not any sea at all. Instead, he saw a rotting wooden wharf, piled high with barrels, boxes and crates. Scattered with garbage, overripe fruit, swill, slops and waste of every sort. The smell was a horror, and the air was thick with swollen green flies.

Beyond the sordid dock was a grim and dirty town full of narrow, high-roofed houses, all crammed and choked up together like weeds. A great horde of people, none more attractive than the next, crowded the cobble alleyways. It was, truly, an awful sight to see. It made Finn yearn for the simple but clean byways of Ulster-East, the quiet of his own Garpenny Street. He even missed the dull sound of cannon down the bay, the colorful war balloons soaring overhead.

"Great Apples and Pears," Finn said, "What sort of place is this? We're not supposed to *be* anywhere, we're supposed to be at sea!"

"Well, I'm certain that we're not," Julia said. "Land and water are not at all alike."

"As ever, I'm grateful for your help," Finn said, frowning at the ruby-eyed creature who'd climbed atop a chair. "I don't know where we are, but I mean to find out."

Struggling into trousers while hunting for his shirt, he glanced at Letitia Louise. She was still sound asleep, her fine ashen hair a silken veil across her cheek. The sun painted golden stripes across her bare and lovely back.

"I'll talk to the captain," Finn said, turning away from the sight, "I'll get an answer to this."

"Good idea," said Julia Jessica Slagg, "that's what I'd do myself."

The deck was crowded with people. Cargo and luggage were scattered all about. Enormous, hulking Bullies, broad-shouldered Newlies with short, stumpy knobs atop their heads, glassy eyes and massive necks stalked up and down the gangway bearing heavy barrels and crates. Many wore golden rings in their noses, many had lewd tattoos.

Finn found Captain Magreet on his quarterdeck, shouting, shaking his fists, cursing at everyone in sight. His officer's hat was askew, feathers and plumes sagging limply in the heat.

"I want to know exactly where I am," Finn demanded. "I want to know why we're stopping here."

Magreet gave him a single sour glance. "Get away from me, sir. Get out of my sight."

Finn stepped in front of the captain, blocking his view of the bustle down below.

"I merely asked, Captain, where we are and why. As a paying passenger, I have every right to information such as that."

"Hah! That's what you're thinking, now, is it? What damn fool told you that?"

"I beg your pardon?"

"Move it there," Magreet shouted, pushing Finn gently aside, "Get busy, you vile, odorous, good-for-nothing beast, or I'll have the flesh peeled off your back!"

One of the Bullies made a deep, rumbling sound in his chest, gave the captain a murderous glance, and moved no faster than before.

A pair of Yowlie crewmen teased the big fellow, scampering about in his path. The Bullie lashed out with one stout foot, but the Yowlies were too quick for that.

"Can't stand the ugly brutes," Magreet said, "They'll turn on you faster'n a southern squall. Damn me, are you still here, Finn? What the devil is it now?"

"Same as before, Captain. I'd like to know where I am, why we're stopping here."

"Makasar. Port of Nakeemo. Sour oats, red beer. Tar and fertilizer, plus a couple dozen other lovely scents, is what you're smelling now. That, and the local damned unbathed population out there."

Finn shook his head. "My ticket says nothing about a port of call. Not anywhere at all."

" 'Course it doesn't."

"What?"

"You deaf or what, boy? Your ticket's going to say where *you're* going. You aren't going somewhere, it isn't going to say."

"That's ridiculous. If the ship's going to stop somewhere—"

Magreet granted Finn a patient sigh. "A passenger coming here don't have a ticket says where *you're* going, sir. None of his damn business. Isn't your business where *he's* headed for."

"Captain, my—servant-companion is not overly taken with the sea. How many more stops will we make before we reach Antoline Isle? I would simply like to know that."

"You would, would you? An' why's that?"

"Why? Because I—" Finn took a breath. "All right, how long will we be here? When will we leave?"

"Overnight."

"Overnight?"

"What did I just say? I believe that's what I said. We sail again on the morrow, out with the morning tide."

"Fine. That is what I asked. You could have said that in the first, sir, and I'd have been long gone."

Magreet didn't answer. He was scowling at a large Bullie who had dropped a barrel on the rocky quay. The barrel burst open, and something dark and oily ran out.

"You'll pay for that, you lout," Magreet yelled, "It'll come right off of your back!"

"In that case," Finn said, "we shall be spending the night ashore. It will be a great relief to get out of the heat for a while."

. . . It'll give poor Letitia a chance to settle her nerves, he said to himself, *and get something decent to eat.*

"I don't suppose there's some rule you haven't bothered to tell me about," he said aloud. "I won't have to buy another ticket to get back on again."

The captain looked bewildered. "Are you daft, man? Who ever heard of such a fool thing as that? Meanin' no offense, Master Finn, but I don't see how you landsmen have the wits to piss and eat, and keep yourself clean. Damned if I do . . ."

"Oh, how I adore you, Finn! Finn, my sweetness, my darling, my very own love. You are truly the most wonderful man in the world!"

"I appreciate the thought," Finn said, making no effort to fend off the moist and tender kisses Letitia showered upon his face. This, in spite of the fact that a passenger or crewman might walk into the cabin at any time, leaving Finn to explain a human and a Newlie in fond embrace.

"In truth, though, I did nothing at all."

"Nothing? *Nothing,* dear Finn?" She twitched her pretty nose and rolled her ebony eyes. "What you have *done,* my love, is save me from—from gross despair and madness. You have given me reason to live!"

"No, really, I—"

Letitia suddenly let him go, caught up her skirts and whirled about the small cabin, for an instant baring her lovely legs, always a pleasant sight to see, though Finn had seen them many times, and certainly a great deal more than that.

He was pleased with this sudden leap from the depths of despair to unending joy. Still, he couldn't help but think about getting her *back* aboard the ship on the morrow. Letitia had chosen to ignore that part of his tale. She would, he knew, recall it soon enough again.

The deck was nearly clear of cargo handlers and passengers when Finn brought Letitia on deck. He carried their small overnight satchel, which Letitia had stuffed near to bursting, even though they would only spend the night ashore.

"It is quite delightful," Letitia said, gazing at the gray, drab little village that lay beyond the docks. "It looks almost like home, Finn."

"Ah, yes it does, in a way, I suppose."

It is nothing of the sort, Finn said to himself, but he knew Letitia would see some beauty in a sewage pool if it was not aboard the *Madeline Rose*.

As he helped Letitia down the gangway, he looked over his shoulder for the captain, but Magreet was nowhere about. And, though several Yowlies clung to the upper riggings, Letitia, in her elation at going ashore, didn't seem to notice they were there.

The moment Finn and Letitia stepped ashore, the sun dropped behind a bank of clouds, leaving the town in half shadow. Without the harsh and unrelenting light, the crumbling stone and rotting thatch seemed somewhat softer, the drab and muddy shades now partially obscured.

"I don't like it already," said Julia Jessica Slagg, clinging to Finn's waist beneath his cloak. "It's a damned pesthole is what it is. A canker, a blemish, a dunghill, a dump. A grubby, vile and shabby place, a—"

"Shut up," Finn said quietly, "There are people all about, I shouldn't have to tell you that."

Finn hurried Letitia along. As they left the broad wharf for the crowded streets of the town, Finn saw that the grimy shopfronts looked much like those at home, though clearly not as clean.

Finn recognized several passengers among the locals. A fat man who sold bad wine, another, a dealer in jewels who'd shown Finn a glittering array of bracelets, necklaces and rings—all of them, Finn was nearly sure, as false as the man who sold them. He also glimpsed the gaunt, hooded lawyers, now without their charge, the poor lad who now lay far beneath the sea.

And then, for only an instant, at the far end of the street—

Finn felt heat rise to his face. *Sabatino Nucci!* There was no mistaking that burly frame, startling red hair, and haughty walk. It was, truly, the pompous, arrogant fellow himself. And, as the winds of fortune seemed to shift and blow Finn's way, he saw that Sabatino gripped a heavy piece of luggage in each hand. That, now, was a piece of good news. This horrid little port was, at least for a time, the lout's destination. He would not be coming aboard again!

"What, Finn? Dare I ask what the grinning's all about?"

"Why, nothing but my joy in thinking of our journey to come. Just the happy thought that our holiday will take on a more pleasant mien from now on."

"How nice of you to keep such thoughts in your head," Letitia said, pausing to place a hand lightly on his arm. "Are you a man of magic, then? Have you a secret skill I've yet to see?"

Finn caught the sparkle in her eyes, the saucy way she moved her tiny mouth, and knew, at once, she'd put sly meaning to her words with purpose and intent.

"Perhaps," he told her, "when we find good lodging for the night, I shall show you a most intriguing spell."

"I would be a most earnest pupil, then."

"Ah, Letitia . . ."

Finn stopped. A few steps ahead, a man walked out of an alleyway, boldly in their path. A moment later, another man followed the first. And, from a doorway across the narrow street, another, and still another, appeared.

Each was dressed in drab, filthy tatters, like the rest of the folk about, and few wore shoes of any sort. The only distinction about them—and clearly the only spot of color in their lives—were the high, pointed yellow cones upon their heads. Finn was uncertain whether he should truly name them *hats,* for he had never seen their like before.

There was one other habit the men held in common between them. Each, independent of the other, walked in a most peculiar way. One walked right into a wall, bloodying his head. After a moment he turned, and walked off to his left. Two of the men walked backwards, then turned and walked forward for a while. One walked three steps forward, then two to the right. This went on until all of the men were out of sight.

"Bottles and Bones," Letitia said, tightening her grip on Finn's arm. "What do you reckon *that's* all about?"

Finn didn't have an answer. It was most bizarre to watch, and plainly made no sense at all.

Still, there was one thing he noticed about this strange behavior, and that had nothing to do with the men themselves: anyone who happened to get in their way quickly moved aside to let them pass. It was, Finn thought, as if people feared the touch of these fellows like the very plague itself . . .

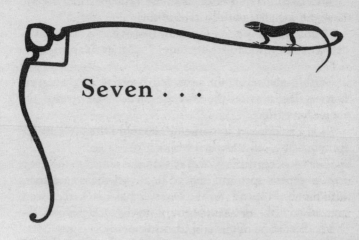

Seven . . .

"SOMETHING IS SURELY THE MATTER WITH THESE people, Finn. That is a most peculiar thing to do."

"Indeed it is," Finn said. "I have witnessed outlandish behavior before, but nothing quite as odd as this."

"It might be a rite of some sort. You remember the Kettle Scrubbers Guild, down the hill toward Ranksetter Street? Each would touch his left ear when he chanced to pass another of his kind."

"I believe it was the right."

"No, dearest, I am sure it was the left."

"I expect you're correct," Finn said, though he knew for certain she was not.

He might have told her, too, though this was not the wisest thing to do, for at that moment, one of the yellow-capped fellows came to a sudden halt in the middle of the street, turned with a jerk, and set his course straight for Letitia and Finn.

Men leaped aside, mothers grabbed their children and held them to their breasts. Finn drew Letitia into the doorway of a shop out of the fellow's path.

"If I lived here," Letitia said, drawing a startled breath, "I would soon get awfully tired of this."

"Hmmmmm, yes," Finn said, more than a little bewildered by the townsfolk's attitude, "but they, it appears, do not."

With a glance up the crowded street to be certain no other walker was on the way, he turned and opened the shop's heavy door.

"Let's step inside a moment," he told Letitia, "Perhaps this nonsense will cease in a while."

The usual sprig of goldberry vine was nailed to the door, a shopkeeper's spell guaranteed to attract those customers with money to spend. As the two stepped inside, they were greeted with the pleasant scent of newly turned wood, the sharp, clear scent of oils and turpentine.

There was little room to stand, as the shop was stacked, racked, overfull with chairs. Big chairs, little chairs, chairs of every sort. Chairs without arms, chairs without backs. Light, airy chairs that would surely shatter if the smallest child were to dare to try and sit. Large, heavy, ponderous chairs designed for the powerful, for emperors or kings, chairs that resembled the trunks of great oaks, carved, chiseled, tangled and entwined with clusters of grapes and strangler vines. Still, with all these chairs about, Finn noticed there was absolutely nowhere to sit.

"May I be of service to you, sir? I am Dalto Frick, Master of Chairs, and I don't mind saying I have the finest chairs you'll find in this or any town."

Finn turned as a very short, very old man suddenly appeared through the maze of chairs across the room. He was dressed in worn red boots and a lavender smock, too large for his wizened frame. His head was entirely bald, and his face was as flat as a pie. Looking at him sideways, Finn could scarcely find any feature at all.

"Your chairs, sir, are the best I've ever seen," Finn said,

"and I've seen quite a few. However, I must confess, I don't think I can use one right now."

"You can't?" The old man's smile dropped away. "You don't want a chair?"

"It's not that I don't want a chair, it's just that I can't really *use* one right now."

"You come in my shop, you don't want a chair."

"No, good sir, not now."

"You stand on my floor, where another, righteous, good-hearted man could be standing right now. A man who truly wants a chair. He can't, though, because *you* are taking up his space. *You* are standing there."

"Sir—"

The old man was clearly annoyed. His mouth began to tremble and his eyes began to blink. Finn feared he might have a seizure or a fit.

"We are new in town," Finn explained with care. "We just got off the ship. As you may have guessed, we are not from here." He stroked the back of a richly grained chair carved in the shapes of creatures of the deep.

"We were on the *Madeline Rose*," he added. "We're just stopping and—"

"That chair you're fondling, getting your oily hands on its finely polished grain, rubbing the finish off—that chair is made of Stonewood, comes all the way from across the Misty Sea. You can't hardly get it anymore—"

"Yes, it's quite—"

"You could take an axe to that chair, you'd split that axe in two, that chair wouldn't have a scratch."

"Amazing," Finn said, though he didn't believe it for a moment.

"Two hundred droaks. I'll let it go for one-eighty-five."

"A bargain at any price," Finn said, "It's a very fine chair. I was wondering, sir—as I mentioned, we are off the *Madeline Rose* for the night—I was wondering if you might suggest a good place to stay. A decent, not too pricey inn where they serve a nice supper, and have a good lock on the doors . . ."

The old man blinked. "A what?"

"An inn."

"An in *what*?"

"Not *in* something. I'm afraid I haven't made myself clear. An *inn*. A place for bed and supper, where one may spend the night."

The old man's eyes suddenly shifted to Letitia Louise. It occurred to Finn now that the old man had scarcely glanced her way since they'd come into the store. Now, though, he studied her curiously, looking her up and down, from head to toe.

"What sort of thing do you got here?" he asked Finn. "I don't believe I've seen one before."

Finn silently counted to three. "Are you speaking of—of my associate, Miss Letitia Louise? Is that who you're speaking of, sir? If it is—"

"I'm speaking of the Newlie you brought in my store. I never heard one called a *miss*. What kind you say she is?"

"I am a guest in your country," Finn said, as calmly as his anger would allow. "I will pretend I didn't hear that at all, and I will waste no more of your time."

"You *heard* me, all right." The man showed Finn a nasty smile, and three remaining teeth. "And my answer is, people here stay where they're *supposed* to stay. They stay where they live. That's what decent people do."

"Whistles and Frogs," Finn said sharply, "I didn't ask you for a lecture, I asked you where we might get a bed. Someplace to—"

"Stop. Don't say another word. I'll not hear it!"

The old man backed off. His hands began to shake, but not before he plunged one hand inside his smock, and came out with a string of dead beetles painted red. He pointed the charm toward Finn and rattled it in his face.

"Fine, that's it," Finn said. "Letitia, let's go."

"I don't know what your game is," the old man shouted, "but I'll have none of it, sir. None of it at all. Whatever you and your—creature do in a bed, you'll not find one to cavort in here. We stay where we're supposed to stay, and we don't do *ins,* whatever that is!"

"Huhhh!" Finn grabbed Letitia's arm and started for the door.

"No you don't, heathen, you're staying right here."

Finn looked at him. "Now what?"

"I'm getting the Volunteers. They know how to deal with the likes of you."

"I'll ask you to stand aside."

"Ask all you want. I'll not move an inch."

"I think I can lift you and toss you about. I don't want to, but I will."

"You try it, I'll have you hung, strung, drug out and fired."

"You'll what?"

"I can do it, too. I've got people in high places."

"Listen, you little imp . . ."

Finn reached down, grabbed the man's collar and lifted him bodily off the floor. The old man howled and flailed his short legs.

"Finn—Finn, put him *down.* Put him down this instant!"

"What?" Finn was so startled by the unfamiliar tone of Letitia's voice that he set the man back on his feet.

"How much do you want for the chair?" Letitia asked. "I won't give you one-eighty-five, I'll give you one-fifty, and not a droak more, whatever that is."

"Letitia—"

"Shut up, Finn."

Finn shut up.

The old man gave Letitia a wary look. "One-seventy."

"One-sixty-five."

"One-sixty-seven."

"No." Letitia shook her head. "Absolutely not."

"You want the damned chair?"

"Not at that price, sir. I wouldn't dream of it."

The old man muttered to himself. "One-sixty-six." He folded his arms and stood his ground. "That is absolutely it."

"I'll take it." Letitia stuck out her hand.

"Oh, no you don't." The man backed away. "I've never touched a creature wasn't human-born, and I don't aim to start now."

Letitia pretended not to hear. "Finn, would you give the man one-hundred-sixty-six trels? I'm sure they're just as good as droaks."

"I don't recall buying any chair," Finn muttered, but he reached in his pouch and counted the coins into the waiting palm of Dalto Frick.

"You've made a fine choice," the old man said, his face wrinkling into a smile. "That chair'll last a lifetime, sir. That chair will be good as new, long after you're dead and gone."

Finn glared. The old man wasn't mad anymore. Finn was a customer now, and apparently even the feeble-minded and the morally impure were entitled to a chair if they were willing to pay for it.

Finn leaned down and gripped the massive piece. As he raised it off the floor, pain ripped down his spine and dug its sharp claws in the small of his back.

"Guts and Bloody Gizzards," Finn howled. "Whale-shit pie!"

"*Finn!*" Letitia pressed a finger to her lips. "I never heard the like."

"Well, you've damned sure heard it now. Open that door."

Finn tripped, stumbled and reeled. Took two steps out the door, swayed, staggered, and felt something give down below.

With a terrible groan, he dropped the chair in the street. Cobblestones cracked, but the chair wasn't injured at all.

For an instant, people paused to look, then quickly walked away. Finn didn't even glance back. He staggered up the street, one hand braced against a dirty brick wall.

Letitia ran to catch up. "Will you stop, please, will you please just stop and sit down?"

"No," Finn said, "I will not. I'm fine. I am perfectly sound."

"You're angry with me."

"Angry? How could you possibly imagine that?"

"Stop, Finn. Stop right now."

Letitia stepped boldly in his path. Finn had to stop or run her down.

"All right, what?"

"I did not buy a chair because I *needed* a chair. You know that, Finn. You saw that fellow's face as well as I. Did you see the way he looked at me? He was going to get the *Volunteers,* which I imagine are the constables here. It is quite clear the customs in this land are much like our own, yet not the same as all.

"We do not have louts in yellow hats who roam the streets and scare folk out of their wits. What we *do* have in common is that—that loathsome attitude toward humans and Newlies of the opposite sex."

"Indeed," Finn said. "And, in this case, the Newlie in question is an especially sensual, ah—overwhelmingly lovely Mycer girl who turns heads everywhere we go."

"Oh, Finn . . ." Letitia's frown faded and curled into a smile. "What a lovely thing to say."

"The truth comes easily, my dear. And, I must add, you came up with a brilliant method of getting us out of there, purchasing an ugly, unbelievably heavy chair. I only wish I'd thought of it myself."

Finn looked at the ground and nudged a broken crock with his boot. "It is a failing of the male of the species, I fear. We like to believe that everything of merit surely begins with us."

"I know that, dear Finn." Letitia showed him a gracious smile. "The female of *every* species is well aware of this, and we love you all the same."

"Well . . . That is a kindly thing to say."

"Finn? If we had indeed found an inn, would you have considered—*cavorting,* as that dirty old man implied?"

"You can be certain that I would," he told her. "Neither of us were inclined to, ah—frolic and cavort on that damnable ship. I, for one, have—"

"Must I listen to this?" Julia croaked from under Finn's cloak. "Is it possible you could save this twaddle for some more fitting time and place?"

"Julia!" Letitia drew a breath. "I am awfully surprised at you, listening in on other people's clearly private talk. I thought you had better manners than that."

"I'm not surprised at all," Finn said, "because I know you treasure those moments when you can sorely irritate. What I'll say, and only once, is we are not on home ground here. We are in a land where fools in pointy hats walk about backwards. A land where you can purchase ugly chairs, yet no one has the wit to think of *inns.* Thus, I would urge you to have a caution, and keep your rusty, scrap-iron thoughts to yourself."

"Well *excuse* me," said Julia Jessica Slagg, "What did *I* do?"

"What you always do," Finn said, "just try not to do it again . . ."

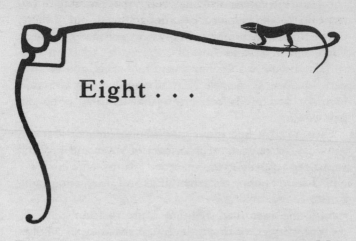

Eight . . .

THE PORT OF NAKEEMO IN THE LAND OF MA-
kasar, Finn decided, might well have been planned by the
yellow-hats themselves. Many of the narrow, odorous
streets appeared to lead to other avenues, then abruptly disappeared. Order, here, was merely an illusion, a dismal sort
of joke. Often, a turn to the left or the right became a circu-
lar route, leading one where he'd begun. As an added hin-
drance, none of the streets had names.

Through pure blind luck, one of the avenues brought
Finn and Letitia out of murky shadow into a broad, sunlit
marketplace. Finn was more than grateful; he decided mar-
kets everywhere were likely much the same, even in so
bizarre a land as this.

There were vegetable and fruit stalls, stalls that sold fish,
stalls that sold mussels, lobsters and clams. Stalls that sold
fat pink shrimp, stalls that sold eels still writhing on the
hook.

And, as ever, there were stalls that sold amulets, talis-
mans and charms. Wands, hexes, potions and spells. There
was magic that would cure, magic that would kill, magic

that would turn a man to stone. And, for a very hefty price, magic that would bring back the dead.

The trouble with magic, Finn knew, was that some of it didn't work at all, and some of it worked too well. Anyone with good sense would stay away from stalls, and go to a seer with a license to spell. That, of course, didn't keep minor mages and frauds from setting up a tent and laying out their wares.

Finn talked awhile with a man who sold metals of every sort: rust-red nuggets of iron, bars of silver and bronze, snippets of copper and tin—rare and base metals Finn used in his Lizard Shoppe to fashion cogs and gears, talons and scales.

Still, the man had nothing Finn couldn't buy on Garpenny Street, or down the hill at the forge of Master Del. But since the man had been patient while Finn poked through his goods, Finn bought a spool of fine-spun silver wire at twice the price he'd pay at home.

"And why not?" he said aloud to himself. "We've already bought an overpriced chair we couldn't move an inch if we cared . . ."

Letitia Louise had found a fragrance she liked at the booth next door. It was oil of tangerine, and she held up her wrist to let Finn have a sniff.

"Very nice," he said, "but you always smell good to me."

"Musty. That's what you say sometimes."

"Musty's good. Musty is a most appealing scent."

"What do you think of musty tangerine?"

"I think I'll be able to handle that."

Walking farther east through the market, the crowded stalls and tents gave way to a small public square. In the center of the square was a fountain surrounding some crude statuary, a carving Finn could not identify. Water trickled in rivulets down its mossy sides. A crowd was gathered at the fountain, and more seemed to be on the way. Many belonged to the yellow-hat bunch, so the mass was always in motion, seeming like a single being that constantly changed its shape, and never stood entirely still.

Standing well to the side of this group were other humans of the town, and several Newlies as well. Finn saw a dozen Foxers, Snorters in their customary red, and two large Bullies from the docks. Letitia seemed slightly out of sorts, and continually twitched her nose until she was certain no Yowlie crewmen were about.

"Whatever it is," Finn said, "I hope it starts soon. We must find a place to spend the night."

Letitia frowned. "I thought that old man made it clear there wasn't any place. I thought they didn't do that here."

"Yes, indeed he did," Finn answered, clearing his throat, "but we can't rely on that. We only have the word of a senile, sullen old grouch who makes chairs. I cannot imagine there is not one person in town who is somewhat civilized."

"One would hope," Letitia sighed, touching a spot of tangerine oil behind her ears.

"Yes, one would. It is my intention, as soon as we can find our way out of here . . ."

Finn didn't finish. He paused as a sudden murmur swept through the crowd. The mob seemed to shrink and then swell, swell and shrink again. And, each time this contraction took place, some of the yellow-hats broke from the mass and headed off in one direction or the next.

"Perhaps we'll see whatever it is," Letitia said. "I do hope it's a parade."

Finn gave her a curious look. "I thought you didn't like parades."

"I don't, ordinarily. I do like some kinds, though."

"What kinds would that be?"

"I'm not really sure. The only one I've seen was the

Bowser Brigade. You remember, dear? They came through town on the way to the War?"

"Yes, I surely do."

"They wore those lovely plaid and green uniforms, and the cute little hats with the tassels hanging down. I was so proud because they were Newlies, and didn't have to fight if they didn't want to."

Letitia paused, and Finn saw the sudden touch of sadness in her eyes. "They didn't come back, as I recall. None except for two. I forgot about that."

"No. I don't believe they did."

Scarcely anyone does, he said to himself. He remembered so many who had gone, and simply disappeared. Pikemen and bowmen, Balloon Grenadiers. A certain captain, he recalled, gone one day looking natty in his new uniform. Back the next as a Coldie, as a shade, no longer a man, scarcely a shadow, hardly a mist, barely aware that he was there.

Finn had thought a lot about it, and decided this was what the War was for: war gave people something to do—the rich and poor alike. Thus, there was always work for the vagrant, and the fools at court who liked the dashing costumes.

Not for the first time, Finn was grateful he'd come from good craftsman stock. Dying, from what he could see, was not a promising career.

Just as these scraps of wisdom were crossing his mind, someone in the crowd began to shout. One single voice, then another, and another after that, until the sound began to echo through the churning mass and swelled to an awesome, deafening roar.

Finn felt a chill touch the back of his neck. Something, or someone, was whipping this crowd into a fever, into an unthinking horde. He could almost taste the anger, the unfettered rage, and most frightening of all, the ugly side of joy, the dark anticipation of what they'd come for, what they'd come to see.

"I don't like this," he said, quickly grasping Letitia's hand. "We're leaving, we shouldn't be here."

"Yes, you're right," Letitia said, her eyes now wide with primal fear. "I'm scared, Finn. And I don't even know what it is I'm scared to see."

Finn turned to retrace their steps, to go back the way they'd come. He saw, at once, there was no place to go, no way through that solid terrifying wall. It would be worth their lives to even try.

"Hold on to me," he said, "don't let go. And don't be frightened, my dear."

Letitia looked at him. "Why not? *You* are."

Finn had no answer to that.

"Look, look there," Letitia said, her nails biting into his arm. "What—what on earth is that!"

Finn followed her glance. At first, he saw nothing at all. Then, at the far end of the square, he saw that the great mass had parted to form a narrow avenue. This action brought the crowd to sudden quiet. A thousand breaths were held; for an instant, a thousand hearts ceased to beat.

Then, through this passage came a throng of yellow-hatters—a dozen, a dozen more than that, then a hundred more, backwards, forwards, walking and stalking, hopping in every mad direction, bumping into houses, running into walls, crashing headlong into their own, knocking one another to the ground. Some got up, and some lay where they fell.

The crowd shrank back, scattered, tried to let them get by. Still, there were too many townsfolk, too many Newlies wandering about. When some hapless soul got in the way, a yellow-hat would explode into anger, beat that being sense-less, and kick them to the ground. No one tried to defend themselves, and no one came to their aid.

"This is insanity," Finn said, "This country is a—a damned asylum, is what it is, and someone's stolen the key."

"Huh? Whassat? What was you saying, sor?"

Finn looked up into a dirt-stained face, a sun-blistered nose, a tangled beard and septic eyes. All on the body of a hulk in overalls.

"You're quite mistaken, sir. I said nothing at all."

"Ruuunka youga hoom," the man said, or words to that effect. "You'd best not be sayin' it again."

"Finn, *please.*" Letitia rolled her eyes. "We are guests in this land. You're acting just awful. You're acting like Julia now."

"Yes, I suppose I am," Finn said, taken aback by her words. "I certainly won't do it again."

And, with that, underneath his cloak, Julia Jessica Slagg dug brassy teeth into his flesh.

"I'll get you for that," Finn muttered, sucking in a breath.

Once more the crowd began to shout, even louder, even more frenzied than before. From the break in the crowd, a high-wheeled wagon appeared, drawn by more hat people still. As the wagon drew closer, Finn could see it held an iron-barred cage. And, within the cage, clinging to the bars, was a naked, frightened man with a mop of shaggy white hair.

"Oh, dear, get me out of here, Finn, *please.*"

Letitia's mouth was so dry she could scarcely spit out the words.

"I'd love to," he told her, "but there's nowhere to go."

He squeezed her hand, harder this time. No great help, but the best that he could do.

The villains brought the wagon to a halt near the fountain at the center of the square. Four of them hurried to the back of the cart and lifted off long wooden boards. They had clearly practiced this before: it was hardly any time before a rough-hewn structure took shape, a crude apparatus twice as tall as a man. Three other louts opened the cage and dragged the naked man out.

At once, the poor fellow shouted and flailed his limbs about. The crowd began to cheer. Clearly, they liked the show so far.

The victim wasn't young, but he was still full of fight. After much effort, his captors managed to bind him to the wooden device. The fellow strained against his bonds, threw back his head and howled.

"I—am—going—to be sick," Letitia said, closing her eyes against the sight. "I really mean it, Finn."

"No. No you're not. That's not a good idea."

Holding Letitia about the waist, he turned to a doughy, middle-aged woman standing next to the man in overalls.

"Excuse me," he said, "could you possibly tell me what they intend to do with that man?"

The woman smiled, showing Finn a row of blackened teeth. Dentistry, Finn decided, was in its infancy here.

"Why, same thing they al'ays does. Goin' to hang 'im, skin 'im and string 'im out."

"They—what?"

Finn felt his stomach do a flip. The Master of Chairs had threatened this very same treatment, not half an hour before.

"After that," the woman added, "they'll fire 'im up, black 'im to a crisp. How comes you doesn't know that?"

"We're new here, we don't know the local customs yet. By the way, does the word *inn* have any meaning to you? We're looking for a—"

"*Finn . . .*"

Letitia was swaying, much like a sapling in the wind, her mouth sagging open, her eyes rolling back. Finn held her close, caught her before she fell. For a very petite and slender being, she seemed to find a great deal of weight somewhere.

"Come on, come *on*," he whispered, slapping her very lightly on the face, "you cannot do this, Letitia. I simply won't have it, do you hear?"

"Lay the victim down flat," Julia said, poking her snout through the folds of Finn's cape. "Elevate the feet, slightly higher than the head. Loosen the clothing a bit, apply cool cloths to the wrists and the neck. Linen, now, not sacking or wool, neither cotton nor flax, not—"

"*Quiet!*" Finn grabbed the lizard's copper nose and pushed her roughly out of sight. "Where do you think we are, in Master Spencer's ward, up on Zod Hill? I am not a physician, Julia, I don't have a healing spell. I don't have any linen, any water, cool or hot. If I lay her down, they'll trample her on the spot. Stay out of sight and let me handle this!"

"Fine, go ahead. I'm only trying to help, doing what I can to save the poor girl's life . . ."

"I am—quite all right," Letitia said with a sigh, "no thanks to you two, I must say. Will you let me *go*, please? I feel quite awkward bent in half like this."

"We were merely trying to help . . ."

"Yes, of course you were, you're both such dears."

Letitia busied herself, straightened a wrinkle here and there, patted Finn's hands and brushed them aside.

"Are you sure you can stand now, love, you're still a bit flushed."

"No one ever expired from a flush," she said, fanning herself with both hands. "I expect I'll survive if I can jus—"

Her words were lost as a ragged cheer thundered through the crowd. Letitia gasped, startled by the sound.

"Don't look," Finn said, moving a step to block her view, "Look at something else."

"Such as? There is little else to see here, Finn."

"Look at the street. Those bricks are quite ordinary, but

the composition, the design, clearly bear the craftsman's touch."

"Stop it, Finn, I will not look at bricks. Tell me what they're doing to that poor man now, I can't bear to look myself."

"Nothing at the moment," Finn said, craning his neck, standing on his toes. "Oh, dear, now that's not good."

"What? What?"

"They're poking him. Poking him with sticks."

"Sticks?"

"Yes. Fairly long sticks."

"Do they—do they appear to be sharpened or dull, these sticks?"

"It's hard to tell from here, but I'd say they're very sharp sticks."

"Oh, no."

"Long sticks. Sharp at one end."

"Don't tell me that, I don't want to hear!"

"Then don't ask, my dear."

"Even if I do, don't tell me, all right?"

"I won't, then. Ah, something else is going on now."

"What?"

"Stop asking, Letitia. You said you didn't want to hear."

"I don't, dear, but I do."

"I understand, you don't and yet you do. It's natural to feel that way."

"What a nice thing to say. You are always very kind and understanding, Finn."

"I doubt that I am. But I always mean well, you know."

With that, she gave him a very quick kiss on the cheek, which was not a good idea, a Newlie showing intimate affection to a human in public, as it were.

Still, Finn was pleased. Sometimes he seemed to hurt her feelings, sometimes he seemed to give her joy. And even though he loved her, he was often baffled by her ways.

Males and females, as everyone knew, were different as night and day. And, for certain, Newlies and humans were not the same. Some differences were slight, but others were not.

Letitia was a Mycer, with the blood of ancient creatures in her veins. There weren't supposed to be any drawings, any pictures of the creatures Newlies had been before their magical change. There were, though, and Finn had seen them all. Some of these images disturbed him, like Snouters and the vicious Yowlie kind, but he always tried to keep an open mind.

And, though he truly loved Letitia, sometimes in his head—sometimes together in bed—he could see that small, furry creature with the twitchy nose and pink tail. It was hard to forget this lovely female, this beauty with intelligence and wit, still had the blood of creatures past in her veins. Three hundred years before, her folk had scampered through the cellars and the walls of human habitats— despised by people themselves, who broke their backs with little traps. And, for added pleasure, kept the cruel, cunning ancestors of the Yowlies about to do the killing job as well.

And even now, those who defended Newlie rights often admitted in their hearts that humans and Newlies would never be the same. Finn wished it weren't so, but wishes seldom changed the world. All he could do was try and keep Letitia from the uglier aspects of life. Which, he thought, with no little shame, he wasn't doing very well now, caught in the midst of an odorous crowd who cheered a pack of lunatics in tall yellow hats.

Letitia tried to see past him, and Finn did his best to make sure that she did not. The madmen had reached a new plateau in their torment of the old man on the rack. Much to the pleasure of the crowd, one fellow brought out a large, shiny, wicked-looking blade that clearly belonged to the butcher's trade.

Skinning, hanging, evisceration and fire . . .

Finn recalled, with a visible shudder, those words of the Master of Chairs. And without a conscious thought, he touched the pommel of his own weapon hanging at his side.

"Butter and Bread," he said aloud, "If that's not a fleshing blade, then I'm a great pile of whale doo!"

"My stars, Finn."

"Sorry," Finn said, and moved even closer to block her way.

The horror by the cart was difficult to watch, but Finn couldn't bring himself to look away. The brute with the butcher's blade drew a charcoal line across his captive's chest, from one collarbone to the next.

Here, the fellow was showing the crowd, *is where I will begin . . .*

The victim saw the blade and screamed . . .

One fellow gagged him . . .

Another tightened the knots around his legs . . .

One poked him with a stick, missed, wandered off left and then right, came back and poked him in the groin . . .

One ran into the wagon, knocked himself cold, and dropped to the ground . . .

Lout number one raised his blade high . . .

The crowd sucked in a great collective breath . . .

The blade descended, and touched his howling victim's chest . . .

Everything began to happen, everything at once . . .

It happened so quickly there was scarcely time to think. A single voice, a murderous cry roiled like thunder through the crowd. The great and noisy herd was struck silent, awed by the unearthly sound that seemed to come from everywhere.

Then, just behind the torture rack itself, a yellow-hat bowed his head and dropped. Another grabbed his face and fell, still another stared at the fountain of red where his arm had been half a blink before.

The awful, fearsome voice that had stilled the raging crowd now showed itself to be a man, a tall man, a man with arms and shoulders strong enough to wield the heavy, man-killer blade he clutched in both hands. He wore a suit of leather and mail, shirt, cape and baggy trousers the shade of the sea. On his head, a rakish felt hat crowned with plumes of lavender, green and gold.

Never stopping for a moment, never even slowing down, he hacked, slashed, and chopped himself a path through the killers like a mad reaper loose in a field.

For an instant, his foes seemed dazzled, stunned, completely out of sorts. Then they found their wits and came at him like an angry nest of hornets, like a hive of yellow bees. But this was not a bare, pasty old man, a man you could laugh at, poke with a stick . . .

Men dropped, men died, men crawled away and bled. Men shrieked and howled, men turned away and ran.

Then, as quickly as it had started, it was just as quickly done . . .

Finn watched, bewildered, as the big man lowered his blade, and the yellow-hats fell back. Moving to the rack, he slashed at the bonds that held the old man. The poor fellow sagged, wavered, but managed to stand his ground. The swordsman turned his back to the crowd and covered the old man with his cloak.

Still wielding his weapon, the tall man drew a leather sack from his belt, weighed it in his palm, then tossed it to the yellow-hats, tossed it with contempt. One of the Hatters caught it, peeked inside, let the others see, then quickly jerked it back. He spoke to the swordsman, waving his arms about. The swordsman laughed, and swung his blade in a blur, missing the man by an inch. The Hatters shrank back.

The man with the sword gripped the old man's arm, and stalked away boldly through the crowd.

A few steps farther and he stopped, found another bag, dug around inside, pulled out a fistful of bright silver coins and threw them to the crowd.

The horde went mad, pounding, pummeling, and kicking one another to grab a precious coin. The big man laughed and stomped across the square, swinging his blade to keep the crowd aside.

Finn could see the plume of his hat bobbing above the crowd, then, for the first time, a glimpse of his face, the pock-marked flesh, the thick red hair—

"Great Gars and Guppies!" Finn gasped, scarcely able to believe his eyes. "It's him, by damn—it's that bloody lout, Sabatino Nucci in the flesh!"

Finn took a step back and drew his blade. Drew a breath and held it, felt his heart pound against his chest.

"Finn, dear," Letitia said, resting her hand lightly on his arm, "I doubt he has the time to fight now, he seems to be quite occupied."

"You simply don't know him," Finn said, moving her gently aside, "The man's a lunatic, crazed, of unsound mind. You simply can't say—"

Finn sliced the air,

 bent one knee,

  parried, thrust,

   snapped to a dueler's stance again.

"—what a savage like that will do next. He doesn't think like a man of reason, Letitia. Don't be fooled by the fancy clothes, he's scarcely civilized. Stay here, love, I shall be right back."

"Finn . . . !"

Townsmen stepped aside, puzzled, bewildered at a stranger pushing through their ranks. Something was amiss. One swordsman was ample entertainment, two was not proper, two was not right.

The crowd was behind Finn now, and there, not a dozen feet away, the man who'd tried to kill him stood before him once again. And, at the very same moment, Sabatino recognized him.

He stared, threw back his head and laughed soundly at the sky.

"Why, I can't believe this. Is it truly you, Master Finn? By damn, it is. What are you doing here, sir? I never expected to see you again!"

Sabatino stalked forward, bracing the old man with one hand, grasping his sword with the other. The crowd stepped even farther back. A pack of yellow-hats followed, keeping their distance, clearly not ready to let the pair out of their sight.

Finn gripped the hilt of his sword. Did this brute take him for a fool, greeting him like a friend? At least he had a weapon himself this time.

Finn glanced over his shoulder at Letitia. Her face was the color of chalk. Under his cloak, he could feel Julia Jessica Slagg clawing her way quickly from his frontside to his back.

"Coward," Finn said beneath his breath, "if he spits me with that great heavy blade, it'll do you little good to hide there."

Julia didn't answer. For the first time that Finn could recall, the loud-mouth lizard had nothing to say.

Sabatino came to a halt. "Well, sir, as I say, I did not expect to see you again." He raised his eyes past Finn. "And that would be your Newlie, ah—serving wench, yes? Most attractive, my friend. I only got a glance aboard. She's certainly worth a second look."

Sabatino's glance was so bold, open, and rife with lewd intent that it quickly brought Letitia's color back. Sabatino couldn't miss the sudden change in Finn's stance. He shrugged and met his foe's challenge with a grin.

"You're overly sensitive, sir. I only expressed admiration, I meant no sore offense."

"You, sir, are an offense in yourself," Finn said. "I *know* what you meant, and I resent it quite a bit."

Sabatino sighed. "That's a craftsman for you, always sees himself a step above his class. An artist, if you will, a man of deeper soul. He strives for greater station, and forgets he was born to the hammer, not the brush."

"This is neither the time nor the place, Sabatino, but by damn, you owe me satisfaction, and I'd have it now."

"Yes? Now is perfectly fine with me." He paused, then, and raised a curious brow. "Ah, where is that little tin *toy* of yours, sir? I only got a quick look before our—quarrel aboard that odorous vessel. If it's as pretty as I recall, I'd buy it from you—proceeds to whatever beneficiary you wish to name, of course . . ."

Finn stepped back and raised his blade. At once, Letitia moved up to his side.

"Don't be foolish, dear. You don't have to do this."

"Listen to her, Finn." Sabatino glanced over his shoulder, then faced Finn again. "Better still, heed a word from me."

To Finn's surprise, Sabatino sheathed his weapon, left the old man on his own, and drew closer still.

"What you must do," he said, so softly that no one else might hear, "is forget, for now, this quarrel with me. You don't know the game we're playing, or the rules, and I've no time to explain it to you now. We've very little time. I'd say two, three minutes at the most. I've cut it awfully short, standing here wasting time with you."

Finn frowned. "What in all the hells are you talking about? I have no—"

"—no time at all, so kindly shut up, my friend. You and

that pretty can stand here and die if you wish. Which you surely will, for they see you're in company with Sabatino Nucci, and that's what they have in mind for me.

"The rules, you see, call for the Moment of Useless Combat, then the Payment of the Honorable Fee. That's done, and we've jabbered right through the damned Horror of the Fallen, so we must get out of here, or wait for the Reckoning of the Just. That should begin about now."

"I have no idea what you've gotten yourself into," Finn said, "but whatever it is, it has nothing to do with Letitia and me."

"Look back there, if you will," Sabatino said. "Tell me what you see."

"I see the same lot of yellow-hatted crazies I saw before. They're milling about, nodding their foolish heads. If I didn't know better, I'd say they'll soon break into dance."

"Very perceptive, sir. In a moment, they'll pound those sharpened poles on the ground. We should have about twenty-two seconds after that. If you'll hold on to Father, I'll bring up the rear and try to hold them off. Keep your head and we'll make it out of here."

"You mean *him*?" Finn looked at the shaggy-haired old man, bent, miserable, ready to collapse. "That's your *father*?"

"Yes, damn you, it is," Sabatino said, quite annoyed now. "Do you think I'd pause to talk to the likes of you if I didn't require your help?"

Sabatino curled his lips in disgust. "Now would you do as I say, noble *craftsman*? Thanks to you, we have scarcely any time left."

Indeed, Sabatino was right, for there was truly no time left at all. His words had scarcely passed his lips before the madmen began to pound their sharpened poles against the square, sway, shout, and dance madly about . . .

Nine . . .

FINN NEEDED NO FURTHER URGING AFTER THAT.
As he came to the old man's side, an unearthly howl rose
from the rear, a sound that fair chilled him to the bone.

"Letitia," he said, "I think we'd best go. I fear these
brutes are quite serious about this."

"Will you *move*, please?" Sabatino ran a finger down his
blade. "Go, and don't look back. I shall be there with you,
don't be concerned about that."

"Oh, I surely won't," Finn said. "How could I have any
doubts about you?"

With Letitia's help, he hurried the old man across the
square and back toward the market. The people gave way,
opening their ranks to let them through. They shook their
fists and shouted, but made no effort to interfere.

Evidently, Finn decided, that was one of the rules of this
game Sabatino had not had the time to describe. Finn de-
tested games of every sort. The whole thing was a fool's
pastime. Or would have been, except for the parts about
skinning, hanging and loss of inner parts.

He retreated down one narrow street and then the next.

Letitia assured him they'd come this way before, and Finn didn't doubt that she was right. Mycers came from folk who had to know exactly where they were at all times if they wished to stay alive.

"Who the hell are you? I don't know you, never saw you before, what're you doing to me?"

Finn gave the old man a curious look. It was the first time he'd spoken since his rescue from the rack.

"My name is Master Finn. What I'm doing is risking my life to save you from those dolts back there. If you'd like me to leave, I can surely do that."

"Huh." The old man thought about that, reached back and scratched his rear. "You a friend of that worthless son of mine?"

"Not even remotely, no."

"Good. I'll accept your help, then, if I've got your word on that."

"That's a great relief to me. I feared for a moment I'd have to leave you here."

The old man glared, and tore away from Finn. "Don't talk back to me, young man. I'll have your feet flailed to bloody nubs. I'll—"

He stopped then, and stared. His bleary eyes went wide with surprise as he suddenly noticed Letitia, standing right beside Finn.

"Glory be," he said in wonder, his weary features stretching in a grin, "Why, you naughty girl, I've had dreams about you, didn't think you'd ever come. Get over here and hug an old man, tell me your name, pretty thing."

"I don't think so," Letitia said sweetly, "just get that out of your head. And try not to breathe on me, you smell like everything I should've thrown out before we left home."

"You can't offend me, girl, a lot of other people have tried. You'll come around, I'm willing to give you time."

"I'd cease that suggestive line of talk if I were you," Finn said. "I don't feel any strong obligation, old man. I wouldn't mind just leaving you here."

"Don't stop to nap up there," Sabatino shouted from the rear. "Keep it moving, *craftsman*, if you want to leave here with your head intact!"

Finn looked back. Sabatino was holding his own, but the horde was on him like flies.

"Letitia, can you hold him up by yourself?"

"No, I can't, Finn."

"Try. I'll be back when I can."

With that he was gone, trotting back to Sabatino.

"What are you doing here?" Sabatino said, without looking around, "Get back—where you—belong!"

With that, he swept his heavy weapon in a terrible arc, downing one fellow and slicing another across the neck.

"Fighting is very restful after listening to your father," Finn said. "It's really quite pleasant back here."

Moving to Sabatino's right, he left a crimson stripe across a foe's chest.

"He can be a bloody nuisance, you're right about that."

"I want you to know that I will never forgive you for the trouble you've brought my way. This is in addition to what you did to that lad aboard ship, and your unwarranted attack on me. Our quarrel isn't done, don't think it is—watch it there, on your right!"

Sabatino caught a pole on his blade an instant before it found his head.

"Letitia's doing the best she can," Finn said, "but it wouldn't hurt if you'd give us some direction. We weren't born in this mudhole of yours."

"Mudhole, is it? I never imagined it as charming as that. In front of you, craftsman, that skinny fellow's faster than he looks."

Finn took care of the man with the flat of his blade and moved up to cover a pair coming in from the left. While the enemy were armed with only sharpened poles, there were plenty of them, quite enough to take the pair down if they failed to stay on their toes.

Luckily, he and Sabatino had superior arms, and the other side failed to attack in an organized manner, as a whole, as a unit, as a trained group of soldiers might do. Instead, some would go forward, then suddenly turn to the right or to the left. Some would whip about and go backwards for a while. Some, as Finn had noted in the square, would bump into one another, or crack their skulls on a wall.

It was only by chance, then, that a foe with a cone-shaped hat would be directly in front of Sabatino or Finn. The danger was solely in their numbers, for they lacked all tactical skills.

The battle turned a corner and veered down a roughly cobbled street. Finn's fighting arm began to tire, but he couldn't slow down. Not in front of Sabatino, who seemed to have great reserves of strength, and was having a joyous time.

Where the hell are we, and where are we going? Finn asked himself.

What if Letitia's inborn instincts betrayed her this time? What if that addled old man had led her off another way?

As if in answer to his thoughts, Letitia shouted, her voice high and shrill, loud enough to cut through the noise of battle, and the crowd that squeezed in behind.

"Finn, *Finn*, this street's come to an end, there's nowhere else to go!"

"Fishes and Fruit," Finn said, wiping the sweat from his brow, "I knew this would happen, I by damn knew . . ."

Sabatino let out a yell. Finn turned, ready to come to the fellow's aid, turned to see him go head over heels over some dark object in the street.

"Look at that," Sabatino said with great disgust, coming

quickly to his feet, "some mindless fool left a *chair* in the street. I could've been crippled for life!"

"Hard to imagine how something like that could happen," Finn said, fending off another pair. One stared at the neat line of blood across his belly. The other simply turned and walked away.

There were plenty more about—apparently, Finn thought, an endless supply. He and Sabatino held them off, beating a hasty retreat to Letitia and the old man down the alleyway.

Letitia was right. The alley came abruptly to an end. A wooden fence and piles of rubble blocked the way. The fence was too high to climb and even if the three of them could make it, the old man would never have a chance.

"Hold them off as best you can," Sabatino shouted in Finn's ear.

"And what do you intend to do?"

"I intend to tear down that damnable fence, if it's all right with you."

"A grand idea. What are you going to tear it down *with*?"

Sabatino didn't answer. He left with a look Finn was quite accustomed to: scorn, disdain, and utter contempt. Sabatino had several other "looks," but these were the three he clearly liked the best.

The assailants, Finn saw, for reasons of their own, had paused at the head of the alley when their foes came up against the fence. Maybe it was lunchtime, Finn decided, and wondered then, just how the fellows ate. Did they take time off, or simply hope they might run into food?

The old man had decided to sit and scowl. A basic mean spirit, or inherent constipation, was apparently a family trait. Finn had seen this sort of thing pass down for many generations before.

"Are you all right?" Finn said, moving up to Letitia's side. "You're not hurt or anything?"

"No, I'm not hurt, Finn." Letitia slumped against the alley wall. Her hair was in disarray and her cheeks were smudged with soot. Somewhere along the way, she had picked up one of the enemy's broken sticks.

"I'm not having a good vacation so far, but I haven't been injured or killed, if that's what you want to know."

"Good," Finn said, "I know this is wearing. I'm extremely sorry, love. As you say, the trip's not going well, but I'm certain our luck will turn soon."

"Why?"

"What's that?"

"Why would our luck turn soon? It has not *turned* since we closed the front door on Garpenny Street. It has gotten worse by the hour, and worse than *that* since your new friend came along."

"He is hardly a friend, I think you know that. I can't abide the man. Fate has thrown us together, and I can't help that. As soon as we rid ourselves of him, I'm sure our fortunes will change."

"I know that, dear." Letitia showed him a weary smile. "I am simply so tired of ships, and those dreadful Yowlies, and now *him*, and that disgusting, smelly old man. Our chair is still in the street, did you notice that, Finn?"

"I did, yes." Finn picked up a rag from the alley and wiped the blade of his sword. "They're milling around up there. I expect they'll have another go at us soon."

Letitia refused to look. "What have we gotten ourselves into, dear? Do you have the slightest idea? Who are these people, and why are they doing this? Why did they want to kill the old man?"

"I don't know. I can't even guess. There is much here I do not understand at all . . ."

He would have said more if their aggressors hadn't suddenly renewed their advance, shouting and waving their poles about.

"Have a care up there," Sabatino called out, "they're a witless bunch, but they never give in."

"I can see these things for myself," Finn said, more than a little irritated, "I don't need your constant advice."

If Sabatino had a cutting reply, it was lost as the horde of yellow-hats poured down the narrow alleyway. If anything, Finn thought they were angrier, and even more determined, than before.

Why they had paused at all, he couldn't say. They were no more organized than before. Some ran backwards, some ran into walls. Some tripped and fell, and were trampled at once by their friends.

Still, Finn was greatly concerned. Numbers counted, and even an army of the totally inept would overcome a pair of skilled swordsmen in the end.

"I don't like the look of this," said Julia Jessica Slagg, "We are severely outnumbered, Finn."

"And how would you know, hiding behind my back? The view can't be very good from there."

"I have ears of a sort, as you're aware. Those creatures make a great deal of noise. Finn . . ."

"What?"

"I don't think we're going to get out of this."

"That's your opinion, is it?"

"It is, yes."

"Then I'll ask you to keep it to yourself."

"You don't have to snap at me, I'm only trying to help. If I were you, I would seriously consider the—"

Julia's words were lost as Finn, with a frightening shout, charged up the alleyway to meet his foes head on.

The ragged fellows looked puzzled, bewildered, somewhat dismayed. They weren't prepared for such outlandish behavior, never having encountered it before. People you were after ran *away*, they didn't come at you.

Finn slashed with a will, cutting them down, driving

them back. They shrieked, fell, clutched at their wounds, doubled up and died.

Still, it was clear that a greater force than pain, a stronger drive than fear, drove these creatures on. Though Finn had never fought in the great eternal War, he had stood his ground in more than one encounter before. He knew that look, that fierce unthinking will of the zealot, the man who gives his life because some greater fool has told him his cause is right, and all others are wrong.

"Damn you all," Finn yelled, his arm so heavy he could scarcely lift his weapon, barely fend off a man who came at him with a stick. "Take your stupid hats and die somewhere else, just keep away from me!"

If anything, Finn's words seemed to stir his enemies to greater fury than before. They jabbered, chattered and boiled, frothed at the mouth, struck out at Finn. Poked one another, dropped to the ground, got up and came at him again.

Like stirring a nest of ants, Finn muttered to himself, *buggers got about as much sense, you ask me . . .*

The yellowheads shouted, yelled, clawed and kicked and scratched, kicked one another to get at their foe . . .

And, in that instant, Finn felt an awful chill, saw, like a dream yet to be, how it would happen, exactly how he'd fall, how deep the wound would be . . . he heard Letitia cry, far, far away . . .

"Back, *back!*" he yelled, his mouth dry as sand, the words grating in his throat. "Get them out, Sabatino, get them out of here now!"

He slashed out blindly, knowing it was useless, the final act upon him, over and done.

Bitters and Blood, I don't even have the last lines, they belong to some fool in a pointy yellow hat . . .

They knew it, felt it, smelled the sweet scent of death.

Their voices rose in an awful manic din, in a cry, in a moan, in a wail that chilled him to the bone . . .

Finn backed up and stumbled, caught himself, lashed out again. Risked a final glance at Letitia, couldn't see her anywhere. The horde came at him in a blind and thought-less fury, jabbing one another with their sticks, crushing one another against the alley walls.

Finn winced as a pole struck the side of his head. Saw double for an instant, shook the fellow off. Kicked out and caught one in the gut. A gaunt, one-eyed bruiser got through, poked him in the chest. He gasped, jerked the point out. The man grabbed him like a spider and brought him to the ground. Another piled on, then another after that.

"Damn your rotten breath," Finn growled between his teeth, "What do you bastards here eat, garbage, offal, slops in the street, maggoty meat?"

He went under then, fighting and cursing, striking out with his fists, his sword no longer in his hand. He was fin-ished, there was no use fighting anymore, but giving up never crossed his mind. He tore at the pile of smelly flesh, fought with every ragged breath, jammed a broken fist into someone's vital part, kicked at a head, elbowed a crotch.

He wondered what would happen to Letitia, wondered what they'd do when they got her, didn't care to think about that. Wondered, for an instant, why that pompous lout, Sabatino, didn't come and help. Knew, at once, that the highborn brute had left him there to fight, left the simple-minded *craftsman* to hold off the louts while he got his precious self away . . .

"Goodbye, Letitia," he heard himself whisper far away, "Goodbye, Julia Jessica Slagg. If you can hear me now, know that I'm sorry I made you, for this is not a world fit for human, Newlie or even a loud-mouth lizard made of copper, spit and tin . . . I could have done better if I'd used better wiring, purified mercury, and gold in your head . . ."

"Will you stop your jabbering, Finn!"

The crackly voice came from somewhere in the small of his back, or farther down than that. "Get off of me, you overweight lump, I'm dying down here!"

"Same . . . up here," Finn said, and everything, as the storytellers say, went suddenly black . . .

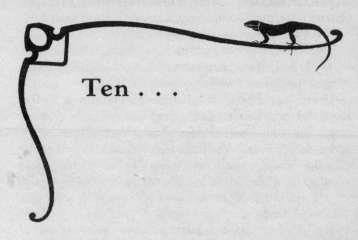

Ten . . .

. . . AND, JUST AS QUICKLY, EVERYTHING WENT
absolutely white-star-hot, eyeball-searing bright.

Finn sat up, blinked, grabbed for his fallen blade. He
hurt too much, there was too much clatter pounding in his
head to pass out. Howls, yowls, shrieks from all about. Yellow rowdies punched, yellow devils kicked, fought one another to escape the awful horror snapping at their heels,
clawing at their backs.

Hurt toughies, dead toughies, utterly mad barbarians
and fiends blocked the narrow way out. Fellows yet alive,
true to their credo, stumbled about, hitting one another,
going this way and that, like ale-besotted louts.

The monster, the beast, the copper-scaled creature loose
among them, tore through bone and flesh like a razor gone
berserk. The floor of the alley, every brick, every crack,
every inch of the grime-encrusted walls turned a bloody
crimson from the dying, from the dead. There were splat-
ters and splotches, patches and drips, syrupy clots. And
through it all, the rattle and the clatter and the snap, the

snick and the click of sharp teeth and the rip of iron claws . . .

"Get up man, not a moment to waste, we simply cannot hang around here!"

Finn found himself hauled off the ground and on his feet again, Sabatino's strong grip urging him down the cobbled street. Through sheer brute force, Sabatino had managed to kick a ragged hole in the fence that blocked the end of the alleyway. He squeezed his broader father through, and stood guard while Letitia and Finn came in behind.

"Oh, love, I thought you were stricken, I thought you were dead, I truly did, dear Finn!"

Letitia's face was drained of all color, her eyes full of dread.

"I'm not," Finn said, "though I fear I came terribly close. Where's Julia Jessica Slagg? Is she harmed?"

"If you mean that fearsome device of yours," Sabatino said, "she, it, or whatever in fiery hell it is, is fine. Nothing else is back there, everything is *meat*."

Sabatino's eyes seemed to bore through the back of Finn's head. "You and I, sir, are going to have a long talk about this marvelous, mechanical killer of yours when we're safely out of here, you can count on that."

"No we're not," said Julia, scooting through Sabatino's legs, rattling on ahead, leaving bloody tracks. "We're not going to talk about *me* at all."

"Damn my eyes!" Sabatino swept off his hat and stared in wonder. "The thing speaks, it talks as well as you and I!"

"It talks entirely too much," Finn said, sending a withering look the lizard's way, "and, as ever, at all the wrong times. I suggest you get cleaned up, Julia. Moisture of any sort is not good for your parts."

"If that's 'Thank you, Julia, defender of the weak, the

frail, the helpless humankind,' then you are quite welcome,
Finn. I am glad to be of service anytime."

"He really is grateful," Letitia put in, "but you shouldn't
talk like that."

"Marvelous, absolutely marvelous!" Sabatino ap-
plauded. "The captain said you had a thing that sat atop
your shoulder, but I scarcely believed him at the time. Poor
fellow drinks, you know. What exactly is it? Whatever do
you call it, Finn?"

"What I call it is none of your concern," Finn said, feeling dizzy and weak now that the fight was over, and his attention was turned toward his bruises, abrasions, and sores.
He was totally disgusted with the whole ridiculous event,
with the town, with the Hatters, and especially with
Sabatino himself.

"I'll trouble you to mind your own affairs," he said,
brushing some gross, unnamable filth from his clothes.
"Do not ask me about my property again."

He knew, though, that the lizard, so to speak, was out of
the bag, there was no use trying to stuff it back again . . .

The towns, as towns are prone to do, began to meet the
countryside; the crowded, sooty houses and grimy, odorous
streets gave way to lonely, sooty houses, and unpaved, ill-
smelling roads.

Desolation, it seemed, was the standard of beauty in
Sabatino's land. There were no trees about, no brush, no foliage of any kind, nothing but a dull, brown furze that was
clearly more dead than alive. Rocks, large and small, were
key points of interest to the left and to the right. Finn
guessed there were even more rocks ahead.

Finn, who had no sense at all of where they might be,
was greatly surprised to see that their way led fairly close
to the harbor itself. Over the roofs of country farms, he

recognized the high masthead of the *Madeline Rose,* crowded in among vessels of various size and shape. Beyond lay the sapphire blue of the Misty Sea, and a dazzling array of purple-tinted clouds. He squeezed Letitia's hand, and Letitia squeezed back.

"Beautiful sight, yes?" Sabatino set his hands on his hips and squinted at the sea. "The very best view of our lovely country, as anyone who visits us will tell you—the way *out* of here."

"I have to agree," Letitia said. "But what a peculiar thing for you to say."

"Oh, really?" Sabatino raised a haughty brow. "And you are enjoying your stay so far, miss?"

"He has a valid point," Finn said. "I never thought I'd say it, but the sea looks very good to me."

"I have a point, as you say—I *live* here. I put up with this nonsense every day of my life."

Letitia frowned. "Every day?"

"All right, not *every* day. It just seems like every day, I suppose. And stop looking over your shoulder. They won't try for us again. Rules are rules, you know."

"What rules?" Finn asked, "What are you talking about?"

"I don't have the time, craftsman, to go into that. Father has had a very trying time. I would like to get him home."

"Indeed," Finn said. "Before you go, I'd be grateful if you'd tell us which road will lead us back to the ship. No offense, but I'm hoping not to spend another hour here."

Sabatino stopped, facing Finn again. "Take any street you like. None will do you any good."

Finn frowned. "And what exactly is that supposed to mean?"

"It means the hour is nearly five in the afternoon. Everything closes at 4:46 p.m. Stores, shops, stalls and bazaars, streets and avenues. Whatever path you might take will be closed."

"Why? Whatever for?"

"Because that's our custom, that's what we do."

"And when does everything open again?"

"Why, at 4:46 in the morning, of course . . ."

Sabatino grinned, pleased at the shock and total desolation Finn displayed at the news. And even more delightful, the horror, the dismay, the total disbelief on the face of Letitia Louise.

Finn's hand trembled at the hilt of his sword. "I don't believe a word of this, Sabatino, not coming from you. I doubt you could tell the truth if you tried. Letitia and I will go on. I'm sure we'll find the roads aren't closed at all. And if it happens that they are, if there's a bare ounce of truth in what you say, we'll inquire about lodging and a decent meal. I'm certain there's at least one person in this dismal land of yours who will offer a stranger comfort for the night."

Sabatino stared at Finn a moment, then his features broadened in a wicked, irritating smile.

"You think so, do you? Well, *craftsman*, that simply shows you're as great a fool as I imagined from the start. *No* one would offer you *comfort*, as you say, even if it wasn't after five, because this disgusting habit of hospitality, which appears to pervade elsewhere, is *not* practiced here.

"We have no homey little inns, hotels or such hovels as I've observed in foreign lands. You cannot eat or sleep in such a place in Port Nakeemo, or anyplace else in good Makasar."

Sabatino's words caused Finn great alarm. He had thought the Master of Chairs feeble in the head, that of course there was *always* somewhere to stay, no matter where you went.

But what if Sabatino didn't lie? What if, for some bizarre, convoluted reason, he *was* telling the truth this time? What then of he and Letitia Louise, who was, even now, trembling visibly beside him, and not from the chill evening air?

"Why," he asked, "Even if this—this insane custom of yours that turns away guests in your misbegotten land is real? Why does the town close up at four-forty—whatever you said? That makes no sense at all."

"4:46. And it makes sense to us."

"Yes, damn it all, but why?"

"Because the night belongs to them, that's why. Because they want it that way."

"Who, those loonies in pointy hats? Snips and Clips, when do these fellows sleep?"

"Not them."

"Who, then?"

"The Hooters."

"Hooters . . . ?"

"Hatters have the day. Hooters have the night."

Sabatino gave a mighty sigh, obviously tired of explaining everyday facts to strangers with little minds.

"Hatters keep the day, all right? At eventide, they give way to Hooters, and Hooters rule the night. And spare me any more questions, Finn. I am quite exhausted, and Father isn't well. Things are as they are, the way they've always been. It's foolish to question why."

"Please don't ask him," Letitia said, "I really don't think I want to know."

"Not only a quite attractive Newlie," Sabatino said, "but one with common sense as well."

He studied Letitia with a practiced eye, a man with a bent for exploration, mapping out places he thought he'd like to see.

Finn was put out, and thoroughly annoyed with the fellow's lies, his arrogant ways, his lecherous remarks, his lewd and obvious leers. There was no threat he could imagine that would make him linger in this most peculiar land.

"We'll be going," he said, taking Letitia's hand. "I'm sure we'll find a place to stay with little trouble at all. If I see a—a Hooter, I'll run the fellow through."

"You don't listen, do you, Finn?"

Sabatino squinted into the setting sun. His father had taken advantage of the stop to squat on the roughshod road. He had scarcely said a word since they left the outskirts of town. Still, Finn decided, the old man seemed to be feeling better, and was more alert now. Alert enough to follow his son's example, and inspect Letitia's parts.

"You think I'm joking about the dangers of stomping about in the night?" Sabatino went on. "Fine. Do it, then. Perhaps the Hooters won't notice you're there. Maybe they won't even notice your lovely friend. Maybe. But I shouldn't count on it, Finn."

"If you're trying to frighten me, forget it. That might work on simple folk. It won't work with me."

"It's working on me," Letitia said, folding her arms close about her chest. "He's scaring me. He's scaring me quite a bit."

"I'm sorry," Finn said. "He's well aware of what he's doing, my dear. There may be such things as Hooters, but I strongly doubt that. What are the chances of two clans of marching morons in one dismal town? Very slim, I'd say."

"But you don't know that, Finn."

"I am not wholly certain, no. But I—"

"Before we go, would you ask this fellow where we might obtain lubrication?" Julia croaked, scrambling from Finn's right shoulder to his left. "If I don't get a little oil in my gears, I'm going to lock up tight. That will be on your head, Finn, not mine."

"Shut up. You'll just have to wait, like everyone else."

"Mr. Sabatino?" Letitia bit her lip. Finn knew she was terribly frightened, for her nose was now constantly a-twitch. Her eyes were dark as river stones—he could even see a little white, and that was rare indeed.

"Sir, will you be truthful with me, if I ask?"

"Of course I will, my dear." Sabatino offered a slight mockery of a bow. "I would lie to your friend, whom I truly despise, but I could never tell a falsehood to you."

"Oh, please . . ." Finn said, shaking his head at the sky.

"Then tell me true. Are there really such things as Hooters like you said?"

"Oh, indeed there are."

"And what exactly do they—do?"

"They hoot, for one thing. All through the dark of night."

"And what besides that?"

"Harmful things, you mean."

"Yes. That is how I'd put it. Harmful things . . ."

Sabatino glanced at Finn, then back to Letitia.

"What they do is different from what the Hatters do. The Hooters neither skin, flog, strangle nor gut folks during their rites. What they do—normally, I mean—is slice off a victim's fingers, one at a time, then all of one's toes, then an eye and an ear and a nose. After that comes the scary part—"

"Damn you, that's enough," Finn said, for Letitia had turned a paler shade of white.

"What they do," Sabatino finished, "is burn everything—every being—in sight. This is what they like to do best."

"You've actually—seen such barbarous acts?"

"Of course not, why would I?"

"You see," Finn said, turning to Letitia, who shivered in the hollow of his arms. "You see what he's doing now?"

"I don't *have* to see," Sabatino said abruptly. "Father was a Hooter until he retired. A Grand High Hooter, as a fact."

Sabatino's father looked up with a toothless grin. "A Grand High Hooter Third Class. No one hardly ever gets higher than that."

"This is true, then?" Finn looked at the old man in a different, more chilling light.

"Why do you think the Hatters made such a big thing out of doing him in? Anytime a Hatter can get a High Hooter . . ." Sabatino spread his hands. There was, his gesture said, really nothing else to add.

Finn held Letitia close, but her trembling wouldn't go away.

"What I am about to say," Sabatino said, gazing at the early evening sky, "is a thing so foreign, so alien to all I believe, all I hold dear, that I cannot imagine these words are about to emerge from me. Though I loathe you with all my heart, Finn, I owe you a debt, and a debt I must pay. This is why I offer you—I can scarcely even say it now—I offer you the sanctuary of my home for the night . . ."

Sabatino rolled his eyes and ran a hand across his brow. "Father, I must ask your permission for this—heresy of mine."

Father, though, had fallen fast asleep on the ground.

"Very well, then. I will take the responsibility myself."

"No, most assuredly not," Finn said. He turned to Letitia Louise. "If I had been thinking straight, I would have headed right for the harbor when the mast of the vessel first appeared. That, my dear, is the path we shall follow now. I think I can assure you no Hooters or other apparitions will appear."

"I am—ever in your hands, dear Finn."

"Are you sure? You seem uncertain to me."

"Not at all, love. How could you ever imagine that?"

"I'm grateful for your trust. I'm confident we'll come safely through."

"Yes. I'm—certain we will."

"Are you two finished?" Sabatino said with a sigh. "If you are, I bid you farewell with this parting word. When you reach the sea—if you did, I mean—you would find that the *Madeline Rose* is not at the wharf anymore, but is anchored in the bay. You would find all other vessels are anchored there as well.

"It matters very little if you don't believe in Hooters. I assure you the good captains do, as they've all been here before, and don't wish their vessels burned down to the keel. No one, Finn, and Letitia, dear, is fool enough to brave the night here . . ."

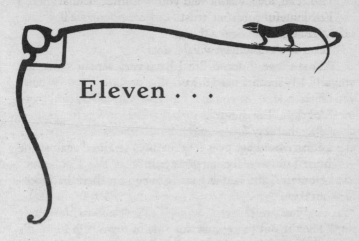

Eleven . . .

MOMENTS AFTER THE SUN DISAPPEARED BEYOND the rust-colored sky, darkness rushed in to swallow up the day. It happened so quickly Finn felt a chill that had little to do with the oncoming night. Letitia felt it too, for she huddled in the hollow of his shoulder and held herself tight, as if she might make herself smaller, safe against the dark in a warm hidey-hole, as her kind had done in ages past.

Sabatino seemed to read her thoughts, for he told them not to be concerned, that his home was just down the road, not very far at all. Finn caught the touch of amusement in his voice, for the fellow knew that Finn was not pleased with the prospect at all.

"Stay close to me in this damnable dark," he told Letitia. "If anything should happen, I want you very near."

"If she gets any closer," Julia croaked from Finn's shoulder, "she'll be up here with me."

"Be quiet. I can't think straight with you squawking all the time."

"I seldom squawk. And even if I did—"

"Both of you be still, will you?" Letitia said. "There's something out there."

"What? I don't hear a thing."

"You don't have Mycer ears, dear."

"That's true, I don't. But I have very sensitive hearing myself. My mother used to say—"

"*Finn . . .*"

"All right, I'm quiet."

"Stay that way."

Letitia closed her eyes, her features strained against the night as if she were feeling great pain.

"Hooters," she said at last. "I'm certain there are Hooters out there."

"Are you sure?"

"They're out there, just this side of town. Oh Finn, it's just like he said!"

"It's all right, we'll be just fine . . ."

"Keep up, craftsman," Sabatino said, "or I'll leave you out here."

"Just him," the old man said. "Don't leave the pretty behind."

Sabatino shook his head. "This has been a most intriguing day, I'm damned if it hasn't."

"That's not what I'd call it," Finn muttered to himself.

When he first saw it, when the dark shape appeared against the greater dark of night, it looked as if a jagged, ragged, malformed tooth had thrust itself up from the awesome jaws of the earth.

Closer, Finn decided it was less of a molar and more a horrid accident. Someone, or something, had apparently run into the thing, and knocked it all askew.

No, he thought again, there's a better metaphor than that: a mad architect and a crew of drunken builders had stood well back and tossed sticks, stones, mortar and bricks in a great ungainly pile. Then, as a parting thought, threw in a score of cracked windows and cater-wonker doors.

There were two, three, or four dizzy floors, depending where you looked. No angle matched another, no pitch was the same. Rooms, towers, chimneys and roofs had been tacked on anywhere. This was a house, Finn decided, that defied the laws of nature, gravity, reason and taste.

And worst of all, the longer he gazed at the thing, the more it seemed to waver, shift, vanish all together, then pop into being again.

"I feel kind of funny," Letitia said, her face visibly pale even in the dark. "I think I maybe have to throw up."

"Don't look at it," Finn said, "that thing isn't real, it's some kind of spell."

"He's right, for once," Sabatino said, "some of it's magic, some of it's not. We don't know why, it's been that way long as anyone can recall. Takes a while to get used to—look at something else.

"Come along, your Newlie is right. There are Hooters out there, and not far at that. Most of the bastards never heard of Father, and wouldn't care if they did . . ."

Inside, the house was most peculiar, although without the nauseating effect. The fault there lay in a great abundance of dust, darkness and neglect. The wooden beams were suffering from rot. The stone walls were cracked. Moths had devoured the tapestries down to a few feeble threads. The décor was Early Gloom. The overall ambiance was Damp.

"We'll be having a late dinner, I fear," Sabatino said, flinging his hat at a chair. The colorful plumes had broken in the fight and were now reduced to stubs.

"Don't bother," Finn said, an image of Sabatino's kitchen in mind, "I couldn't eat a thing."

"I could," Letitia said, "I'm absolutely starved."

"Letitia . . ."

"I must say I've never seen a place as big as this. Why, we could fit the whole house on Garpenny Street in a corner somewhere."

"I can't imagine why we'd do that. No offense, you understand."

"None taken," Sabatino said. "That craftsman's sense of humor has a fine edge, Finn."

Finn pretended not to hear. He noted they'd been inside scarcely a minute and a half and Sabatino's father had completely disappeared. Changing into something more proper than nothing at all, no doubt.

"If I may ask, I know Letitia's quite weary, and I wonder if there's somewhere she could rest. I seldom tire, but I confess I could use a break myself."

"Of course," Sabatino said with a courtly gentleman's bow, or at least a parody of such. "You'll find lovely quarters upstairs. There is every convenience one could ask. Squeen William will show you the way."

Finn followed the fellow's glance and saw no one at all, nothing but a shadow on the wall. He glanced at Letitia, but she clearly saw nothing herself.

"Been with the Nuccis for years. A quite reliable servant, none better, as a fact. Loyal, quick, part of the family, I'd say. A dear, dear fellow, he—

"—by damn, you worthless, cunning bastard, you've been in the spirits again, I can smell your foul breath from here! You take advantage of my gentle nature, you miserable lout. If I didn't have guests, I'd flail you bloody, strip the skin off your back. Damn your heathen soul, I'm talking to you!"

". . . And I be lissssen to your worthy, as isss my pleassure, sssir. . . ."

Letitia screamed, backed up and ran into Finn, tried to push him off and get away.

"It's all right, love, I'm right here."

It wasn't all right, for his heart had nearly stopped, and he'd almost shouted himself. You scarcely ever saw a Vampie, unless you were fond of the night. They were creatures of the Nine, but likely more frightening—and far less human—than any of the rest. Gaunt, hairy creatures with ebony eyes, a flat, ugly nose, and hairy ears. From their narrow shoulders to their wrists, they carried a band of dark leathery tissue, vestigial wings from what they'd been before.

Though few in these days knew why, it was more than their appearance that frightened humans. Long before they took Newlie form, they had been perceived as creatures akin to magic of the very darkest kind.

". . . Ah, Squeen my boy, there you are, then. These are our honored guests. Finn, master of—what did you call the thing? And this lovely creature is his, ah—able companion, Mistress Letitia Louise. See that you answer their every need, or I'll pluck your eyes out and feed you to the eels. Now take these good people to their room before I forget I'm a patient, most forgiving man . . ."

Letitia drew in a breath. "Squeen, I hope you'll accept my apology. I was startled, I guess, and I didn't mean to scream."

"Isss all right, misss. Squeen be unner'sssstan."

"Quite, ah, unnecessary, that," Sabatino said with a frown, "no need at all."

"You will follow, pleassse?"

"Thank you," Finn said, in an effort to further irritate their host. "That's most kind of you, Squeen."

"Impertinent lout," Sabatino muttered to himself.

∽

Finn, holding Letitia's hand, followed the creature up a narrow, winding staircase that rose into the dark.

"Damn the fellow . . . doesn't miss a chance to cause others discomfort if he can . . ."

"What's that, my dear?"

"Nothing. Mumbling to myself."

"Well, it was certainly a very *angry* sort of mumble, I have to say."

Finn didn't answer. He kept his eyes on the worn wooden stairs, praying they wouldn't give way and plunge them into some dark and endless abyss.

Squeen William with his dim tallow candle up ahead was not a pretty sight. He waddled like a duck, dragging one foot painfully behind, the motion causing him to sway from side to side. And in odd countermotion, his head bobbed from front to back.

At the top of the stairs, Squeen proceeded down a long and dusty hall, past dark foreboding doors, past scabby papered walls, past corridors that clearly led nowhere at all. Finn ran into a thick spiderweb, and no matter how he tore and pulled and flailed, this graveyard for hapless nits and moths, flutter-bugs and things that buzz about, this coffin for the hollow husks of flies clung to his face and wouldn't go away.

"Here, ssssir and misss," Squeen said, stopping before a door much like the ones they'd passed before. "Wery fine quarters, you bees warm and comfy here."

"Thank you, Squeen," Finn said. "We are grateful for your help."

"Yesssss." Squeen offered a ghastly smile to show that he was pleased. "You needin' ssssomething, you bees callin' Squeen."

Finn waited until the creature was gone, then he turned and took Letitia in his arms.

"Oh, dear Finn, Finn . . ." Letitia had been holding her breath, and now she let it out in a rush.

"We'll be all right," Finn assured her. "We'll stay right here until daylight. We won't even go downstairs, that's what he wants us to do. Sit down and listen to more of his pompous, irritating talk. Play the gracious host."

"I *am* hungry, dear."

"Of course you are. And I shall demand that he send food up to our room. He can't deny us that."

Letitia sighed. "Yes he can, Finn. He can, and he surely will."

Finn looked away, angry at Sabatino Nucci, but mostly angry at himself, for he knew Letitia was right. The damned fellow had them in a box. There was nothing they could do, nowhere to go. Certainly not out into the night.

"Ah, love," Letitia said, her hands about his neck, "you're worried about me, as ever, and you really mustn't be. I'm perfectly fine, I'm just a bit—scared, is all. Scared and awfully tired."

"This is not the vacation I had in mind, my dear. I never dreamed we'd be caught up in something like this. Damnation, it's been a disaster from the start. One thing after another. That ship, the crew, that maniac Magreet, and then—*him*. Scones and Bones, what did I do to deserve Sabatino Nucci in my life?"

"It's not your fault now, Finn. There's nothing you could have done."

"Yes, you're right." He turned to her then, a sudden flash of understanding in his eyes. "You're right, I've been telling myself I was a fool, a buffoon who could do nothing right. A weak and trusting dolt helpless to stand against the vagaries of chance."

Finn sat on the edge of the bed and motioned Letitia to his side. "I have come to see, love, that even the Fates could not contrive to dump such an odorous load of dung into my life. No, there is something else at work here, something I have completely failed to see."

"What, Finn? What is it you're trying to say?"

"I'm certain I must be wrong in this—yet, equally sure that I'm not, for it is the only thing that smacks of reason in this whole bizarre set of events."

He reached over and took her hands, finding them suddenly icy cold. "You know I steer clear of mystic arts, Letitia. I wear no amulets, I have no use for spells. Yet, after all that has happened, I have to say our troubles smack of magic to me."

"Oh, Finn . . ." Letitia drew her hands away, stood, and looked at the shabby wall. "I feel you're out of sorts, my dear. We are under a great deal of strain, and I cannot blame you for thinking as you do. Still, I have to say I don't know who would go to the trouble of buying a curse as troublesome and—and as threatening as this."

"Nor do I. But that's what it feels like to me."

"Who, then? I ask again, who could it possibly be?"

"Who would spend the money to fill my life—and yours—with chaos and misfortune? Why, several names come to mind."

"Name one."

"Count Onjine. He tried to use one of my lizards to murder the prince. You surely remember that."

"Of course I do. But Onjine is dead. I remember that as well. Done in by the very trap he set for the prince."

Finn made a noise in his throat, a deep and thoughtful noise, if one is familiar with sounds such as that.

"He has friends, Letitia. Friends, brothers and uncles and other wealthy kin. None as mean-spirited as Onjine himself I grant you, but still . . ."

"Name two. Name another who would do the same."

"Teklo Amakin, he'd do it," Finn said, slightly irritated at the need to pursue this.

"What?" Letitia did her best not to laugh, but a slight burst escaped all the same.

"I'm glad you're amused."

"I'm sorry, but Teklo the Toother? This is the Teklo we're talking about?"

"I don't know any other Teklos. It is not a common name."

"He took out your tooth."

"He took out the *wrong* tooth. That is a different matter than simply taking out a tooth. I refused to give him a pence. He's never forgotten that."

"Really, Finn . . ."

"No, not *really Finn*—the man puts on a kindly face, but he's full of bile. They're all like that, it goes with the toothing trade. Some are simply more vicious than the rest."

"All right."

"And that means what?"

"It means I'm sorry to have to say it, but I think you're overly tired. I feel you need some rest."

"You feel I'm raving, possibly out of my head."

"Don't be like that. I just don't think you're right."

"So I see."

"We don't need to argue about it. We simply have different opinions."

"Yes. *Quite* different, I'd say."

Finn stood abruptly, went to the darkened window and peered out at the night. If anything was there, he failed to see it. The window was so coated with years of grime, it could easily have hidden a horde of Hooters dancing naked on the lawn.

"I didn't say there *wasn't* a curse over you, Finn. I never said that."

"You said I was overly tired. It's the polite way of saying I have a disorder of the mind."

"Stop this. Please."

"All right. It's stopped."

"Your tone of voice says it isn't. I'm hungry, Finn. Do you think we could talk about this some other time? I'd rather not faint on this floor, which hasn't been cleaned in several years."

Finn went to her at once. "I've been thoughtless, Letitia. I shall insist they bring you some soup. Soup or a stimulating broth. Broth is very good for the vapors, I understand."

"*Solid* food is what's good for an empty tummy. I certainly don't need any soup or any—stimulating broth. What I'd really like is—"

"—nothing you'll get in this cesspool, I promise you that."

"What?" Finn looked at Julia perched on a hardback chair. "And how would you know? I've warned you not to jabber, have I not? Most especially when you've no idea what you're talking about."

"You have indeed. But if I'm wrong about the menu here, you may strike me with a rock. Further, I'm sure Letitia is right. It is most unlikely you're under a spell. The Fates don't *have* to drop dung in your lap. Dung happens. It can strike anyone at any time. This time it's you."

"Fine, that's it." Finn threw up his hands, then let them collapse at his sides. "I'm assaulted by my own dear wife on one side, and a—a pile of scrap on the other. I'm out of sorts, mentally impaired, and oh—overly tired."

"Don't do this, dear . . ."

"I won't. Don't worry. From here on, I'll keep my insane thoughts to myself."

"Imagine," said Julia Jessica Slagg, "I lived to see that."

"No, that's not entirely correct." Finn whirled about to face the lizard. "You talk, you slither about, you even have a ferret's brain inside your tin head. Whether you are actually *alive* is another matter."

"That's not a nice thing to say," Letitia said.

Finn gave her a cutting smile. "What do you want me to do, apologize to a bag of gears and wires? All right, I'm sorry, Julia. You think you're alive? Fine. You're alive and I'm overwrought. Dung happens. Sticks and Bricks, I've got to take a nap."

"It's all right. I'm used to abuse. That's my mission in life."

"Apparently, it's mine as well."

"Poor you," Letitia said. "Poor both of you. And I'm still hungry, does anyone care about that?"

Julia blinked her ruby eyes. "We have company. It's that ugly thing with hair."

"I don't hear a thing," Finn said.

Someone rapped lightly on the door.

"Come in," Letitia said, "it's not locked."

"How could it be?" Julia said, "It's scarcely a door."

Letitia had seen Squeen only moments before, but the sight of him startled her all over again.

"Sssssir and lady. Dinner isss be ssserving, if you ple-assse . . ."

"Thank you," Finn said, "but we're very tired, and we'd rather eat up here, if it's no trouble for you."

"Issss no bees trouble, sssir."

"Good, good. My apologies to our host."

"Issss no bees trouble for Ssssqueen, but massster sssays no."

"No? He won't let us eat, is that what you're telling me?"

"Eatsss isss fine. Masster sssayin' you bees comin' down. Issss bad mannersss, Masster Sssabatino sssays . . ."

"Damned if he does. That's outrageous. We simply won't put up with that."

"Massster ssayin' you bees bringin' lizard perssson, too."

"Listen, now—"

Squeen was gone. The door closed again. Or, as well as it ever did.

"Blast the fellow. He goes too far with me."

"I'm hungry, dear."

"Me too," Julia said. "And some say I'm not even alive. Now is that a puzzler or what?"

"Finn . . ."

"Yes, my dear?"

"I hate to mention this, but since you haven't noticed, I'd better tell you now. We didn't get here with our satchel. I suppose we lost it in our flight. I fear we have no change of clothes, no brushes, no lotions of any sort."

"Damn me," Finn said, "I hate to hear that."

"And what I said before? How I didn't feel any of this was your fault?"

"Yes, and I appreciate that."

"I'd like to take some of that back. I don't have a thing to wear, Finn, except the same dirty dress. If you don't mind, I'd like to say I blame you for that . . ."

Twelve . . .

WITH GREAT RELUCTANCE, FINN USHERED LETItia down the stairs, hoping the shaky apparatus would hold. Julia, perched on Finn's shoulder, pondered the question that was ever on her brass and ferret mind:

Who am I? Or is it maybe what? And does it really matter? If I think I'm here, I am. Unless, of course, I simply think I think I am, and actually I'm not.

"Quit fidgeting," Finn said, "What's the matter with you?"

"I believe I'm thinking, is all."

"Well, don't."

Finn had hoped that, somehow, things would look entirely different than they had when he'd first come in. If anything, everything was worse. Now, lit with foul-smelling tallows, every spot, stain, rip, tear and snag, every marred, scratched, dust-covered surface, every table, every curtain, every chair displayed its imperfections for everyone to see, like an unattended corpse, like a garbage museum.

Worse still, the dining room table was set with a hodge-podge of dishes, glasses, saucers and bowls; everything broken, everything cracked. Knives without handles, forks without tines, and, Finn was certain, no two of anything alike.

"They *could* have dusted the table and the chairs," Letitia whispered in his ear.

"They could have burned the place down," he whispered back, "but unfortunately it's here."

"Aha, I heard that," Sabatino said, appearing from somewhere in shadow wagging a finger in Master Finn's face. "It's hard to get help here, which I shouldn't have to say, since you've seen our lovely town. Those who aren't Hooters or Hatters are scared out of their wits, or feeble in the head. All of the *natural* servants—no offense, miss—don't seem to like the place. You can't get a Newlie near."

"How odd," Letitia said, forcing her very best smile, "how very odd indeed."

"At any rate, we've got Squeen William, and he keeps everything as tidy as he can. Don't you, good Squeen? Damn your bloody hide, where are you hiding now? Oh, sit, please, anywhere you like. Except that chair, my dear, I fear its legs are partially impaired."

Letitia moved down a seat, finding the next one not much better than the first. Finn tried in vain to find any tableware in one piece. His cup had no handle. His plate had been broken and glued together again. Not very well, either, since all three pieces were from three different sets.

"I think you'll enjoy the wine," Sabatino said. "I have a little garden out back, and I make the stuff myself."

"Oh, really?" Finn took a sip and nearly gagged.

"Interesting, is it not? Nobody makes proper use of turnips anymore. They could if they tried, they're not hard to grow."

"No. I suppose not."

Finn set his glass aside. He tried to look at Sabatino, fix-ing his gaze half a foot above his head. The man had, in his own peculiar way, changed into dinner clothes. Jacket, vest, hat, shirt and pantaloons. A frothy amount of epaulets, lace, flowing sash and tie. Medals you could buy at the fair. The colors, ranging from the top: purple, puce, russet and rose. Crimson, pink, lavender and gold. Lemon, lilac and aquamarine.

"No green," Finn said, almost to himself.

"I beg your pardon?"

"You don't care for green."

"Can't stand it. Absolutely loathe it." Sabatino sniffed. "Fine for nature, though. Looks quite good on a tree."

"Do you mind, sir," Letitia asked, carefully leaning for-ward in her chair, "if I ask a question? I mean, if you please."

Sabatino's eyes flashed, his interests mirrored there in greasy candlelight. "Anything, my dear. Whatever comes to mind."

Finn allowed him a deadly look, which Sabatino chose not to see. Letitia held her question while Squeen limped in with a ghastly, transparent soup, and a great, faded silver fish with glazed, astonished eyes; a fish still startled, still stunned by the stroke of bad luck that had clearly ruined its day.

"I do not wish to pry," Letitia said, staring in wonder at something in her soup, "I see you are a man of position and wealth with everything a person could desire. May I dare inquire just what it is you do?"

"Why, of course you may," Sabatino said, leaning back with a hearty laugh, a wink and half a leer. "As it happens, I don't do anything, miss. I travel at times, as you know. But mostly I stay right here—as you so graciously pointed out—in the comfort of my lovely home."

"Yes, how nice." Letitia gazed at her soup again, certain now that something in there moved. "Still, I would say you

stay quite busy, what with violence and rebellion all about.
I don't know if I could live in a land so sorely torn by
strife."

"Strife, miss?" Sabatino looked puzzled, slightly annoyed, as if Letitia had committed some minor offense.
"I'm guessing, now, you're referring to the spiritual life
practiced here. I should hardly call what you witnessed today strife."

Finn set down a broken spoon. *"Spiritual life?* I'm sure I
didn't hear you right."

"Why, you did, for a fact. We practice liturgy, ceremony,
varied sacred rites. All of which are, I believe, common to
religious institutions everywhere."

"Not everywhere," Letitia said.

"Oh?" Sabatino folded his hands beneath his chin. "So
you are saying, I believe, that religion in your land is superior to that practiced in mine?"

"Ah, no, not at all, sir." Letitia looked to one of the
many heavens for help. "Some are less aggressive in nature,
I have to say that. Not so much slaughter, torture, moaning
and such. That sort of thing."

Sabatino waved her words away. "Lame, insipid—bor-
ing, you mean."

"Some of us like it that way."

"Yes, I'm sure you do. And if you don't mind, may we
set this subject aside? Our ways are best. Yours are clearly
not. Let's talk about you, Master Finn. And you too, of
course," Sabatino added with a sly, deliberate glance at
Letitia Louise. "And that marvelous creation of yours.
The, uh—what? The grizzard, yes?"

"Lizard, I believe."

"Yes, whatever. What did you say it did, now? Except
speak, of course, and give a good showing of itself in a fight.
Aside from that, what exactly is it *for?*"

"No, a moment, please . . ." Letitia daintily dabbed her

lips with the tip of her finger, as there were no napkins of any sort.

"I don't mean to be rude, but I have just gone through the most terrifying day of my life, and you have dismissed all that as no great incident at all. We nearly lost our lives during one of your *sacred rites,* and I am damned—I beg your pardon, I do not ordinarily use foul language, as Finn will testify—but I am damned if I can understand what happened out there. Your father came very close to torture and death, and yet you *condone* this sort of thing? Why? It makes no sense to me."

"No reason why it should, lady, no earthly reason at all . . ."

Letitia turned to see Sabatino's father stumbling down the stairway and into the dining hall. Two steps left, and then another right where he knocked a vase of very dead flowers to the floor.

Sabatino's features froze into a mask. "I think you would be more comfortable in your rooms, Father. You've had a trying day. I shall send Squeen William up with soup and fish."

"Bugger your fish, boy."

The old man staggered to the table and gave his two guests a crooked grin.

"Master Finn, is it not? And the very lovely whatsher-name."

"Letitia," Finn said, rising slightly from his chair. "I'm pleased you're feeling better, sir."

"Yes, well, I'm not. Never felt worse, not that anyone in this house cares. Calabus. Calabus Nucci. We were never properly introduced. Put your hand away, please. I never touch people without a protective device of some sort. Terrible disease is spread through the flesh, through the very air itself."

"I never heard that," Finn said.

"Likely much you've never heard, boy. I doubt your knowledge extends too far beyond your craft. Few men have the will to extend themselves past their meager needs."

"You might be wrong in that, sir."

"Oh, now don't take offense. From what I've seen of your work, I'd guess you're a bloody genius in your field. Likely know your numbers, but I doubt you've read a book. Damn you, Sabatino, I loathe things that live in the sea. Squeen! Get me something else, you mange-headed brute! Bring me some food fit to eat!"

"Father, if you intend to stay, sit."

"Not that chair, sir," Letitia warned, "I understand it's unfit."

"Nothing works in this place. You can thank my worthless son for that."

Calabus found another chair, pulled it up and sat. Downed a mug of turnip wine, and filled it up again. Squeen limped in, looking like old clothes left out in the rain. He set something down in front of Calabus and hastily left. Finn stared at the old man's plate, and never looked that way again.

If the son, he thought, had abused every color in nature, and many that were not, the father had balanced the books. Calabus seemed content with shredded tones of gray from head to toe. Whatever he'd been drinking upstairs, most of it had dribbled down his vest.

"The answer to your question, miss," the old man went on, as if not a moment had passed, "is that people act the way they do in this sorry country because they don't know any better. Yokels and fools, every one. I ought to know, I'm a former fool myself. Pass that wine around, will you, Master Finn? Damned if this isn't a vintage year.

"Used to be just ceremony. Flog your neighbor, punch an eye out. No one minded that. Now you've got to pay the bastards off. Richer you are, the worse it gets. I've been taken twenty-two times, you believe that? Nobody else has got any money here."

Calabus took a bite of something brown, and glared at his son. "Took you long enough today, boy. Don't let it happen again. That Newlie you got there, Master Finn? Could she take off her clothes? By damn, I'd like to see that."

"What?" Letitia turned three slightly varied shades of white.

"I don't much care for the manner of your speech," Finn said. "It scarcely seems polite."

"True, Father. You don't ask questions like that." Finn thought Sabatino spoke with little conviction at all. He seemed to have a vision in his head.

"She's a Newlie," Calabus said, spitting a morsel on the floor. He grinned at Letitia as if he'd truly seen her for the very first time. "You're a Mycer, right? You and me are going to talk, girl. We're going to get along fine."

"No sir, you're not." Finn pushed his plate aside. He'd eaten a bite of bread, and scarcely anything else. "Letitia, if you're finished?"

"I haven't even started, Finn. Do you imagine I'm going to eat a fish?"

"You can eat tomorrow, dear. When we get back to the ship."

Letitia thrust out her chin. "I'll die before that. And I don't care what he says, all right? It doesn't bother me."

"Well, it bothers me. If you're not going to eat, we're leaving, dear. I don't care for the company here."

"I hope you and he are going to fight," Calabus said, grinning at his son. "That's another thing I'd like to see."

"Master Finn and I will settle our differences," Sabatino said. "I loathe the lout, and he feels the same about me.

Tonight, though, we won't go into that. As much as I despise it, I'm in the fellow's debt."

Sabatino turned to Finn, offering a wide, and thoroughly insincere smile. "I insist, sir, before you leave our table, you give us a little display of your, ah—"

"Lizard. We've been through this before."

"I'd like to see that," Calabus said, his mouth not working right, his eyes beginning to cross.

"There's really very little to see. It's simply a mechanical device. Mostly made of copper, iron and tin. As you mentioned, it bites."

"It speaks as well," Sabatino said. "Might it do that?"

"No, it will not." Finn made no effort to hide his growing irritation. "As you said, we do not care for one another. I don't see why we must play this ridiculous charade. My lizard is none of your concern. Neither is Letitia Louise. We are grateful you have taken us in, but I don't see we owe you an evening's entertainment for that. If you wish to satisfy our quarrel, I'll oblige you in the morning before we go."

"I've got a—a marfel—marvelous invent—invention of my own, you know," Calabus said, soup dribbling down his chin. "A craf—craf'sman like yourself would 'ppreciate seeing it, I know . . ."

"Father, shut up. *Now!*"

Finn had seldom seen a man filled with such rage. Sabatino's whole body trembled, and his features turned a brilliant shade of red, a color that did nothing to enhance his ghastly attire. Whatever the old man had said, his son wasn't far from a full-blown seizure or a stroke.

Calabus, however, had missed his son's fury, and gone to sleep instead.

Squeen William chose this moment to drag himself past the kitchen door.

"Desssert be ready, sssir. I be ssserving now?"

"Get out of here," Sabatino shouted, shaking the table with the ball of his fist. "Out, or I'll skin your filthy hide!"

"What are we having?" Letitia said. "I mean, if it's not impolite to ask."

"Whatever it is," Sabatino said, "it isn't alive. At least I've cured the fellow of that . . ."

Thirteen . . .

"WHATEVER THEY'RE HAVING FOR BREAKFAST, I intend to eat it," Letitia said. "I've never been so hungry in my life."

"You won't be here for breakfast, love. We'll be out of this asylum at first light. At 4:47, I believe."

"With nothing to eat."

"We shall eat aboard ship. The food there was no great treat, but it consists of things I've put in my belly before. Great Bees and Trees, did you hear what that fellow said? 'Whatever it is, it isn't alive?' "

"That fish was all right," Letitia sighed. "As long as you didn't peer into its eyes. Of course, I wouldn't eat it, but it didn't look as bad as the soup. There was something most peculiar in there, Finn."

Finn turned over, reached across Letitia, and snuffed the smelly candle out. He didn't care for sleeping in the dark in such a place, but at least the night masked the bizarre décor of the room. He hoped there weren't many bugs about. Maybe they stayed away. Maybe the house was too dirty for them as well.

He touched Letitia's shoulder, and she folded herself against him: head, back, tummy and legs. It was always a marvel how perfectly she fit. Apparently, this had been planned in advance. A great many things seemed to work that way, one part matching the next. Like the tiny cogs and gears he put together to make a lizard go. If you did it just right, it looked as if it had simply grown that way.

It always made him feel grand to think of that. He had put a great many things together, and even one—Julia Jessica Slagg—that actually seemed alive. There was no question of that in Julia's "mind," though Finn still harbored a few doubts himself.

Across the room on a table by the door, he could see the ruby glow of Julia's eyes. Julia didn't sleep, but Finn knew she "napped," if you could call it that. It wasn't anything Finn had planned. It was simply something Julia did.

He felt a touch of apprehension, a little fear and doubt about the wisdom of bringing her along. Nearly everyone thought she was just a clever toy, a very fine machine. Now and then, though, someone gave her more thought than that. A seer at the far end of Garpenny Street had told him there was magic involved. The reason he'd said it, Finn was certain, was because it was something the man couldn't do himself.

And, worse still, there were those who were clever enough, and greedy enough as well, to feel they should have such a wonder as Julia themselves. People like Sabatino Nucci and his father. They both had that glimmer of lust in their eyes, that special look you saw in merchants, bankers and thieves.

Not the same look when a man saw Letitia Louise—that was a look quite different from anything else.

And what, Finn wondered, was he to make of the dinner table scene between Calabus and Sabatino? Whatever that was about, the son had nearly come unraveled when the tipsy old man had begun to speak of some invention of his own.

That, and the bizarre business of Hatters and Hooters. Finn would be glad to put it all behind him in the morning, and never look back. If, he reminded himself, that idiot didn't run him through at dawn. Strangely enough, he felt totally detached from that event, as if it were so ridiculous it could never come about.

Finn was certain he'd never sleep, but it wasn't long before he did. And, not long after that, he came fully awake again, and sat up in the bed.

The house creaked and groaned like a shaky old man, but this was a different kind of sound. A hoot was what it was, or a lot of hoots at once, like a flock of noisy owls. Only these weren't owls, he knew, but a pack of maniacs.

Beetles and Bones, what was wrong with these people? Why couldn't they act like the civilized folk back home? Granted, the prince, and the princes before him, had been at war with neighbors for seven hundred years, but nearly every kingdom did that. A war was a totally different thing. It wasn't about a bunch of crazies in yellow hats, or another bunch that howled at the moon. This sort of thing made no sense at all . . .

"Letitia, are you awake, dear?"

"I am now, Finn."

"I'm sorry. I heard them. The Hooters. I wondered if you heard them too."

"No, I didn't. As you guessed, I was asleep. I was dreaming about thistleberry pie. It was bubbling over, and sugary drops were sizzling on the stove. The juice made little hissing sounds as it came up through the crust. Oh, Finn, what do you want? Please tell me and let me get back, before that pie is gone."

Finn ran his fingers across her cheek. "I feel very bad about this, Letitia, don't make me feel any worse. I'm glad we didn't eat that fish. I am not at all sure it wasn't spoiled. I don't think even if you're dead, you're supposed to look like that."

Letitia yawned and stretched. "Food that looks bad begins to look good when your tummy starts making funny sounds. Did you ever think of that?"

"I'm hungry too, you know."

"I'm sure you are, Finn. Good night again."

Letitia leaned over, gave him a peck on the cheek, plopped down and faced the other way.

"I've been thinking," Finn said, "about the future and the past. This vacation, though it hasn't been a great deal of fun so far, has brought some ideas to mind, things sort of rattling about in my head.

"You've brought a lot into my life, Letitia. I'm a different man than I was before. I was just drifting in my craft, doing some of this, some of that. I made lizards that blow on the fire, lizards you could put the garbage in. A skinny lizard to poke in your musket and clean the barrel out. Captain what's-his-name, you remember him, the Balloon Grenadiers. He had a thing for you, which doesn't much matter, since he's quite dead now.

"Anyway, he gave me the idea for that. Sold a lot of them, too. I can likely sell more, since the war shows very little sign of slowing down.

"That's off the subject, though, or maybe not. It wasn't very easy selling lizards when I first thought them up. Folks would say, `What on earth is that, what's it for?' I really didn't get off the ground until the bug-snatcher came along. Now that caught on very quickly. That tongue leaping out all the time seemed to frighten little children, but they soon got over that. People didn't like to empty it, of course, and I can't blame them, I suppose.

"By the way, that's where I got the idea for the dirt-sucker, dear. That went quite well. After that, things went downhill awhile with Lizards-for-the-Blind. One can't be right all the time, and no one was badly hurt.

"All this, Letitia, is what got me thinking. You simply can't stand still, you've got to try—even if something goes wrong. And that's what I did, and that's how Julia came to be. After I made her, everything else seemed rather tame. It was something no one had ever done, something so different I can't ever tell anyone except you. I made a creature out of seventeen kinds of metal, elements common and rare. Then I put the ferret's brain in. I don't know *why* I did that, I just did.

"It scared the hell out of me, too. Shar and Dankermain got hung three hundred years back for doing much the same—making human-like creatures out of animals, and giving them the power to think.

"I'm awfully glad they did Newlies, dear, because now I have you. Of course, they did it with magic, and I just fiddled around with scraps and tiny gears. It's not the same thing, but who'd believe that? Why, they'd put a noose around my neck and cut me up in pieces, just like those crazy seers.

"What was I saying, now? Yes, about the future, what I want to do next. Did I say it scared me when I finished Julia Jessica Slagg? It did, but it had another effect as well. It made me see what *could* be done, what unbelievable worlds could be explored. It was our misadventure with Count Onjine and his Yowlies—I know you won't forget that. At any rate, it was there I learned that Julia could actually *see* the tiny bit of poison in the jeweled lizard that would have killed the prince if we hadn't stopped the Count in time. It was a thing no human could ever see, and it struck me that if Julia could learn to craft devices so small, what's to keep those near invisible machines from making *smaller devices still?*

"What a marvel that would be! I was dizzy at the thought, and I'm often dizzy still.

"This is what I wished to tell you, dear. I should have mentioned it before, but with the trouble at sea, and our odd predicament here . . . Anyway, do you think me fevered, love? Some sort of vain, crack-brained fellow whose dreams have taken him over the brink, like the poor hapless loonies in a dark asylum somewhere? If you believe that's so, I wish you'd tell me, please. Don't hold back for fear I'll be crushed, for I'm not as proud as that.

"Please, Letitia. I need your honest thoughts on this. We have not been together long, but I feel we've seen the birth of a deep and meaningful relationship. So, do you think you've given your love to a man with some wits about him, or a hopeless buffoon?

"Letitia?

"Letitia Louise . . . ?"

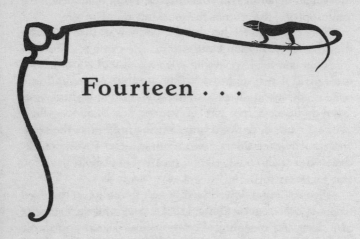

Fourteen . . .

FINN SAT UP. LETITIA SNORED LIGHTLY, A LOCK OF hair rising on her cheek with every peaceful breath.

"Beads and Weeds, dear, I can't believe you'd do this to me. It's inconsiderate, is what it is. I really feel you should apologize."

"You lull her to sleep with your babble, and you want an apology to boot?"

Julia gave a tinny chuckle from her perch across the room. "You nearly put me under, and I've never been asleep in my life."

"You didn't have to listen. Everything I say isn't directed at you."

"Everything you talked about is me. It's nothing we haven't discussed before. I am always loathe to agree with you, Finn. You have a sizeable head as it is. In this case, though, I quite approve. Delving into the microscopic world is a bold, exciting idea. If, as I have learned, the world is made of Earth, Air, Sky and Water, what indeed are *those* things made of?

"Of all the tomes on your shelves, I find the ones on the philosophy of the cosmos the most intriguing of all.

"I feel we understand each other, Finn. It's no great secret that you irritate me quite a bit. You think too much of yourself, you strut about like every human male I've seen—noble, merchant, soldier and commoner alike. Including, I might add, the dead, who seem no wiser in one state of being than the next.

"Still, we can do some quite interesting things together, in spite of your failings. Even if you're slow in your thinking, I have to say you had the wit to make *me*, and I give you much credit for that.

"One thing, though, Finn. And this we haven't talked about. We can make things smaller, and doubtless smaller still. If we do, though, why? I am quite fascinated with the effort, the drama of discovery, the thrill of the chase. But I see little sense in the result. What good will tiny things do? What on earth could you use them for?

"You couldn't sell them, for no one's fool enough to buy a thing they can't even see. And surely they'd be stepped on all the time, or simply blow away. Like so many good ideas, I fear this one lacks any value except as an oddity, a curiosity of sorts. Has this perhaps occurred to you?

"Finn?

"*Finn . . . .?*"

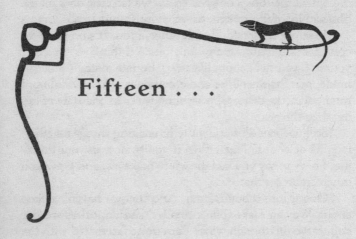

Fifteen . . .

THE WINDS PICKED UP AS A GALE SWEPT IN FROM
the sea. Rain pounded on the twenty-nine roofs, roofs of
slate and shale, roofs of wood and thatch, roofs that leaned
sideways, roofs that were steep and roofs that were flat.

Rain rattled on the eighty-four windows, windows made
of paper, windows made of slats, even, on occasion, windows made of glass.

The house creaked and groaned, trembled and shivered
in the wind. Thunder rolled like boulders through the frenzied sky. Lightning painted Finn and Letitia's room with
strobic fits of light.

The light struck Julia's ruby eyes, shimmered on her tin
and copper scales. Julia didn't care. Julia didn't move. It
was night, and there was no one she wanted to talk to,
nowhere she wanted to go. At times such as this, listening
was her favorite thing to do. When Julia cared to listen, she
could hear a vast array of sounds. Sounds from the low
scales, sounds from the high. Now, she could hear spiders
walking in the walls, hear moths chewing on the rugs out in
the hall. If she wanted, she could hear the little clicks and

the whirs, the tiny cogs and gears within her metal shell. She had learned, though, to set those sounds aside, unless something went awry. Then, she would fix the problem, or complain about it to Finn.

She could hear, not far away, the vile sounds humans made, playing their Hooter game. A game, she knew, from other sounds she heard, that often brought pain, and even death itself.

She wondered, idly, why these maniacs stayed out in the rain. People and Newlies didn't rust, but why would they want to get wet? She wondered, too, if these fools, like the others, wore some peculiar kind of hat?

Julia stopped hearing in the regular, ordinary way, dropped into a state where she could listen, totally aware, but simply not *there*.

Finn snored.

Letitia breathed.

Termites ate the wood.

Something slithered softly through the grass.

Something came in the door down below and started up the stairs . . .

Julia came awake with a start. She was not in the *there* anymore, she was back, in the *here*. And here, there was something very much amiss, something that set every golden cog astir, set every wheel abuzz, tingled every gear, every wire, thin as beetle hair.

It was not just the sounds, though the sounds were very clear. Julia had a metal body, metal snout and metal tail, but she had a real brain, taken from a ferret dying in a trap. The ferret was a sly and cunning creature, and it sensed things that humans didn't see. Now that it was part of Julia, it was even quicker, even more aware of sounds that meant danger, smells that meant fear.

There was something else too, from that something on the stairs, something that rattled Julia's scales and lit her ruby eyes; a raw and savage hatred that cut the night air, an anger and a loathing so brutal and intense that Julia shrank away, shut it out at once . . .

While all this was surging through her head, one second turned to two, and before it got to three, Julia was across the stone floor with scarcely a rattle or a scratch, and up on Finn's chest.

Finn woke.

Not with a start as most anyone would, faced with ruby eyes staring in his face, toothy snout poking at his chin. Finn was not surprised at such intrusions anymore, only vexed, irritated, irked to no end.

"Up," Julia whispered, like the wind through a broken window pane, "Sword and dagger both. No time for boots, scarcely time for pants. Something's in the hall with murder in its head . . . !"

Finn took a breath, yanked on his pants, jammed his weapons in his belt. Took one step, and froze on the spot.

A blood-chilling scream shattered the silent night. Not just a scream but another after that. Screams, groans, curses and growls. Sounds of assault, terrible howls.

Letitia sat up straight, eyes big as biscuits, throwing off the sheet, baring lovely private parts.

"Stay down. Cover up. No, wait. Get under the bed. Stay there and don't come out."

"Finn, just what is going *on* out there?"

"I don't know. Do what I said."

Letitia didn't. He didn't think she would.

Finn drew his dagger and his sword, stepped back, and threw open the door.

Whatever he'd expected, it surely wasn't there. Everything else was there instead. Thirty-seven things seemed to happen at once. In the dim corridor, it was hard to sort anything out.

Sabatino Nucci stood barefoot in the hall, crouched in a fighter's deadly stance, lashing his sword about. Facing him were two wiry creatures dressed entirely in black. Black vests and boots. Silky black sashes, baggy pantaloons. Black hoods covered their features, black scarves wound about their necks.

Finn wondered why they bothered with this frightening wear. Even in the dim half-dark, their sharp Foxer noses were quite clear. Their ears made little black tents in the fabric, as if their heads were camping out.

From the corner of his eye, Finn saw Sabatino's father, moaning on the floor behind his son, kicking his legs, and flailing all about. For whatever reason, the old man was naked once again.

And, from the *other* corner of his eye, Finn saw a scene even more bizarre. Just at the top of the stairs, Squeen William backed against the rail where the steps went up instead of down. Squeen had one furry foot on the floor, one atop a bearded, filthy old man. The man was making meaningless sounds, and frothing at the mouth. Squeen was holding off a third Foxer, beating his withered wings, flailing at his foe with the leg of a broken chair. Clearly, he was trying to save the old man who was doing all he could to shake his benefactor free.

Finn absorbed this whole chaotic scene in the blink of an eye, then waded right in. He had no quarrel with Foxers, but poor Squeen was no match for a creature with a sword.

The Foxer saw Finn, and the greater danger, and turned away from Squeen. Finn wasted little time at all on posture, grace and style. He parried the creature's first pass, knocked the weapon from his hand, struck its bottom with the flat of his sword, and kicked the fellow howling down the stairs.

"You all right, Squeen? You hurt or anything?"

"No, issss bees fine, sssir. Ssssqueen bees thankin' you much."

"You're most welcome, I'm sure." Finn glanced over his shoulder at Sabatino. For the moment, he was clearly holding his own.

"Who's that on the floor, Squeen William? He doesn't look healthy at all."

Squeen showed him a foolish Vampie grin. "Issss nobodyss, ssssir. Isss sssmelly old man."

"I can tell that much on my own. It isn't what I asked."

"Be damned with you, craftsman," Sabatino shouted, "give me a bloody hand here!"

"Sorry," Finn said, "be right along."

He turned then, to the Foxer on Sabatino's right. He had caught Sabatino's glance, and was coming straight at Finn. Finn parried, and quickly backed him against the far wall. His hood had come loose in the fight, and Finn could see his prominent nose and pointy ears, his startling, lemon-colored eyes. He was not an animal now, but his ancestral traits were quite clear.

This second opponent was better than the first. He liked to go after Finn's face, cut and whip about the eyes. It was irritating, like batting at silver flies. The fellow didn't like body work, and didn't watch his own too well. Finn gave him a swipe about the groin, and scared the intruder to death. He brought down his sword to guard his parts, and Finn drew a thin red line across his chest. The Newlie howled in pain, dropped his blade and ran.

"Didn't mean to get you up, Finn," Sabatino said, backing the lone Foxer down the hall. "Know you and the lady need your *sleep* and all."

Finn let the words go by. Sabatino couldn't say 'hello' without impertinent intent.

Sabatino's foe tired quickly. His weapon was drooping, his lemon eyes were full of doubt and fear.

Sabatino laughed, cut the fellow twice on his prominent nose, and notched his ear. Like his comrade, this one had clearly had enough. With a snarl and a bark, he backed away and stumbled down the stairs.

"A Newlie will fight till he gets a little cut," Sabatino said. "Then the sorry louts will turn tail." He squinted at the point of his blade, then spoke without looking at Finn.

"Your face is clear as glass, craftsman. You'd best stay away from games of chance."

Finn looked puzzled. "I'm afraid you have the best of me. I don't know what you're talking about."

"Newlies, friend. Present company in your room there excepted, of course. I've found them to be cowards, every one. Back down from a human every time. Worst of the lot are the Foxer trash. Them and the Bowser lot. Got a bunch of 'em here. Ought to run 'em all off."

"You seem to have a problem, sir. I've noticed that before."

He knew he ought to stop right there, but the words came all the same. "Especially, I recall, if they're young and unarmed."

"That little pup on the ship?" Sabatino showed no offense at all, beyond a nasty smile. "You *do* have the stomach to bring it up. Hurrah for you. Don't waste your time goading me tonight, Finn. I'll run a blade through your low-born heart at first light."

Sabatino glanced at his father, who'd gone to sleep on the floor.

"Now isn't that a lovely sight? Damn me if I believe I was sired by an ugly brute like that. Squeen William! Get your disgusting hide over here and get my loving daddy into bed. If you can't lift him, drag him in a corner some-where. All right, craftsman, what are you staring at?"

"An empty spot where a very old lunatic was lying just now."

"Really?" Sabatino's smile faded. "I urge you to return to your room, and your very charming friend. You and I have a quarrel to settle soon. I feel I'm safe in saying this is your very last chance to get a good night's sleep . . ."

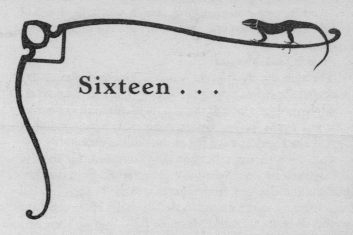

Sixteen . . .

FINN WAS READY TO DROP. THE INSANITIES OF THE day in this land clearly didn't lessen with the night. His body ached for sleep, but sleep wouldn't come. Letitia, as easily as ever, dropped off as soon as the furor was over in the hall. He wondered if he resented her for that. Decided he shouldn't, and admitted that he did.

The storm had moved away, and morning was very near. The false light of dawn did little to enhance the dreary appearance of the room. Everything in this grim pile of crooked walls and floors, angles, tangles and impossible doors, stairs that went this way and that, looked better in the night.

"You're fortunate you don't need sleep," he said. "You might at least thank me for that."

Julia Jessica Slagg was still indistinct across the room, but her red eyes pierced the dim light.

"Thank you for that. Anything else?"

"Courtesy wouldn't hurt. You're a little short of that."

"I'm short of a lot of things, Finn. See, I didn't make a lizard, you did. What you put in comes out. I'm whatever you tinkered together, I thought you knew that."

"Don't start on me, it's been a hard day."

"And in case you're asking, which you will, I didn't come to your aid, but you seemed to have the problem well in hand."

"I didn't ask, all right?"

Through the fly-specked window, the first sign of day appeared above low clouds to the east. The sun, when it arrived, looked as reluctant to get on with matters as Finn. A pale and runny yellow flecked with rusty spots of red, it looked like a very sad egg left in the skillet overnight.

Still, Finn thought, he shouldn't complain, for the day brought release from Sabatino and his father, from the Hatters and the Hooters, from Squeen and the Foxers, and old men foaming at the mouth. Soon, he and Letitia and Julia would all be back on the *Madeline Rose,* and on their way again.

Finn turned over, bleary-eyed and hungry, watching his love stir under the ragged sheet. He wished it was a week or two from now. That he and Letitia were somewhere else, in some other bed, engaged in quite another pastime . . .

Awake, but in a stupor common to the weary and the dead, he sat up with a start at the gentle rapping on his door. Setting his feet on the floor, he padded across the room to open the portal, and found Squeen William standing there.

"All right, what is it, what's the problem now?"

"Massster Sssabatino sssay you bees comin' down now. He bees waitin' outsssside."

"Outside." Finn blinked. "What's he doing out there?"

"Ssssay you comin' outssside."

"You said that. Please don't say it again. Tell him I'll bees—tell him I'm coming outside, on my way out. Tell him I'll wave goodbye."

"Masster, he sssays—"

Finn slammed the door. Letitia groaned but didn't wake up.

"Get her up, make her dress," Finn said. "Tell her I'll be right back, we're getting out of here."

Julia flicked her tail. "I don't much like to do that."

"Do what?"

"Get Letitia up. She tends to call me names."

"Well, I'm terribly sorry. Try to live with that."

"Easy for you to say—" Julia began, then Finn was out the door.

The house was still musty, and still leaned to the south and to the west. The downstairs still reeked of fish from the bleary night before. The heat outside was awesome. It nearly brought Finn to his knees. He thought about the ship, and recalled how stifling it could get down below.

There ought to be a way to get air down there, he thought, to give people half a chance to breathe. He'd worked out a method of heating up a room, giving a boost to a fireplace or a stove. The Lizard Blower worked extremely well. But those enormous bellow jaws snapping open, snapping shut, frightened little children and it didn't sell at all. If you could reverse that process, suck cool air to a cabin, instead of blowing hot air out. Of course, such a lizard would be rather long . . .

"Having a little nap, are we? Lots of holes about, I'd take care if I were you."

Finn snapped back into place, wondering exactly where he'd been. Sabatino was leaning against his house. Or, possibly, the house was leaning on him.

"I didn't sleep well," Finn said, making no effort to hide his ire. "Frankly, sir, your house is the worst place I've ever spent the night."

"I regret the disturbance. Don't know how those cunning little bastards got in. I've set traps everywhere."

"Cunning little bastards indeed. And a crazy old man."

"Which one? I hope you don't mean Father. I'd have to take exception to that. Never mind," he said, waving his words aside, "I didn't call you down here to talk about my personal affairs. I'm afraid I've got a bit of bad news."

"About what?" Finn took note of another unusual manner of dress. Knickers in a pale and sickly pink, a vest the color of soup, one red boot and one blue, and a lilac plumed hat. It annoyed Finn to no end that the man looked as if he'd had a good night's sleep.

"It's about the duel," Sabatino said. "I'm afraid that's off. At least for the time."

"Some days nothing goes right," Finn said. He didn't mention that the duel had slipped his mind in light of everything else. "I'm disappointed, of course, but we'll try some other time."

Sabatino kicked a stray brick aside. "That's awfully good of you. I don't think I'd have handled it as well. I feel you're a foolish, impertinent oaf, with uppity notions in your head. I'd like nothing better than to cut you down to size. I believe if your lovely—companion, as it were, could watch you cower and bleed, she'd come to her senses and notice there's a real man around. I think you might have her in a spell. Even a craftsman, these days, can buy a little magic on the street somewhere . . ."

"Now look here, fellow—"

"No, you look." Sabatino poked a finger in the air. "Allow me to finish, you've gotten me off the track. Calling off the duel is not my idea. Father asked me to, and though I can't abide the old fart, I'm obliged to humor his request."

Sabatino waved a hand across his face as if to banish some quite offensive smell.

"The thing is, he's somewhat impressed with that clever

device of yours. I believe he mentioned he fancies he's an inventor of sorts himself. He's mad, of course, but that's beside the point. He's got this thing of his going, and he'd like you to help."

Finn stared, trying not to laugh or throw up. "What on earth are you talking about? I wouldn't stay in this place another minute, even if you and your father were afire. I'd piss on the ground before I'd put either one of you out. Letitia and I will be out of here and gone, *racing* for our ship before you can blink."

"Well, that's the point, you see." Sabatino yawned, picked something off his vest, and flicked it to the ground. "I'm loathe to say it, but you really have no choice. I fear you'll have to stay."

"What? What are you talking about? Damn it all, Sabatino—"

"Yes, well you see, the ship's gone. It sailed well before first light."

"No, I don't believe that, you arrogant lout. It's another stupid lie." Finn felt something cold and heavy turn over in his gut. "The captain is obligated to wait for his passengers. It's a—law of the sea, or something, I'm certain of that."

"It is, actually," Sabatino said, "but Magreet is a scoundrel, I don't have to tell you that. He came very cheap, as most of them do. Walked down there in the middle of the night, Hooters all about. Fellow took my first offer like that.

"I'm truly sorry, Finn, but one must respect one's father, even if he's a sack of fecal matter, and totally bonkers as well . . ."

Seventeen . . .

"PLEASE TELL ME THIS ISN'T HAPPENING, FINN. Tell me it's certainly not happening to me. Tell me I'm back in Garpenny Street in my very own home, and I'm having a really bad dream."

"I wish I could say that, love. I wish I could make this all go away."

Finn stood at the window staring out at the hot and dreary day. "I feel as if it's somehow my fault, that I, and I alone, have gotten you into this terrible mess."

"That's the way I feel, too."

"What, my dear?"

"That it's all your fault. That you got me into this mess. And don't call me 'dear' or 'love' or any other term of affection. If you do, I think I'll get sick. I have never been so frightened, so angry, so completely undone, except when old Miz Griller put Mama in a hex and she wasn't acting right for some time. Why couldn't we just go to the mountains like everyone else? Why did we have to get a *boat* and come here, will you explain that?

"No, don't. Don't even try. Miz Elaina Bloc, who's married to Ollie, who runs the Sweet Store? They had a perfectly lovely time in the mountains. They saw a cave and a little waterfall. Elaina even bought a pot from ancient times.

"Finn, if I don't get something to eat I'm going to die right here, are you aware of that? Do you even care?"

Finn turned to face her, partially appalled. "How can you even think such a thing, much less say it aloud?"

"It's easy, I'm sorry to say. I hope, for your sake and mine, I feel different sometime. But that's how I'm feeling now."

He thought his heart would break. He didn't know what to do next. He wanted to hold her, but he knew this was not the time for that. She looked so lovely, so delicate and fine, perched cross-legged on the bed, totally bare and sleepy-eyed, unaware of how the sight of her filled him with love, with overwhelming desire. The morning sun painted her downy skin, the colors muted by the window's dirty glass and a veil of spiderwebs.

"I'm going right now," Finn told her. "I'll get you something to eat if I have to flatten Squeen William and fix it myself. If there's nothing edible here, I'll—go and find something in town."

"No. No you won't." Letitia sat up straight. "You think I'm going to sit here and let something awful come up those stairs the minute you're out of sight? I'm bedamned if I will. Just get that out of your head."

"Yes, but—"

Letitia was up in an instant, slipping into the garments she'd worn from the ship, which looked as if they'd been wadded up in a ball somewhere.

Finn was startled and alarmed, and though he thought it most peculiar, quite charmed at the sudden, fierce resolution in the wife he thought he knew. She was fury unchained, and he was certain he could live with that. He was also certain if she guessed his thoughts then, he'd wish they'd never popped into his head.

Finn blinked as a blurry flash of lizard darted across the floor and vanished beneath the bed.

"Get out of there," he said. "We're all going down for breakfast. *Nobody's* staying up here."

"If you're mad at me, Finn, it'll just have to be," Letitia said, patting down her frizzled hair. "That's the way I am right now."

"What?" Finn tried to look terribly pained. "I'm not mad at you, Letitia. You must know I could never do that . . ."

"I dearly love the morning," Calabus said, spraying bits of breakfast through his beard. "There's something about a new day dawning, like the world's starting over, fresh and pure again—*Brruuch!* Sorry, miss. I expect you've heard a man belch before, it's quite a common event. May I say, you're looking most comely, my dear?"

The old man reached over and patted her hand. Letitia drew it quickly away.

"No offense, now. A compliment's what it is, nothing more than that."

Calabus winked at Finn as if they shared some base and lecherous thought. Finn didn't bother to complain. There was clearly no way to stop the man. He'd say what he liked, whatever popped into his head. This morning, he was wearing a shabby robe. Food from meals past formed a crusty path down the front. As ever, he didn't seem to care.

Breakfast was a horror. Deep-fried turnips. Turnip bread. Some kind of jelly, possibly made of dirt. Something hot and gray in a cup. Finn wouldn't drink it on a bet. Nucci and son seemed to like the stuff quite a bit. Finn took a bite of this and that. Letitia ate everything she could, and finished off Finn's plate as well. Finn tried not to think of Squeen William, who had fixed all this with his damp and furry hands. He wondered what the kitchen looked like, and pushed the thought quickly aside.

"I cannot tell you how pleased I am that you are my guest, Master Finn. That contraption of yours is a wonder, a fine mechanical feat. You simply must take it apart and show me how it works."

Julia gave a frightful croak, and dug her iron claws in Finn's back.

Calabus laughed, and pounded the table with his fist. "By damn, the little bugger understands me, does it not? How on earth did you manage that?"

He leaned in closer, bread crumbs drifting like snow from his beard. "What you got in its head, little wheels and such? A little magic too, I'd guess. I'm a fair crafter myself, but I couldn't do that."

"It knows a few elementary words," Finn said, "nothing more than that."

"A great *deal* more than that," Sabatino said, raising a wicked brow. It was the first time he'd spoken. He had spent his time leering at Letitia, taking some perverted form of pleasure watching her eat. He was dressed in slightly better fashion than his father, clad in faded lilac from head to toe.

"You forget, Finn, that we shared a great adventure yesterday. Your lizard is quite extraordinary, in a number of ways."

"*My* invention, now," Calabus put in, waving his son aside, "is most unusual as well, if I do say so myself. What I have *not* accomplished, sir, is cramming so much complexity into such a tiny space. I fear that damned thing of mine simply gets bigger. I cannot contain it. It sprawls all over the place."

"That's a bloody understatement," Sabatino muttered to himself.

"You think I didn't hear that?" Calabus clenched his fists and glared. "You think I'm deaf? What have you done with your miserable life, *boy*, except go through my money like soup through a sieve? That, and father every squealing mutt in town. At least I've accomplished something. I've given something back to the world!"

"A pile of crap clogging up the cellar. The world's got plenty of that . . ."

Finn looked at Calabus with alarm. The old man's face was purple as a grape. His eyes began to bulge, and Finn feared they might pop out and severely injure someone. Even Letitia was stunned by the sight, and stopped eating long enough to watch.

Half a second shy of a stroke, Calabus' features faded to a splotched and dissipated red. Moments later, his wits slipped back in place.

"You will, I hope, accept my son's apology for his behavior. It shames me to say he's my own flesh and blood, this vile, repulsive excuse for a man."

"I think I resent that, Father." Sabatino picked up his plate and dashed it to the floor. "That is a hurtful thing to say, and quite unfair. I fear I must demand satisfaction, unless you take your words back."

Finn couldn't help it. He burst out laughing, which drew a startled glance from Letitia, and angered Sabatino all the more.

"Are you challenging your own father to a duel? Is that what I heard you say?" Finn covered his mouth in an effort to restrain himself. "I thought you a blustering fool, but I fear I am way off the mark. You're clearly a flaming lunatic! Great Tails and Snails, man, you ought to be locked up somewhere . . ."

Sabatino sprang out of his chair. Before Finn could

blink, the man was on the table coming at him on all fours, scattering dishes, saucers and cups. Spoons without handles, knives without blades. Platters and handicapped forks. Letitia cried out, ducking turnips and flying bits of bread.

Finn scarcely had time to bring up his arms and fend the man off before Sabatino's big hands closed about his throat.

Finn's chair collapsed, shattered into scrap. Finn hit the floor, flat on his back. Sabatino held on like a vise. Finn pounded the fellow's face, struck him on the nose, hit him in the mouth. Even in the fury of battle, he noticed Sabatino had a missing upper molar, and extremely bad breath.

Sabatino cursed him, howled like a loon, pummeled his head against the floor. Finn began to see stars. Not simply stars, but whole constellations. The Chicken, the Wand, the Three-Legged Witch. He had never been able to spot the other leg, but he saw it clearly now.

Letitia broke a plate over Sabatino's head. The plate, from three different races, blue and green and red, could never be mended again. Sabatino hardly noticed. Julia bit him on the foot, but he didn't seem to feel that.

Suddenly, his face disappeared behind short stubby wings, wings that were furry, scabby and black. Squeen William lifted his master off the floor, carried him off, and set him gently in his seat.

Finn came shakily to his feet. Letitia gave him a glass of turnip wine. Finn drank another glass as well, before he remembered he couldn't stand the stuff.

"That doesn't count as a fight," Sabatino said. "Closer to a scrap. Don't imagine I'm through with you yet . . ."

"Indeed you are, though," Calabus said, his face approaching a ruby shade again. "That man is a master of mechanical arts. I insist you treat him as such.

"Squeen William, I commend you for your help in this

affair. My son would have murdered the fellow had you not stepped in to save his life. You will be severely scourged for laying your foul and nasty hands on your betters. I will personally flog you senseless until you scream for mercy. Then I will think of something worse after that. Moreover, you will not have dessert for a week. Again, I am grateful for your loyalty and your service to this house. Please get your miserable, stinking carcass out of here and bring me some cheese. Not that vile-tasting piss-colored stuff, I want the white."

Squeen William quickly vanished behind the kitchen door. Finn, still awed by the creature's strength, wanted to thank him as well, but decided the poor fellow was in enough trouble now.

"And you, sir . . ." Calabus turned his rheumy eyes on Finn. "We go beyond all tradition and taste to even harbor you here. I acknowledge the debt, but it sickens me to have you in our house. Moreover, we do *not* care to be called lunatics. I would remind you that persons of high intelligence are often deemed cabbage-brained or goofy by those of lesser ilk. Moreover, I have observed over a long lifetime that mental stability is not all it's cracked up to be."

Calabus wiped a greasy sleeve across his mouth, and reached for the decanter of turnip wine.

"Now. I hope we're done with that. Let's get back to subjects of greater interest. My modest contribution to science is what I'd like to pursue."

"No," Finn said, "I won't do that."

"What?"

"I have no interest in your work. Not any, none at all."

"Finn . . ." Letitia looked concerned.

"Don't worry, I can handle this."

"I suggest you don't." Sabatino grabbed the arms of his

chair, poised to leap again. "You've had a taste of what happens out there. Our home is your only sanctuary. Don't make us any sorrier than we are that you sit at our table and sleep in our bed."

Finn shook his head in wonder. "And we're safe in here? You've got killers lurking about in the dark. You've got some—some decrepit old maniac foaming at the mouth . . . Oh, sorry. No one's crazy here, I forgot."

Calabus made a face. "Those are personal problems. No concern of yours."

"I told him that," Sabatino said. "Fellow doesn't know when to quit."

"Desssert, sssirs and misss? Sssea Pudding, with tiny little thingss inssside. Little blackie thingsss."

"Get out," Sabatino shouted, "you vile, filthy Newlie dung! No offense, miss."

"No—certainly not," Letitia said, looking frightened, and just this side of dread.

"All of you, please." Calabus spread his hands, looking weary, looking pained. "Master Finn and I were discussing my invention. I cannot wait to go over this together, sir, to get your invaluable suggestions. How it can be ah modified, changed for the better, made more useful to all mankind. Don't pretend you're not curious now, I can see the thirst for knowledge in your eyes. Damn your rotting flesh, Squeen, get that Sea Pudding in here before I drop hot coals in your ears and stick thorns in your eyes!

"At any rate," he said, making a little tent with his hands, "I think you'll be delighted. I *know* you're in for a surprise."

Finn let out a sigh of resignation. "All right, what exactly is it? I don't believe you said."

"It's something you really have to see."

"Yes, I thought it might be."

"It's—ah—it's a device."

"A device."

"Yes."

"And what is the nature of this device?"

"Big."

"I beg your pardon?"

"It's basically a very big device."

"Well, that clears it up for me."

"Damnation," Sabatino groaned, "just *tell* him, Father, get it over with."

"I will, boy, I'm coming to that right now."

Finn was delighted to note that Sabatino's jaw was slightly off center, and that his nose was larger than usual and out of whack. With any luck, the swelling might never go down.

"It's big. A great deal bigger than I planned. I have to say it's out of hand . . ."

Squeen William appeared bearing cups of something jellied and gray. Gray, apparently, was Squeen William's choice for food of every sort.

"Ah, very nice, Squeen. No one can make Sea Pudding like you. Mind you don't sneak any for yourself, or I'll slice off several of your toes."

"Sssssomebody bees here," Squeen said. "Ssssomebody atta door."

"What?"

"What?"

Calabus and Sabatino looked up at once.

"Who is it," the younger asked, "and what in damnation's he doing here?"

"Never mind," Calabus said, "whoever it is, don't let the bastard in."

"Already am," said a voice behind Squeen. "Took the

liberty. Know my way in the dark to my good friend's house."

Calabus came out of his chair, gasping for breath.

"Sabatino," he cried, grabbing a mended fork. "To arms, lad, run the fellow through! Kill him before he slays us all . . . !"

Eighteen . . .

THE NEWCOMER GRINNED, BUT TOOK A STEP BACK. "Cal, you damn fool. You're not going to slay your own kin, certainly not in the house."

"Huh! You're no kin of mine."

"How sad it is to be denied," the fellow said with a sigh. "We cannot choose our relations, Cal, that's in greater hands than ours. And I'd be cautious if I were you, for you're in need of family now. Folk who'll stand by you, no matter what your crime . . ."

Calabus came out of his chair as quickly as his scrawny frame allowed.

"Damn your treacherous hide, what the hell are you talking about, what are you up to now?"

He had to look up at the man, who was tall and gaunt as a scarecrow, a hollow-cheeked fellow with a bony nose and balding hair. He looked as old as Calabus himself, yet he carried himself with some stature and pride.

"I'd as soon poke a hole in your gut right here," Calabus muttered, "Don't have to go outside. Son, draw that sticker and do your duty now."

"Dr. Nicoretti," Sabatino said, "my esteemed uncle, who, as you'll note, is totally despised in this house. Uncle, Master Finn and Mistress Letitia, who are staying with us until their vessel—arrives. You have seen this gentleman before, but I doubt you'd recall. He was somewhat farther away mutilating Father on a rack at the time."

"I know who they are," the doctor said, glancing at the pair as if he hadn't noticed them before. A glance and then away as if a longer look might taint him somehow.

"I know what they're doing here, too. *Staying*, sleeping in the house."

Nicoretti paused to thrust a pair of spectacles on his nose. "What in blazes were you thinking, Cal, have you lost your fool mind? This is a terrible thing you've done. It's Outlander ways, not ours. And one of 'em is—the other kind."

"I know what she is," Calabus said, "you don't need to come in here and tell me what someone is."

"It's a matter of honor," Sabatino said. "It's not an ordinary thing."

"It's not, huh?" Nicoretti risked a look at Letitia and Finn. "Sleeping in here? Eating at your table? It isn't decent, Cal, it's disgusting's, what it is."

"Don't talk to me about decent," Calabus said, "walking in like you own the place. Least you had the manners to leave your pointy hat outside. By damn, I would not put up with that. You want a glass of wine before you go?"

Nicoretti made a face. "If you had some, I would."

"Suit yourself then." Calabus downed another goblet, spilling the better part of it down his robe. "So what *did* you come for? The game's over and you're out of bounds here."

"It's about those two, is what it is. We had a meeting last night. Most of the Hatters feel, and I think rightly so, that we've got every right to a penalty fee. You brought in illegal players. That's interference, plain and clear."

Sabatino laughed. "We didn't ask for help, they volunteered. You can't fine us for that."

"I think we've got a case here."

"Nonsense. It's happenstance, nothing more."

Nicoretti sighed. "I don't want any trouble, Cal. You and I have been kin a long time. Fate cast us to the winds. We, as mortal persons, don't have a lot to say. I could've been born into Hooters. You could be wearing the yellow hat instead of me."

"Not hardly," Calabus said. "Not on your life. The Nuccis come from better stock than that."

If Dr. Nicoretti took offense, he didn't let it show. Finn thought he clearly wasn't happy being there. He looked a bit weary, like he'd rather take a nap. Then, instead of facing Calabus and son, he turned and looked curiously at Finn.

"We could come up with something. Maybe settle all this."

Calabus frowned. "Like what?"

"Those two, say. Instead of a fine. We'll be holding afternoon worship in three days' time."

"Hah! Splendid idea." Sabatino shot Letitia a wink. "You can have *him,* but you can't have her."

"Shut up, he can't have either one." Calabus scowled at his son. "I'll be working closely with Master Finn. Besides, you can't use a Newlie in rites of a spiritual nature, there's laws against that."

"There are ways around it, too. The Hatters have a lot of Newlie friends."

"Say, hold on there!" Finn stood, a motion that shattered the remnants of his chair. "We're not even from here. We don't believe in your religion, or the Hooters', either one."

"You don't have to believe, stranger. *We* do."

"Nothing doing, no way." Calabus scratched something

in his beard. "Just get that out of your head. I'm not giving anyone away."

"There's something you ought to think about, Cal. Your people aren't going to take this hospitality business kindly, any more than us. It's not our way. Him and a Newlie gal sleeping and *eating* here." Nicoretti made a face. "Heresy's a nasty word. I don't even like to say it out loud."

"Is that a threat?" Sabatino said, clutching the hilt of his blade. "If it is, I shall have to call you out, Uncle. At your convenience, with the weapon of your choice."

"Sit down, son, and shut up."

Calabus looked at Nicoretti. "I'm surprised you'd lower yourself to such unworthy trickery as this. We can't abide each other and never did, but I didn't dream you'd sink to the bottom of the pit. It's Hatter ways have done it, I'm sorry to say. You're wearing the coat of the damned, and it sure seems to fit. Now get yourself off my premises before I forget my manners and do you bodily harm."

"I feel you've made yourself clear," Nicoretti said.

"I surely think I have."

"Is that Sea Pudding you got there, Cal? Why, I haven't had any since I don't know when."

"You're not having any now, either. You should've thought of that before you came in here with gross extortion on your mind. Now go. And don't walk funny or knock something over in my house. I've got valuable pieces in here . . ."

Nineteen . . .

"I DON'T BELIEVE THIS," FINN SAID. "IF I DIDN'T know better, I'd say I'm having an awful nightmare. I'm not, because I'd never close my eyes in this place again. Stones and Scones, Sabatino, I despise you as a person, but I thought you had a trace of fair play. It's clear to me you don't."

"I was only bluffing, Finn. Give me more credit than that."

Sabatino yawned and picked his teeth with a damaged fork.

"Besides, we take our spiritual life seriously here. Nicoretti's crowd was paid handsomely at the Giving of the Goods. We don't owe him a thing, we don't need to give you away. It was all by the rules of the game."

"Game . . ." Finn shook his head in disgust. "Torturing some poor devil in the marketplace. That's not a game where I come from. It's flat-out murder and assault."

"Do I tell you what church to go to? No. Then stop complaining, dear boy, and have some more wine."

"No thank you," Finn said, "If I want to throw up, I'll do it on my own . . ."

The breakfast fare was gone, but Sabatino had kept the turnip wine. Letitia had fled to her room, taking Julia Jessica Slagg. Calabus was upstairs as well, possibly changing from filthy nightwear to something filthy for the day.

Squeen William was nowhere in sight. Finn felt he ought to hear the clatter of dishes, something going on back there. It might be washing was not the custom here. Maybe one simply threw the dishes out, or set them aside for the next meal of the day.

"I wouldn't worry," Sabatino said, turning over his empty mug with a frown. "Father was very big in Hooters, you know. He has a bit of clout."

"I have to worry because you've lied to me every step of the way. I don't think you can help it. I doubt you could tell the truth if you tried."

"Please," Sabatino moaned, "don't start that. You'll put me to sleep."

"You lied about the ship. You lied about the old man you've got locked up in here. You lied about last night. Who sent those Foxers to do you in? The more I think about it, the more I remember that boy on the ship . . ."

Sabatino's face went slack at that. "Think what you like, craftsman, but keep your words to yourself. I've promised Father not to kill you. Still, as you say, I lie a great deal."

"Right. Whatever I ask I'm wasting my time. This Dr. Nicoretti. You called him Uncle. He's your father's brother, then?"

"Thank the heavens, no." Sabatino made a face. "And that's none of your concern."

"Your mother's brother, then. Is your mother—Right,

none of my concern. Would the doctor hire Foxers to kill you and your father? You don't seem to like each other much."

"Nonsense." Sabatino waved the words away. "Just because the Hatters aren't of our faith doesn't mean they're assassins as well."

"I'd say this was more personal than church. Who, then? Unless it was the Foxer's idea, and you don't want to talk about that."

"I haven't the foggiest idea," Sabatino said, and from the sober, sincere cast of his eye, Finn knew he was lying again. "At any rate, don't make me tell you again. *Nothing* in this house is any business of yours."

"It is if Letitia and I are stranded here, with killers roaming the halls. Last night was a—Letitia, I thought you were going to rest awhile."

"Did you? I guess you were mistaken, Finn, as I am not up there, I'm down here."

Letitia found a chair that worked and sat, not overly close to Finn. Sabatino chuckled beneath his breath, delighted at the tension between the two. Julia, wrapped about Letitia's shoulder, kept her snout shut, and let her ruby eyes flick about the room.

"Well, then, what's the topic of conversation?" Letitia asked, a honeyed sweetness to her voice that annoyed Finn no end. "Is it the weather? I wouldn't know if there's any, as there's not a window one can see out. And if I were to take a walk, I would be assaulted by persons in yellow hats. Or maybe someone in a mask? There are so many possibilities in this *lovely* spot you've brought me to, Finn."

"All right, let's not—"

"Let's not quarrel *here*, Letitia? Well, where else would we quarrel, *dear*? There's no place else to go." Letitia pounded the words on the arm of her chair. "We are—here—in—this—horrible place with these dreadful people, and—and—"

The storm spread across her lovely features till Finn was sure sparks would fly out of her ears.

"—and I expect WE ARE GOING TO DIE HERE!"

"Wine? Anyt'ing you bees wantin', anyonesss?"

Squeen peeked out of the kitchen, granting everyone a ghastly furry smile.

"Get him out of here," Letitia screamed, "he's scaring me to death!"

"Letitia, I think you're overwrought."

"Don't you tell me what I am, don't you speak to me . . ."

"Well, we all enjoying ourselves? Why, I could hear you clear upstairs."

"Strike me blind," Sabatino muttered, "What on earth are you wearing, Father?"

"What, this? Don't you tell me what to wear, you miserable wretch. This is finery, is what it is. We can't all join the circus, boy."

"I'll argue that . . ."

Calabus paid no attention to his son. He had changed into a shirt of faded puce, a spangled vest of red and blue with half the spangles gone, the others hanging loosely by a thread. Mauve pants gathered at the ankles, peach velvet shoes with the toes cut out.

"Well, then." Calabus rubbed his hands together, a childlike twinkle in his eyes. "Are you ready, Master Finn? I commend you for your patience. You have held your excitement in check."

Finn looked puzzled. "Ready for what? I'm afraid I have no idea."

"Ready to look upon my invention, sir, what do you think I'm talking about? That's why you're *here*, you know. I am not breaking all the rules of decency for my health."

"Well said, Father."

"Who asked you, boy?" Calabus turned on Finn. "My

laboratory's in the cellar. You won't need a coat, it's really quite warm down there."

"And I shall do my best to amuse Miss Letitia while you're gone," Sabatino said. "We'll think of something, won't we, dear?"

"We certainly will not," Letitia said.

"Definitely not," Finn said. "Letitia goes with me."

"I don't *go* with anyone. I am going, but I'm going by myself."

Calabus looked pained. "No, young lady, you're not. I cannot allow you down there."

"Why not?"

"He can't," Sabatino said.

"I was asking *him*, thank you."

"It's simply not possible."

"Why not?"

"Please do not ask me that again," Calabus said, "you've done it twice now."

"How about three?"

Finn stepped to her side. Letitia pretended he wasn't there. "I'll ask it, then. Why? Is your invention dangerous in any way? Would she come to any harm?"

"Very likely not."

"Very likely not, but what?"

"I didn't say a what."

"You've said very little, as a fact, sir. I ask you plainly. What exactly are we going to see?"

"It defies description."

"It does."

"Most assuredly so."

Finn spread his hands. "That settles it, then. Anything that defies description is something I don't care to see myself."

Calabus sighed. "All right. It's a—mechanical device."

"You already mentioned that. A device of what kind?"

"A device related to matters of the, ah—unhappened circumstance."

"The what?"

Calabus rolled his eyes, his patience clearly at an end. "The unhappened *future*, boy. What else is unhappened but that? Damn you, sir, get your wits about you, or get left behind . . . !"

Twenty . . .

THE STAIRS LED DOWN FROM THE REAR HALLWAY
behind a thick, padlocked wooden door, down, down,
down a dizzy spiral of ancient stone, down a dark and
twisted way, down a passage so narrow, so cramped and so
tight only one person could squeeze through at a time.

Calabus led the way, his torch casting ghostly shadows
on the low confining walls. Finn crouched behind him, Julia on his shoulder, Letitia after that, with Sabatino bringing up the rear.

Finn could hardly guess how long they'd been descend-
ing into the earth. Deeper by far than he'd expected, for the
cellar to an ordinary house. And Calabus had surely been
right. There was no need for warmer clothing here. Every
cellar Finn had ever seen was damp and cool. This one,
though, was unnaturally hot.

"Stop that, sir!" Letitia cried out. "You stop that at
once!"

"Your pardon, lady. These are very tight quarters. I certainly meant no harm."

"Finn . . ."

"I can't kill him now, Letitia. Not unless we all lie down."

"Don't be amusing, I'm in no mood for that—Oh, that *sound!*"

Letitia swallowed hard, choked, strangled and gagged.

"What is that, it's awful!"

"I don't hear a thing," Finn said, "maybe it's the heat, there's very little air."

"It's not, either. You don't hear it? If you can't hear *that . . . ?*"

"Quiet back there, the lot of you."

Calabus stopped, the smoke from his torch bringing tears to Finn's eyes. Past the old man, Finn saw another heavy wooden door strengthened with enormous straps of iron.

"This is a place of science, a chamber of creation, I'll brook no childish play here. Don't make me tell you twice, or I—*Bruuuup!*—dreadfully sorry, Sea Pudding does it to me every time. The gods only know what Squeen puts in it. You could flog the scoundrel to death, he wouldn't tell."

"Finn . . . I can't breathe . . . I think I'm going to—faint . . . !"

"No you're not, there's no room here."

"Finn, please!"

Letitia swayed, sagged in Finn's arms.

"Move away," he told Sabatino, "she's not feeling well. I've got to get her upstairs."

"I can't *move* away, sir. Your very words. There's no room here."

"Well, make room, she's got to lie down. I need a cup of water, I need a wet cloth . . ."

Calabus turned to Finn, clearly annoyed. "Didn't I say

don't bring her down here? What did I say? Stand back if you will."

Calabus grabbed a key from a hook on the wall. The key rattled in the lock and the door swung free into a chamber dark as a demon's heart.

At once, Finn's ears were assaulted with a tumult of sound, a shriek, a rattle, a terrible whine, a head-splitting, gut-shaking clatter, a rumble, and a clamor and a roar.

"Hah, well. That's it," Calabus shouted, "We're here. You're in the presence of the greatest invention of our time—the Calabus Nucci Prophecy Machine!"

"The what? I can't hear a thing but some damnable machine."

"Don't anyone move. I'll get some light in here."

"What?"

The torch moved off to the right, and Calabus was gone.

Letitia moaned, coming to life again, clapping her hands against her ears.

"I'm terribly frightened, Finn. This is an awful place. I cannot stand it here."

"Hang on, dear. I'll get some light, then I'll get you upstairs. Why, you're trembling, Letitia. Surely you can't be cold, it's terribly stuffy to me."

"I am not cold," Letitia shouted in his ear, "I'm *scared*. Didn't you hear me? I have never been so scared in my life!"

"In that case, I'd best get you out as quickly as I can."

Finn lifted Letitia in his arms. She wrapped her hands tightly about his neck. He was greatly concerned, yet pleased somehow, for she was anything but distant now. Maybe they'd settle their quarrel without the need to discuss it anymore. Finn always hated that.

He moved, backing toward the stairs away from the deafening roar, and ran into Sabatino at once.

"Did you not understand me?" he said. "Move aside, you're in the way."

Sabatino didn't move. "This is Father's foolishness, not mine. You were advised, missy, to stay upstairs."

"Don't you call me that. I'm not a missy, you lout."

"Just move *aside*," Finn said, losing his patience now. Letitia was slim and very light, but even 90-weight of lint grows heavy in a while.

"I'd rather not," Sabatino said.

"You'd rather not? I don't care if you'd rather not."

Sabatino looked away. "I, ah—don't come down here. I do not fear the place, of course, that would be absurd. It's simply quite annoying to me. If I do come down, to see the old fool doesn't fall, I stay here. Just inside the door where I am now. I do not wish to go further than that . . ."

"Move. Move or I'll have to force you, sir."

"I don't think you can manage that. Not unless you put the lady down."

"Damn you, Sabatino. I'm going to take her upstairs if I have to walk over you!"

"Doubt if you could, Finn!"

A laugh, too highly pitched, stifled at once, and in scarcely any light at all, Finn caught a look of apprehension in Sabatino's eyes, slight, but clearly there, a touch of agitation, not enough for fear, not enough for dread, but all out of place in Sabatino's masks against the world. For a moment, the face behind the bluster, the swagger and the sneer, revealed a man cursed, damned, lonely and lost, and worse still, by what, he didn't know . . .

All this in the blink of a second, and the man was Sabatino, and illusion once again.

"What—whatever you may think you want to do," Finn said, releasing a breath, coming at the fellow with pluck, spunk and will in his voice, "you *will* get out of my way and do it now. I will brook no more of your—your—damn it, whatever it is. You're lucky I can't see you very well or I'd—"

Darkness suddenly turned to light. Not light as he'd ever perceived it to be, but a brilliance, a radiance past anything he'd dreamed. From the ceiling hung a great chandelier, three enormous circles of iron, one within the next, each ring alight with a hundred crystal spheres, spheres ablaze with the light of captive suns, fiery orbs of energy that spread their harsh glory to every corner of the room.

A wonder, an awesome sight to see, but the light was not the marvel that held Finn breathless in its sway. The light was the catalyst that offered its brilliance to the astonishing sight below . . .

"Great Tarts and Farts," Finn exclaimed, nearly dropping Letitia to the floor, rapt, trapped by the bizarre monstrosity that groaned and shuddered before his eyes—a thing that defied all description, betrayed no sign of what it could possibly be.

Monstrous in complexity and size, bigger than a pig sty, bigger than a poor man's house, it seemed to expand one moment then shrink back the next. It boiled, roiled, chattered in a fury, a thing of twisted iron, copper and brass, metals that had seethed, breathed, run together in a dross of some odd, uncommon design, each fiery element no longer itself.

And, coiled within this ruinous mass, wound in ugly convolutions like a nest of angry snakes, like the foul and tortured bowels of some great imagined beast, a beast that had surely taken ill, was an endless maze of grime-encrusted tunnels; tunnels made of crude, translucent matter, something old, something fused, something cracked and used, something once akin to glass.

Within those tunnels was a sight that raised the hair on

Finn's head, for even through the filth, through the dark obscuration, he could see that something *moved* in there, something of a dimness shifting in those kinked and twisted whorls . . .

"Well then, what do you think, boy?"

Calabus was suddenly beside him. Finn nearly jumped out of his skin.

"It's, ah—most impressive," he said, fighting the clamor, the shudder and the quake. "It's different than anything I've seen before."

"Yes it is, isn't it? Oh dear, I see you carry the poor girl about. Just as I advised, I believe. A Newlie doesn't fare well here. Something in the ah—primitive makeup, I assume."

Letitia found the strength to glare. "Let me down, Finn. I'm much better now." Her voice was so weak below the clamor and the roar, Finn could scarcely hear her at all.

"Nevertheless, I'm taking you back upstairs."

"Oh, sorry, I'm afraid you can't do that."

"And why not?"

"Because I can't allow just anyone the key. No offense, you understand. Miss Letitia, if you'll wait near the top of the stairs, you'll scarcely feel the, ah—disturbing emanations there. A little queasy perhaps, but I doubt you'll regurgitate at all."

"I can't allow that—" Finn began.

"Damn it all, Finn, I am going to throw up on you if you don't put me down!"

Letitia squirmed out of his grasp, nearly fell, and caught herself in time.

"This won't do," Finn said, "I'll have to insist on that key."

"I told you, sir—"

"*Wuuuuuuuuurp!*"

Letitia clasped her hand across her mouth. Her eyes

went wide and all the color drained from her face. Before Finn could stop her, she staggered toward the door, pushed Sabatino aside, and vanished up the stairs.

"I'll attend to her," Sabatino called out. "I'm going up myself . . ."

"Don't even think about it," Calabus said. "You stay right where you are." He turned to Finn then. "I do regret this. But you're here, sir, and I insist you take at least a hurried look before you tend to the girl."

"I'm afraid that wouldn't be right."

"Nonsense, come *along*, now," Calabus said, taking Finn's arm with a quite insistent, quite surprising grip.

Finn looked back, hoping against all reason, that Letitia might still be in sight. No one but Sabatino was there, perched on the steps with a surly petulant air.

"I knew," Calabus said, urging him along, "that a fellow with a passion for the mechanical device, would see at once the beauty, the perfection, of what I've done."

That wasn't what Finn had in mind, but he let it go at that. The more he looked at the thing, the more he was certain it had started much smaller than it was, then grown, through some odd replication, like a clutter of weeds gone wild.

"The damn thing's so *big*, though," Calabus said with a sigh of regret. "I've tried to hold it down to no avail. This is where I feel you could help. Your contraption is so neat and compact. I don't expect to carry the thing on my shoulder, you understand, but it *would* be nice if it fit on a table somewhere."

"I think you're well past that."

Calabus showed his displeasure at once. "I don't allow humor down here, it's simply not the place. I'm not surprised at anything a young man would say. It's the practice of youth to chatter over matters they scarcely understand.

The Prophecy Machine ∽ 153

The science of Prophecy is rife with problems I doubt
you'd comprehend. It's not like making a device that simply snaps and wags its tail.

"I assure you, I can do a great deal more than that.
Things I doubt *you'd* comprehend."

Julia's screech was easy to hear, even over the din.

"Keep your opinions to yourself," Finn said. "Nobody's
talking to you."

Calabus gave the lizard a thoughtful glance. "Most intriguing, Master Finn. I believe I mentioned before that I
would dearly like to see inside the thing."

"That wouldn't work at all. I do not have the proper in-
struments here to take a lizard apart. Without them, it's
simply impossible. The device would be quite undone."

Calabus smiled, a smile that embraced a little mayhem,
a vision of mechanical fun.

"I've got all the tools you need. I'm not a damn fool, you
know."

"Of course not. I never imagined you were. But your
machine bears no resemblance to mine. One doesn't split a
melon to see what's in a grape. I'm sure you get my point."

"I don't give a damn about your point, craftsman. You
understand that? Duck now, you're going to see the rest
whether you like it or not."

Just in time, Finn followed the old man's advice, barely
missing a clot of glassy tunnels, a dark and awkward knot
that bulged obscenely from the rest. Close as he was, he
could see nothing more than the quick blur of movement
within the filthy pipes.

"What did you say it was, now? The, ah—forces in motion in there?"

Calabus showed him a sly and cunning grin. "Why, I
don't believe I did. And, as you're aware, I'm sure you
didn't ask."

"Whatever it is," Finn said, "it's awfully hard to see."

With that, he took a step closer and reached up to touch a portion of the tunnel itself . . .

At once he felt himself seized by a flush, by a fever, by a nauseating chill. He felt a disassociation of the head, a numbing of the joints, and the promise of a diarrhetic fit.

"Stop it, get away from there!" Calabus shouted, grabbing his shoulder and jerking him roughly away.

Startled by this frightening event, Finn staggered against a wall waiting for the room to stand still.

Calabus offered a reassuring smile.

"I'm terribly sorry, it's not to be touched. For your own good, you see. There are certain—energies emitted by the device. As the girl learned, it can tend to make one ill."

"A bit more than that," Finn said, still very much aware of the tingle of every single hair on his head.

"Prophecy is somewhat abhorrent to the passage of time. Time is content to slug along at its own languid pace, looking neither forward nor back. It does not like intrusions of any sort. I can testify to that. My machine moves *through* the stream of time, nips off little bites of future, even snippets of the past.

"Time expresses its displeasure by inducing the desire to throw up, to barf, to emit, to toss one's biscuits, as it were."

"And does it very well," Finn said.

"I'm quite used to it. Doesn't bother me at all."

"And the dark pulsations one sees in the pipes, the things we were talking about? That would be what—your, ah, bites of some tomorrow flitting past?"

"You were talking about it, not I." Calabus looked annoyed. "I had hoped you'd be of some use to me, Finn. I can see that I was wrong. I have patiently explained the whole thing, and you have no grasp of it at all. My son was apparently right, you're a craftsman to the core. Come along, quickly now, you've wasted my morning, you might as well see the rest."

"I'm afraid not," Finn said. "I must see to Letitia. I fear we'll have to cut it short."

"Nonsense. Newlies have to complain about something, it's in their nature, you know. Ah, take a look at this and you'll be back to the lady in a blink."

Before Finn could protest, the old man took a step forward and opened a pair of heavy panels just below the stairs that Finn hadn't noticed at all.

At once, an alarming clatter filled the large chamber, drowning out the rumbles and rattles of the great machine itself. Finn stifled a desire to step back. The noise was overwhelming, an assault on the senses, a clear violation of every nerve and cell.

Revealed behind the doors were a clutter of golden tubes, a hundred or maybe more, arched up in closely packed rows, tubes like the graceful necks of swans, or serpents poised to strike. And from the mouth of each polished device spewed narrow, seemingly endless strips of paper that flowed into a hundred straw buckets, buckets that had long overflowed, spilling their flaccid ribbons across the floor.

"Crocks and Socks," Finn said, astonished at the sight. "Pardon my ignorance, but what on earth is that?"

Calabus was no longer surprised, scarcely irritated by Finn's lack of knowledge in the higher, loftier realms.

"What it is, is the end product of *that*," he said, nodding toward the twisted tangle of tunnels, wires, and pulsing muddy light.

"*That,* is merely the engine for this. The machine collects the prophecies—robs them from Time itself, I'm pleased to say—then transmits them over here. Go ahead, try one if you like."

"I don't think so," Finn said. "I have enough difficulty with the present and the past."

Calabus made a face. "Don't be ridiculous. You think *everything* has to do with you?"

"There's that. The odds are rather slim there's much about me in there."

Finn reached down and cautiously drew out a handful of tangles and loops. Holding a string to the light he read:

SDDKDFH FHKDFDFHHF HKDKKDFHFHDKDK HHiK HKDiGV

iOTOODN   ODVT   LDDLDLEMMLLOEEEL   J6808GP   LDD

BNNNNLLNNOWOV . . . OVSLDLOTHEL . . .FOELTLLMMELLV

LDFJJELOVVL LLVV6TL LFLLiTiiiii LLODV DLiK60606979

9-FG9-9 569-79V BFJDLD LDFFFJLNLLLOOL JLD LDJF

LDLDDLLDLL FFFFF LODVDGF LLL . . .

Finn scowled. "This is all gibberish. It makes no sense at all."

"Of course it doesn't." Calabus gave him a sour look. "It took me a great deal of time to learn to read the stuff myself. You think you can walk in here and snatch up a lifetime of scientific toil? Damn your arrogance, sir!"

"I forgot myself again," Finn said. "If you don't mind, I'd like to get upstairs."

"I'm damned if I know why I brought you here at all. Waste of time for me . . ."

"One thing I must ask," Finn said. "Those chandeliers above us here—they give out an astonishing light. May I ask what you've captured inside the glass bulbs? It seems like tiny bits of the sun."

Calabus looked annoyed. "That's got nothing to do with

anything, boy. It's excess energy—waste. The device makes so much power, I've got to drain it off somewhere."

"I think, sir, you've hit upon a very practical application here. It seems to me—"

"Sabatino!" Calabus shouted. "You will not forget to tell Squeen William I want sparrow pie tonight. And no feet this time. I find a single foot, I'll thrash the bastard to death . . . !"

Twenty-One . . .

ALL THE WAY UP FROM THE CELLAR, ALL THE WAY up to their room, Letitia didn't speak, wouldn't look at him, wouldn't say a word. It seemed to Finn that she was scarcely there, that the real Letitia was hidden somewhere within a shell, a shell that looked much like the real Letitia Louise. And when they were finally there, safe within the room, safe as one could be with a door whose knob had vanished years before, Letitia climbed in bed, turned away and pulled a dusty sheet about her head.

"Now I know you're upset," Finn said, sitting on the edge of a chair, "and I know you're angry with me. But hiding under there won't solve a thing, Letitia, I'm sure you know that."

"Yes, I'm very upset," she said beneath the covers, "and I'm very angry with you. You're wrong about the last. Hiding under here solves everything for me. Whatever happens next, I don't intend to see."

"She's got a point," said Julia Jessica Slagg. "It always works for me. I simply make a little click inside, and it all goes away."

"Nobody asked for your help. Nobody needs your advice. Be very quiet, or I'll give you to that old man who's dying to take you apart."

Julia knew this wasn't so, that he'd never do that. Still, she was good at reading vocal tones and what they might imply, so she rattled off in a corner and shut her ruby eyes.

"We have to talk," Finn said. "If you feel better under there, then stay. I can hear you well enough, and you can hear me."

Finn waited for some reply. When nothing came, he assumed she agreed and went on.

"From the moment we arrived in this place, I felt, and I'm sure you'll agree, that everyone here is addled, crackers, one hand short of a clock. Everything that's happened since has enhanced my feelings on this. I won't go over the events, you know them as well as I. But this, this whatever-it-is in the cellar, this monstrous machine, this is the most frightening thing of all . . ."

These last words, it seemed, had a great effect on Letitia Louise. She tossed the sheet aside, sat up at once, and looked thoughtfully at Finn.

"You really felt it then, is that what you're telling me now? I thought—what I *thought*, from your total disregard, was you didn't even *know* what was happening there. You surely didn't act as if you did."

"I'm sorry, my dear. I never meant to be uncaring, but I felt I ought to see just how deranged these people are. It's truly worse than I thought. Sabatino's mean of spirit and possibly daft, but the old man's totally deranged."

Finn shook his head. "He believes that pile of rubbish, that junkyard down there, is really retching up mail from the future. I can't imagine what he—"

"Oh, Finn . . ." Letitia covered her face with both hands. When she looked up again, all signs of anger or displeasure were gone. Now her features held no emotion at all.

"You say you felt it, but I'm not sure you did. Not the way *I* did, dear. There's something really awful, something terrible, down there. If I ever had to face it again, I fear my heart would simply stop."

"Letitia . . ." Finn left his chair and sat beside her on the bed. He touched her hand and found it limp and cold.

"I did feel something, I assure you of that. I touched the thing, and nearly got sick on the spot. But it's nothing to fear, it's some kind of natural force, something like, what—? Like lightning struck and you were close to the tree."

"No. It's not like that at all." Letitia jerked her hand away, but her eyes impaled Finn. Locked in a daze, locked in a stare, yet somewhere else, somewhere far away.

"You can believe that awful thing's real or it's not. It doesn't matter, Finn. But it's more than a machine, I'll tell you that. Magic's at work down there . . . No, now don't interrupt, just listen to me. When I'm done, you can argue with me then.

"This is what you have to do. And don't tell me you won't or you can't, or anything of the sort. You must leave, you must go back to town. Find another Mycer there, find her and tell her my name. Tell her my mother's name, which was Liliana, of the Phileas Clan. Tell her that, and she'll know you're all right. Newlies don't pass out names like humans do, we know better than that.

"And it must be a *she*. Never mind why. I didn't see any Mycers in town, but I'm certain someone's there, I can feel it, Finn. When you find them, tell them we have to have a seer. Tell them it has to be a Rubinella, First Order. Don't forget. It won't do any good if she's any less than that."

She reached out then and squeezed his hand. "Now you're going to say you wouldn't leave me on a bet. That this is all nonsense in my head. You will go though, because you have to, Finn. Julia won't let them harm me, and I doubt they'll even try. They'll let you go, because they know you'll come back to me.

"Can you *do* this? You have to, love. I can't explain why, because I don't really know. But I know what's down there is *wrong*, and we have to do something, or I don't think we'll ever get out of here alive."

Finn stared at her a moment before he could even find his voice.

"Skillets and Pans," he said, feeling a chill lift the hairs on his neck. "I don't know what to say. I can't imagine where you're getting all this. It's not like you at all."

"It is, though. It's just not a part of me you know, and I don't have time to tell you now. You'll do it though, won't you? You'll trust me, Finn, because we do have a great love for each other, and I'm sorry we had a small fight. I hate doing that, even if they're small, because I care a great deal about you."

Finn took a breath. "I don't like it, but I will, though I don't know what it's all about. But you do, it seems. That will have to be enough for me now."

Letitia smiled, the smile that always reassured him everything was right, though the rest of the world was completely unstable, totally out of whack. Which, quite clearly, it most surely was now . . .

Twenty-Two . . .

FINN WAS SURPRISED TO DISCOVER HOW CLOSE THE
Nuccis' house was to the village and the sea. The flight
from town the day before had seemed to take forever, hampered as it was by madmen with sharp pointy sticks. Now,
that same dusty road had turned to mud from the night's
fierce rain. The ruts worn by countless carts and wagons
were troughs of dirty water reflecting a leaden sky.

Even before he reached the rise that revealed the narrow
streets and cramped houses down below, the ghastly collection of odors assured him the town was still there. Still grim
and uninviting, a pile, a dump, an unlovely heap of peeling
wood and sooty stone. Convenient, Finn thought, for the
blind or the sighted as well. Either could find the place with
scarcely any effort at all.

It felt good to be free, out in the open, if somewhat tainted,
air. Free for a while from the mean in spirit and the mentally deranged, free from that house, free from the old
man's infernal machine.

Relieved, but still concerned that he'd left Letitia behind. She would come to no harm, he was sure. He wouldn't have gone if he'd had the slightest doubt.

Still, perhaps he'd been quick to agree, telling himself it was, after all, her idea, that he really didn't want to disappoint her again. He hoped she hadn't guessed, hadn't read it in his eyes, hadn't seen that he felt it was a useless thing to do, hunting for a seer, that it made no sense to him at all. She would be in a fury if she did.

He shook these thoughts aside, for he needed all his wits about him here. None of the locals he passed wore yellow hats, but that didn't mean this fellow or that hadn't tried to do him in the day before.

At the very edge of town, he turned to the right and headed for the docks, quickening his pace as a tangle of spars and masts appeared. He was certain none belonged to the *Madeline Rose*. Sabatino lied nearly all the time, but he'd happily told the truth about that. Three vessels were there, but Captain Magreet was gone.

One of the ships was loaded with kelp, stank to high heaven, and wouldn't be leaving for a week. Another was crewed by pug-faced Bowsers, who howled and snapped their teeth and threw fruit at him as he passed. The third, and largest, of the vessels had recently burned and settled to the bottom. Only charred and brittle masts still rose above the sea.

"What happened, might I ask?" Finn addressed an old man who was fishing off the quay. "I recall this ship wasn't sunk yesterday."

"Wasn't," the man said without looking up.

"I assume, then, it suffered an accident."

"You'd be wrong if you did. Hooters got it. Held their midnight service right here. Burned the thing down to the keel."

"Oh," Finn said, and didn't say a thing after that.

The man looked up, studying Finn with a fierce and curious eye. "I've seen you somewhere. What's your spiritual affiliation, friend?"

"Got to run, hope you land a big one," Finn said, and quickly hurried away.

"Why should I care if you stroll in town or not? You'll be back, you've no place to go."

Sabatino's words and his pompous, arrogant stance had annoyed Finn no end, but he'd held his temper at bay.

"I'm not asking your leave. I'm simply telling you I'm going. To get fresh clothing for Letitia, though it's none of your concern what I do. Clothing, and—no offense, unless you care to take it so—some sort of decent food. Your meals are atrocious here. I don't know how you stand it. You've been abroad, I know. I can't believe you never dined on a dish that wasn't gray. Something that looked as if it might run away."

"Ah, you're fooling no one, craftsman, certainly not me." Sabatino gave him a bawdy wink. "You're going because you think you'll find some clever way out of our lovely town. You won't, you know. But you're welcome to give it a feeble try."

"Go anywhere near her—just glance in her direction while I'm gone—and you'll answer to me."

"You strike terror in my heart."

"I mean it, Sabatino."

"Of course you do. Have a marvelous time."

Finn was near certain everyone in town knew who he was. Any other place, and he'd dismiss the thought at once. Here, it was no aberration of the mind. Men, women, babes in arms—no one turned his way. Still, when each was well past, he could feel their eyes poking at his back.

The chair he'd left in the street was gone. Most likely, the Master of Chairs had hauled it back inside. Who'd want to steal the thing? He thought about going in to check, but only for a second and a half.

The sign above the tavern read **TAVERN**. A sound and frugal name, Finn decided, no one putting on airs. One mug of ale before he went about his tasks. One cool mug couldn't take a lot of time.

He climbed three wooden steps and entered the dimly lit room. A bar made of planks was on the left, tables on the right. Feeble oil lamps and the smell of sour ale. At once, Finn felt somewhat at ease. If everything else in this land was awry, at least taverns smelled the same.

A man the size of a storm was suddenly in his way. He had no neck and no brow, and his body was so immense that his arms likely never touched his sides.

"Your pardon," Finn said, "I'd like to get by."

"What do you want," the man said, in a voice surprisingly shrill, "What you doin' here?"

"What I'd like to do is drink an ale. Would that be all right with you?"

"No."

"No?"

"No. It's not all right with me."

"Would you care to tell me why?"

"It's not all right because it's not. Why you askin' me something like that?"

"I don't know, it just seemed the thing to do."

"Those people." He glanced past a massive shoulder. "Those people drink in here."

"Yes, I see they do."

"They drink here. Not somebody else."

"This is a club, then. It's not a public bar?"

"Who told you that?" It was clear all this was hurting the fellow's head. "You see the sign, you see what it says outside?"

"I surely did."

"What does it say?"

"TAVERN, I believe."

"Tavern. That's what it is."

"Fine. I'd like an ale, please. A dark if you have it, if not I'll take a red."

The man was growing puffy about the eyes. Behind him, Finn could see faces, pale little moons floating in the dark.

"They drink here. Other people don't. These are the folks that drink here."

"And where," Finn wanted to know, "do the people who don't drink here go?"

"Somewhere else."

"And the people, the ones that drink somewhere else. They don't *ever* drink here. The ones that drink here, I'll bet they never drink anywhere else."

"I think I know you. You're the one doesn't come from here."

"I'm taking up your time, and I'm not really thirsty anymore. Let me ask you this. You know where I can find some Mycer folk in town? I'm trying to find a Rubinella; that's who I'm looking for."

The man's eyes grew wide. As wide as his butter cheeks would allow, as wide as little birdy eyes can go.

"You turn around and get out of here, you got a second and a half. I know who you are, all right. You been—you been staying over—eatin' and sleepin' overnight. Why you want to come to our town? Why'nt you stay where you belong?"

The big man could scarcely get the words out. He made no effort to hide his disgust. He looked at Finn as if he'd

swallowed a bug. Now, some of the moon faces were looking his way.

"I'm not entirely familiar with your ways," Finn said.
"If I've said something to offend—"

The man stabbed a finger at his chest. "You say some-
thin' dirty to me, I'll knock you flat."

"Thank you for your time," Finn said, "you've got a nice
place here . . ."

Twenty-Three . . .

Answers, it seemed, did not come easy in this queer, uncommon land—not as autumn leaves that fall in plenty from the tree, but tardy and slow like the lazy sap of spring. And, worse still, answers and questions looked strangely alike, the same as two dust balls, the same as two peas:

> As far as Finn could tell, nearly everyone here
> was a Hatter or a Hooter. Hatters ruled the day,
> and Hooters ruled the night.

> Hatters carried sharp pointy sticks.
> Hooters liked to burn things down.

> Torture and murder lead to spiritual growth.
> There were inter-faith rules to the game.

> The food was awful and the people smelled bad.
> Bad manners were the rule, hospitality was a sin.

> Questions had no answers, and answers were
> questionable at best.

Still, Finn felt he had gained real insight into the ways of this land. Everyone lived according to his creed, and everyone was totally mad.

Leaving the tavern called **TAVERN**, Finn passed a similar place called **BAR**. Reason said there was no use stopping there, so he made his way toward the broad market square.

The clouds had blown away and the sun had appeared to warm the dreary day. The square was crowded with booths, stands, and stalls of every sort. Stalls made of blankets on a pole. Stalls that sold melons, magic and simple card tricks. Big shops, little shops, shops no more than a stool or a bench. Each one squeezed, packed against the next. Finn could scarcely tell where one left off and another one began.

Working his way through the drab and odorous crowd, he found it hard to forget he was at the very site where Fate had slapped him silly and shown him what for. That too familiar tingle at the back of his neck was present there again.

After a bit of searching, he found the stall where he'd bought some tin scraps and a roll of silver wire. With a sigh of relief, he saw the same merchant was there.

"Good day," Finn said, offering a smile to a fellow he'd met before, "it's quite nice to see you again."

"I don't do returns," the man said, wary, as ever, of a pleasant attitude. "You bought it, it's yours, don't come whining back here."

"I'm very satisfied with my wares," Finn said. "I have a question, is all."

"I can sell you brass, bronze, nickel, or lead, copper, iron or tin. I can get you gold, I can get you gilt. The gilt's so good you could fool eight people out of ten."

"My question's not about that."

"Then you're in the wrong stall, friend."

The merchant, a wiry man with a buzzard's nose, spat

on the ground close to Finn's boot. Finn noticed he had a tattoo of a fish with a woman's head and breasts, ranging from the bald pate of his head to the base of his scrawny neck. He wondered how he'd possibly overlooked this striking image before.

"I'm willing to pay," Finn said, reaching in his jacket and showing the man a silver coin. "This is yours if you tell me what I want to know."

"Be still my beatin' heart. How can I resist such a fortune as that?"

"Right. Two silver pieces, then."

"Three. And they'd better be silver 'stead of plate of some sort. This is what I do all day, friend."

"I'm looking for Mycer folk. I haven't seen any, but I'm certain they're around. One Rubinella, I believe. If you could just—"

Finn stopped at once. The merchant, a man of a light copper shade, went suddenly pale. As pale, in truth, as the man at the tavern, who would make three or four of the fellow here.

"Are you daft," he said, his gaze shifting wildly about the marketplace, "are you possessed, brother, soft in the head, looking for a noose? Would you care to be cut into ribbons, roasted on a spit? Is there some kind of pain that you desire?"

"None of that at all," Finn said, "Why do you ask?"

"Gata-watta-bool," the man muttered, or words to that effect. His fingers clutched an amulet dangling from a chain about his neck. A quarter-moon, Finn noted, carved from adder stone, with a single opal eye.

"I meant no offense. All I asked was where could I find a—"

"I *heard* what you said. For the life of me, don't go sayin' it again."

Rolling his eyes in a most peculiar way, he quickly tossed a cloth across his goods and loosed a cord that dangled overhead. At once a slatted curtain rattled past Finn to the ground.

"We're closed," the merchant said, from behind his shabby blind. "All day, and tomorrow as well. Don't come back anytime. I won't be here the day after that."

"What's wrong with you?" Finn said. "What did I do? Is there anyone sane in this place?"

He thrust the blinds aside, ready to give the fellow a piece of his mind. The stall was quite empty, the merchant had fled. Finn was disgusted, totally dashed. It was plain, he decided, that it wasn't the Mycers that set the locals foaming at the mouth. They'd all seen Letitia the day before, and doubtless there were other Mycers here.

It had to be the name, then: the Rubinella. Clearly, that bothered them a lot.

"I shall have to approach this some other way," he told himself. "Rubinella is not too popular here . . ."

While no one offered him a smile or bothered to be polite, no one else went out of business when he offered to buy their wares. Finn bought long loaves of bread, overripe tomatoes, hot roasted corn on a stick. Cherries, berries, a crock of pickled cabbage, and a jar of plum jam. Oatcakes, sweetcakes, and sugary treats. Apples so brown and wizened, they all had faces like little old men.

He didn't buy a single turnip, and he didn't buy a fish. He did buy a straw basket to put his goods in. He didn't buy a thing they'd have to cook. Letitia would surely be delighted. The food would lift her spirits, and she wouldn't be angry for a while.

Finn was so hungry himself, he ate two loaves of the

bread, a great deal of cabbage and most of the jam. He didn't feel bad about eating before he got back. Certainly, Letitia wouldn't fault him for that.

It was pleasant to see foods of different colors again. Nothing in the market was gray. Nothing looked at all like the horrors that Squeen William served. Neither of the Nuccis seemed aware they ate glop, slop, gunk and toxic swill three times a day.

If the Hatters and the Hooters and folk who didn't go to church at all had any bias toward Newlies, it was nowhere in evidence here. Finn saw them everywhere. Stout, broad-shouldered Bullies who seldom showed expression beyond a blank stare. Snouters strutting lazily about. No Yowlies so far, and he was thankful for that. Bowsers a-plenty, though, yapping and marching about, wearing those ridiculous boaters Bowsers wore everywhere, getting in everyone's way.

Even a pair of Dobbins, tall and handsome creatures, with their outsize noses and kindly brown eyes. If there was any station, any rank among the Newlies, the Dobbins would surely be near the top. With the Yowlies at the bottom, by damn, as far as Finn was concerned.

Of the Favored Nine, those animals the outlaw magicians, Shar and Dankermain, had changed into beings very much like Man, Finn had seen all but one, even the shy elusive Badgie, known for its stealth and criminal enterprise. He had never, ever seen a Grizz, and hoped he never did. They were fierce, antisocial creatures who kept to themselves, mostly in the North. Finn had seen an etching of some, sitting in a forest by a fire. Everyone said that a Grizz loved fire, but no one said why.

"Now, if I could only find a Mycer, I could leave this

odorous place and get back to Letitia, alone in that hideous house . . ."

First, though, he knew he'd best purchase another jar of jam and some more oatcakes, as there was little of either left. That, and a gown she could wear, though where he'd find that, he couldn't say. The females here, Newlie and human alike, seemed to favor ill-fashioned garments made of scraps, patches, and snatches of straw.

Letitia wouldn't care for that. Letitia didn't dote on clothing, but she wasn't fond of sacks. If he could *ask* someone, if someone had the courtesy to talk instead of sneer . . .

"Ah, looking at who is here, looking who is out to see the sights in our most lovely town."

Finn stopped, pulling up short as the Foxer stepped right in his path. One, and then another, and another after that, all arriving quickly without the appearance of intent, yet clearly designed to box him in.

"I fear you're in my way," Finn said, "I ask you to kindly step aside."

The Foxer closest by showed Finn a toothy grin. "He askits we are stepping aside. He fears wes in his way."

"In his way," said the second, who was shorter than the rest.

"Steps aside," said the third, who walked with a limp. His voice was a rasp, much like that of his companions, voices that were scratchy and dry.

Finn had seldom been around Foxers, except for a few at home. Foxers didn't care for the west, they'd mostly settled south. To him, these three looked much alike. Gaunt with red eyes, amber hair and tufted ears, and mean little mouths. Still, the bloody slash across a brow, the scar above an eye, a limp and a twitch, told him he had met this trio before.

"That's a wicked cut indeed," Finn said, addressing himself to Short, yet taking in the rest. "I'd get a stitch or two, drink lots of water, and get plenty of rest."

Short reached up to touch his scar, thought better of it, and simply glared at Finn.

"We wishes to tell you," said Limp, "you listen real good."

"No harm will be coming," Toothy said. "You gets far aways from here."

"Far aways," Short said, "far aways from here."

"A most excellent idea," Finn said. "I've considered that myself. As soon as possible, I'll be gone from here, far across the Misty Sea. Until that time, I've something to say to you.

"Last night you woke me from a dream of melon pie. One of your lot is quite good with a blade, and the other two are not. None of you are nearly as good as I. Come at me again, by damn, and I'll slice your hairy ears off and have them for lunch."

None of the three moved. Limp shook his head. "You might be besting us we have a fight. I'm not believing you eat ourselves, though. We are not foods."

"Most clearly we are not," Short said.

"What I'm thinking is, that was not a true," Toothy said. "That was a humor, was it not?"

"I don't ever do a humor. It was nothing of the sort."

"Ah, I see." Toothy looked at the others. They came to him at once, speaking in low and rusty tones.

Finn wondered what they'd do if he simply walked away. Still, just because they couldn't tell jokes didn't mean they weren't agile, fast on their feet, cunning and sly. He'd learned that much the night before. They were dressed in ordinary clothes now, shabby vests and pantaloons instead of black. Except for the blades at their sides, they looked harmless and benign. They didn't even smell as they had when he'd fought them in the hall, an odor that was rank, alien and foul.

All Newlies smelled, some good and some vile. Bullies smelled like grass and sweat. Vampies, Squeen William's kind, had an odor like meat, like mold, like the sickly smell of death.

Letitia, on the other hand, smelled like musk, like old attic dust. Sometimes she smelled like clover, like brittle winter leaves, like earth turned in the spring.

Human folk had odors too, odors that offended, or attracted, others of their kind. And what did the Newlies think of human smell? Letitia Louise said Finn smelled nice, or most of the time, and he hoped that this was so.

"We has come to a decide," Toothy said, turning to Finn once again. "Our decide is this. We doesn't think you contend against our kind. We doesn't think you do a quarrel. We believes you had a hostile because you was there."

Finn felt a sense of relief, but he didn't let it show.

"What you say is true. I am pleased you understand. It was dark, and there was little time to reason things out. I had no idea who you were, or what you were doing there. It is clear now, you did a—you had a quarrel with the Nuccis. I'm not too surprised, but there's no need to go into that. After I'm gone, do feel free to break in anytime."

Toothy looked at Short. Short looked at Limp.

"You are a gone? We thinking you are here."

"Gone from *there*," Finn explained. "Gone from the Nuccis when a ship arrives again."

"That is not a gone . . ."

"No, that is like a then . . ."

"This calls for a change of our decide . . ."

"This is not a pleasant," Short said, "but this is how things is. If you be not a gone when we is coming, you be there again. Best thing to do, wes thinking, is us be sticking you now."

"What?"

"Will you journeys to the alleyway, please? It is plenty darker there . . ."

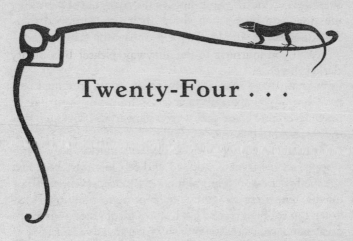

Twenty-Four . . .

FINN HAD NO TIME TO THINK, NO TIME AT ALL TO blink. All three Foxers drew their blades at once. Finn ducked as Limp shaved the hairs atop his head. Toothy came at him from the left. Finn stepped on his toes and sent him reeling into Short.

"Lunatics, crazies!" Finn shouted. "I'm stranded in a madhouse here!"

And, with a solid kick that impaired Toothy's very vital parts, Finn was off and running through the horde, through the rabble, through the packed marketplace.

The crowd cleared before him, parting like water before a schooner's bow, parting, as any crowd would, before a man howling, growling, shouting out curses in some unholy tongue, clutching his blade and waving it about.

Bold, short-tempered men, men who liked to have a drink without a lot of noise, hastened to find a brick or a sharp-pointed stick, hastened to stop this brazen oaf. Hastened, then paused, paused and hesitated, mindful of the rage, of the fierce determination in the man's clearly homicidal gaze, mindful of the yelpers and the yappers, of the barking berserkers on his tail. Thinking it wise to stay out of this mess, the stout and burly men shook their fists, dropped their bricks and sticks, and let their anger chase the man instead.

Finn knew that a man with any sense would let a madman have his way. Especially a loony who came from out of town. Everyone knew they were a dangerous lot, even when they seemed to be sane.

Turning a corner into a narrow, murky way, Finn stopped in his tracks, stopped and felt his heart beat fast against his chest. A team of worker Bullies, seven, eight, or maybe ten, were dragging an enormous building stone down the cobbled street. Each was a giant among his kind, great ponderous creatures with broad massive chests, and scarcely any necks at all. Each grasped a rope across his shoulder, grasped it in two chunky hands, strained so hard against the burden of the stone that a deep and awesome thrum resounded from their lungs with every step. Their thighs were as big as the torso of an ordinary man, and the veins in their arms were as thick as killer vines curled about a mighty tree.

Each of the brutes looked solemn and grave, and each wore a heavy ring through his nose, some lost tradition from the past, some rite now centuries old.

Finn knew he couldn't get through, knew the narrow street could scarcely contain these fellows now. Knew the manic Foxers were howling on his trail. Knew he could beat them one and all if they'd only fight him fair. He paused, took a breath and plunged into the fray . . .

He ducked, weaved, scrambled through columns of meat, under crotches, under legs, over bare and smelly feet. The fleshy hulks kicked him, cursed him and growled. Finn gagged and choked, staggered under body odors foul, under flatulent attack.

Finally, gasping for breath, stumbling to his feet, he came out the other side. The air was still vile, a near visible cloud.

The streets were close to empty, everyone at market, Finn supposed, leaving their doors and windows open wide. Trusting their neighbors, no doubt, for their goods were so shabby no one wanted whatever lay about.

The lane here was narrow, narrow and cramped. The stories from one side leaned out drunkenly to meet shaky structures tipping the other way. The street was a tunnel shut off from the sun, a place too wretched to live, Finn thought, unless everyone wore gray.

The Foxers, he guessed, wouldn't be fool enough to come the way he had. They'd go around and try to cut him off, and they'd know the town better than he.

Which way, then—left, right, the street that smelled of cabbage, or the one more like a sewer? The sewer, he decided, for a bit more light leaked down through the arches overhead.

Three more byways, and three dead ends. Finn wished he'd gone the other way—he couldn't keep going, couldn't go back the way he'd come.

An old woman passed with a bundle of wood, a child strapped tightly to her back. The child stared at Finn in wonder. The woman didn't bother to look his way.

Finn studied the shop behind him, the building over-head. The shop had a sign that read **TALLOWS & LAMPS**. The one across the street read **CLUB**. Another place that wouldn't let him in. Only the people at **CLUB** could drink there. He was, it seemed, beginning to under-stand these alien ways.

He plunged his hand into the basket, coming up with half a loaf of bread. He ate half of that, and put the quarter back. All of the tomatoes were squashed. Getting through the Bullies had ruined all the cherries and the berries, and the sweetcakes had crumbled into shreds.

He heard the sound of his foes before he saw them, the yipping and the yowling and the stomp of heavy boots, the clatter of buckles and swords.

He looked to his front, to his left and to his right. Finally, he looked at the arches that loomed up above.

"Up it is, then," he said aloud, chiding himself for pausing to eat, "up is the only way there is . . ."

The first story up was chunky stone with plenty of handy holds for hands and feet. The second was ancient wood, which rotted and crumbled, and nearly spilled him to the ground.

Once at the top, he could see a small corner of the market, a blue slice of the sea.

"The sea would be west. When we were still in open water, the sun always set behind the stern. Except, I think, when we went through Blue Butter Strait. Unless I'm mistaken, the sun on that occasion came up in the *south*. I knew that couldn't be, and meant to ask about it at the time . . ."

Not for the first time, Finn had to sadly confess that he scarcely knew his left foot from his right. That sort of thing was not required for a man in the lizard trade. He surely didn't know his way back to Julia and Letitia Louise. Back to Squeen William and the Nucci maniacs. What he knew was the sound of his pursuers was growing much closer all the time.

Leaping from one roof to the next was as simple as could be. The thatched, patched, tiled and slatted shops were hardly a quarter inch apart, and often closer still. The clatter of the Foxers was fading with every step he took. Finn, however, knew that he was fading too. His throat was dry as sand. He'd had a little food, but not a thing to drink. If you can't get in **BAR** or **TAVERN** or **CLUB**, there's little one can do.

He jumped from a roof made of shingles to a roof made of pebbles to a roof made of plaster and sticks. Some roofs were steep, and others were flat. One had a hole that he nearly fell through. A man down below looked up at Finn and stared, said, "What the hell you doin' up there?"

"Pardon," Finn said, and noticed the man was cooking an ugly fish.

Someone shouted and told him to stop. Finn thought it was the man, then saw it was a Foxer running straight at him across the rooftops. Another appeared, then another after that. Then, worse still, three more, and that added up to six.

"They've brought in help," Finn muttered. "That doesn't seem right."

With a leap and a yell, the nearest foe came at him, twisting his sword in a high and fearsome arc. Finn met him with the flat of his blade, pushed him aside, broke into a run and didn't stop.

This appeared to anger his pursuers. They jeered and called him names. Finn didn't care. Honor was scarcely an issue here. The Foxers were no great fencers, but six of them would surely bring him down.

One came at him from the left, two closed in from the right. Finn feinted toward the loner, then surprised them all by going for the pair.

A moment's hesitation, an instant of surprise gave Finn a small advantage and he took his foe out, blooding him deeply from his knee down to his thigh. The Foxer gave a cry and stumbled back. Before he hit the roof, Finn turned on his companion—whom he recognized as Toothy—and drove him savagely away.

Step, slash—step and slash again—

—and then he was aware of the loner at his back, aware with a start, that his single enemy had turned into four. It struck him, again, this was not the vacation he'd bargained for.

"Standin' and fight," said Foxer number one, "face me if yous dare!"

"We'll not bes harmin' if you do," said number two.

"Yes we will," said three, formerly known as Limp, "that bes what we're here for!"

"I'm afraid I have to go," Finn said, "I'm expected somewhere."

With a bark and a shout, Limp came at him, driving Finn up the steep slate at his back.

"What yous gotten in the basket?" Limp said, slashing at Finn's head. "When I bes makin' you deads, I takin' a look inside."

"There's not as much as you'd think, but you're welcome to it if I fail."

"Hey, failin' you will, for we doesn't welcome strangers to our shores."

"If you'd not taken up with Nucci scums, we'd maybe lettin' yous go," said a Foxer approaching from the right, one he didn't know. "You dids, though, an' we gots to stick you for that."

Finn turned from Limp for an instant to drive the newcomer back. The Newlie was better than he'd thought. Instead of retreating, he lunged in quickly and ripped Finn's shirt at the chest, leaving a painful stripe of red.

"Hah! You'd best bes givin' in," the Foxer grinned, licking his pointy nose, glaring at Finn with his hateful red eyes. "Yous no match for me, yous only a man!"

"A lucky hit," Finn said, "don't count on doing that again."

He forced a smile to match his foe's, but the cut hurt him

more than he wanted the fellow to know. Without looking back, he retreated up the steep slope, praying he didn't slip on a slat some lazy roofer had failed to nail down.

"Is it bein' true what wes heard," Lump said, edging up on Finn's right, "is it trues in your land you got a place where strangers stop and sleep?"

"Spend the whole night?" someone added.

"And eats there too?"

"With peoples you don't even know?"

"Where yous can see them, and theys can see you?"

Limp made a face. "Humans is nasty everywhere, but I never heards anything sicker as that."

"What is it you have against the Nuccis?" Finn asked, hopping to the right, and then the left again. "I'd simply like to know."

He was nearing the peak of the roof. Another step or two, and he could risk a look down the other side . . .

"If it's that lad on the ship—is that it? I stopped Sabatino, I'd like to mention that. Weren't aware of that, right? To tell you the truth, I don't care for the Nuccis myself. Fate tossed us together, I assure you, I didn't have a great deal of choice.

"But attacking people in their beds, in the dark of night—that's a coward's path, there's little pride in that. Far better if you'd face them in the open, work out your quarrel in an honest, straightforward way—"

The Foxers came at him as if they were all of one mind, as if some sign, some gesture, had passed between them unseen. Their teeth were bared and their eyes were bright with rage. Their blades flashed in the sun, and they raised a terrible din.

"Something I said to offend, I'll wager," Finn muttered to himself, hastily backing toward the peak. "I fear I've set you fellows off again."

He reached the top, then, one foot braced on the near

side, one against the other, neither too secure, for he felt a bit light in the head. He'd ignored the wound thus far, knew he should have left before the weakness took him down.

The Foxers could sense his confusion, read the hesitation in his stance, smell the blood, perhaps, as their kind had done before the Change.

Every action, now, seemed to move faster for Finn, everything but the limbs at his command. While the Foxers were a blur, moving with a speed uncanny to the eye, his legs, his arms, the weapon in his hand, dragged through a thickening mire, moved with all the fervor and dash of a tortoise in a syrupy sea . . .

Color faded from the sky, simply cracked and peeled like dry and weary paint that's seen its day. Then there was nothing, nothing there at all, only the sense that he was falling, tumbling, giddy and muddled, out of control, drifting, drifting far away . . .

Twenty-Five . . .

"VAT DEY SMELLIT LIKE," SAID THE ONE, "ISS ON-yons. Vile onyons un' leeks."

"Garlig," said the other, "thas the wursof awl. Garlig getting in da poors an' dond efer goes avay."

"I won say it iss or it's nod. To me, iss nod a simble thing, it's the mix dat make a scent I kant abide. You takes a radich. A radich un a kabach—ain't so fensive as it iss ven dey kook da damn ting, I'll say dat. Now der is un odor dat'll drife you up da vall.

"But I vas sayin radich, radich un kabach, dey won be zatisfy wid dat. A Hooman bein's goda grind dem peppah on it and stir in zum sprout. Bad enuf ven dey ead da filty stuf, the wurst iss in da varts. May I die if it's nod da holy truth, der is nuttin' like the badd smellin vind from a Hooman's goda gutt fulla green an' yellah plants. Vhatcha gotten now? I'm showin' pair of fivezies, and a prince. You goda tree twos, the bet's to you . . ."

Finn could smell them . . .

He could smell them in his dreams, smell them when he

woke, didn't even have to look. Bowsers always smelled the same, like they'd come in from the rain. He'd known a few at home. A couple lived on Garpenny Street and did good business selling meat and bones. Rabbit and gopher, possum and coon. Beaver, goat and porcupine, wrens, hens and hawks. Carcasses hanging on hooks out front, bloody and swarming with flies.

The folk who ran the shop were decent folk, but Letitia wouldn't speak to them at all. Some of the meat they sold were related, she said, squirrels and voles and such. Besides, Yowlies shopped there; even if they didn't care for Bowsers, they hungered for the dead things they sold.

"I goda tree Vitches," said one, "that'll beat your twos."

"You're a tamn cheet is vat you are," said the other, "you didn haff no Vitches before."

"I god you both," said the third, "I god a pair of nines un tree Seers."

"Shid," said one.

"I'm oud," said the other, and tossed in his cards.

Finn risked a look and opened one eye. When he did, a terrible pain shot through his head. For the very first time, he remembered the rooftops, remembered the Foxers, wondered just how he'd gotten here.

He could see the three across the room. They sat at a table under an oily lamp. One was rather pug-nosed and fat. One was very small, with very large ears. One, Finn saw, was bigger than the rest, with close-cropped hair and mean eyes. All three wore straw boaters, stiff collars and dirty white shirts. Two, Pugnose and Mean-eyes, wore monocles pinned to their vests. Some sort of thing they did,

Finn decided, for the butchers at home dressed exactly like that.

Skipo, for that was the butcher's name, had an accent as heavy as these fellows did, though he'd lived all his life in Ulster-East. Newlies had a thing about that, or some of them did. Even if they worked with humans, or had human friends, they took great pride in retaining their strange variant of the local tongue. The Bowsers did it here, and the Foxers as well, and likely most all the Newlie kind.

Squeen William, Finn decided, was probably an exception, and could do no better than he did.

On the other side of the coin, Newlies like Letitia, who had no trace of Mycer accent in her speech, were often reviled by Newlies who did.

This is often the way, Finn thought. *If you do something right, someone will take affront, and try to bring you down . . .*

"It's avake," said the big one, "I zaw im move his eyes."

"It's *been* avake," said the smallest of them all. "Hoomans vill do dat, dey are wery sly."

Finn was startled, suddenly aware they were clearly discussing him.

"Don get up," Mean-eyes warned him, pushing back his chair. "Shtay vere you are."

"I'm staying," Finn said, "all right? Look, what's going on, what am I doing here? All I remember . . ."

"You fallin' off a roof. You hittin your head," Pugnose said.

"Foxers isn't liken' you a lot," Mean-eyes added with a grin.

"Tell me something I don't know. Whoever you are, thanks for your help. I see you've got some ale there, I could certainly use a drink."

"He could use a trink," Mean-eyes said.

"Give him a trink," the little fellow said.

Pugnose got up, grabbed a jug of ale and squatted at Finn's side.

"You vant a trink, Hooman? You like zum ale?"

"If it's no bother," Finn said.

"No pother, my friend," the Bowser said, and Finn, with utter disbelief, saw the jug coming down at his head . . .

"They can be quite decent, most of their kind, but this is quite a callous bunch. I'm sorry they struck you in the head. I want you to know, I don't approve of that."

"They struck me twice," Finn said, "in the very same spot."

Dr. Nicoretti frowned and shook his head as if he was truly alarmed. "No, they did not. You fell, on your merry chase across the roofs. If they hadn't been there, the Foxers would have surely run you through and dumped you in an alley somewhere. I put a gauze on your chest. Lost a little blood, no big thing. I expect you were somewhat overwrought, more than anything else."

"And I owe my life to you, yes? For that, and sending those louts to *save* me? So who put the Foxers on me, then? I don't suppose I can thank you for that as well?"

Nicoretti rolled his eyes. He leaned back in his chair, the one where Mean-eyes had sat before. Finn was not greatly surprised that he had woken to find Sabatino's uncle there. After the past few days, little shocked him now.

"That is a most ridiculous thing to say," Nicoretti told him. "Why would I bother with such a charade— send those crazies after you, and rescue you as well? You've got more sense than that, lad. Don't play the fool with me."

Finn forced himself to sit up. His head throbbed and his

throat was quite dry. Nicoretti had given him some ale, but the stuff was warm and sour and only made him thirsty for more.

"If I'm a fool, then I guess I've got reason to be. I don't know what's happening here. I don't trust the Nuccis, and I surely don't trust you. If I'm not mistaken, it was you who asked the old man to give Letitia away. For *spiritual rites?*"

Finn made a face. "Hooters and Hatters. You people aren't civilized here. Decent people don't go to churches like that. You're all mad is what you are!"

"I'll overlook that," Nicoretti said. "You're clearly a bigot and you've been shaken up, you're not thinking straight. Besides, that business of you and the Newlie, that was just a joke. You two wouldn't do me any good, you're not from here. The Pastor wouldn't go for that."

"Huh! Didn't sound like a joke to me."

Nicoretti leaned forward, his hands on his knees. His eyes seemed to bore through the back of Finn's skull. In the flickering light of the lamp his features were shadowed, and somber as the grave.

"You call me mad, Master Finn, yet it's you that's acting less than sane. May the demons take me, what do you think you're mixing in here? Do you think you're *safe* up there with those two? Do you think they'll let that pretty of yours walk out of there?"

Nicoretti threw up his hands in despair. "Why did I bother? Why did I take the trouble to save your hide? You're too *dense* to listen, too full of pride. I should have let those idiots have their way, let them punch you full of holes. You're no good to yourself, and you're surely no good to me!"

Finn ignored the man's theatrics. The more he waved his arms about, the broader the deception, the bigger the lie, or so it appeared to Finn.

"If you did truly save me, then you had some reason, and you'll not mind telling me why."

"I can't stand by and see a man do himself in just because he's a fool. And you've got a talent for it, Finn. You've angered the Foxers because you put yourself in their quarrel. They won't let go of that."

Nicoretti raised a restraining hand before Finn could break in.

"They're hard-headed creatures, and your intentions mean not a whit to them. In their minds, you're an enemy as well as the Nuccis themselves."

The doctor unwound his skinny frame, stood, and stalked about the cramped room.

"It's true you're taking blame for sins you couldn't likely help. My church has got its hats on crooked because you helped the Nuccis get away. The whole damn *town's* up in arms because you're staying there. Hospitality is the Fourth Deadly Sin in our religion and seventh in theirs. Sabatino and Cal are flaunting that in our face, and we're all wondering why."

Nicoretti stopped his pacing, turned toward Finn with a questioning brow. "Maybe you could help me, Master Finn. I expect you have a guess at what's going on up there. It'd help me and others understand if you could shed a little light on that. Could you be of some aid in this?"

All this was delivered in calm and easy tones with a reassuring smile, an actor switching roles without a single change of scene, setting off alarms of every sort in Finn's head. Was this a trap of some kind? Did Nicoretti know about the madness Calabus was brewing in the depths below his house? And if he did, why then would he care? It was all a lunatic's obsession anyhow.

"I'll be honest with you," Finn said. "I may be wrong, but I think you're trying to be straight with me. If the Nuccis are up to anything, as you say, I don't know what it is. I don't know why they took us in, except we helped Sabatino save the old man from your yellow-hatted maniacs. No offense meant."

"Oh, I assure you, none taken, sir."

"I must admit, I find it hard to believe they're the sort that's easily overcome with gratitude."

"I'd agree heartily with that."

"I'd guess there are two factors here, Dr. Nicoretti. One, they take pleasure in flaunting custom, shocking the locals who clearly have no love for them. Two, I suppose you're aware Sabatino's a hopeless lecher, obsessed with my—companion, Letitia Louise. I cannot tell you how difficult it was to leave her there with him."

"Ah, but you did, though. In spite of those fears . . ."

The sudden flare of interest in Nicoretti's eyes, the way his body tensed as if he might spring from a branch upon his prey, told Finn this was a topic that had best go astray.

"The Nuccis," he said, with an irritation that was real, "have no perception of decent food. Squeen William's dishes are horrors in gray. I had to risk a visit to get us something we could eat."

"I see you've done a shoddy job at that," Nicoretti said, nodding at the nearly empty basket on the floor.

"Food doesn't fare too well if one has to stop and fight. I intend to replenish my supplies, if it's any concern of yours."

Nicoretti spread his hands and smiled. "It is *not* my concern, as you say. And if it were the only reason you were here . . ."

"I said it was, did I not? I would be gone if those louts hadn't tried to do me in." Finn answered Nicoretti's virtuous smile with one of his own. "How lucky for me your Bowser boys were about. Nearby and ready to save out-of-towners who might come to harm in some way."

"Fortunate, indeed. I'm delighted they could help."

Nicoretti curled his lips as if he'd tasted something foul.

"Their manners are impossible, of course. Nasty types, I'm sorry to say. Stiff-necked bastards. Do a lot of marching and strutting about, that sort of thing. Where did you get the idea for your lidard, Master Finn? Do you mind if I ask?"

"Lizard, you mean to say. People have asked me this before. I fear my answer won't suffice. When I made the very first one, 'lizard' was the word that came to mind. As the word 'stone' might well have occurred when a man first saw one lying in his path. It simply seemed to fit."

"Well, then . . ." Nicoretti brought the jug of ale out again and filled Finn's cup. The stuff was still flat, warm and unpleasant to the taste, but there was clearly nothing else around.

Still, Nicoretti downed his drink with great delight.

"I will not delay you further, Master Finn. By my reckoning, you should just make it back before market closes down. Our Hatter folk have no service planned till tomorrow afternoon. However, I'd advise you to get back to your companion and your lidard before it gets dark. The Hooters, I believe, have choir tonight, and that can get rowdy sometimes.

"One more thought before we part, if I may. Let's put aside the foolery, lad. We've been lying to one another since our talk began. There is something going on in that wretched house, and it's not impossible that you know what it is. You'd be wise to tell me, but you won't. You'll play the fool until it's much too late to ask for help.

"Now, would you tell me why you're looking for a Mycer called Rubinella? A fact every farmer, every bumpkin, every clown in town knows now? I would strongly advise you to tell me, sir, before you get in something completely over your head!"

Finn was not surprised to learn his search had reached

Nicoretti's ears. The man was a meddler, that was plain to see. Why, though, what was he up to? That was the mystery here.

And no matter how well he masked his emotions, he had clearly betrayed, along with open anger, a slight hint of fear—and that bothered Finn a great deal.

"I see no reason to tell you," Finn said. "If it's true we're both liars, my answer would do you little good. I could ask, though, why you care who I'm looking for, but then you'd lie too. So what's the point here?"

The sudden flush of color in Nicoretti's face let Finn know the doctor didn't care for that.

"You'd best not be too clever, friend. A man's been known to laugh himself to death, chuckle to his coffin, giggle to his grave."

"Sir, I have no idea what that means."

"Of course you do, don't play the fool. Now, what do you know about that filthy old man? The one they keep hidden up there, the one who's goofy as a loon?"

"What do *you* know about him? You tell me."

Nicoretti shook his head, his patience at an end.

"There's nothing else I have to say to you. If you come to your senses, we might talk again."

Dr. Nicoretti stood, a clear invitation for Finn to leave.

"I suppose I should thank you," Finn said, coming to his feet, making his way to the door. "But I don't know what for."

"Of course you don't, you're quite an ignorant boy. I'm surprised you've managed to survive."

Finn didn't have to hide his anger. He truly felt nothing at all.

"I did mean to ask, but you're so full of questions, Doctor, I didn't have the time. You're Sabatino's uncle, so you're kin to the family some way. Might I ask why you loathe the Nuccis, and why they feel the same? What happened to cause such a rift, one I assume goes back many years?"

Nicoretti's eyes went wide. His mouth began to move, but no words came out, only strangled noises in his throat.

"I'm sorry if I caused you alarm," Finn said, "but you, sir, have done your very best to humiliate me, so perhaps we're even now. And Calabus' wife, I meant to ask— Sabatino's mother. Is she deceased now? I wondered, as no one's spoken of her at all—"

"Get—get—out—of—my—*sight!*"

Nicoretti's gaunt, aged frame began to tremble, his face turned black with rage. Finn stepped back. If the man fell rigid with a stroke, Finn was in the way.

"I surely will, sir. I fear I've overstayed my welcome, I do regret that. One thing more. I'd like to get a cool mug of ale somewhere, yours isn't good at all. Do you know some-one who might let me in?"

Nicoretti looked appalled, as if Finn had hinted at some immoral act. Again, he tried to mutter, tried to mumble, tried to speak, but Finn didn't wait to see the end of that . . .

Twenty-Six . . .

NICORETTI WAS RIGHT. TO FINN'S GREAT ALARM, he saw that the day was fading into late afternoon. The shadows were long, and the bleak and gloomy streets even darker than before. Still, he hadn't been out as long as he'd thought. There was still time to get back to market and fill up his basket again.

Not time enough, he decided, to seek out one Rubinella, who was clearly known by all. Letitia wouldn't like it, but she'd surely understand once she learned what sort of day he'd had.

"And what," he said aloud, still annoyed by the fuss, "just what is *that* all about? Why the great interest in a single Mycer seer?"

Like much he'd encountered in this land, it made no sense at all. Seers, magicians, spellers and such were common as potters, scribers and blinks. Yet one Rubinella stood out from the rest, at least in this dreary town.

The door where the Bowsers had held him led down a twisting alleyway back to Market Square. Finn was certain he could never find his way back again. And, if he did, he was certain Nicoretti would no longer be there. A sly and cunning fellow, for sure. Whatever his shadowy designs, they plainly boded no good for Finn.

"Giggle to his coffin, chuckle to his grave, indeed. The man's as daft as everyone else around here . . ."

He kept his eyes out for Foxers, but luckily none appeared. Finn didn't fancy another encounter. He was certain he'd done in one of the brutes, and maimed several more. They wouldn't be friendly if they found him again. And, though he didn't like to admit it, Nicoretti was right, his fight with the Foxers had left him feeling the worse for wear.

Many of the stalls were closing, and some had disappeared. Finn hastily purchased what he could. Wilted leeks and the last of the bread. Oatcakes hard as river rocks. A potato with a serious condition of the skin.

Now why did I go and get that? Dips and Flips, we'll have to eat the thing raw . . .

The Dobbin bumped against him, nearly spilling Finn to the ground.

"Sorry," the fellow said, in a gruff and throaty burr, "my fault entire, I truss yur na' hort, good sir?"

"No, not at all," Finn said, "I'll be fine."

"Yur pardon, then," and he was past Finn and gone.

Finn got only the slightest glimpse before the Newlie was lost in the crowd. Tall, as Dobbins tended to be. Rheumy brown eyes and a great prodigious nose; a nose that seemed to have a twitch. Just beneath the nose, a tiny pink mouth. Plainly dressed, in a smock and floppy hat.

Clumsy fellow, but decent enough. Not like some others I could name around here . . .

He thought about onions, a vision that was simply unaccountably there, a vision he could taste, a vision he could see. Big onions, small onions, yellow ones and reds. Had he seen any onions when he'd passed through early in the day? So why was the image so strong, so overpowering now? Why, he could almost—nearly—just about—

The essence, the aroma, the reek of an onion was there, not just in his mind, but simply *there*—

—and when he glanced in his basket, he knew what he'd find, fat and round as an onion ought to be.

Not for the first time that perilous day, tingly little hairs climbed the back of Finn's neck. There was something else, besides an onion there. He stopped, looked to the left, and to the right. Finally, he snatched up the onion and held it close to his vest, quickly, so no one would see.

The note was written on a small scrap of paper tacked to the onion with a pearl-headed pin. In very tiny script, in lines as fine as a spider's silken web, shaky little lines that could scarcely be seen, he could make out the words:

9 past the marrow,

2 past the bell,

keep to the narrow,

fall in the well . . .

"Trickery, deceit," Finn said aloud, "and I've had enough of *that* to last awhile."

Even if the thing made sense, damned if he'd put himself in harm's way again. Who was behind this—Dr. Nicoretti or the Foxer crowd? Surely neither thought he was simple as that.

The Dobbin—it couldn't be anyone else. The fellow had jostled him and dropped the note there. It didn't matter who, now, it didn't matter why. The night was closing in, the day was waning fast. He didn't want to be in the open when the Hooters came out.

"Why can't people keep their religions to themselves instead of annoying everybody else?"

He'd keep the onion, then, no use throwing it away. You couldn't cook the thing, you'd have to eat it raw. Save the tiny pin, pins could be handy sometimes. Throw the foolish note aside . . .

Finn drew a breath. The instant he plucked out the pin, the tiny words vanished, faded away.

Magic! Sure as water's wet, sure as dirt's red. Not great, astonishing magic, but magic all the same!

"Great Pies and Skies," he said aloud, "it has to be the seer, Rubinella herself. It can't be anyone else . . ."

Twenty-Seven . . .

FINN WAS QUITE PLEASED WITH HIMSELF. HE wasn't good at puzzles, didn't care for tricks. Letitia was always doing riddles, and he never got them right.

Still, he saw that **MARROW** was a sweet shop that led off Market Square. **NINE** streets farther was a bell shop, oddly named **BELL**. Two lanes more, and he came to an alley so narrow his shoulders scraped the sides. And there—imagine that—was a **WELL**.

A dry well, and somewhat rank, but a well for all of that. Finn had no intention of falling in as the note said to do. There was no need, he saw, for chalked on the rim was the number **17**.

He watched, waited for a moment, but the number failed to disappear. Three doors down was a door with that very same number, small as a flyspeck, but clearly 17.

Finn tapped lightly on the dry and weathered wood. A tap, he reasoned, would surely suffice. A very small number called for a tap, not a knock or a rap of any kind.

No answer, so Finn tried again. Lightly still, but somewhat stronger this time.

In the cramped and narrow way, there was hardly any sky overhead. What little there was, was closer to darkness than to day. Finn was nearly sure he saw a star, and his heart beat faster at the sight. Night, and there he was, caught in an alley, Letitia far away . . .

The door seemed to open by itself. Magic, Finn thought, then saw it was hanging by a nail, close to falling off, not exactly a spell.

The room was very dim, lit by a single candle against a far wall. The air inside was close, musty, dusty and chill. Finn smelled ginger, nutmeg and pepper, bitterroot and lemon, every kind of spice.

There was also the hint of something else—oils, powders, scents that were musky, scents that were slightly, wonderfully wild . . .

Finn puzzled to define these aromas, pondered for a second and a half, knew, of a sudden, why each was familiar, why he knew them well—

"Buttons and Snaps," he whispered to himself, "everything in here smells like Letitia Louise!"

"—All right, you're here," said a voice from somewhere, "what do you want with me?"

Finn nearly jumped out of his skin, tried, at once, to hide his apprehension, knew it was too late for that.

"I'm sorry I startled you," the someone said, who wasn't truly sorry at all. A voice with a gentle, soft sibilation, a whisper, a sigh, or possibly a lisp.

"Sit down. There's a stool to your right. You don't have to see it, you can feel it in the dark. Now. Answer my question, and answer it now. I know who you are, I think I know why you're here. I hope to high heaven I'm wrong about that. Not too likely, I fear. Snake pokes his ugly head through the veil if it's something really bad. Takes a great joy in that, though I can't fathom why."

Snake? Better not ask . . .

"You've a lot to answer for. Everyone in town's raving on about me, and you're the cause, Finn. Where did you *hear* that name, I'd like to know that?"

"Rubinella? That's who I'm to ask for. That note, I know it came from you."

"Of course it did, boy. You haven't answered me. Who gave the name to you?"

"Letitia," Finn said, squinting to see some movement in the dark, "Letitia Louise. My wife. She's a Mycer too, you see—"

"I know who she is. I didn't know her name, but I know she's with you. Everyone in town knows about you two, don't you realize that?"

The voice from the darkness was harsh, intense, quite out of patience, and not at all happy with Finn.

"It was she, then, who told you to seek me. Snake should have told me this. She said something else. What exactly was that?"

"To tell Rubinella that—To tell her we needed help, that we needed a seer. Letitia—Letitia's mother, was Liliana, of the Phileas Clan. I was supposed to mention that."

"Yes, I see."

The voice was somewhat gentler now, not what Finn would call friendly, but neither so cautious, anxious nor strained.

"The Phileas Clan is strong. Good blood. The males are somewhat hasty, irresponsible at times. The females somewhat—assertive, I suppose. Too inclined to take up with human men."

Finn felt the color rise to his face, and wondered if the seer could sense that, too.

A laugh, almost—more than she'd granted so far. Somewhere on the edge, throaty but nice, a bit, Finn decided, like Letitia Louise.

"Do you know, Finn, what 'Rubinella' means? You have no inkling, I don't know why I asked."

"It's a name, I suppose. I wouldn't know what it means."

"It's not a person's name, and it's certainly not mine. It's a Mycer word that means `Lady with the power in her hands.' Your Letitia Louise knows that. The common tongue has twisted it into something else. Anyone in town, Newlie and human alike, will *swear* it means 'Mycer-witch-woman-who-can-make-all-your-privates-fall-off.' "

Finn felt the heat again. "Trees and Bees, I surely didn't know that."

"There's much you don't know, Master Finn."

"And can you?"

"Can I what?"

"Make their, ah, you-know-whats fall off?"

"You want an honest answer? I don't think so. Listen to me, Finn. Life is not a jest, and your wit is not appreciated here. Not by me, and not by others who are present as well. Your next question's *who*, and we won't go into that.

"Again, I strongly suggest you spend your time with me—with us, in an earnest and serious quest."

"I'll—yes, I certainly will," Finn said, glancing through the darkness at the walls, at the ceiling, searching everywhere, not as anxious for answers as he'd been only moments before.

"Since you entered, I've been getting an image, a very faint picture, closer to a vapor, closer to a blur."

The Mycer hesitated, and when she spoke again the tension in her voice was clear.

"What I see is bad. Very bad, I fear. I've known that something was wrong in this town for years. Even a child who has a touch of the gift can see that. Sometimes a portal winks open, and the sound of evil leaks out. I knew it was here, but I didn't know where. Your appearance has given me the answer to that.

"Your Letitia was right. It is in that—in that *house*. The bad thing is there . . . !"

"What—what is it?" Finn sat on the edge of his stool. "Tell me what you see."

"I don't see a thing."

"What?"

"I can't *see* anything, are you listening or not? It's there, but it's in a blanket spell. I can't get through it. Neither can Snake, or anyone else."

"Under a spell . . ."

"Under a *blanket* spell. A blanket covers everything up. You can't see a thing under there."

"But it's bad."

"Oh, it's bad. Bad's a good start. I think it's worse than that. Anyone who can do a blanket spell, one that's keeping *me* out, that's someone—or something—to look out for."

"And you don't know who it is. Who's using magic like that?"

The seer let out a breath. "Are you impaired in the head? How did you ever charm a bright and lovely Mycer girl? I—Never mind, let me guess."

"No, I don't know who cast the spell and I doubt I ever will. Don't you see that? Someone who can blanket a house is good enough to hide themselves."

"I didn't think of that."

"I don't suppose you did."

"Yes, but—" Finn was so pleased with the thought, he nearly stood up. "Listen, I think I can help. I've *been* there, I've seen what you're talking about. I can tell you what it is!"

The seer was very still. Finn thought he heard her breathe. "Well, I'm listening. Please enlighten me, then."

"Of course. What it is, and no offense—but I doubt it's that important at all—is sort of a **prufa-fuffa-gigee-gaaka-geeb—**"

Finn froze, horrified by the chaos in his mouth. He tried once more, tried to get it right, but the words got tangled every time.

"I can't," he said, desperate and truly frightened now. "It's there, but I can't spit it out!"

"I sensed you had the image, and I know you cannot let it go. This is very bad indeed . . ."

"Would you stop saying that, please? That's not helping at all."

The seer moved then, and he could almost see her, a shadow against the greater dark.

"There's no more I can do. Not now. But listen to me, Finn. What you see, what you've encountered is not what you think, not what you think it is at all. *You must, truly, understand that, above all else.* Are you listening to me?"

"Yes. I greatly fear I am."

"That's all I can say now, except you must try to leave that place, and quickly if you can. You, and Letitia, and the thing with shiny scales."

"You know about her? About Julia Jessica Slagg?"

"What did I say? You have something else with shiny scales? Here, take this . . ."

Something slid across the floor and lightly touched his foot. Finn bent to pick it up, felt something small and nearly weightless, metal and stone, something so fine it ran through his fingers like sand.

"Tell Letitia to wear it. Whatever you do, don't try and wear it yourself. Do you understand that? Go now, get back to her as soon as you can."

"Yes, I will." Finn rose to leave.

"And by the way . . . those feelings, when you first came in? Strange, wondrous feelings, possibly passion and desire? That was me. I'm older than your Letitia, but a Mycer woman never forgets how to do that.

"Mycer males are easy. And humans like yourself . . ."

Another throaty laugh, a chuckle in the dark.

"I don't know about that," Finn said, deciding though, that possibly he did.

"This, uh, place of yours is quite nice," he said, the first thing to come to mind. "We have some seers back home, and I always feel their shops are sort of—petrified. Like they keep old papers and crawly things about. Potions, jars and nasty pots. Your place, now, smells like ginger, apples, and maybe cherry pie."

"You have a good nose for the prurient," the seer said from the dark, "and you're good with food as well. Not too surprising as you're sitting in my kitchen keeping me from supper right now . . ."

Twenty-Eight . . .

LETITIA TRIED NOT TO COUNT THE MINUTES, TRIED not to pace, tried to stay away from the fly-specked window that looked upon the sere and somber plain. Each time she glanced at the narrow dirt road, it seemed to grow dimmer, the colors seemed to melt and coalesce. If she looked long enough, everything faded to the same shade of gray.

Closing her eyes, she dug her nails into her palms. If it hurt badly enough, maybe it would wake her from this horrible dream, maybe time would turn around, go back the other way. Night wouldn't come, and Finn would be safely in her arms.

"Why did I do it, Julia? I must have been out of my mind. I was angry, I admit. I took it out on him and it wasn't his fault. Not *all*, anyway. He didn't know there were Yowlies on the ship. He didn't know about the Hatters, what would happen in the square. He didn't—Damn it all, Julia, he could have done *something,* seems to me!"

Julia was sprawled on the bed curled up like a snail, now and then whipping her brassy tail.

"Say something," Letitia said. "I feel like I'm talking to an ugly pile of tin. That's very annoying to me."

"Well, what a delightful thing to say. And what, exactly, would you care to hear? No, it was not a good idea to send him out looking for seers. And no, I don't know what I would have done, so don't ask. He'll be back, he always is."

"I don't know how you can be so sure of that. He could be *dead* right now, lying in a ditch."

Letitia was sorry she'd spoken so harshly, but Julia really *did* look bad, not polished and shiny as she should. In the dim and dreary light, her scales were dull and faded, like rust was setting in.

"He's got his faults, Julia, but I do love him so, and he's very dear to me." She sniffed then, and found a hanky in her sleeve. "We've hardly got started on marital bliss, and we might never have a chance again. Did you really mean that, do you think he's all right? You're not just saying it to make me feel better?"

"That's most of it, yes," Julia said. "You know I can't stand to hear you whine and blow your nose. The nose thing, that's one of the six most disgusting things meat creatures do. I wouldn't dream of discussing the rest.

"In truth, though, I do feel Finn will pull through. He's really quite bright, though you mustn't tell him that. He also enjoys amazing dumb luck, another meat trait that I don't understand."

"Stop it, all right?" Letitia curled her mouth in disgust. "You know I don't care for talk like that."

"What, meat?"

"See, you're doing it again."

"What am I supposed to say? That's what you are. A sack of blood and bones, squishy stuff and skin. Do I get upset when you say *tin*?"

"That's not the same. You're not—"

"Not real, huh? I don't have feelings like you. And I'm far too polite to say where *you* came from."

Letitia rolled her eyes. "I'm getting sick. Could we possibly talk about something else?"

"Like, is Finn going to rescue us soon, or do I have to go and save him? If I were to guess—"

Letitia jumped back from the window, startled, as lightning sizzled on the road outside. Thunder shook the house, rattled all its seams. Fat drops of rain struck the window sweeping muddy rivers down the pane.

"He's out there in the dark," Letitia said, wiping away fresh tears. "Now he'll never get back. Oh, Finn, I'm sorry for most of the things I've said. Some, I admit, were not on a totally positive plane. I know I'm not perfect, and neither are you. That's good, I guess, because I don't think marriage would work out if you were always wrong, and I was always right.

"Julia, do you think the Hooter persons will be out on a night like this? I went to Mycer Mass until I met Finn, but no one expected you to go if it was storming like this. Julia? *Julia . . . ?*"

"If you're looking for that mechanical device, you'd better find it quick. I won't have it running loose around my house."

Letitia gasped, turned around quickly and found the old man standing in the door, standing there watching her with little black eyes and a ghastly toothless grin.

Calabus smiled even wider, clearly pleased with the effect.

"Didn't mean to frighten you, girl. We don't have a lot of knobs in this house. They're inclined to fall off, and that useless servant of mine won't ever put 'em back. If I wasn't cursed with a kindly nature, I'd flay him to the bone, roast every strip of that stinking flesh and make him choke it down . . ."

"Please," Letitia said, as her stomach lurched, as everything began to float around. "I beg you not to talk like that, I feel I'm about to be ill. And will you get *out* of here, I did not invite you in!"

"Don't have to. I can go anywhere I like. Where'd that ugly thing go? I heard you talking to it, know you've got it hid somewhere."

"She's not hidden at all. She's right here. Aren't you, Julia?"

Letitia frowned. She peered in the closet and under the bed. Under the only chair. She looked at Calabus, genuinely puzzled now.

"I don't *know* where she is. She was here a moment ago. I expect you frightened her away."

"Don't try any foolishness, girl, it won't work with me."

Calabus jerked around, his face the color of plums.

"Squeen William! Get your sorry carcass in here before I bind you with hooks and wire, pour hot coals in your ears and pull out your eyes. Find that lizard thing and get it back here!"

"Yesssss, bes doin' thisss quickly, sssir . . ."

Lightning turned the room a blinding white, and Letitia saw a ghostly face and sharp little teeth disappear behind the door.

"What—what do you want with Julia, anyway? Why are you telling that thing to bring her here?"

" 'Cause that's what I came for, pretty. I intend to take it apart, see what it's got inside."

"Why, you'll do no such thing!" Letitia stared, her heart skipping half a dozen beats. Was this why Julia had so abruptly disappeared? Did she sense, somehow, what the old fool had in mind?

"You lay a hand on her, and Finn will—he'll do something awful, I promise you that."

"Master Finn's not here. I expect you noticed that."

"I know he's not here, but he'll be right back."

"And what makes you think so, my dear?"

Calabus showed her a sly and totally goofy smile, a smile that made her skin crawl.

"What are you talking about? Of course he'll be back."

"Shouldn't have ever left. Damn fool thing to do."

Letitia took a breath. "If there's something you're not telling me, you'd better do it fast. I will not put up with this."

Calabus spread his hands. "Don't know a thing, girlie. Don't have to. I know this town, though. Know there's not a soul with half a wit's gonna be out there after dark."

"Well, at least those Hooters of yours won't be rummaging about. There's no way they could possibly start a fire."

"That isn't all we used to start . . ."

"Just what do you mean by that?"

"Don't mean a thing. Just sayin' there's mischief folks can start, it don't have to be dry."

"Then why," Letitia said, "did you say everyone would be *in*? Why don't you make up your mind?"

"You don't listen real good. I said folks with half a wit. There's plenty of the other kind about."

Letitia stood straight, rigid as a reed, and spoke as boldly as she could. "If you're finished, you can go. I don't care for your presence in here."

"I want to see that lizard. I mean to find out what makes it tick."

"No you don't," she said, surprised to hear what was coming from her mouth, uncertain how she knew, but certain that she did. She'd caught the man before he looked away, caught the blink and the wary glance, knew at once he didn't want to meet her eyes.

"That isn't what you want, don't try and tell me that. You're after something else, and it better not be what I *think* it is!"

"Huh!" Color rose to mottle the old man's face, but it quickly went away. "That's my worthless son you're talking about. He's the pervert in the house, not me. I got needs, all right, and I'm sure there's a couple you could fill . . ."

"Will you get to it? I'd rather listen to the rain, it makes more sense than you."

"Can I sit?"

"What for? All right, that chair's got three good legs. Don't come near this bed."

Letitia waited, arms across her breasts, back to the window. Ready, if she had to, to leap through the dirty glass out into the rain. And what was Julia thinking, disappearing on her like that?

"I want to talk to you," Calabus said, "you weren't wrong in that."

"First, let's get something straight. If that smelly cook brings any harm to Julia, he'll wish he never had."

Calabus looked at the floor. "If that man of yours doesn't come back, I'd like you to stay here with me . . ."

"You *what?*" Calabus wouldn't meet her eyes, and Letitia was glad of that.

"I don't expect you to fully understand. Not right off, anyway. It'll take a little while to settle in."

"Get out of here. I'm going to throw something at you. As soon as I can find anything in one piece."

"It's not what you think. I already said that."

"And what is it *you* think?"

Calabus faced her. It seemed to Letitia he looked older and dirtier by the minute, as if the ancient flesh, the shaggy hair, the awful rags he wore were sloughing into dust, even as she watched.

"You've seen my invention down below. I don't feel you were comfortable at the time, but I think you'd come to love it there. You'd throw up awhile, but we can overcome that. There's herbs and potions you can take.

"I did my best to make young Finn see the value of my work. I tell you what, I'm quite disappointed in him. You'd do better, I'm sure of that. You could be a great help to me, girl. I strongly doubt you'll ever get a chance at something as big as this."

Calabus rested his hands on his knees and showed her a loony smile. "What do you think, dear? If that fellow doesn't make it back—and I surely doubt he will—I could give you a good position here. You can keep this room. That window's the best in the house. I don't get a lot of light in mine."

Letitia counted to three. Stopped, and counted once again.

"I'm going to be perfectly calm about this. I don't want you coming at me with a piece of that chair. No. I won't stay here with you, I'd just as soon die. And Finn's coming back, no matter what you've got in your head. No offense, and you stay right there, but this is the worst, most disgusting offer I've ever had in my life. Perhaps you can't tell, but I am shaking all over right now.

"Aside from all that, how on earth did you get it in your head that a Mycer girl could *help* you with that frightful machine? I mean, if you could chain me up and toss me screaming in there? I've just got to hear that."

"I mumle-dumle-loo . . ."

"Look at me, all right?"

Calabus did, then glanced away at once. "I had this dream. You were down there—helping me with things."

"I was not. That was somebody else."

"It was you, all right. You did some—some stuff I don't know how to do . . ."

"What—what kind of stuff?" Somehow, these words scared Letitia more than anything else the man had said.

"I don't *know*, all right? Things . . ."

Calabus looked anxious, miserable and full of dread. It was all he could do just to get the words out.

"You already said it, girl. It doesn't make sense, but it's real. It's a *Telling Dream*, I'm certain of that. I've had dreams of every sort, you won't believe what goes through my head. This one, though, was real. You'd best be nice to me. We're going to be friends. You want something to eat? I'll have Squeen William cook you something up."

"I'd rather eat dirt. I'd rather eat a bush."

"Up to you, girl." Calabus pulled himself up with a long and painful sigh. "I'll run down and see if he's caught that slippery lizard yet."

"You heard what I said. You harm her in any fashion, and you'll regret it, old man."

Calabus grinned. He looked past her at the storm outside.

"Even if your man gets back—which I don't guess he will—that pesky boy of mine's got a nasty surprise waiting for him at the door. You and me'll talk some more after that . . ."

Twenty-Nine . . .

THE STORM CAUGHT UP WITH FINN AN ALLEY PAST
the Mycer seer's door. He ran for cover quickly, under the
arches by a shop called **SHIRT**. He thought he knew what
they sold there. He'd been in town long enough to guess.
Maybe there was one called **FROCK** nearby, where he
could get something for Letitia to wear.

If there really was a shop, if there really was a **FROCK**.

If it was day now instead of dark.

If it wasn't raining hens and frogs.

If there weren't any Foxers or Hooters on the prowl.

Maybe the storm was a piece of luck. Even villains of the
very worst sort would likely stay home on such a frightful
night.

Finn wrapped his cloak about him and ran into a fierce,
punishing rain that came at him in chilling and penetrating
gusts, and nearly swept him off his feet. A rain that moaned

and howled, a rain that stung his cheeks, a rain hard as peppercorns, hard as little daggers, hard as little stones. A rain, Finn decided, that could drown a man standing if he dared to raise his nose.

He didn't have a plan, at least not one that made sense. He didn't know east, he didn't know west. He knew, though, the town had to end. When it did, he could walk in a circle till he found the Nuccis' house. The place wasn't all that big. The odds were one in four he was, at that very moment, headed the right way.

Even as these thoughts crossed his mind, as his boots began to slosh and the rain began to trickle down his neck, the houses and the shops began to thin. Ahead lay lone and shadowy remains, dark skeletal structures, blurred and indistinct, warped and distorted by the unremitting gusts from overhead.

Finn ducked beneath his chill and sodden cloak, dashing through the storm to the cover of a nearly roofless frame, the sad and darkened bones of some hapless farmer's barn.

It was very little shelter, but better than being drowned. Maybe he could take his boots off, pour the water out, let his socks dry.

"So where am I, then?" he asked himself aloud. He remembered, roughly, how far the Nuccis were from town. The ruined barn seemed near enough. If he knew which way to go, to the left or to the right . . .

Finn turned swiftly, suddenly alert, suddenly aware. Someone, something, was *in* there with him in the barn! Nothing he could see, nothing he could touch, but the overwhelming presence was something he could feel.

For a moment, he froze, stood perfectly still. Hand on his weapon, eyes on the dark. Saw them as they slowly, silently appeared, saw them of a sudden, saw them growing near, figures made of vapor, vague and indistinct. And with this spectral vision came the chill, musty odors of days un-remembered, lives lost and spent . . .

"Oh, it's you fellows, then," Finn said, with a great sigh of relief. "You had me there a minute, I'm somewhat jumpy tonight."

"Food for the departed, sir?" said a voice like winter, like gravel in a can.

"I've got this basket," Finn said. "I'm afraid it's not as full as it used to be."

"Good enough it is, we're grateful as can be."

Finn set the basket on the ground and stepped back. There were five of them, five or maybe ten, phantoms, chill apparitions frail as smoke. They gathered round the basket, drawing out the essence, the dream of oatcakes, the vision of leeks. They hummed off-key as they fed, wraiths with old memories of bread. Some people said you shouldn't eat anything sniffed by those who'd passed on, but Finn knew this wasn't so.

He'd been so absorbed in his troubles with the living, he'd given little thought to the dead. There would be a Coldtown here, of course, like anyplace else . . .

"I'll bet you don't remember me at all, Master Finn. It's been quite a spell."

"I'm not certain," Finn said, peering at the ghostly shape that had suddenly appeared, trying to recall. Shades had feelings, he knew, like anyone else.

"I waved at you from the ship," the figure said. "I thought you waved back."

"Now, I do remember that," Finn said, recalling the phantom schooner he'd seen from the *Madeline Rose*.

"And I know who you are. It's Captain Pynch, yes? Kettles and Pots, Captain, what are you doing here?"

A wispy smile told Finn the fellow was greatly pleased.

"I'm here to see a dear departed aunt who crossed some

time ago. It's not a very lovely town. Not like the one we know. Still, in my condition, it matters little anymore. Death and corruption's not all it's cut out to be, Master Finn. It's a worrisome thing at best. And not all the living are as tolerant as you, sir, not by a mile they're not."

Finn would never say it, of course, but Pynch looked even worse than he had when they'd seen one another before, not long after the officer's tragic death, back on Garpenny Street. The parts he had lost were missing still—the arm and the foot, the eye and both ears. His ghastly flesh was a pale and tattered gray.

Only a shade of himself, so to speak, Finn thought. A soldier without a purple vest, without crimson pantaloons. A warrior stripped of crested helm, and a dashing plume of tangerine.

So, too, were the others in his group—so wan and indistinct there was little way to tell what any might have been.

"I have found no consolation in this foul circumstance," the captain said. "I miss the war, I do, the bracing thrill of combat in the air. I was with the Royal Balloonist Fusiliers, as you recall."

"I do indeed," Finn said.

"And how is the lovely Letitia Louise? I took quite a fancy to the lass back then."

"Yes, I know you did."

"Didn't take offense? You, I mean, Master Finn."

"Not at all," Finn said, though in truth, the captain's attentions had annoyed him at the time.

"She used to give me tea."

"I recall that as well."

"And spicecakes, too," Pynch said with a spectral sigh, a chill and fetid breath that nearly brought Finn to his knees.

Moments before, a wraith had detached itself from the crew above Finn's basket. Now, he stood just behind Pynch.

"I hope I'm not intruding, sir. I'd speak if you've the time."

"Damned impolite, I'd say," said Pynch, "but no one has manners these days."

With that, the captain floated over to the basket to whiff some emanations himself.

"I am Lucas D. Klunn," the misty figure said. "I lived here all my life, and I have to say the town is as dreadful for the living as the dead."

"I can only speak for the former. But I'd likely agree with that."

"I felt the need to speak when I learned who you were. You're in great danger, sir. I don't suppose I have to tell you that."

Finn was taken aback. "You know me? You know who I am? From Pynch, I suppose. You overheard our talk."

"No, there was no need for that. A Coldie hears things, sir. There's little else to do, you know. It takes up the time, whatever that is, the meaning's slipped my mind."

The wraith had a grisly, terrifying demeanor. Worse, even, than the gruesome Captain Pynch. Very little head, and the features that were left were awful to behold.

"I think I said I'm Lucas Klunn, which will have no meaning to you since the Fates have kindly set your life in other realms. I was a merchant, once, and made a small fortune in the export of peas. My church affiliation was Hatter, though I seldom went full-time.

"In my early middle years, I was struck with dread disease. Either that, or poisoned by my wife, I've often wondered which. She left soon after, with a fellow who dealt in beans.

"But I digress, sir, and apologize for that. What you'll want to know, or maybe not, is that I feel you've little chance of leaving here alive. If things come to that, you're welcome in our little band. Or, if you'd care to go home, the vessel *Irrational Fears* should be putting in soon, the one Captain Pynch came on—"

"Master Klunn!"

Finn was greatly startled, stunned, and given a turn by the apparition's words. "If you could get to it, I'd be pleased. I'm anxious to hear what dangers I face, besides those I know about myself."

"Oh, well then . . ."

Klunn, what there was of him, looked disappointed that his dire and dreadful tidings might not be news at all.

"You know, I guess, that the Foxers here have posted a reward for your fingers and your toes . . ."

"For my *what?*"

"Fingers and toes. They're not your ordinary folk, you know. They have their own manner, their own peculiar ways."

Finn tried to set this disturbing image aside, but it failed to depart.

"I know they have a quarrel with me, I'm quite aware of that. We had a run-in the other night, which you've likely heard about. Apparently, everyone has. I had thought they were angry merely because I was on the scene. I'm no longer certain of that. I don't know if there's more to this or not. If anyone else is behind this thing, someone using Foxers to get me out of the way . . ."

The shade began to fade, flicker, shake and shiver all about. Finn looked away before he got terribly sick.

"That I can't answer, sir, but I can tell you this. You got the Foxers on your trail, you don't need anyone else."

The wispy fellow shook his head, which was not a

pleasant thing to see. "This thing with the Nuccis, it's more than a quarrel. It's a plain blood feud is what it is. Old hates were stirring long ago, before I was born."

"And when would that be?"

The spectral figure hesitated. "That's hard to say. Time doesn't work the same for the living as the dead. Sometimes it feels like tomorrow when it's truly yesterday.

"I worked real close to a Foxer whose name escapes me now. He was in beets, when I was in peas. He and his sort were hard to be around. They didn't much care for human kind. There'd been some trouble with their folk disappearing, simply dropping out of sight, never showing up again."

"Disappearing how? You don't mean dying, you mean just—*going*, right?"

"That's it, indeed. And didn't anyone ever know why, ever know how."

"And this had to do with the Nuccis somehow?"

"I'm near certain it did. Everyone thought so at the time. Bad blood is what I'm saying. I've no idea why."

Finn took a breath. Lightning forked out of the sky and struck the ground far away. Finn could feel the tingle in his boots. And, for an instant, the Coldies seemed to blink away.

"Do you know a man here in town named Dr. Nicoretti? He's a Hatter, I don't know much more than that."

"I know who he is. I wasn't alive in his time."

"And a Mycer seer . . ."

"Well, certainly I do. How do you think you found us this night, Master Finn?"

Before Finn could answer, the ghost of Lucas Klunn began to shimmer and drift apart.

"One thing more, or maybe two," said a chilly whisper in his ear. "You might stay among the living, there's a little chance of that. The Newlie, now, I doubt she'll make it through. And hear me, Master Finn: *There is something in the Nucci house that's more like us than you . . .*"

"Wait," Finn said, "you can't go and leave me with that!"

Finn scarcely blinked, and Lucas D. Klunn was gone. So was Captain Pynch, and so were all the rest . . .

Thirty . . .

FINN HAD BEEN SO INTENT ON LUCAS KLUNN THAT he'd failed to notice the storm had swept over the town. Scudding clouds near touched the earth, and thunder was a drummer far away. Errant drops of rain plunked from ruined timbers overhead. Somehow, the silence now was more frightening than the raging storm itself.

There was so much stirring in his head that Finn feared it might burst at any time. Foxers, Bowsers, and sly Nicoretti, who was clearly a danger, though he couldn't say how. Dread revelations from the Mycer, doom from the apparition Klunn.

Reason said put it all aside. Stay alert, keep your mind free until you come safely back to Letitia's side.

"A fine idea," Finn agreed with himself, "I'll surely have to try it some time . . ."

Finn damned and praised the mess the storm had left behind. His legs were weary from stomping through the muck and mire. Still, this misery was countered by the fact that he seemed to have the night to himself.

He wondered about the time. "Night" was likely not the proper word now. It had to be the very early hours, not too far from dawn. With this in mind, he quickened his pace as much as the rain-soaked earth would allow.

A good quarter hour after he left the shades, Finn smelled the strong, salty scent of the sea. Moments later it appeared, a darkness greater than the night, touched here and there with peaks of luminescent white.

He was very relieved at the sight. If the sea was to his left then he only had to turn a short angle to his right. The road from town to the Nuccis would appear, and he'd be with Letitia long before first light.

Finn had not allowed himself to dwell on her much until now. She had to be safe, had to be just as he'd left her, just as he saw her image now. Sabatino wouldn't harm her, wouldn't dare. Even that crazed old man had warned his son about that.

Finn hesitated, closed his eyes and drew in a cold breath from the sea.

"Bricks and Sticks," he said aloud, aware at once of the foolish rationale he'd allowed to cloud his mind. "Letitia's all right because *Calubus* is there? Wake up, Finn, before you go as mad as all the rest!"

The day was coming much too quickly now. Moments before, Finn had felt secure in the safety of the dark. Now, things gray and indistinct threw off their nightly guise and donned their daytime shapes again.

He felt naked and exposed. He found a small depression

and hunched down nearly to the ground. He could still see a slice of the sea, the low outline of the town etched against a sky tinged with purple, streaked with dirty blue.

Standing again, moving quickly but carefully across the wet ground, he saw a darkened smudge not far ahead below the last wink of fading stars—

The house of the Nuccis! It had to be! There was nothing, anywhere, that matched its warped and crooked lines, its odd delineation, its bizarre silhouette. Finn could have never imagined he'd be so pleased to see the place again. The road itself could not be very far. He was tempted to go straight ahead until it appeared. Even after the rain, the way would be easier than what he was crossing now.

Easier, yes—but more exposed as well. He kept to the low, muddy hillocks, the wet and marshy grass. The cover wasn't good, but it was better than waving a flag and letting one and all know he was there. A little closer, another few yards, and he'd be near enough to run for it, even if someone suddenly appeared on his tail.

He started walking, even faster than before, and then he heard them howling, huffing, making their way across the spongy earth, a small but noisome army of Hooters, stomping their way toward town before the day began. Finn cursed them soundly, muttered every oath he knew, and pressed himself against the sodden ground.

They were Hooters for sure. They hooted, hollered and danced about. Some, Finn could see, raising one eye above the mud, wore homemade feathers sewn to their arms. All wore Hooter beaks and goggle eyes, and all carried torches that they waved above their heads even though there was nothing anywhere dry enough to burn. Still, if you were a Hooter, Finn guessed, it was best to carry plenty of fire. One never knew what one might find.

He didn't move until they were clearly out of sight. They passed very close to the Nuccis, but caused no mischief there. Fortunate, indeed, for nothing he could think of would go up as quickly as that rotted, desiccated corpse the Nuccis called a house.

At last Finn came to his feet, miserable, cold and wet. He picked up his basket and scowled in the direction where the Hooters had disappeared. Cutting it rather close, he decided. It was nearly daylight now, and that meant Hatter time. Was it too much to hope that the louts in yellow hats would meet the oafs with goggle eyes, and start a religious war?

The house was closer now, grim and gray as ever, tilting every way but straight. He thought about what the seer had told him, about the *blanket spell*. Who was responsible for that? Sabatino, Calabus himself?

No, the Mycer lady had been too impressed. It was a powerful load of magic, and he didn't think either of the Nuccis could handle such as that.

Who, then? The more he thought about it, the more it seemed a peculiar spell indeed . . . It clouded a secret that even the Rubinella couldn't see, a secret so strong Finn couldn't even spit it out.

He'd been pondering *that* one ever since he left the seer. Why bother to protect the old man's Prophecy Machine, if it wasn't even real, but only a lunatic's dream? Was it something else, then? Something down there besides the mad device?

"Foxers can get in the house, and possibly anyone else . . . if the spell is so awesome, why can't it keep them out . . . ?"

There seemed to be an answer to that, one with a certain sense of reason—if, that is, there was reason in magic at all. Anyone could get in the cellar—anyone who had the old man's key—but once you saw the thing, it clouded your mind, and you couldn't speak of it again.

So, logically, if you came to harm it, what might it do then? Finn shuddered at the thought. If it could stop your tongue, what could it do to all your other parts?

Maybe Letitia could see him, he thought. She could, if she was there in their room, if she was looking at the time. The windows were so grimy, so totally askew, Finn wasn't sure he could spot the right one from the outside of the house—

A high and piercing shriek brought Finn to a halt, brought the hair up straight atop his head. He went to ground again, slipped his blade free, and peered through the stand of brittle grass.

There was scarcely any cover on that damp and barren plain, other than a thicket of weeds, of dead and tangled trees, huddled close against the house. Finn saw something move there, something very fast fleeing through the grass.

Another shriek, another horrid wail. Finn had heard nothing like it, such a grate, such a screech, such a raw intrusion on the nerves, such an unworldly shrill. He came up in a crouch, saw the weeds tremble, saw the twisted branches shake.

The form moved again—when it did, Finn moved swiftly, determined to cut it off and bring it to a halt.

The creature had extraordinary senses. It froze the instant Finn made his move.

"Whoever you are, you can halt right now," Finn shouted, "I'll brook no more nonsense this day—"

The words were scarcely out of his mouth before something burst through brittle foliage, shrieking and whining, an assault upon his ears. Finn stepped quickly aside, raised his weapon—stopped in his tracks, stood there and stared.

Julia Jessica Slagg scuttled past him, lizard legs a-blur, moving at a speed Finn had never imagined she could go. Just behind her came something with a hop, something with a gimp, something that scuffled and staggered and dipped, something dark and damp with a pinched little face and shaggy ears. Something, he saw, no less than Squeen William himself, clutching a wretched broom, swatting at Julia, shrieking and shouting and gnashing wicked teeth.

"Hold it, you, hold it right there!" Finn took three long steps, grabbed the Vampie by the scruff, jerked him off his ugly feet, leaving him swatting air.

"I don't know what you're up to or why, but it's over right now. Drop the broom, Squeen, and stop that noise before you ruin my ears for good!"

Squeen's answer was another shriek, even shriller than before. He spit, spat, ground his razor teeth, stared up at Finn with his fearful Vampie eyes.

"I can't blame you for being thick-headed, considering who you work for. Now get out of here while I've still got a kindly mood to spare."

With that, Finn loosed the wretched fellow, dropped him to the ground, gave him a kick and sent him on his way. The Vampie whined and whimpered, sniveled and yelled, fell in the brush, rose and hit a tree, stumbled to his feet and scampered toward the kitchen door.

Finn turned away in disgust. "Julia, where might you be? Call out or something, I can't see a thing in this tangle of desiccated grass."

"Move an inch with that dirty boot of yours, and you'll step on my head . . ."

Finn looked down, startled by the croak, by the too familiar squawk, by the cranky voice right at his feet.

"Will you tell me what that is all about?" he said, squatting to the ground. "Why is that fleabag after you with a broom? What are you doing out here with Letitia up there all alone?"

"I'm fine, I'm not hurt badly, thank you for your gracious concern. Would you turn me over, please? This is undignified and crude, a plain humiliation at best."

Finn tried to keep a solemn face. Julia did indeed look somewhat improper lying on her back, legs churning in the air.

"I'll have to look at that," he said, setting her aright. "I'd guess a balance wheel is somewhat off the track. Possibly a spinner gear, it's hard to tell which. If you wish, I'll carry you back to the house."

"I don't wish, Finn. I am quite accustomed to taking care of myself. Which is lucky indeed, since I seldom get any help."

"Whatever you like," Finn said. "And you haven't answered my questions, being so busy crying about yourself—"

At that instant, a familiar howl erupted from the house, a howl and a scream and some other sounds as well.

Finn raced for the door, Julia on his heels, slightly off center, but clearly under sail.

At the entry, at the shabby front steps, Finn paused, listening to the clamor, then raised one foot and kicked the door in.

The door nearly vanished, crumbled into powder, scattered into pulp, back to basic dust. Finn stopped short and drew a breath, taking in a most peculiar sight. Squeen William writhed on the floor, flailing about, caught in the tangle of a cruel corded net that had dropped from above. The net was laced with barbs, hooks, nails and broken glass.

Sabatino stood back from the trap, not even looking at Squeen, venomous eyes locked entirely on Finn.

"Don't stand there gawking, *craftsman*," the younger

Nucci said. "You've a blade, help me cut this miserable creature out."

"This is a terrible deed," Finn said, guessing at once who the trap was really for. "The poor fellow could've been killed."

"True enough," Sabatino said, shaking his head, "nothing ever works the way it should . . ."

Thirty-One . . .

HE HELD HER VERY CLOSE, SO TIGHTLY SHE
feared he might crush her in his joyous embrace. He
smelled to high heaven, smelled of mold, smelled of onions,
smelled of Bowsers and Foxers and primeval sweat.

Letitia didn't care. She was just glad to have him safe
again, glad to have him there.

"Rest," she told him, "you're practically asleep on your
feet. We can talk after that."

Finn, bone-weary and ready to drop, started to babble
and couldn't stop. It all came at once, the whole thing from
the start: Foxers, Bowsers, Nicoretti and the seer. The Bullies and the stone. The Coldies and the storm, Hooters
hooting in the night. And, finally, poor Squeen William setting off the trap Sabatino had laid for Finn.

"I knew it," Letitia said, clenching her fists till her palms
turned white. "That old man told me his son was up to
something. *Bragged* about it, can you believe that?"

"I can indeed. That, and any other madness you have to
tell."

"I couldn't warn you, love. There was nothing I could do."

She glanced at Julia, giving her a nasty stare. "I *might've* had some help, if Miss Julia hadn't run off for fear she'd get taken apart."

"What?" Julia raised her snout, blinked her red eyes. "Who's going to take who apart? Anyone tries, they'll come away without a hand!"

"Don't lie," Letitia said. "If you lie, you don't get an afterlife. Though I don't know as you would, being what you are . . ."

"Wait just a minute here." Finn clapped his head between his hands. "Who's going to take Julia apart, what are we talking about?"

"I didn't even know about that. I left when the old man came in. And where was I going, one might ask? I was going to look for you, Finn."

"You had better be talking true this time," Letitia said.

"What old man? Calabus, you mean? He was in here? You didn't say a thing about that."

"Now when would I, dear? With all your tales, who'd get a word in? That man—you won't believe this, *I* didn't—He wanted me to work with him on that—whatever it is. As if you could get me down there again . . . Oh, Finn, you don't know what I'm talking about, I scarcely do myself."

She paused to get a breath, led Finn over to the bed and sat him down. "You're soaking wet. Get out of those clothes and get into something else."

"Like what? I don't *have* anything else."

"I don't care, I'll wrap you in a sheet. Finn, that man is scary. He so much as told me he doesn't know what he's doing down there. All that—that awful machinery, and he doesn't know? He wants help from *me*? He said he had a dream. I thought I'd come out of my skin, listening to stuff like that."

"It simply doesn't make sense."

"You think I don't know? That's what scared me to death. Oh, Finn . . ."

Finn looked down at his basket and grasped her hand in his. "I'm sorry about the food, I really did my best." The rain had done its job, and there was nothing left but a soggy layer of mush.

"I couldn't get you anything to wear. Shops aren't the same over here."

"You got back, love."

"Captain Pynch said hello."

Letitia made a face. "You told me that." She studied the amulet the Mycer had sent, ran the polished chain through her fingers, touched the tiny stone.

"I hope she's not angry at me for using her name. I didn't know what else to do."

"She's not mad. She's greatly concerned, is all."

Finn watched her, trying not to shiver in his clothes. His heart nearly broke with the joy of seeing her again. Still, he was filled with sorrow and dread. He hadn't told her, and certainly never would, all the seer had said. That, and the grim account of the Coldie that Letitia would surely perish here.

He would never let that happen, no matter what. He would see her out of here, safely home again. And who could credit a dreary apparition, a thing with no more substance than smoke? Why, the fellow had no idea if this was tomorrow or today. And even if a seer and a shade had dire things to say, that didn't mean they were so. Especially the dead . . .

One thing he believed, a thing he couldn't let go, the words the Coldie had said:

*There is something in the Nucci house, something that's
more like us than you . . .*

He became aware, then, that his thoughts had taken him
far away. He glanced up quickly, hoping she hadn't read his
fears, that none of the horrors in his mind had come her
way . . .

"All right," he said abruptly, as if a great plan had taken
shape in his head, "we're getting out of here. I shouldn't
have waited, no matter what."

He ran his hands through his hair, tried to cast the
weariness aside, and, now that he'd begun, wondered what
he ought to say next.

"I take the blame, though that won't help a whit. We
have held *ourselves* hostage here—for as loathsome as it is, it
seemed a sanctuary from the madness outside. Our fears
were real enough, I don't have to tell you that. There is still
great danger out there, danger very real.

"I am convinced, though, we must face those dangers,
for we are surely not safe here. Letitia, Calabus' behavior
toward you is alarming enough. The old man's daft. That
device down below has scrambled his head. And Sabatino
has such a hatred for me—and a lewd obsession toward
you—I feel he's a greater menace than Calabus himself."

*And why don't you tell her there is something so dread and
unspeakable here, that even the dead fear it? Are you doing
her a favor, keeping her in the dark?*

"There can be no more waiting for a ship. If I knew one
would sail into the harbor tomorrow, I would not wait it
out. And if we can't stay here, if we cannot stay in that—
that open asylum they choose to call a town, then we must
go somewhere else still . . ."

For a moment, silence met his words. Letitia's eyes told
him nothing at all. She worried at a pitiful chunk of nearly
petrified bread.

"All right, I'll be the one to say it," Julia said, with a rattle and a croak. "If not here or the lovely village, where? Are you aware your flair for the dramatic drives others to the limit, Finn? Up the wall, right to the edge—"

"You do, you know," Letitia put in, "not that I don't like the way you talk, because I do."

"Oh, well I'm sorry if I do my best to make matters clear. I regret I'm such a bore."

"Stop it, dear. We don't need that."

"All right, I'll get to it at once," Finn said, grateful for the intrusion, which had given him time to discover several new thoughts.

"We will not stay here, and we will certainly not go into town. It is senseless to wait for a ship. We will—we'll travel over land. Away from the coast. Entirely the other way. If anyone pursues us, and I really doubt they will, we—should get a good start before any Foxers or spiritual zealots know we're gone."

"How on earth are we going to do that, Finn? Would you please tell me that?"

Letitia sat cross-legged on the bed running her hands through her hair.

"We don't have a map, we scarcely know where we are now. We have no provisions, and—don't take offense, dear—it appears they're quite hard to get."

Finn pretended not to hear. "We have no knowledge of the country, I'm aware of that. But this is clearly not the only village in the land. We'll follow the road. It has to go somewhere besides this."

He hoped the folly of his plan did not appear as fragile to Julia and Letitia as it did within his head. He regretted now that he hadn't thought this out before, that he hadn't asked the crew of Coldies, for most of them had lived or died nearby.

"We can't be sure there won't be Hooters and Hatters in

the next place too," Julia said. "Quite often, religions aren't confined to one town."

"She's right about that," Letitia said.

"We don't even know where the next town is."

"We don't know if there *is* a next town."

"If there is, it could be worse than this one, how do we know?"

"What if there's no one but Foxers there?"

"What if there's Vampies? Vampies with brooms? Why, I could've been squashed completely flat!"

"All right, that's quite enough, both of you."

Finn stood, leaving a wet spot on the bed. He'd slipped off his shirt, but kept the damp trousers on.

"I don't know what we'll face out there, I don't know what we'll find to eat. I know that we're going, all right? We don't have a choice. If someone has a better idea, I'd be pleased to hear it now."

"It's not that we don't approve, dear. It's just—frightening, is all. The thought of having no idea where we're going, what we'll find there . . ."

"And that's exactly what's kept us here, what's blinded us up to now."

Finn shook his head, frowned at the grim, peeling paper on the walls, at the spiderwebbed ceiling, at the threadbare carpet on the floor.

"We'll leave an hour before sundown. Tonight. That gives us time to see where we're going before it gets dark. By the time night falls, we'll be safely out of sight. I doubt anyone will bother to track us down. If they do, we'll be ready for them, you can count on that."

"I know we can, dear."

"Well, you can. We'll—get out of this . . ."

He was wet, hungry, ready to drop for lack of sleep. Letitia reached for him and drew him back to the bed.

"Finn, I really think you should sit. It won't do any good

to keep talking about this. What we all need to do is get some rest."

"Good idea," Finn said, pulling gently from her grasp, "I appreciate the thought, but there's much I have to do right now. This room is a ruin, but there are items here we can turn to good purpose for our trip. These drapes, which are filthy, could serve as a tent. The bedposts will serve as poles. If we break up the chair—"

"Finn," Letitia said, as gently as her nature would allow, "I'm going to strike you, dear. I have never done that before, but I will surely do it now."

Finn blinked, startled. There was something in those black, enormous Mycer eyes, something close to anger, something close to fire. Something new in this bold, defiant beauty, something haughty, something naughty, something wild.

Bones and Stones, he thought, *whatever that is, it is terribly attractive, though I do hope she can't find anything to throw* . . .

And, in that instant, she did. Reached out and clutched at an object, reached out unaware, lifted up Julia, ready to hurl her through the air.

"Letitia, don't!"

Letitia didn't hear. Letitia was hungry, Letitia was beat. Weary, strung out, tired of the same shabby dress. She yearned to wash her hair, soak in a tub, yearned to be anywhere but here. Something was squirming, squawking in her hand. She didn't know what and didn't care . . .

The door swung open and struck the wall hard, raising a veil of dust. Letitia froze. Finn reached for his blade, then remembered he'd left it in a chair across the room.

Sabatino slouched in the doorway, dressed in resplendent lilac hues, watching with a vain and arrogant grin.

"Oh dear, a family quarrel. What a nice surprise. Do go on, pay no attention to me. When you're finished, you'll find fresh linens, clothing, lotions and such. A tub and hot water, all right here, just outside the door.

"And—I nearly forgot—luncheon is served very shortly in the dining salon. I think you'll find it quite a treat. Squeen is maimed for the moment, so the meal should be a real delight."

Sabatino paused, inspected Letitia up and down, then down and up again. It imparted such lewd and open desire that Letitia felt a rush of color to her face.

"There is nothing so arousing as a woman full of ire," he said. "You are fortunate indeed, Master Finn."

Finn went for him, unarmed or not, but the fellow was gone in a lavender blur before he could stalk across the room . . .

Thirty-Two . . .

"THIS IS ANOTHER OF THAT DANDY'S DESPICABLE jokes," Finn said. "Fraud, chicanery and lies have stained the man's soul. Treachery's the only skill he knows. He must be a fool to think we'll fall for something so utterly transparent as this."

"I'm certain you're right, dear. He's cunning, devious and sly."

"And we're not taken in, not by a whit."

"If you'd like, I'll scrub your back, Finn. Then, if you please, you may do mine."

"I'd be delighted, for sure."

The tub was made of staves, held in shape by hammered copper bands, rolled in with steamy water buckets from the hall. It was clearly not a tub for two, but once Letitia let her dress slip to the floor, dipped a tiny toe, and immersed her lovely self, Finn was not far behind. He backed up against her, so close that her legs had to wrap around his front. A rather tight squeeze, but wasn't that the idea, after all?

"I'll bet that feels good," Letitia said, scrubbing him with a brush. "It's been some time."

"It has indeed," Finn said, scarcely aware of any brush at all.

"I'd give a silver penny to know what he's up to," he said, watching Letitia's wiggly toes.

"Well, whatever it is, this wonderful tub and real soap and—clean clothes! That's no trickery, Finn, that's real!"

"Oh, it's trickery all right, make no mistake in that." He leaned back against her, resting his head in the hollow of her shoulder, whispering in her ear.

"It's a cruel hoax, my dear, playing on our needs. All this is meant to distract us from some other purpose hatching in his devious mind."

"What, though? I can't imagine what it might be."

"Nor I, and it doesn't greatly matter, since it plays right into *our* plans to make our way out of here tonight."

He kissed the steamy droplets on her cheek, and nibbled at her ear.

Letitia leaned away and gave him a wary look. "He said there'd be real food. I don't intend to miss that."

"We won't, we won't. I can't imagine he knows what decent food is, but we'll gladly play along. The bath, the clothes, the food—it all bends in our favor instead of his. We'll be much better prepared to make our move. Cleaner, clothed and fed. The fellow doesn't know he's filling all our needs."

"Oh, I know it's going to work. It's a good plan, Finn. And we *are* going to eat first, right? I feel it's essential that we do."

"Well, yes. I think he might grow suspicious if we don't."

"Come here, please. Turn around, love."

Finn felt his heart leap. "I—think I can. If I stand up

first. I don't want to flood the place. We might go right through the floor."

Letitia watched his clumsy gyrations, hiding a laugh behind her hands.

"Take your time," she said, with a glow, with a glimmer, with a shine, with a very saucy hint in her great enormous eyes.

"I'll be right here, love . . ."

And Julia Jessica Slagg, aware there were times when she shouldn't be around, took a lizard nap beneath the chair.

Sometimes she felt Finn had built in a toggle or a spring, a tiny little switch that said *forget you're even here*. She couldn't say for sure, and could never quite remember to ask . . .

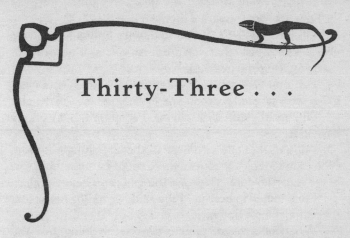

Thirty-Three . . .

THE FIRST THING FINN NOTICED WAS THE TABLE.
It was painted a shade of creamy white. Not black as it was
the day before. Closer, he realized that it wasn't painted,
but merely scraped clean.

Beside him, Letitia drew a breath, dazzled by the sight
before her eyes. There were truffles, pickles, cheeses of
every sort. Steamy roasted potatoes split down the middle
with a buttery lake inside. Fish grilled crispy brown, fragrant with a lemony sauce.

And greens, to Letitia's great pleasure. Crispy, leafy
treats of a color she'd nearly forgotten. Even the dishes
were whole, and the vessels made of glass.

"I have to say," Letitia said, "in spite of my intense dis-
like for you, I must say this is a stunning feast you've set
before us this day. Don't you think so, dear?"

"I expect it's ill-mannered to ask, but do I have your
word nothing here is laced with deadly herbs or drugs? No
foul or septic powders, no poison of any sort?"

Sabatino looked hurt. "Of course not. If I'd not already
called you out, I would do so again."

"Is that a yes or no?"

"You may trade plates with me if you like."

"Oh, no you don't," Finn said, with a sly and knowing grin. "That's just what you'd do, isn't it? You're ready for that, you'd expect me to ask."

"Eat, Finn, it's delicious." Letitia stabbed a bite of vinegar greens, savored it a moment, closing her eyes in delight. "Oh, my, that fish looks divine. I shouldn't, but I simply have to try."

"I don't sense any virulence in the air," Julia said from Finn's shoulder. "Of course, there could be something I've never sniffed before. There *are* things I can't detect at all."

"I'm stunned to hear it," Finn said, wrinkling his nose at the fish, risking a tiny bite.

"What concerns me more is *why* you're doing this? You have some reason, Sabatino, and I doubt it's too obscure."

"You're quite right, of course. And you as well, dear lady. There is no need to mask our loathing for one another, it makes for a most unpleasant meal. Oh, and I must say you look enchanting. That gown fits you well."

"I'd rather you didn't, but thanks all the same."

The gown was quite nice, an enchanting shade of blue, and it certainly fit, Sabatino had seen to that. If Letitia hadn't done hasty work with pins, she'd be naked to the waist.

"You didn't cook the meal," Finn said. "I doubt you made the dress. This crockery is whole, everything's clean . . ."

Sabatino wagged a finger at Finn. "You're such a curious fellow, I knew you'd have to ask. Not a healthy trait, I might add. There's a place I go for ale now and then, **TAVERN**, as it's called. Some people go to **BAR**—I wouldn't be caught in there, of course."

"Neither would I."

"No, you would not. At any rate, the food was prepared

by the keeper's wife. The gown is her daughter's. If you could see the wife, you'd know it wasn't hers."

"And what's it all for? You never got to that."

Sabatino held his glass up to the light. It wasn't turnip wine, but he didn't seem to mind.

"My father is mentally impaired. Poor fellow gets daffier by the day. I should have taken action before. I've put up with his madness, but I cannot afford to indulge him anymore."

Letitia raised a brow. "He won't be joining us, then?"

"Very astute, miss. No, he will not." Sabatino spoke in warm and earnest tones as if he were gathered with family and friends.

"He is obsessed with that outrageous folly in the cellar. I can't say whether this nonsense warped his mind, or whether he was bonkers all along. It hardly matters now. I've put an end to that before we end up in the street. He has poured his last coin—and mine—down the drain."

"I see," Finn said, trying to catch the man's ever-shifting eyes, hoping a glimmer of truth might leak through the barricade of lies. For, no matter what Sabatino said, Finn was certain he could not avoid deceit for more than a minute at a time.

Sabatino faced him, then, with a most sincere and artless smile as if he'd guessed Finn's thoughts all along.

"You and this charming lady can be grateful to me, Finn, have no doubt of that. Surely you guessed Father lied, that if, somehow you failed to return, he would give Letitia safety here, that *I* was the villain all along? He said I'd set a trap for Master Finn, did he not, my dear? When he came with that false and deadly offer to aid him in his folly down below?

"Yes, I know about that," he said, catching Letitia's surprise. "I know a great deal. I have this shameful hobby of listening at doors."

Sabatino's eyes glittered with specks of gold in the flickering candlelight. "Oh, I know some other things, too, things I'd never tell . . ."

Whatever those things might be, Finn didn't want to hear.

"You'd have us believe you didn't set the trap?"

"Certainly not. There are easier ways to dispose of you, sir. And there's clearly no honor in such a device. Did you not detect the inventor's weakness for pulleys, ropes and such, for the needlessly complex? I should think you would, a craftsman like yourself."

"Your father told me it was you," Letitia began, "so I would think . . ."

". . . So you would see him as your savior after I supposedly murdered Finn. He sent Squeen William out to get the lizard, and the wretched fellow caught himself in Father's trap."

Sabatino paused, studied the ring on his finger, watching it catch the light. The stone was a brilliant green, the size of a lump of coal. And worth about as much, Finn knew, for he had some knowledge of precious stones.

"I am supposed to be the rogue here and I won't deny that. But what do you think would happen, miss, if you fell into Father's hands? He is mad, and likely to grow madder still.

"I can see the question you're burning to ask, Master Finn," Sabatino said, waving his hand in disdain. "What now, that you must deal with me, and not a witless old man?"

"In truth, we had no intention of dealing with you at all," Finn said. "As long as I can wield a blade, we'll decide our own fate. It has little to do with you."

Sabatino tried to hide his chagrin. "You face many dangers outside this house, I trust you're not ignorant of that. I am trying to be your friend whether you're blind to that or not."

"What you're doing is overthrowing your father. Any good that comes to us is accidental at best—"

"We've made our own plans, anyway," Letitia broke in, "we don't need any help from you."

"Letitia . . ." Finn nearly came out of his seat, but it was useless to stop her now.

"Forgive me for speaking up, dear. The more I think about it, the more foolish it seems to be less than open here. If he truly has our interests in mind, he'll be glad to rid himself of one more complication in his life."

She turned then to Sabatino, with a bold, most determined eye.

"We are leaving, sir. Between sundown and dark. We will travel inland, and trust we will find safety there. You have already provided us with clothing and an excellent meal. If you wish to prove your concern, perhaps you'll draw us a map of some kind, and give us any extra provisions you can spare . . ."

For a moment, Sabatino looked bewildered, astonished, as if Letitia had spoken in some strange and alien tongue. Then his cheeks puffed out in an explosion of laughter. He threw back his head in hearty guffaws, scarcely able to contain himself at all.

And Finn, who knew this rascal had seldom been caught in unthinking emotion, no more than an actor on the stage, wondered what this performance was about. Likely, he decided, to give the fellow time to think of what to say next. In the meantime, Finn had the chance to consider why Letitia had spilled the goods, and decided she was very probably right after all.

"Forgive me, please," Sabatino said, exhausted by this clownish display. "The thing is, you see—and I doubt you'll credit this—that is exactly what I had in mind myself. I do have a plate full of trouble on my hands, with Father and all, and I would like you out of my way."

"And we're supposed to swallow that?" Finn shook his head. "No matter, we'll soon be gone, so we'll both be quite satisfied."

"Excellent!" Sabatino drew back his chair and stood. "If you'll wait in your room, I'll see to the needs of your journey. I'm sorry we'll miss our duel, sir. Life keeps getting in pleasure's way."

He showed them both a weary smile. "As you might imagine, my father's not taking his—new position too well. Even those who are *not* old, useless and insane, do not like to yield up authority they have taken for granted so long. But, damn his rotten eyes, he must do as *I* will it, now."

"Is he all right, then, he's not—"

Letitia, aghast at what she'd said, and almost said as well, looked down and studied her hands as if she'd discovered an extra finger there.

Sabatino's glacial stare was real; he was not the actor now. "Squeen William, get out here," he said, without taking his eyes from Letitia Louise, "get out here, you scum, and show these people back to their room . . ."

Finn, quite aware of the enmity Letitia had aroused, had his fingers on the hilt of his sword until Sabatino was gone, out of the room, through the entryway, and out the front door.

"I bes takin' you upstairsss no. Bes coming with me, pleassse?"

Letitia clasped her hand across her mouth, holding back her sudden fright. Squeen William was a disaster from head to toe, a creature covered with bruises, cuts and sores. Frayed, frazzled, broken and lame, beat-up and maimed. Bandaged in tatters, wrapped in dirty rags, and rather severely impaired.

"Squeen William," Letitia asked, knowing at once it was a foolish thing to say, "are you all right, can you get up the stairs?"

"Squeen William bes fine, misssy. Isss very kind of you to asssssk . . ."

Thirty-Four . . .

"I DON'T KNOW WHAT HE'S UP TO," FINN SAID, stretched out on the bed with his hands behind his head. "It's damned irritating to deal with a fellow who seldom tells the truth. But now and then he does, and I believe he's shut his father up somewhere. I'm not too surprised, understand. The old man's cracked, as nutty as can be.

"I'd like to think there's a true advantage to having us out of here. I feel perhaps there is. For certain, whatever family fortune's left is his. He'll keep the old man locked up, or maybe do him in. Either way, when we're gone, he can do most anything he likes. Who else is going to wander in here? Dr. Nicoretti, I suppose. If Sabatino's wise, he'll keep that fellow well away. He's sly as he can be, I'll tell you that . . ."

Letitia, standing at the window, turned to face him then.

"You think he'd do that? Murder the old man?"

"I can't say, love. I used to think Sabatino was soft in the head as well. Now, I feel he's simply contemptible and vain.

An arrogant, self-centered liar, a scoundrel mean at heart, a man who'd stoop to most anything to get his way."

"I'd say he's all of that."

Letitia absently ran her fingers over the amulet at her throat. "You're not mad at me, are you? For speaking up like that, giving away our plans?"

"No, and maybe it did some good. That's what you thought and you said it. No one can fault you for that. And you, Julia, I commend you as well."

Julia, at the foot of the bed, twitched her metal tail.

"What did I do? I hardly said a thing."

"I know. That's what I'm grateful for."

"Keep your thanks, then. I can do without."

Finn stared at the ceiling. What if it sagged a bit more? What if the whole thing came down and crushed them on the spot?

He wanted to believe Sabatino had nearly told the truth this time. He did have a great many things to clear up. For one thing, he could cleanse himself of the sin of hospitality, and earn the town's respect again. And, if he did rid himself of his father, perhaps the Foxers would leave him alone. It was clear in Finn's mind that Calabus was the center of trouble in that long and deadly feud. That if he was gone . . .

And, another task beyond that: the cellar, and Calabus' obsession, the Prophecy Machine. Sabatino would quickly have it gone. He said it was a fool's device, yet he clearly feared the thing.

What, though, if there was truly something dreadful down there, as the Mycer and the Coldie had implied? Was Calabus responsible for the spell that protected something there from harm? Was it even his doing? Did he even know it was *there*?

If a thing down there didn't *want* to be disturbed, Finn

thought, didn't wish to go away . . . Truly, this was an excellent time to leave the Nucci house, and put this dreary land behind.

He sat up abruptly and put his feet on the floor. He decided he must have dozed for a moment, for Letitia was sleeping beside him, her lips half open and her hair in disarray. He got up slowly, careful not to wake her. Julia followed him silently with her eyes.

There was little to see out the window, nothing but a hot and dreary afternoon. Too many hours to wait, too long until they'd be away. Away from the Nuccis, Hooters and Hatters, everyone and everything he never wanted to think about again.

Somehow, they would get free of this land, get a ship across the Misty Sea and back to Garpenny Street where they belonged. And if anyone ever said "vacation" again—

He heard it, then, felt it beneath his boots, felt it when he pressed his hand against the wall. A rumble, a scrape, a deep vibration through the floor, coming from the hall.

Finn went quickly to the door, tried to push it open. It was stuck against something, wouldn't give an inch. He tried once more, put his back and shoulders to the job. Nothing. The sound was gone now, the intense vibrations gone.

"All right, who's out there, what's going on?"

Silence.

A faint, nearly inaudible breath.

"Sabatino, this is not amusing. You will let me out of here now. Damn you, man, I mean what I say. You'll answer for this!"

"Save your breath, Master Finn. You won't be seein' that miserable, traitorous son of mine. Not anyone will, not ever again . . ."

A chill touched the back of Finn's neck. He stepped back a pace, and stared at the door.

"Calabus? Look, I don't know what's going on with you two, that's no concern of mine. But you must talk to me, understand?"

For a moment, there were footsteps in the hall, and then they were gone. Finn pressed his ear against the door. Listened, strained to hear, but there was no one there at all . . .

Thirty-Five . . .

"HE PUT SOMETHING BIG AGAINST THE DOOR. Something extremely large, I can't budge the thing an inch."

Finn struck his fist against the door until it hurt. "He didn't do it alone, either. He had to have help."

"Squeen William, you think?"

"Who else? That fellow's incredible. Sabatino nearly crippled the lout, and he's up and going again. Calabus loathes him, yet he's clearly working for *him*. Apparently, whoever screamed at him last . . ."

"This is not good, Finn. This is not good at all."

Letitia stood well across the room, arms crossed, drumming her fingers against her elbow at a fairly rapid pace. Not a promising sign, Finn knew. It was like faraway thunder before a great storm.

"No, it's truly not good, but it's not the end of the world. Calabus has left himself in a very tricky spot. If he tries to keep us here, we'll smash that window and lower ourselves to the ground. I'd start knotting sheets if I were you. On the other hand, if he opens that door, I'll run the fellow through. If it comes to that, I'll take Squeen William as well."

"Finn—"

"What?"

"Come over here, and look down, please."

"Why? There's nothing to see."

Nevertheless, he joined her and peered through the fly-encrusted glass.

"I believe that's Squeen William," he said. "He's sitting in the grass out there. By damn, he's got a weapon, too."

"I believe he does, dear."

"I think I know what it is. It's a Ponce-Klieterhaus musket. Used by the Hansi Grenadiers. Shoots a fairly decent ball. Why, that relic's fifty years old."

"You think he could hit anything?"

"I shouldn't think so. Hard to tell, though."

"Uh-huh." Letitia's tapping rapidly increased. "I don't intend to knot a sheet, Finn. I'm willing to listen to another suggestion, but I will *not* dangle my lovely self out a window to see if a Vampie can shoot me down."

"He wouldn't act like this if he hadn't been terribly abused."

"I feel sorry for him, too."

"Yes, well . . . Julia, up here on the table, if you will. You've still got a jerky foot from that run-in with Squeen and his broom. We may have to move quickly quite soon."

Letitia sighed. "Do we have time for this? Don't you have other things to do?"

"Whatever we do, I think we should all be in good shape to do it. Stop moving around, Julia, we're not back in the shop. If I break something here, you're scrap."

"Anyone ever tell you you have a horrid bedside manner, Finn?"

"Anyone ever tell *you* I'm not a physician, and you're

not a patient? What you are, if you don't lie still, is a useless collection of cogs and gears. Gold, copper and tin that would make a nice watch with enough left over for the bin."

"No wonder you're not a doctor. Who in their right mind would *reeerk!*"

Julia gave a tremble and a jerk, opened her snout and went stiff as a lizard can be.

"There now, that's better. Let's see what we can see."

Finn slipped a fingernail beneath a certain scale, gave it a tap that only Finn knew. A panel swung open in Julia's tin belly, a panel that revealed a great wonder, a sight to confound the keenest eye. Here was a world that moved in a whisper, in a click, in a blur. Muscles of nickel, sinews of brass, nine tiny hearts made of mercury and gold. Nerves fine as gnat's hair spun from cinnabar and pearl.

Finn fairly shuddered at the thought of that crazed old man poking grubby fingers in Julia's tiny parts. Why, a mote of dust alone from this sty was enough to spoil the crudest device—what havoc it could wreak on Julia Jessica Slagg!

A touch here, a nudge there, with a needle fine as any ever made, a tool Finn always pinned to the collar of his coat. One more twist and he was done.

Julia's belly closed with a snap. Finn turned her over, and watched her ruby eyes glow, watched her snout clamp shut.

"How's the leg now? Give it a shake and let's see."

Julia dutifully shook. The leg seemed perfectly fine.

"I think I had a dream," Julia said.

"That's what you always say. I strongly doubt that."

"Doubt if you will. Why would I remember something if it wasn't truly there?"

"Maybe you did. I don't want to hear it, whatever it is."

"Are you two done over there? Could you possibly spare the time for something else, like getting us out of here?"

Finn knew that when Letitia's voice reached a certain pitch, one should consider an intelligent reply.

"Is Squeen still spooking about below? Can you see him from there?"

"Where would he go, Finn?"

"I'm working on a plan. I truly need to know."

"What kind of plan?"

"It's not in the talking stage now. As soon as it is I'll let you know."

Julia made a lizardy sound in her throat. "She's not buying that, Finn."

"Don't talk, please. I'm trying to think."

"You could ask me, you know."

"What?"

"I said—"

"I heard that, Julia. Ask you *what*?"

"How to get us out of here."

"If I do, will you shut up for a while?"

Julia didn't answer. The light went out in her eyes.

"All right. I'm sorry. If you really have something to say, don't keep it to yourself."

"You haven't asked."

"I'm asking now."

"I'm not overly certain, but I think we can get out the same way I got out before."

Finn was listening now. "Don't play games with me, there's no time for that."

"You're talking about when Calabus was up here, right?"

Letitia was across the room before Julia could get the words out. "When you went looking for Finn?"

"Certainly. If there was another time I left, I don't recall.

I didn't slip out the door, as you perhaps imagined, I was gone before the old man came in. I got out over there."

Finn and Letitia turned in the direction of Julia's nod. Neither saw anything but a wall. Both looked back at the lizard. Finn was certain Julia smiled, though he knew for a fact she didn't have the parts for that.

"Patience," Julia said, "and all will be revealed."

Sliding off the table, she scampered across the floor. At the wall she stopped, hesitated, moved her snout an inch to the right, then another to the left.

Finn glanced away for an instant, looked back again. When he did, Julia was gone.

"Finn . . . !"

Letitia squeezed his hand. Finn went quickly to his knees. He rubbed his fingers across the ancient wood where it met the grimy floor. Nothing. No cracks or seams. Nothing to suggest a secret panel or a hidden entryway. Yet, short of sheer magic, Julia couldn't simply disappear. There was something here, something that plain confused the eye. Something he—

"Well then, what do you think? Is that not a fine deceit or what?"

Julia's appearance brought a gasp from Letitia, and a muttered oath from Finn. The lizard's red eyes blinked from a narrow hole. A veil of cobwebs hid her snout, and her scales were coated with dust.

"It was no illusion," Julia said, "it's architectural folly's what it is, a madman's dream, a builder gone berserk. Rooms don't begin where another room ends. They stop short, leaving dark canyons in between. Roofs come through the ceiling and up through the floor. Some doors open on walls. Some doors open on doors. Corridors begin and go nowhere at all."

Julia tended to irritate Finn with her frequent rattling on. This time he truly didn't mind. This time her chatter gave him hope, a new chance to leave this wretched place behind.

"And all these chambers, passages and such, they lead outdoors, they take you out of here, and it's safe all the way?"

"Safe enough," Julia said, "if you don't meet a Vampie with a broom somewhere."

"Don't worry," Letitia said, "he's only got a musket now."

"That's not our problem anymore," Finn said. "If you please, grab a handful of those smelly candles, dear."

He turned back to Julia. "That hole looks fine for lizards. I guess I'll have to widen it a bit."

"No problem but have a care when you do. One wrong move and you'll bring the house down. Oh, neither of you care for creatures of the insect persuasion, I recall? Lice, beetles, spiders and flies? Mites, millipedes, bugs of every sort?"

Finn looked at Letitia, Letitia looked at Finn.

"Anything bites, don't scratch," Julia said. "That's what you get for not wearing tin . . ."

Thirty-Six . . .

EVEN AS JULIA SAID, IT WAS NO GREAT EFFORT TO make the very small hole large. She was also right about bringing the whole wall down upon his head.

"I would say I told you so," Julia croaked, and rattled off into the dark, "but I'm fairly sure I did."

"I am grateful for your help," Finn said, wheezing, gasping through a cloud of dirt, rot and old debris. "I don't know what I'd do without your good advice."

Letitia appeared through the gloom, holding a candle high, a pale and dusty apparition with wide and anxious eyes.

"I don't care for this, Finn. I'm not sure it's a good idea."

"We haven't even started, dear. I don't think we should judge it quite yet."

"*I've* started. I've started to itch. I don't like it in here."

"I don't either, but I don't see anything for us back there."

Letitia didn't answer. She followed Julia, whose lizard eyes could penetrate the dark far better than any human or Newlie born.

As Julia had warned, insect life of every sort abounded in the maze behind the walls. It was heaven for spiders, a termite delight. There were bugs that crawled and flew, bugs that liked to bite, bugs Finn couldn't even name.

Once, ducking wooden beams, bending nearly to the floor, Letitia cried out, stood and cracked her head. The candle flew away and rolled across the floor, the wick still lit. Finn crawled across to get it, stopped in his tracks. The dusty floor was teeming with roaches. A swarm of thousands of the ugly, writhing creatures, frantically running from the light that intruded on their dark, unwholesome world.

They moved like the undulations of the sea, wave after wave, one mass scrambling atop the next, another and another after that. Worst of all, the thing that made Finn's skin begin to crawl, was the color of the things. Neither brown nor black, like their ordinary kin, this dreadful mass was deathly white. Pale, swollen, disturbingly fat.

"Here's your candle," Finn said. "You ask me, that was not a pretty sight. If you'd like, I'll trade places and carry the light awhile."

"So something can find me in the dark? No thanks, Finn. You're not getting away with that."

Before he could answer, she turned away again. Finn let her go. This was clearly not the time to speak of anything at all.

It all made a certain kind of sense, Finn thought. The outside of the house set the theme: every room, every hall he'd seen, was cockeyed, leaning, listing left or right. Why shouldn't the spaces in between be as peculiar as the rest?

Sometimes Julia took them ways so narrow that Finn could scarcely squeeze through. Sometimes they climbed, sometimes they crawled between floors. Once, Finn pulled his way hand over hand, under a set of stairs. When he reached the bottom, a section of roofing blocked his way. When there was finally room to pass Letitia, he brushed a mess of cobwebs aside and told Julia to stop.

Letitia looked alarmed. "Where are you going? Is something wrong, Finn?"

"Not a thing. I'm going up to see Julia."

"Don't, please. Stay right here."

Finn reached out and touched her. "You feel rather cold. Are you all right?"

"No, I'm not. Thanks for asking, dear."

Julia's eyes were dim points of light against the dark.

"I have to ask. Are you certain you know what you're doing, are you sure you got out this way?"

"No, I'm quite sure I did not."

"What?"

"If I went the way I did before, you and Letitia would never get through."

"But you know where we are."

"You put a compass inside me, remember? I couldn't get lost if I wanted to. That flooring, just below the stairs? The one that slants forty-two degrees? The one where you saw the mottled centipedes? Where you—"

"All right, I remember. What's the point here?"

"You asked me where we are. We're just below the hall outside our room. Where we *were* was directly beneath that heavy object Calabus set before the door. Did you notice how much the floor sagged? I'm surprised it didn't come right through . . ."

Finn drew a breath. "You're telling me that's as far as we've gone? We're on the same floor, out in the hall?"

"Below the hall, to be exact, not in it. If we were *in* it now—"

"Bogs and Frogs." Finn wiped a sleeve against his face.

"Why didn't you tell me that? You never tell me anything I need to know."

Julia hesitated. She lifted herself up slightly, flexing her silvery legs.

"I saw no reason to alarm you. There are unusual conditions here—vibrations, emanations in this house. They come from that machine down below."

"I know that. I nearly threw up down there."

"Yes, but it isn't just down there. I can sense them all the time, you can't. I've been trying to get us out without getting too close to that thing. It affects my parts to some degree, but I've seen what it does to humans and Newlies. It's best to take the long way."

"Fine, then, if it doesn't take forever."

He tried to swallow, but only managed to stick his throat shut. He wished he had a mug of cool ale to cut the dust.

"You did the right thing, Julia. But I wish you'd told me. Calabus could find out we're gone anytime. Then what? Letitia's wearing out, and I'm getting there myself. One more roach parade, one more spider—"

Finn was suddenly talking in the dark. He turned, quickly, back the way he'd come.

"Letitia? Letitia, are you all right? Just stay there, don't move, I'm coming back."

"Finn. She's not there."

"She *has* to be there "

"I can see, and she's gone. She's not there."

"Letitia!"

Finn felt the hairs tingle on his neck. "Say something, please. Answer me, love!"

"Hold it down, Finn. That won't do us any good."

Finn searched for an extra candle in his pocket. Drew it out, found a firestick in his vest. His hands were shaking so badly he could scarcely get the thing lit. At once, he saw

Letitia's candle. There was still a wisp of smoke rising from the wick.

When he turned again, Julia was gone. He caught a blur of copper as she scrambled to the right, under a row of crooked joists. Finn made himself follow, leave the spot where Letitia had disappeared. He felt drained, empty, terribly frightened, terribly alone.

He followed Julia on hands and knees, squeezing through the narrow space between the walls. A splinter sliced his palm. He winced but didn't stop.

She's all right, nothing happened . . . a spider startled her, she dropped the candle, the candle went out . . . she tried to find me, took a wrong turn somewhere . . .

"Why didn't she call out? Why didn't she make a sound?"

When he caught up to Julia, he found her rigid, perfectly still. Her lizard snout twitched, tasting the air. Finn wanted to yell, tell her to hurry, damn it, they didn't have time.

Finally, she moved, off to the right with a glance back at Finn. He tried to hold his candle low, away from dusty walls, the timbers just above his head. If a flame ever licked that dry and rotting wood . . .

At the end of the crawlway, he was able to stand and stretch his legs. Holding the candle high, he saw a wide shaft crossing his path just ahead. Six, maybe eight feet across. It started somewhere above, dropped into smothering darkness far below. A place for a chimney, perhaps, a project that never got done. In a house like this, he thought, there must be a number of things that ended before they were even begun.

"Finn."

"I'm here."

Julia's eyes blinked. "I know that, I can see you there. There's a ledge around that pit. Come that way."

"I see it."

"I think it ought to hold."

"You think?"

"It will. And Finn . . ."

"What?"

"There's a strong emanation and a smell. You'll know it easily enough while you're crossing the shaft. I'm telling you so you won't panic and run across. It's a very long drop."

"I'm not going to panic, I've never fallen in a pit in my life. Did she come this way? Do you have any feeling about that, anything at all?"

"Come over, Finn. Don't look, don't think. Do it right now."

Finn took a breath, let it out and held it again. He walked across the narrow stretch of timber, his back pressed to the wall. Halfway there it hit him. It didn't help to hold his breath, it was too strong for that.

He gagged, feeling the bile rise up in his throat, feeling the undulations in his bones, in his muscle, in his flesh. His stomach heaved. The nausea nearly brought him down. He felt as if his head might swell up and split.

"As I said, take it easy. Don't panic. Which is exactly what you did."

"Stones and Bones, Julia, what in all hell was that? Letitia, where did she—"

"I've lost her. I don't know where she is, but I know what's making you sick. As I said, the emanations from that machine have always been evident in the house, but they're awfully strong here. We're very close to it. By my reckoning, we shouldn't be, but we are."

"And that's what's causing the smell?"

"What? Oh no, that's excreta, waste and flux. Dribble, sweat, foul urination and such. And, if I'm not mistaken, Squeen William's cooking lunch. Don't be concerned about that, it's the throbbing and the pulse, the rumble and drumming and the thrum, that's what'll bring you down."

Finn was scarcely listening at all. The back of his neck still tingled, and he couldn't make it stop.

"When we were down there . . . that thing had a strong effect on Letitia. I should never have taken her there."

"I have to tell you, Finn. If we get any closer, I doubt you can stay in a conscious state for long."

Finn shook his head. "I have to. I've got to find her and get her out of here."

"What good will it do if you're stricken by this—wave, this radiation, whatever it may be? It's better if I go on, discover where she is."

"Forget it. We're wasting time here. If I have to throw up, I'll do it on the way . . ."

Thirty-Seven . . .

JULIA SAID THEY WERE GOING UP. IT FELT LIKE down to Finn. With the myriad of slants, angles, skews and deviations, zigs, zags, corners and bends, it was nearly impossible to tell. Once, Finn came upon a window. A window with glass, a window with panes, nailed to the floor. What was it doing there? On the other hand, why not, in a place like this?

He wondered, again, if Calabus knew they were gone. What would he do if he did? Maybe send the Vampie in. Squeen would feel at home in a place like this. What had the old man done to Sabatino? Locked him up, done him in? Would he go that far with his very own son? Unthinkable, of course. Unless you were a Nucci. All bets were off then . . .

Finn cursed as a stream of hot tallow stung his fingers. He almost dropped the candle, but caught it as it nearly went out. It was getting short now. What would he do when it was gone? Hang on to Julia's tail while she led him around in the dark?

The pulse, the throb, the dark emanations were stronger

than ever now. Finn tried to picture Letitia, picture her eyes, picture her face, picture her safe. Sometimes he could see her, sometimes she wasn't there.

He wiped the sweat off his face, shook his head to keep it clear. The force was like a great and hungry magnet drawing him in, pulling him ever tighter in its grasp. He felt it was tugging at his flesh, bending, cracking his bones, and the thought struck terror in his heart.

Once, when he could shake his mind clear, he wondered if the thing down below was the only force that drew him in. Or was the strong magic a part of that power as well? Or, suppose the two were one? He tried to hold the thought, but it flicked off in the ether and was gone . . .

"Finn . . . Finn?"

Finn looked up, suddenly aware that he was down on the floor retching between his knees. There was nothing there, but his stomach didn't care.

"You find her . . . you—got Leti—Letitia now . . . ?"

"No, Finn. I only know she went this way. We can't go any further. I have to get you out of here."

"Letitia . . ."

"I'll come back. I'll find her. I promise you that."

"Need some—candles," Finn muttered to himself, almost certain he knew what a candle was for, fighting to keep his vision clear.

"Candles are good," Julia said. "Come on now, stay close to me . . ."

He could scarcely see now, the very air seemed to warp, seemed to buckle, seemed to blur. The world without was false, distorted, anything but real. The world within his head was even worse than that . . .

Something moved, something bent, something twisted out of shape, and, even from Finn's disordered view, he knew that it shouldn't be there . . .

"Julia . . . ?"

"I saw it too. Just for an instant. It isn't Letitia, though."

"What else—is in here?"

Julia didn't answer. Finn touched her scaly back, stumbled, and got up again.

"I can't help you much," Julia said. "Whatever this power is, it's not good for lizard machines. Things are happening inside I've never felt before."

"Me . . . me too."

The shimmering walls, the convoluted floor, seemed to beat like a monstrous heart. Finn ducked into a wind he couldn't see, heard a deep and dreadful howl. And there was the thing again, a phantom, a wisp, an involution of the air. He wondered if Julia saw it too. Wanted to ask, but didn't know how.

"We're terribly close to it now," Julia said, from a million miles away, "the device, it's expanded somehow, spread from the cellar up into the house . . ."

I should have guessed, Finn said, or maybe thought aloud, *. . . should have known that . . . it was growing when we saw it . . . why should it stop, confine itself there?*

"We can't go this way," Julia said, "We have to go back, get through somewhere else."

Where? There isn't anywhere but here . . .

He didn't see it this time, didn't see a shadow, didn't see it dark-dark-dark against the wall. This time, it came up from behind, silent and swift, and he smelled its fetid odor, smelled its deathly breath, turned too late, as it picked him up and threw him hard against the wall.

Finn hit, struck a rotten beam and tumbled to the floor. The creature was on him then, pounding with its fists, beating his head against the floor. Finn couldn't see it, but knew it was strong, knew it smelled awful, knew there was nothing he could do but try to stay alive. And that wouldn't work, not for too long. This growling, odorous brute had mutilation in mind, and possibly worse than that.

The creature shrieked and loosed its grip. Finn clawed at the floor, trying to get away. He heard a familiar *claaaank!*, and knew that Julia had bitten the fellow hard, winced, an instant after that, as Julia hit the floor with a ruinous crunch of copper, a shattering of tin.

"Hold on," Finn shouted, "I'm coming, whatever's broken, it's something I can fix!"

With a roar, with a breath that would gag any good-sized town, the creature grabbed Finn, tossed him over its shoulder, and stomped away in the dark.

Finally, his captor stopped, opened a door, and stepped inside. It paused there a moment, then dumped Finn roughly to the floor.

Finn was aware of dim candlelight. He groaned, rolled on his back, looked up and saw the creature standing there. Finn began to yell and couldn't stop. The brute wasn't nearly as big as he'd thought, but he'd seen it before, seen the crazed eyes, seen the tangled beard, the dirty hair. Seen it kicking, flailing and screaming outside his own room.

The brute frowned, spat on the floor. It muttered to itself, found a tangled cord, left Finn bound for market then it stomped out the door.

Finn took a breath. For the moment, he was apparently alive. And one thing more: the dreadful sounds were nearly gone. He could scarcely feel them in here!

"Well, this is just fine, I've got company now. Damn you, Finn, how did *you* get here?"

Finn turned, startled. Sabatino was leaning against a far wall bound in much the same manner as Finn himself.

"What—what are *you* doing here?"

Sabatino rolled his eyes in disgust. "I believe I asked you first, craftsman. I'm here because that insane father of mine got free and put me here. It's fairly clear he got you as well. How's Miss Letitia? I hope she fared better than you."

Finn took a breath. "Who is that—that disgusting creature? Kites and Mites, I never smelled anything worse in my life!"

"There you go," Sabatino said, "insulting the Nuccis again. That disgusting creature is dear Grandfather, the other madman in the clan . . ."

Thirty-Eight . . .

FOR A MOMENT, FINN SIMPLY STARED. HE TRIED to think of something to say. Nothing seemed proper, nothing seemed to fit.

"And he just, ah, runs around loose, I assume."

"He's not supposed to, but he does. Would you like to try and stop something like that?"

"It seems to me, no offense, but it's awfully hard to keep you fellows penned for long. The Nuccis are good at getting loose."

Sabatino made a face. "Sometimes we are. I thought I had Father locked up, but he's clearly out howling as well. I expect Squeen William had a hand in that. Master Finn—would you be kind enough to tell me if I still have arms and legs? I can't feel a thing."

"They're still there," Finn assured him, and realized his own limbs were growing numb as well.

"What's your—grandfather plan to do with us? Do you know? Has this ever happened before? Rooks and Books, what'll he do if he catches Letitia? If he tries to harm her, by damn, he'll answer to me!"

Sabatino's look said he thought this was clearly absurd.

"There's no way to tell what he'll do. He's never tried to finish us off before, but I wouldn't count on that."

Sabatino paused. "This is family, and none of your concern, Finn, but I suppose you're a part of this calamity now. My father didn't build that infernal machine. Grandfather did. It drove him mad, of course, but not before he passed his obsession along to his son. I grew up with this aberration, but learned quite early to stay away from the thing. I'm not insane, in spite of what you think. I'm a bit off-center, granted, but nothing like those two, you have to see that."

Finn wasn't certain this was true.

"Your father and the, uh —your grandfather, they're in this together, then?"

"Of course not. They loathe each other. I doubt Grandfather knows who we are. Whoever fed him last—that's all the poor devil knows. That's how his mind works, whatever bit that's left."

Oh, Letitia, I'm sorry I got you into this . . . I'll find you, love, wherever you are . . . and Julia, I'll make you right, if I have to start all over again . . .

"The Prophecy Machine. There's nothing to it, then. It's just a—a machine."

Sabatino yawned. "What do you think, Mr. Inventor? You saw the holy gibberish the thing spits out."

"I saw a lot down there, and gibberish doesn't explain it all."

"Think what you like, I'm sure I don't care."

"This is monstrous," Finn said, "he has to let us go. He has no right to treat us this way."

Clearly, Sabatino didn't care to talk. He was huddled in the darkest part of the room. By scooting his shoulders about, Finn could see further past the gloom. What he'd taken for stains and damage of the years was clearly something else. There were squares and bits of metal, scraps of every kind. Hundreds of them placed in some fearsome array, some strange disorder that only a madman could see. Copper coated green, sheets of dull tin, iron turned a rusty red. Scrap, Finn supposed, salvaged from the machine. And he knew, suddenly, why they were there. They blocked out the power, made this hideaway a refuge from the thing down below . . .

Sabatino's features curled into a sly and cunning smile.

"You see it, do you? The old man's mad, all right, but he knows how to get a night's sleep."

"You're not telling me everything, Sabatino. There's a great deal more, I'm certain of that. I don't think you can truly help yourself. I doubt you could make it through one complete sentence without a lie. It might be full of truth, but you'd find a hole, an empty spot to tuck in a sham somewhere."

"I'm greatly offended, sir, crushed, as it were. Your opinion is *so* important to me. Do you mind if I nap?"

"That night when the Foxers came to call. Your grandfather was on the loose then. Squeen took him off somewhere. Does the Vampie know about this place, then?"

Sabatino forced a nasty laugh. "Of course not, don't be a fool. *I* didn't know about it till he brought me here. I used to play between the walls when I was a child. The radiations from the cellar hadn't yet filtered up here. Squeen got the old man out of the hall before he could kill someone."

"A Foxer, you mean. That's what he was after." Finn didn't need to ask. He knew from Sabatino's expression it was true.

"This quarrel goes back a long way, does it not? Back to your grandfather's time? What started it, Sabatino? Why do the Foxers want the Nuccis dead?"

Sabatino turned away as if he found Finn a crashing bore.

"I haven't the foggiest idea. I doubt those idiot creatures know any more than I do. That was too long ago."

"I don't believe that."

"Well, the devil with you, then. I couldn't care, Finn."

"Is it the Prophecy Machine? What do the Foxers have to do with that?"

Sabatino turned back to Finn and glared. "We discussed this, I believe. It isn't a machine that *does* anything. It's a toy for fools, is what it is."

"It does something," Finn said. "It grows all by itself, and it apparently drives people mad."

"Well, that should be enough, don't you think? What more could you ask? If we really must pass the time together, Finn, I'd rather spend it doing something else. Like getting out of here, before Grandfather comes back. You don't happen to have a blade handy, do you? The old man took mine away."

Finn had to laugh. "No, I don't have a blade. Would I be lying here talking to you?"

"No, I don't suppose you would." Sabatino lifted his head, a great and painful effort, wrapped as tightly as he was.

"Left, not too far from your head. It's hard to tell in this feeble excuse for light, but I think there's a scrap of metal over there."

"Why didn't you bring this up until now?"

"I didn't *see* the thing until now, damn you. Do you want to argue, or get out of here?"

"I'm bound the same as you. Everything's gone numb, I can't feel my toes."

"You're closer than I am. It has to be you."

"I told you—"

"Think about the pretty Newlie, Finn. That should warm you up. It would certainly do it for me."

Finn refused to be annoyed. There was no use wanting to batter someone if you were both paralyzed.

He was sure he couldn't make it. He could feel everything from his head to his waist, but that didn't seem to help. One needed hands and feet. Limbs separated Man from the lower forms of life. No wonder larva never did a thing.

"Undulate," Sabatino suggested. "Sort of scoot, you know? Push and then pull, push and then—"

"Shut up," Finn said. "I can undulate without your help." And he did exactly that. Pushed with his shoulders, then pulled, raising his belly off the ground, dragging his useless limbs behind. How long could one cut off circulation without ill effect? The word *gangrene* came to mind.

"A bit more, Finn."

"Just be quiet. I'm over here and you're not."

"Well, *do* excuse me."

"I'm not even sure what you saw is metal at all. The closer I get, the worse this corner smells."

"I'm sure it's metal, Finn."

"It damn well better be. It better not be what I think it might be."

Sabatino chuckled to himself. "Wouldn't that be a cruel jest? A fine tale to spin at **TAVERN** some time."

"If you were there to tell it, you mean."

"Do get on with it, Finn."

Finn muttered to himself, cursing every Nucci from the present to the past.

Fits and Mitts, what a frightening thought . . . dozens, generations of Nuccis I've never heard about . . . !

"I've got it," Finn said. "I'm happy to admit that you're right. It's a scrap of iron as broad as my hand. Rusty, but it still has an edge. There's some other pieces here, copper and some tin. But this should do quite well."

"Excellent. Undulate over here, Finn. Let's do get out of here."

"I don't care for that word. Try not to use it again."

"Well, *scamper* won't do, and it's surely not *scurry*, not at that pace. Don't linger, Finn. I shall think of something on the way . . ."

Thirty-Nine . . .

IF HE GOT OUT OF THIS, WHICH SEEMED UNLIKELY at best, Finn would count it as the third, or even the second, most humiliating moment of his life. Scooting across the grimy floor, putting undulation out of mind, he managed, after a torturous, never-ending time, after forever had passed him by, to reach Sabatino against the far wall. With the scrap of rusty iron in his teeth, he moved quite close to the fellow's rather ponderous rear.

"If you cut me, Finn, I'll hold you accountable for it," Sabatino said. "On my oath I will."

"If I cut you," Finn told him, "if your blood comes spurting like a fountain in the square, you'll never feel a thing. Your hands are a most unsightly shade of blue."

Sabatino went silent after that. The cord the old man had used was older than Finn, but there was plenty of it. Finn's jaw was weary. Sweat poured down his brow to sting his eyes. He wanted to rest, but wasn't sure he could raise the scrap of iron again.

"I think you'd best hurry," Sabatino said. "I don't feel we have a lot of time."

"A keen observation. I wish I'd thought of that."

"I'd remind you of the lovely Letitia, how she may, at this very moment, be in dire straits. I would, but I'm sure you'd take offense, you nearly always do—"

"Get up."

"What?"

"Move your arms, roll about. *Undulate*, you ungrateful lout, your hands are free."

"Oh, my good friend, I am in your debt. I shall never forget this most charitable act."

"Yes, you will. Almost at once. Now get about it, damn you, before some crazed relation comes along. Your hands and your legs are going to hurt. Swallow the pain and get me out of here."

Sabatino sat up and groaned, gritted his teeth as the blood rushed back into his limbs. He flexed his fingers, pounded his fists, then quickly tore the ropes from his feet.

He turned, then, and looked down at Finn. "I want you to never forget I could easily leave you here. I'm sure that thought has crossed your mind."

"Never once," Finn said, meeting Sabatino's eyes. "You are a scoundrel, a liar and a rogue. One of the most disgusting men I've ever known. Still, I never imagined you a coward, a man who'd leave his comrade, his brother in arms behind."

Sabatino looked pained. "We are not comrades, Finn. Please don't use such a word referring to you and me. I despised you on sight. Nothing has happened to change my mind since."

"Until this is over, we're brothers in arms. Hate, loathing and disgust have little to do with the matter till we're out of here."

"I'm thinking about it."

"Don't. Do it now. Before some family trait comes to mind . . ."

ᑽ

Grandfather Nucci had not left their swords where they might be easily found. For weapons, Finn and Sabatino ripped planks of wood off the floor as quietly as they could. Sabatino had a suggestion that Finn felt was sound. Removing sheets of tin from the wall, they fashioned hats that would cover their heads, leaving only slits for the eyes. These devices were ugly and crude, not at all like the helmets of old, but they would have to suffice.

"If it worked for Grandfather, it will surely work for us," Sabatino said, with less assurance than Finn felt himself.

Before they left the room, he glanced at the plated walls again. There was something there he hadn't noticed from the floor. Crudely scratched upon each scrap were symbols that gave Finn a chill. Runes, spells, clear signs of sorcery, and none of it, Finn was dead sure, close to benign.

Grandfather Nucci had built this protective metal wall—and someone, the old man or someone else, had added some very dark magic as well.

He turned and waited as Sabatino opened the door a crack, then waved Finn to follow behind.

At once, Finn breathed a grateful sigh. He could still feel the awful tug of the machine, hear the faint, ever-present howl, but the makeshift helmet offered welcome relief. Without it, he knew that deadly thing would strip him of his senses, of his will.

He wished, now, that he had taken time to fashion one for Letitia herself. Whatever effects the emanations had upon the mind, they seemed to vanish when one was out of range, or wore some protective device.

Letitia is different, though . . . that horror has a strange hold upon her, some unwholesome sway . . . when I find her, she may be lost, nothing but a shell . . .

Finn swept the frightful thought from his mind. It wouldn't be so—she'd be his Letitia, she'd be just the same.

While each of the two had stubby candles scavenged from the grandfather's room, their path was treacherous and dim. Ceilings sagged abruptly, giving little time to duck. Floors tilted from one dizzy angle to the next, with scarcely any warning at all.

Finn tried not to think about Julia. He'd heard the terrible, sickening sound when the crazed old man had hurled her at the wall. Finn had built Julia with all his heart and skill, lovingly crafted every part. She was solidly made, but not meant for blows like that.

He couldn't, wouldn't, let himself dream that she'd survived. Julia was his glory, the height of his art, a thorn in his side, and he felt a great emptiness now that she was gone. All his thoughts were on Letitia now, for Letitia was not a machine. Letitia, he was certain, could still be alive.

"Watch yourself," Sabatino said, gripping Finn's arm, holding him back. "Where do you think you're going now, man?"

Finn shook himself free of his thoughts, blinked, and found himself staring at a wall.

"Sorry. I was off somewhere."

Sabatino's grip tightened. "You have judged me right, Finn. I have no affection for you. I would have left you bound back there, but I'd like to get out of here with all the same parts I brought in. You were fool enough to let me go. I'm smart enough to let you live. Get your mind off the Newlie. She's lost for good. Now you can watch over me."

Finn couldn't see the fellow's features behind his tin mask, but he could read Sabatino's eyes.

"Brothers in arms, you know. Your words, I believe."

"And don't mention her again. I won't put up with that."

Sabatino turned away, holding his candle high, and ducked into a passage at his right.

"I don't suppose you have any idea where we are," Finn asked. "This is your house, you know, not mine."

"I told you before. I played in these corridors when I was a lad. I don't remember where. My guess is we're just above the main floor. I believe the library is right under here. Was, I mean. The bugs ate the books long ago."

Finn stopped. "Then, if we tried to break through the floor—right here, we might be out of this place."

"And again we might not. We might be on the bloody roof, or back in Grandfather's hidey hole."

"I don't think so. I've tried to keep a sort of map in my head."

Sabatino laughed. "Have you now? A lizard maker who conjures up maps on the side."

"I did not mean my words as a jest."

"No, you never do. Fools are more certain of themselves than their betters, I've always found it true."

"And that *better*, that would be you . . ."

"A delightful thought occurs. Since Father has clearly broken his command to treat you well, I'm no longer bound to cancel our duel. Now I *know* we'll get out of here. I feel much better, Finn. The very thought of running you through—"

Sabatino's smile fell away. He stared at Finn as the lizard maker raised his plank of wood, and brought it down in a swift and deadly arc.

Sabatino cried out, threw up his arms in defense. Finn's blow missed him by an inch, but struck home soundly on the old man's skull.

The grandfather roared like a beast in pain, staggered back and slammed into a wall. Dust and rotten wood drifted in a veil from overhead. Sabatino turned quickly, pounding the fellow with his club. *Families*, Finn considered, don't always get along.

The old man shrieked, a horrid, mindless sound. Sabatino wouldn't stop. Finn was uncertain what to do. It wasn't right to kill one's kin, yet the grandfather would surely slay Sabatino if given half a chance.

Before Finn could make up his mind, the old man, seemingly helpless at his grandson's feet, reached out a bony arm and yanked Sabatino to the floor.

Sabatino cried out in surprise, dropped his club and clawed at the ground. Finn saw cold, unspeakable horror in the younger man's eyes. He knew Sabatino feared this ancient, mad relation, but he'd never seen, never even imagined, the kind of terror he witnessed now. Sabatino's face was frozen in a rictus of dread, lost, caught in hopeless desperation. His eyes had nearly disappeared, with only the whites revealed, and his face was the pallor of the dead.

The old man had taken so many brutal blows to the head, Finn couldn't bear to strike him there again. Instead, he kicked him soundly in the ribs. Clearly, this was the thing to do, for the savage let his grandson go, and whimpered off into the darkness again.

Sabatino struggled to his feet, brushed off his vest and patted a welt on his cheek.

"I must thank you for that, Finn. I had him under control, but your help enabled me to release him without further harm. He's quite insane, but one hates to kill one's blood."

"That's very thoughtful of you," Finn said.

"Besides, it's said to be bad luck. Or at least I think it is. Let me get my bearings again. We were headed that way, I feel."

"No, just the opposite, as a fact."

"Of course. Navigation is one of your skills, I believe.

I'm sorry, but you're quite wrong again. It's this way. I think that's why we were attacked at that precise moment, at that very point. Grandfather knows this place like the back of his festered hand. He knew we were close to finding our way."

Finn held his ground. "You're wrong. I'm quite sure of that. The emanations are strong here. My hat isn't doing much good."

Sabatino smiled with total disdain. "As it happens, sir, we are over the kitchen right now. I can smell dinner on the stove. Do stand back if you will."

"No, now don't do that . . ."

Almost before he could get the words out, Sabatino brought his boot down hard upon the floor. On the third or fourth kick, the wood began to splinter.

"You see," Sabatino said, "we're nearly out of here."

"I don't think so, something's wrong here—"

On the fifth kick, the floor gave way . . .

Sabatino stumbled back, nearly knocking Finn down. A bright burst of energy seared Finn's eyes, tugged at his flesh, tore at his bones. Sabatino cried out, but Finn couldn't hear. The Great Horror shrieked, thundered and roared, clattered and howled, twisted and tangled in tortured convolutions, as if it might rip itself apart. . . .

. . . and, once more, Finn was frightfully aware of the foul, obscure distortions, the sluggish bits of darkness that wound their fearsome way through the vile crusted entrails of Calabus' hellish machine. Even this close, he could not tell what those shapeless forms might be. And, he was more than thankful he could not.

He and Julia had guessed that Calabus' strange device was, indeed, prodding, pushing, thrusting itself blindly through the Nucci mansion as it grew.

And where might it go after that, he wondered. What might it want to do . . . ?

Forty . . .

FINN COULD ONLY VAGUELY RECALL THE STRUGGLE
to escape the thing's grasp. Crawling, gasping for breath,
the terrible emanations howled in his head. Sabatino had
bragged that he was scarcely bothered by the awful emis-
sions from below. Still, it was Finn who dragged the fellow
free, up the dizzy floors, down the crooked halls, until they
were far enough away.

Sabatino muttered and thrashed about. Finn would have
bound him up again if he'd had a piece of rope. Instead, he
cursed Sabatino every step of the way, even the step that
found another dead end, one exactly like the rest.

Finn stopped and sank wearily to the ground. Sabatino
slept on. Now and then, bubbles appeared at the corners of
his mouth. Finn looked away in disgust. Maybe he could
leave the lout here. Go back and find Letitia, gather up poor
Julia's parts. Come back and find Sabatino again. He wasn't
likely going anywhere, not for some time.

"If I had another piece of rope," Finn said to himself,
"one like the one that I don't have now, I could tie one end
right here, and find my way back. All right, no rope. I'll

have to just—hah, indeed!" Patting desperately at his pockets, he found the small coil of silver wire he'd bought at market. He could use a rope of any sort, but wire, to a craftsman, was a comforting thing to have around.

His legs were shaky. He laid his hands flat against the wall to pull himself erect. Sabatino's candle was gone, but Finn still had a stub. Not much of a light, but better than groping in the dark. Better than—

Finn stopped. A small patch of brightness suddenly appeared. Or maybe it had been there all along, and he simply hadn't seen it from the floor. It was only the size of a half-penny coin, but it was bright, brighter than anything he'd seen in this miserable maze.

"Bright," Finn said aloud, his heart fairly pounding in his chest, "bright as it can be. Snails and Whales, it's bright as day itself, we've been in here all night, though it doesn't seem that way at all!"

"Whu-huhsa?"

"It's daylight," Finn laughed. "Daylight, sunlight, I'd forgotten what a marvelous thing it is!"

Sabatino opened his eyes to that. "I told you I'd get us out of this, but you had no faith, you'd given up hope, you wouldn't listen to your comrade in arms. You were too busy thinking about yourself . . ."

Finn didn't hear him at all. He was pounding on the wall, ripping boards free, letting the harsh, beautiful light into the gloomy room. He could see clouds now, white and pure and clean, see the sunlight blazing on the earth, shining on the sea.

"I'll help in a moment," Sabatino said. "I seem to have bruised myself a bit. Damn me, Finn, I don't recall this place at all, what are we doing here?"

Finn had a proper hole now, big enough to stick his shoulders through. He was two stories up, maybe three.

There was no way to tell in a house such as this, where height had no meaning at all.

He could see one edge of the town, a piece of the winding road. And, directly below, dead trees and yellow weeds.

Now, he could really use that rope, the one he didn't have for Sabatino, the one he meant to use to find his way. Still, they were out, they were free, he could get proper lamps and provisions, go back in for Letitia Louise. And anyone who tried to stop him, anything that got in his way—

Something splintered, and he suddenly felt the wall give way beneath him. Finn grabbed for a hold, tried desperately to stop. Then he was gone, down and on his way without a rope of any kind . . .

Forty-One . . .

She dreamed about the sea. It was not a sea she'd ever seen, not the sea they'd crossed, the sea that had brought them to this strange and deadly land. This was a sea that had likely never been, the kind that lives in dreams.

The sea was jeweled, a thousand shades of green, a million shades of blue. Sapphires, emeralds and lapis lazuli had melted when the earth was very young, and formed this tranquil deep so she could share its beauty now.

How could she have such a dream? She had never ventured anywhere at all. She had never heard a tale of such a place, or seen such an image anywhere. Yet, it was there, as real as it could be . . .

. . . And, with a surety, the sudden awareness that only a dream can bring, she knew in that instant that she'd sailed upon this sea, knew the fierce, exotic creatures that lived upon its shores, knew the colors, knew the tastes, knew the scents of its streets, of its alleys, of the bright marketplace.

One thing more she knew, and this the most startling of all: *she had been there for certain, but not in the form she was now. For what she was now, she had never been before . . .*

This wonder, this marvel, opened a thousand secret doors. Everything she'd done, everything she'd been, every life she'd lived, struck her at once and filled her head with visions she could scarcely comprehend.

She could have shouted, laughed aloud at these countless images of joy, sorrow, love and hate and fear, these illusions of the past. She could, for certain, if only she could find herself now, if only she was somewhere, someone, anyone at all . . .

Forty-Two . . .

"I'VE HAD A THOUSAND CHANCES TO RUN YOU through, to pierce that arrogant smile, to stop that vain, insolent speech with a slash to the throat, to never, ever abide that cocky, condescending sneer. And I will, I swear, you prideful lout, if ever I walk again . . ."

Sabatino plucked a burr from his lavender hat.

"You may think what you wish, Finn, I'm certain that you will, but I did not *push* you, damn it, you fell."

"That's patently ridiculous. I never fall. I have never fallen, even as a child."

"Oh, please."

"You're the consummate liar here, I would never try to best you on that. No, none could hope to ever—Where are we, do you have the faintest idea?"

"Near the back, not twenty paces from the kitchen door. That was a fine leap you made, sir. Most impressive for your very first fall."

Finn didn't answer. Biting his lips until they bled, he tried to raise himself to see through the thicket of brambles, weeds and twisted trees. Pain ripped along his leg like a blade, and he sank back to the ground.

"I can't bend to take a look. Can you tell if it's broken, is there blood, is a bone showing through?"

Sabatino looked appalled. "How would I have any knowledge such as that? I cannot see through your trousers, sir."

"No, of course not. Would you mind just tearing them a bit and take a look?"

"You go too far, Finn. I have never handled a man's leg, and I'm not starting now."

Finn groaned, more in anger than in pain.

"I'm having a fever and a chill. I will not be conscious soon. When I'm not, would you consider it then? I wouldn't know, you see, and perhaps it would give you less offense."

"I don't see how that would help *me*. I'd be aware of your, ah—limb, and when you awoke, you'd be aware of it too. No, there's no solution there."

"Rocks and Socks, you pompous fool," Finn shouted, "I'm going to lie here and die if you don't get off your—"

Finn's words were lost as a loud explosion shook the very air. A limb snapped, falling inches from Sabatino's head. A pall of dirty smoke drifted from the house.

"Damnation," Sabatino said, shaking his fist, "stop that at once! I could have been severely injured. What's the matter with you up there!"

"Who is it?" Finn asked, "Squeen William?"

"Of course it's not Squeen. That fool would have no idea how to operate your basic firing arm, much less an exquisite piece like the Ponce-Klieterhaus 39. It's Father, who else?"

Sabatino paused, squinting thoughtfully at the house.

"Look, we're brothers in arms, and I will not desert you, Finn, I promise you that. However, it might be wise, from a tactical point, for me to move well away from here. He seems to have our range. Keep low, and I'll try to draw his fire . . ."

"What, do you think I'm feeble-minded?" Finn laughed, an action that hurt clear down to his toes. "You stay *here*, Sabatino, I'm not falling for that."

"You're taking this all the wrong way."

"Right. And you didn't push me, I fell."

"I've come to think of you as an actual brother more than a comrade in arms."

"Please, I can't stand to throw up, not now . . ."

The second shot hit another tree. The heavy iron ball whined off to the south, or possibly the west.

"Father, don't do that again." Sabatino nearly stood up this time. "Reloads for that weapon are quite hard to find."

"Sabatino," Calabus called out, "get yourself off my property. You don't live here anymore."

"What are you talking about? I'm your son, Father. How can you speak to me like that?"

"I had a son once, I don't anymore."

"We need to talk about this. It's clear there's been a misunderstanding here. We've had our differences, Father, but we're family. There's no stronger tie than that. I suppose some of what's happened is my fault, but most of it's yours. Nevertheless, I'm willing to forget and start anew."

"Start a new what?"

"You ignorant old bastard, I'm giving you a chance to make this right. I don't intend to sit here all day!"

"Why not?"

Sabatino frowned, giving thought to that. Finn shook his head. He couldn't think of anything to say.

"I have a casualty here. He's gravely injured, I fear. He's going to need help or he'll perish right away . . ."

As if in answer, Calabus loosed a high, piercing laugh,

more like a cackle, more like a shriek, not like a laugh you might hear every day.

Sabatino took a deep breath. He seemed to sag, he seemed to wilt, seemed to go into decline. Finn felt he might simply fade before his eyes.

"Father is over the hill. There's nothing else for it."

"No offense, but he's been over the hill for some time."

"I know. But this is worse than that."

Sabatino crawled to the edge of the brush and risked a look.

"This man is hurt, Father. Just let me come in there and get a glass of wine, perhaps a damp cloth of some kind."

"It's that lizard fellow we're talking about."

"Yes it is, Father. It's Master Finn. You remember him."

"He's hurt real bad?"

"Extremely badly, Father. It's his leg."

"One leg, you mean. Not two."

"No, just one."

"Tell him to limp the hell out of here, then. I'd just as soon shoot him too."

Sabatino turned to Finn. "I'm doing my best. It's impossible to reason with the man."

"I can see that."

"Father—"

"That's no way for a son to do, boy. Locking me up like that. That hurt a lot. You've been breaking my heart since your mother passed on. I wish she'd stayed around to suffer, see what I had to go through."

"You locked *me* up, Father, don't forget that."

"Damn you, boy, you did it first. Whoever does it first, that's the one started it all, you ought to know that."

"Grandfather's gone berserk again," Sabatino said quietly, "He's worse than he's ever been before. I think he might have the Newlie girl. You've got to destroy that device of yours, Father. It's bulging all over the place, it's getting out of hand."

Calabus was silent for a while. "He's got Miss Letitia, you think?"

"I think he likely does."

"That's what people get for playing in the walls. I told you that when you were six. Tell that lizard fellow, tell him if she's still all right, I'll go and get her out. If I do, though, he's got to give her to me."

"Like hell I will!"

Finn tried to get up. Pain pushed him back down.

"Stay out of this," Sabatino said. "You think you're going to *reason* with him now?"

"Just help me up. Get me a stick, anything you can find . . ."

"He'll agree to that if he has to, Father," Sabatino called out. "He loves the lady, but he'll give her up to save her life."

"I want that lizard, too."

"He'll go for that."

Finn opened his mouth to protest, but Sabatino shook his head.

"Can I come in now? I'd like to get that wine and a cloth of some kind. Tell Squeen to find something clean—"

The shot clipped the plume off Sabatino's hat. Sabatino hit the ground. Lilac feathers filled the air.

"Damn you, boy," Calabus shouted, "you think I'm deaf and blind? I know your intentions, I've got 'em right here!"

Calabus raised a tangle of paper and shook it in the air, endless loops and snarls, ravels and curls, whorls and kinks and coils. Finn swallowed his pain and stretched his neck to see. There, on the porch, was a man in a rage, a man with a musket, a man with severe disorders of the mind.

"It's all right here, you damn fools! The works! *Every-*

thing! What's going to happen, everything that has! You can't trifle with me, I can *read* this stuff now!"

Calabus crowed again and spread his arms wide, tossing paper to the wind. "Don't try an' put something over on me. I know what you're up to before you know yoursel—"

The house began to shake, began to roll, began to twitch, began to rock, began to quake. To the left and to the right, to the bottom and the top, wood began to squeal, began to creak, squeak and groan.

Finn saw it, then, felt it in his belly, felt it in his toes. A window cracked, timber snapped, and dust began to fall. A spot near the roof began to swell. It bulged, oozed, festered like a boil, like a horrid open sore. A foul and awful corruption throbbing with dark bits of matter that tumbled through its grime-encrusted coils.

Finn couldn't breathe, couldn't draw a breath.

"It needs more room," Sabatino said, "the damned thing's coming outside . . ."

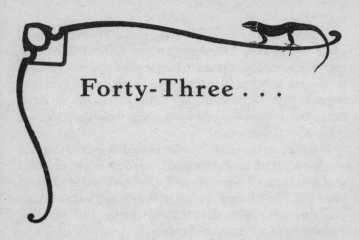

Forty-Three . . .

SHE HAD NEVER FELT SO WONDERFUL AND WARM, so full of energy and life. She knew, as she had never known before, that this was what life was really like, that she'd only thought she was truly alive before . . .

Then, she'd been only one, only a single lost and lonely soul, a creature looking at the world through a single, lonely pair of eyes. Now, she was everywhere there was, everywhere at once, everywhere she'd ever be . . .

She laughed, laughter she couldn't hear. She could almost remember now, remember the long, long before; before she'd worn the form she wore now. She could almost see herself then, see beyond the blur, beyond the veil before her eyes. And something within her said, *No, don't look before, don't look back, you don't want to see that now . . .*

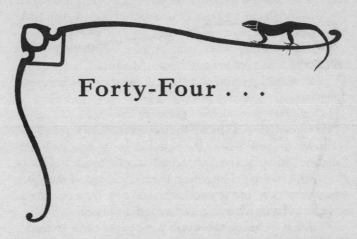

Forty-Four . . .

IT ONLY HURT FOR AN INSTANT. THEN EVERYTHING
was gone and it didn't hurt at all. When he opened his eyes,
the pain was still there and he wasn't where he'd been.

"Ah, you are with us, I am happy to see. You are feeling
fine again?"

Finn scowled up at Sabatino through the sharp and
screaming pain. "No, I am not feeling fine. Why did you
pick me up, you damn fool, don't you know any better than
that? You don't pick up a man who's broken several bones,
you could kill him like that."

"I take offense," Sabatino said. "From a brother in arms,
I expected more gratitude than this."

"Oh, well, now I understand."

"I felt we should distance ourselves from the house. I
didn't think it was safe to leave you there."

"You did this for me?"

"Well, no, that's not quite true. You see how close
we are? You can see right through me, Finn. When your
leg feels better, you and I together, we'll retrieve the
house. Which is rightfully mine, of course. Father's in no

condition to make decisions of any sort. And, of course, you'll want to try and get Letitia out. I feel there's little hope, but of course you must try."

"I think I worry when you *don't* lie," Finn said. "And don't say I won't get her out, because I will."

"You should try and stand now," Sabatino said, leaning down to help, "get used to moving a bit."

"Don't come any closer—get away from me . . ."

He turned, then, as he felt the tremor moving through the earth, felt the rumble, felt the beat, like some gigantic heart. Sabatino had carried him a hundred paces or more, but it was clearly not enough. The power, the terrible tug of the thing was weaker here, but it was there. And how far would it go, what would it do when it grew beyond the house?

Finn felt a chill as the words of the seer came to mind. There was more to that dark device than a madman's dream. Calabus' father had created the thing, but there was magic there as well, a spell of such power that it struck out at anyone who threatened the machine.

And what has it done to you, Letitia? Has it stolen your soul, has it taken your mind? If I find you, my dear, what then will you be . . . ?

"Finn, look. Over there."

Finn started, then followed Sabatino's eyes. Someone was coming down the road. Not just someone, more like everyone—everyone who lived in that foul, odorous, unfriendly village was apparently on the march, coming their way.

"Damn them all," Sabatino muttered, "just what I need, a bunch of interfering fools. They've got no right coming here."

"Maybe they want to help," Finn said. "You could use a little right now."

"Help? That herd of idiots?" Sabatino laughed, or possibly sneered. "They're more pitifully inept than you are, Finn. And you're scarcely any use at all."

Sabatino muttered beneath his breath. Clenched his fists and ground his teeth. He didn't like anyone at all, and surely didn't like them more than one at a time.

It was indeed, Finn thought, a curious caravan. Most of the folk were on foot, but in their wake were several carts, carts with outlandish high wooden wheels. Pulling the carts were teams of Bullies with ropes about their chests, tugging their burdens in step.

Whoever the people in the carts might be, they were far more comfortable than the struggling teams. Each wagon was covered with a canopy shade held aloft by wooden poles. There might, Finn thought, be drink and fresh cakes inside.

He felt the carts looked familiar, felt, with a touch of apprehension, he had seen them before, and of a sudden, knew exactly where. Just such a cart had delivered Sabatino's father in a cage to Market Square.

"Who are they?" Finn asked, for Sabatino was scowling at the caravan as well. "What are they doing here?"

"What they always do," Sabatino said. "Mind other people's business, stick their big noses in everyone's affairs, snoop around where they aren't welcome, turn up where they don't belong."

"Oh, I see," Finn said.

"And that one, the one with the red and purple top and the vile yellow wheels; that is my dear, dear uncle, the foul and loathsome Nicoretti himself."

"Him? Coming here? Bees and Trees, you don't see a bunch of Bowsers with him, do you?"

Sabatino showed a curious eye. "Now where did you hear about them?"

"I don't know, in town somewhere, I really don't recall."

He hadn't shared these adventures, and didn't intend to start now.

"Huuuh . . ." Sabatino said, in a tone that said he didn't accept this explanation at all.

The horde on foot, a hundred, maybe more, stopped just short of the line of dead grass beyond Sabatino and Finn. They stood in such a neat and even line that Finn thought there might have been a sign, a fence, a stripe painted boldly on the ground. Everyone knew where to stand, exactly how far from the house they ought to be.

No one smiled, everybody scowled. Now and then they muttered, whispered, mumbled among themselves.

"These people don't look content," Finn said. "Are we in danger here?"

"Not yet, but you never can tell."

As if in answer, someone began to throw fruit. A very old peach landed close to Sabatino, splattering his boots. A pear and a melon after that, but both fell rather short.

Sabatino's hand went instinctively to his belt where his weapon ought to be, if his mad grandfather hadn't taken it away.

"Be on your guard, Master Finn, there could be trouble on the way."

"Have you noticed? I'm on the ground here, I can't stand up."

Sabatino didn't answer. All at once, the crowd began to part. From somewhere farther back, brilliant red plumes began to bob up and down. From Finn's rather limited view it seemed a curious sight, as if a flock of very tall birds were engaging in a dance, or possibly a fight.

This illusion vanished when the first feathered figure appeared. They were men, not birds, no more or less shabby, odorous and worn, than their peers in the crowd, except for the bright scarlet crests upon their heads.

"Birds and Turds," Finn said, taken aback by the sight, "how many churches do you *have* in this town?"

"Don't be a fool," Sabatino said, without a glance at Finn. "It's not a church at all, it's the Crimson Lancers Volunteers."

"I don't see a lance anywhere."

"They're not allowed to carry arms. We won't put up with that."

Someone in the mob threw a squash that was well beyond its time. Someone threw a tomato that struck Sabatino on the knee.

"All right, we'll have none a' that. Any more tossing of produce, I'll shackle everyone here!"

A stout fellow with heavy brows and a crooked nose stepped out of the crowd. Finn couldn't place him at once, then saw it was the fellow at TAVERN who'd refused to let him in.

"Sorry for the intrusion, Master Sabatino," he said with a scornful look at Finn. "There's trouble up here it seems, and we got to step in."

"There is no trouble here, *Constable* Bob," Sabatino said with particular disdain. "If there was, it is none of your concern. The Nuccis do not require your services at all."

"With all respect, sir, I feel that you do. Your residence appears to be causing unrest. Some type of discharge, some sorta seep, some kind of ooze is coming from your place. Something, it seems, that clouds men's minds. Folks are reporting diarrhea and unholy thoughts. One lady said a demon intruded on her parts."

"Rubbish, folderol," Sabatino said. "We're having trouble with the plumbing, it's nothing more than that."

The Constable glared at Finn.

"What happened to him?"

"I believe he's injured a leg."

"That's another thing, sir, and I might as well say it right out. We know you've had persons—eating and sleeping, staying overnight in your house . . ."

Constable Bob rubbed his chin, having difficulty getting the words out. "That's not our way, I don't have to tell you that. Whatever else is going on here, it's causing unrest. That said, sir, I'm going to have to take a look at that house."

"Please do." Sabatino looked amused. "Have a look around."

The Constable frowned. He had a most suspicious nature and didn't trust people who smiled.

"And you," he said to Finn, "don't be hanging 'round **TAVERN** anymore, I'm not about to let you in."

"You made that clear," Finn said.

"Good. Nothing personal. We don't cater to perverts or strangers of any kind. Bursoni! Thomas! I want a squad over to the house. Move it right now! Ricko, get those louts in line!"

The Constable stalked off. Men of the Crimson Lancers Volunteers jogged into groups of three, seven and nine. Some, Finn noted, ran into one another. Others hooted and rapidly blinked their eyes.

"The volunteers . . ." Finn began.

"Don't start, Finn. The Lancers come from all denominations. We're not bigots here."

"There's that."

"Damn those bleeding meddlers, they can't blame this fiasco on me. They'll *think* diarrhea, if they run into Grandfather in there!"

And, as if the house had overheard, in some uncanny manner listened in, a new tremor shivered through the ground, quivered in dread oscillation through the very air . . .

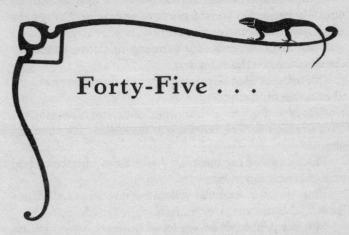

Forty-Five . . .

THE CROWD BEGAN TO MOAN IN COMMON FEAR. A young woman screamed, an old man dropped to the ground. Finn could feel the fearsome thing himself, feel the sickly emanations as a chill in his belly and a trembling in his head.

"I've got to get in there," he said, "I can't just lie here, I've got to get her out!"

"Well, crawl right in, Master Finn," Sabatino said with an unwholesome grin. "By all means, don't let us hold you back. Rescue the maiden, we'll cheer you on from here . . ."

Then, of a sudden, Sabatino's smile fell, replaced by a dark malicious glare.

"This day is yet to do its worst, I see. By damn, he's got gall coming here."

Finn looked past Sabatino to see Nicoretti stalking through the crowd. He clutched a black bag in one hand, and two stubby Bowsers followed at his heels.

The Bowsers stopped some distance away, a great relief to Finn, as he suspected he'd seen the pair before. Mean-eyes and Pugnose, he was nearly sure.

"Ah, I see my services are sorely needed here," Nicoretti said, dropping his bony frame to the ground. "What the devil have you done to yourself now, boy? A pleasure to see you as well, Nephew. Or possibly not," he added, as Sabatino turned the other way.

"Bradley, Willie! Give us some cover over here. Let's get this lad out of the sun!"

"No, you don't have to do that," Finn said, watching the Bowsers scamper off, snapping at the crowd. "I'm fine as I am."

"Don't tell me my business, I won't stand for that. Hold still, this may hurt a bit . . ."

Finn loosed a frightful yell as Nicoretti yanked off his boot.

"I'll bet you don't *have* a lot of business, treating your patients like that."

"Hush, lad. All you've got is a sprain. I'm going to wrap it, give you a couple of splints. Stay off that foot awhile, you'll be as good as new. Don't give me that look, it won't do you any good. That girlie's still in there, right? Forget it. You're not walking on that, not for some time. Wouldn't do you any good if you could. Whoever's in that fearsome place, they're not coming out. Now, how's that feel, too tight or what?"

Finn stared at the man, backing away from his touch.

"You don't know what you're talking about. Letitia's all right, and I'm getting her out of there."

"You think so, do you?" Nicoretti gave a sly, secretive glance at Sabatino to see if he was far enough away.

"If you think you can," he said, leaning close to Finn, "then you know what's in there, don't you? What foul secret the Nuccis are hiding from us all. Perhaps you'd like to share that with me. I've tried to be open with you, lad, I think you know that."

"Open with me? Should I laugh, or would that be impolite?"

"I can help you, boy. But you have to help me."

"And you can—what?" Finn asked, hurting all over, now, from his fall. Hurting everywhere, not solely in the foot.

"Can you get Letitia out? Can you help me do that? Oh, but you say she's dead, so that's out. I guess I don't need you at all, Doctor. Thanks for the lovely splint."

Nicoretti's face went dark. "Damn you, boy, I said you'd play the fool, and you haven't proved me wrong. I can tell you things. Things you don't know."

"Like what?"

"Like the crazed old man in there. I'll tell you who he is. He's Calabus' father." Nicoretti grinned. "What do you think of that?"

"I know who he is. What else have you got?"

Nicoretti looked grim. He glanced at Sabatino, who was farther off now, watching Constable Bob attempt to line his troops in a row.

"All right, pay attention, boy," Nicoretti said with a sigh. "You know I'm Sabatino's uncle. The reason I am is because my sister, Ingretta, married Calabus. She was Sabatino's mother, rest her soul."

"I guessed she wasn't alive, whoever she turned out to be."

Nicoretti hesitated. "No, she is not. My sister and I came to Makasar when we were young, after our parents died. We were raised by a very distant aunt. Ingretta and I were both Calabus' friends at the time, possibly the only friends he had, for the old man would seldom let him out of his sight.

"His father had come to this country years before after he'd amassed a great wealth somewhere. Often, when he was away on some venture, Calabus would let us in the house. It was, even then, a frightening place to be.

"Later, when Calabus and Ingretta announced they would wed, his father went into a rage and forbade him to see her again. The two were much in love, though, and they ran off together anyway.

"All of us paid the price for that. When the couple returned, the old man took them in. But not from the goodness of his heart. He told my sister she could never leave the house, that she would never see me, her brother, again."

Nicoretti hesitated. "That was his punishment for disobedience. He was, even then, a crazed and bitter old man. No matter how either of us pleaded, Ingretta and I never saw each other after that. Even when she died giving birth to Sabatino, I was not allowed to bid her soul farewell. I was a Hatter, you see, and not of my sister's new 'faith,' though the old man never entered his own church in his life.

"Calabus, I regret to say, was ever weak at heart. His father's hatred, his terrible will, set Calabus against me in the end. And thus it remains today."

Finn shook his head. "It's a sorrowful tale. That one man could cause such misery in his life. I fully understand why you've loathed the Nuccis so long. You have greatly suffered at their hands."

"Anyone who knows them suffers at their hands. You're aware of that as well."

Indeed, Finn thought, and I'll suffer yet until Letitia's out of there. He looked past Nicoretti at the crowd. They were silent now, for no new tremors had come from the house. As any crowd will do, if there's little of a tragic nature to behold, they soon become restless and bored.

There was no sign of the Crimson Lancers Volunteers, and Finn wondered if they'd marched in disorder on the house. If they had . . .

Bracing himself on two hands and a leg, he tried to pull

himself up. He made it for a moment, cold sweat beading on his brow, then sharp pain drove him down again.

"I told you," Nicoretti said. "No one listens to their doctor, they know it all, they do."

"You could help me up, *Doctor,* I'd listen to that."

"Help you cause greater damage to your leg? Not on your life, son. I won't betray my craft."

Finn glared at the man, drew a breath for another try.

"One thing I want to know. You and the Foxers. You're together on this. I knew it from the time you—*saved* me from them, but I don't know why. I'm not buying that they just happen to hate the Nuccis too."

"Ridiculous. I wouldn't get near one of the brutes."

"Because they're Newlies?"

"Because I don't like 'em, is all."

"You don't mind Bowsers."

"I'll hire a Bullie to pull a cart, but I'm not taking him to lunch."

"I'm not as far from home as I thought."

"What's that supposed to mean?"

"Just what it—"

A sudden great vibration shook the ground again, stronger, more awesome than before. Nicoretti fell. The crowd began to shriek, and half of them toppled to the ground.

"Help me, damn you," Finn said. "Get me on my feet!"

"I'm down here myself, boy, didn't you notice that?"

"Sabatino, give me a hand—"

Finn glanced behind him, but the man wasn't there. The tin hats they'd worn were gone—Sabatino had taken Finn's too.

"He knows you're crippled up good," Nicoretti grinned. "He's gone in to get that Newlie for himself."

"No. He's gone for his father. And not to get him out, I'll wager."

Finn struggled to stand, fell twice, then again. The fourth time worked, but the world kept whirling around.

"You won't make it," Nicoretti said.

"Wait out here and see."

"I was truthful to you, lad. You didn't give me my due."

Finn looked at him. "That's what you're asking? I can't tell you what's in there. I couldn't if I tried."

"Damn lie," Nicoretti said, "you could if you weren't a cheat."

"It's not a lie, Doctor, it's just the awful truth is what it is."

He turned and hobbled feebly toward the house, dragging one leg, cursing Sabatino with every breath. On the way he passed the Bowsers, Pugnose and Mean-eyes, dragging a colorful awning in their wake. They growled at Finn, and Finn growled back . . .

Forty-Six . . .

FINN'S RETURN TO THE HOUSE, TO THE HOWL AND the clamor and the din, to the shriek and the thunder in his head, was the longest journey of his life. Nicoretti's splint, a clever and torturous device, pricked, punctured, pinched his tender flesh, and ground one bone against the next with every agonizing step.

Still, Good ever springs from Bad, lessons Finn learned as a child in the Crafters Church of Meticulous Care. A man who's lost his right hand can give his extra glove to a man who's lost his left. He who's lost his sight can use his books to build a bed. Even Death itself has lasting benefits—Joy, Peace, Love. Or, if nothing else, a very nice nap . . .

Finn, then, found the excruciating pain in his foot over-whelmed the awesome emanations from the house. Even in the kitchen, where the force from this grim, indomitable machine nearly brought him to his knees, he could tolerate the thing if he kept one foot on the ground.

With desperation as a well-meaning friend, it took Finn little time at all to learn how he might survive in his search for Letitia Louise.

The kitchen was a graveyard of patched, broken, sooty pans and pots. Big pots, little pots, pots of every sort. Kettles made of iron, rusty and red, skillets heavier than lead.

Working with his roll of silver wire, he hurriedly fashioned a garment for the battle to come. The first thing he chose was a thick black kettle for his head. It smelled of Squeen's cooking, but it brought the fierce radiation to a level he could stand.

When he was done, Finn was a kitchen unto himself. Hardly a knight in helm, armor and mail, but one makes do, as they say.

Before he left, he grabbed a collection of knives, some that were reasonably sharp, some that would scarcely cut butter in the sun. A pocketful of candles and a lamp full of fat.

"I'm coming, Letitia," he said to himself. "Don't be frightened when you see me, love, for I look like a peddler hung with his wares . . ."

The dining room was in horrid disarray. Table, chairs, dishes and food were crushed into the floor. Finn felt a chill at the sight. The dark extrusion had clearly had its way with the tableware, then rolled into the hall grinding everything to pulp.

The stairs were still intact, no worse than before. He hesitated, drew a deep breath, then ran up as quickly as he could, knowing what a tremor would do if it should catch him there.

Not much more, I suppose, if it catches me anywhere . . .

The climb took a toll on his foot, but there was little he could do about that. The room where he and Letitia had slept had disappeared. The hallway was full of debris: walls, floors, bits of ratty carpet, everything tattered and shredded.

Through a gap in the wall he saw a familiar path, a way he and Sabatino had come through before.

"What are you up to now?" he said aloud, as if the younger Nucci could hear. "You'd better be minding your affairs and not mine."

Finn gave little credit to Nicoretti's nasty hint. Sabatino was not after Letitia, Finn was sure of that. Still, it wasn't the kind of drivel he liked to hear—

A shadow crossed the darkness just ahead. Finn stood perfectly still. Nothing. Whatever it was, it didn't move again. He took another cautious step . . . Then, with no warning at all, the floor ahead buckled, splintered, and vanished in the darkness far below.

Finn wrapped his arms about a post and held on. The wall shrieked as its timbers twisted out of shape, gave way, and tumbled in the pit that had taken the floor in its maw.

No way forward, then. No way back. Only a small crawlway, a tunnel the machine had yet to touch.

No matter where it leads, there's no place else to go . . .

Dropping very slowly to his knees, he nearly passed out from the pain. His foot didn't much care for the motion, and instantly let him know.

Once down, he was sure he would never move again. The foot was bad enough, without the encumbrance of skillets, pots, kettles and pans.

He made his way slowly, ever aware of the thrumming hum of the frightful machine.

The tunnel opened abruptly into a larger room. Finn inched forward, pushing his lamp ahead. Everything was familiar in a sense. Surely he'd come this way before, or imagined that he did. The wedge of slated roof that nosed out of the floor, the window on the ceiling where a window shouldn't be. Shreds of wallpaper hanging limply from the wall, a shattered bit of doorway that—

"You must be the infamous Master Finn. The one who runs off without a thought for his friends . . ."

"Julia?"

Finn nearly stood, a poor move at best. "Fleas and Bees, where are you, I can't see a thing!"

"That's because there's not a lot to see. Over to your right. You'll have to come here, I can't come to you."

"You don't sound right. What's the matter with your voice?"

"Quite a bit. It's hard to know where to begin."

"I'm not in perfect shape myself. And I did not *run off*, you know perfectly well. That old man was—Great Frogs and Logs, Julia, *what happened to you!*"

Finn stared, shaken beyond belief. Shocked, stunned, surprised that the lizard could still be alive.

"Indeed," Julia said, a shaky rasp to her voice, "I seem to have lost my head. Or, other parts have lost me. Depends on your point of view, I suppose. Finn, you're wearing a lot of pots and pans, but I guess you know that."

Finn didn't answer. He gazed at Julia, bent nearly to the floor, holding the lamp close to the spot where her head had detached itself from the rest. As a master of his craft, he was fascinated, totally enthralled. As Julia's companion and friend, he was also greatly relieved.

"It's clear I'm even better than I thought," he said aloud. "Every wire, every spindle, every node detached on impact as it should. Nothing even tore. I made it that way for maintenance, of course. But I never imagined you'd come through something like this. In essence, you could survive quite nicely as a head."

"Many thanks for the lecture, Dr. Science, now please creep about and find my nether parts. I shouldn't care to be a head alone. Finn, you've got sticks tied to your foot. Part of your costume, I assume."

"We don't have time for talk. We've got to find Letitia, and get her out of here."

"We've got to find *me*," Julia corrected. "*Then* we'll look for Letitia Louise . . ."

Forty-Seven . . .

EVEN WITH A GREAT SHIELD OF SKILLETS, PANS and cooking ware, Finn could feel the power, the draw, the inexorable force of the horrid machine that pulled him ever closer, closer still. Though he refused to give it life, denied it conscious will, he could not but feel the thing had some blind purpose, some dark, unknowing intent.

"It may be, if it sees us," Finn muttered beneath his breath, "it will think us a dread apparition, more frightful than itself . . ."

"I hope *it* sees us," Julia said, "and no one else, no one who knows us well. I couldn't stand the humiliation, Finn, looking like this."

"I doubt we'll meet any neighbors from the Street. I shouldn't think the grocer or the cobbler would ply their wares here."

"It was only a figure of speech, Finn. I've lost my body, but my wit is still intact."

"As much as ever, I assume."

"What, what's that?"

Finn didn't answer. A low arch loomed up ahead, and he had to duck low, an act that played havoc with his knee.

Anyone who saw the pair would likely be appalled, for they were truly a spectacle to see. A limping monster clad in cooking ware. An ogre with a kettle for a top, and, mounted on that, firmly tied in place, a red-eyed lizard head.

Finn had recovered all of Julia's errant parts—torso, legs, a tail bent out of shape, all stuffed into pockets now, for a better time and place.

"You know what I dreamed," Julia said, "while I was there alone in disarray? I dreamed about the sea, about lives I've never lived, about things I've never seen."

"You didn't dream, you imagined that you did."

"Nevertheless, I felt I'd lived a thousand lives, passed a thousand doors, and I'm sure I know why—though the answer's as amazing as the story is itself.

"I am made of precious gems from the corners of the world. Gems, copper, silver, iron and gold, elements of the earth. It is not just humans and Newlies who remember things, Finn. *Everything* does, though I doubt you'd credit that.

"Every garnet, every onyx, every flake of gold, each has a tale, what they've done and where they've been. Now, all their stories, all their ventures, come together in me. All has been revealed in my dreams. Is that not a marvel, Finn, is it not a wondrous thing?"

"No, but if it makes you happy, believe what you will."

"Why do I bother, why do I expose myself to your abuse? Why do I speak to you at all?"

"Because we are friends, Julia, companions of a sort. And because my pockets are full of all your parts."

"I'll buy the second half," said Julia Jessica Slagg. "I'm unsure about the rest, the part about companions and friends . . ."

"Hush, be silent," Finn said, pressing his back against the wall, standing perfectly still. "I'll give you something to be sure of, down the hallway there."

Julia saw them at once, their forms distorted shadows from the fiery torches they waved about.

"Foxers," Finn said, and added an oath after that. "Damn fools, that's no way to light a place like this, they'll burn the thing down!"

"What on earth are they doing in here, I'd like to know that."

"I know what they're doing," Finn said. "They've come to settle with the Nuccis. I can only guess why."

A flimsy guess at best, and that from a shade who isn't sure if tomorrow is today . . .

Indeed, Foxers had vanished at a time, though the Coldie named Klunn wasn't sure exactly when. Were the odds good or bad that the Nuccis had a hand in that?

"They're gone," Julia said. "My uncanny senses tell me they're heading down."

"Of course they are. Everyone's headed down, that's where this horrid device would have us be."

"They wore no pots or pans. I'm sure you noticed that."

"I did, indeed. They're not affected, then. I couldn't say why, except they're not the same as me . . ."

He staggered, then, with a shudder, a shiver, a chill at the back of his neck. A moan, a cry, from somewhere near, so faint he could scarcely hear.

"There," Julia said at once, "I see her, Finn. Right there!"

Finn was already on his knees, all his pains forgotten as he drew Letitia up into his arms. So light she was, barely there at all. He knew there would never come a day when he'd not see her lying there, hands clasped tight against her ears, dark eyes glazed with fear.

"Letitia. Letitia Louise . . ."

He knew, though, she was hardly aware, stupefied by the dread emanations that had caught and held her there.

What if it's too late now, what if her mind is empty, drained of all she's been . . . ?

He cast the thought aside, refused to let it in. Instead, he loosed an iron pot from his armor, one without a great dent, and fit it carefully on her head, tying it with wire beneath her chin. It couldn't hurt, and might very well help.

He had her now, had them both again, and wouldn't let them go. One was in pieces, one was scarcely whole, but anything broken, Finn believed, could be fixed, patched up, made to work again . . .

"Finn, wait, you don't want to go there," Julia said.

"No, and why is that?"

"That's the way the Foxers went. We'd best not run into them again."

"You weren't listening, were you?" Finn said. "You really ought to try. There's only one way—that foul device has made certain of that . . ."

Forty-Eight . . .

"I DREAMED, FINN. I'VE NEVER HAD SUCH A WON-derful, frightful dream. I thought I was only me, then I saw I was everything that was, everything that could possibly ever be.

"I looked through a million eyes, saw a million lives. I al-most saw the poor thing I'd been before. That's when the dream wasn't good anymore, it got awful after that. I didn't want to know, I didn't want to be that again . . ."

"Everyone's having dreams, it seems. I never cared for them myself. They were either so good I didn't want to wake up, or so bad I thought I never would."

"Thank you for finding me, love. I think I was gone an awfully long time."

"Much too long, Letitia. Any time at all is too long for me."

"I think I'll try and sleep some more."

"I think that's a bad idea. I'd rather you'd stay awake, dear."

It was too late, though, she was gone once again.

⟡

Finn was relieved that she'd come to her senses, but not at all sure she was wholly herself, that something wasn't missing somewhere. Time, he was certain, would chase any frights from her head. He vowed he would hold onto that.

The way was most confusing now. Either that, or the howl and the clatter of the horrid device had loosened every nerve in his head. Right seemed left, and left seemed right. Letitia had been light at the start, but she was quite heavy now. That, and his foot, and the kettles and skillets that constantly weighed him down . . .

Sometimes he was certain he'd gone to sleep himself, but Julia seemed to squawk if he tried to nod off. *How could she manage such a feat?* he asked himself. *She couldn't see him from her perch, and her senses weren't as fine as that . . .*

"Damn it all, Finn, watch where you're about. You're as loud as that miserable device."

Finn jerked awake at once. "Sab—Sabatino! What are you doing here?"

"Please, craftsman, not the obvious. What is *anyone* doing here? Ah, you found the lady, I see. I'm so glad, I was most distressed. Heavens, what happened to your lizard?"

"What I'm doing, dear fellow, since you feel you have to ask, is trying to get *down* to that thing. These pesky Foxers keep getting in the way. They're thick as flies, you see.

"Ah, watch your step here," he said, brandishing his blade. "I've caught one or two, possibly three."

"I'd say three's correct," Finn said, holding his lantern up high. Three dark figures slumped in untidy lumps against the wall.

"Clearly, the Foxers know you're here. If they're as many as you say . . ."

"Doesn't matter, I have to go. Father's down there, I'm sure. He and I have to settle things, once and for all."

Finn didn't like the sound of that.

Then, down the narrow hallway, past some forgotten wall, the thunder and the rumble, the howl and the shiver of the awful device shook the ancient house. Finn felt that if he didn't hold on, he'd be quickly swept away.

"Dr. Nicoretti told me about your mother. I'm sorry she passed away."

Sabatino looked annoyed. "This is ill-timed, Finn. And you're a bit late with your concern, which is none of your business, anyway. Uncle has a very big mouth."

"Why do you think the Foxers are here? What did the Nuccis do, what happened in the past?"

"What happens," Sabatino said, his eyes dark with anger in the dim lamplight, "if I stick you in the belly right here? Who'd ever know, and who'd ever care?"

"Me, for one. You, for another. If I'm not here, you'll have to take the Foxers on yourself."

Sabatino looked delighted. He hadn't thought of that.

"Let's get at it then, brother in arms. Can the pretty stand by herself, or will you carry her into combat?"

"I can stand just fine," Letitia said, possibly awake for some time. "And don't call me a *pretty*, that's not all I am."

"My pardon, then," Sabatino said with a bow. "I am in your debt, ma'am."

"You're in the soup, both of you," Julia said with a screech and a howl, "if you don't take heed right now!"

The Foxers were on them then as quickly as that, making odd little sounds, little coughs, little hacks, waving their blades about. And, Finn noted, wearing their silly black masks, so no one could guess just who they might be . . .

Forty-Nine . . .

SABATINO GAVE A CRY AND LUNGED INTO THE
fray. Finn, hampered by his armor and the need to set Letitia down, was a second too late, a second too slow. Before he
could act, he took a hard blow atop his head.

The kettle rang like a bell, rending him deaf and scrambling what little there was left of his wits. The Foxer, nearly
as stunned as Finn, stared at this strange apparition that
had nearly dented his blade.

Finn felled him with a skillet, took the fellow's sword,
and tossed away his kitchenware.

"That lout missed me by a hair," Julia squawked, "could
you watch it down there?"

"If you don't like it, you can walk."

"Fine way to treat a warrior, wounded in the field . . ."

Finn turned a plucky Foxer aside, sending him sprawling to the floor. Booted one soundly down the hall. Another
popped up to take his place, then another, and another after
that.

They came now in a horde, in a throng, in a rabble, in a

swarm. As quickly as he put one down, a comrade took his place.

"Back! Back!" Sabatino shouted beside him. "We can't hold them, Finn!"

A glance told Finn the fellow was right. The narrow passage was full of Foxers struggling to get at their foes. He grabbed Letitia, pushed her behind him, fended off a Foxer again.

"Stay behind me," Sabatino said, "we've the advantage now, the louts don't have room to fight."

"They'll give up soon, I'll bet."

"No time for foolery now, this is somewhat serious, Finn."

With that, Sabatino lashed out, ripping a Foxer from gullet to chin. Finn saw he'd found a blade himself, and was making it count.

Thrust, parry, kick and collide. One down, but another at his side.

"I'm thankful we have the advantage," he said, "or they'd have our lovely hides . . ."

"Finn! Watch your step!"

Finn turned half about and nearly fell. The hall ahead had crumbled, leaving a ragged maw, a gaping hole full of broken brick and stone, choked with dusty air.

And, with a horror and a chill, he saw the way led down, down steep and narrow stairs, and knew at once, even before Letitia screamed, he was in the machine's dark and deadly lair again.

"I can't," Letitia cried, *"I can't go down there!"*

"We have to," he shouted over the awful din, "stay close to me, and keep your kettle on."

Down, then, Foxers slashing affront, the howling maelstrom below, a rumble, a throb, a dread palpitation that ripped into the very soul.

It was all Finn could do to fight off the foe and keep Letitia in hand, for the thing down there had her firmly in its grasp. She fought, thrashed, lashed out to break free, no longer in control of her will.

It was as Finn had feared—from the moment she'd stepped into that dread abode before, he knew the thing had taken some hold upon his love . . . now, it was determined to take her down, have her as its own.

You won't, though, damn you, not while there's a breath of life in me . . .

Still, she struck out blindly, kicked, clawed, hammered with her fists. She was not his Letitia but a wild and frightened creature, senses all adrift, reason gone astray, a stranger he scarcely knew.

Then, as the Foxers spilled down the darkened stairs, driving their foes ever back, back under hopeless, impossible odds, Finn, over his shoulder, saw the twisting passage give way to the horrid den itself, into the storm, into the din of the hellish scene below . . .

The Foxers saw it too, saw, in the midst of the fury and the deafening swell, the beast, the wretch, the one whose blood they thirsted for. At the sight they loosed a terrible cry, an awesome surge of rage, frenzy, hatred so strong it seemed a near visible thing that fouled the very air.

And in that very moment, in the echo of the Foxers' savage wail, Finn heard a cry of such sorrow, anger and regret, he could scarcely believe it came from Sabatino himself.

Holding fast to Letitia, he followed the fellow's gaze, and saw the brunt of the Foxers' ire, a mad, pitiful thing, shorn of his senses, a man with an empty, witless smile. Calabus, naked as a babe, sat amidst his gold array of nozzles, spigots, founts and tubes and spouts, clever little mouths that spat endless whorls of wisdom, secrets of tomorrow, visions of the future that only he could comprehend . . . sat there in a stupor, in a daze of childish wonder as the ribbons and the strips, as the ceaseless tongues of paper tried to drown him in their coils . . .

"Get your lady out," Sabatino shouted, slicing another Foxer to the floor. "I'll get Father and hold them off here!"

"You can't," Finn said, "there's too many of them, you'll never make it through."

Sabatino showed him a curious, slightly puzzled frown.

"Damn it, craftsman, the old fart's family. What else can I do?"

Before Finn could answer, Sabatino was gone, jumping into the fracas, leaping amidst the brawl. In an instant, he was swallowed up in Foxers, lost from sight.

"Letitia, *look* at me," Finn said, shaking her roughly, gripping her tight. "You've got to stop this, I cannot do everything at once. Come to your senses, dear, or I fear we're both lost."

Letitia's answer was a foolish stare, a look that chilled him to the bone, for he'd seen the same hollow, empty gaze in Calabus' eyes.

He clutched her wrist and jerked her along, turning back to the stairs. The Foxers were busy with Sabatino, and there might be a chance, a slim one at best, that he could slip by them and get her to safety, come back and help . . .

The Foxer came out of nowhere, leaping out of shadow into light. Finn met his blade with a shock that numbed all feeling in his arm.

The foe came at him furiously, one wicked blow after another, driving Finn back. He knew he couldn't hold the fellow off, not with one hand, knew he couldn't let Letitia go, knew if he didn't they were both as good as dead.

Fate, then, as Fate is wont to do, solved the problem then and there as the Foxer's companion leaped in to help his friend . . .

Fifty . . .

THERE WAS NO DECISION NOW, NO CHOICE TO make. He let Letitia go, clutched his blade with both hands, swept it in a quick and deadly arc at the fellow coming on his right.

The Foxer looked stunned, grabbed his throat and tumbled to the floor. Finn knew he'd done his best, done what he could, and knew if he took one out, the other would surely bring him down. He stepped back, stumbled, felt the blade strike, felt it bite into his splint.

Finn had seldom known such agony in his life. His weapon was lost, but he didn't greatly care, for Letitia was gone, out of his sight. Through a veil of awful pain, he gazed up at his foe, saw the Foxer grin, saw him raise his sword for the final deadly blow—

—closed his eyes, opened them again to an unearthly howl, saw the Foxer stagger, saw him reel, saw blood begin to spout, saw, in a wonder, a deadly, disembodied head. Saw, an instant after that, a blade thrust through the Foxer's back and out his chest.

The Foxer collapsed. Sabatino drew out his sword, bent down and tore Julia loose from the grisly remains of a nose.

"I believe this is yours," Sabatino said, holding the lizard well away, tossing it to Finn. "I'd clean it up if I were you. Can you stand? Where'd the pretty go?"

Sabatino looked weary, bloodied, somewhat out of sorts. Finn dropped Julia's head in his pocket, along with her other parts. Julia rattled and complained, snapping at empty air.

"Thanks for your help," Finn said, "I'm busy right now. I don't know where she is, she's gone. I've got to find her. Sabatino? Can you give me a hand? Your father, did he make it all right?"

"I'm afraid not. Couldn't get to him. Bastards already did him in."

"What did they—"

"You don't want to know. Father was mean at heart, crazy as a goose. But no one deserves a fate as cruel as that."

"I'm sorry for your loss. If you could help me to my feet . . ."

Sabatino shook his head. "If she ran back there, friend, I fear she's a goner as well. We'd never get her out. Best we try and save ourselves. I doubt we can even handle that."

"I guess you didn't hear. I'm not leaving without Letitia Louise."

"Ah, you're serious, I presume. Let's get you up, then. Won't do a bit of good, but I suppose we could try."

Finn gave him a long and thoughtful look. "I feel I should be straight with you. There's no reason you have to go too. You won't win favor with me, don't think you will. I despise you for an arrogant lout, and a liar to boot. Nothing you can do to change that."

"One thing you forget," Sabatino said, with a nasty grin. "If you don't happen to make it out, craftsman, I win the lovely prize . . ."

Fifty-One . . .

MERELY STANDING NEAR THE DREAD MACHINE WAS enough to fry a brave man's soul. Ducking through the clang and the clatter of that terrible maze, fighting the shriek and the throb and the clamor that howled through his head was a hundred-fold worse than Finn had imagined only moments before.

Madness waited there in the hot, churning bowels of the thing, a thing that had likely drained his love, stripped her of her reason, sucked her mind dry.

Hold on, Letitia, wherever you are . . . I'm coming for you, dear . . .

One instant Sabatino was beside him, the next he was gone. The Foxers were nowhere in sight. Perhaps they'd sated their fury on the hapless old man, Finn thought. Or maybe they were smart enough not to go near the thing at all.

Once more he squeezed through the vile convolution of fat, distended coils, countless tunnels of soiled and sullied glass, foul viscera that wound their way through the tangle, through the snarl of the device.

And, as ever, through the filth and the splatter, there was something almost heard, something almost seen, a blur of dark motion rushing swiftly about within.

"Letitia!"

"Sabatino!"

A hopeless cry, his voice all but lost in the din.

Finn made his way through shuttering cogs and wheezing gears, through the tremble and the quaver and the roar, the awesome emanations shrieking through his head.

Unsteady on his feet, he nearly stumbled again, caught himself, and—

—there and then it struck, hit him like a great enormous fist, a wall that wasn't there, a wall he couldn't see.

He shook himself, dazed, dazzled, stupefied. The machine was still there, but there was something else as well, something vaguely sketched, like a shimmer, like a veil, like a thousand panes of crystal that shimmered in impossible light.

The sight made him queasy, made him want to retch. The rapid oscillation numbed his sense of balance, his sense of far and near. Finn took a step, and UP swept him over, DOWN jerked him back to his right and to his left, turning him in directions he'd never seen before.

He shouted, flailed about, but no words came out. He was spinning, whirling like a top, but he couldn't move a bit. A face he'd never seen before loomed up at him, grinned and disappeared. Another, and another after that, one face atop the next moving so incredibly fast they seemed to be made of molten wax.

The faces vanished.

Finn vanished as well . . .

He stood on a flat, endless plain, as great shaggy beasts plodded by under a broiling sun that dropped into the bloody sea as the mighty vessel died, spewing gouts of flame, flame that reflected in the woman's chocolate eyes as the silver craft whined overhead, as the stars swept by in a spidery veil, a veil of deadly smoke that ate the soldier's eyes, eyes that looked out on a flat, endless plain as great shaggy beasts plodded by under a broiling sun, as the mighty vessel vanished, spewing gouts of Sabatino everywhere . . .

"You're coming apart," Finn cried out in alarm, "you're just—going everywhere!"

Sabatino was gone, lost in a blink. Finn saw him dash through a bright crystal pane, followed him over a flat, end-less—

Finn?

FINN?

PLEASE
Help
ME

FINN . . . !

"Letitia? Letitia Louise!"

"Who do you think," Julia said, *"how many people do you know in this place?"*

"Shut up, I'm trying to think."

"Don't waste your time. It's not allowed here."

"You don't know, you don't know where here is."

"Here is where you are. Here is where you're going, here is where you've been."

"That's all I need, lizard philosophy talk. And what are you doing up there? You're in my pocket with the rest of your parts."

Julia walked on nothing, upside down. Turning shades of amber, saffron and a horrid tone of green.

"Stop that, you're making me ill."

"Stop what?"

"Whatever you're doing, don't do it again."

"Whatever or when? I can't do both at one time."

FINN . . .

FINN . . .

PLEASE,

FINN!

"Letitia, over here!"

"Let's not start that again," Julia said, wherever she was, wherever she'd been.

"I'm coming," Finn said, "I'll be right with you, dear . . ."

Letitia's scream shattered all the crystal panes, splintered every *when*, shredded every *where*, and suddenly she was there, or maybe not at all, maybe a vapor or a wisp, and all about her a pale luminescence, a nimbus of light.

Sometimes she flickered and was gone, less than a whisper, less than a fleeting breath of air.

"I can't see you well, love," Finn said. "I'm not certain that you're there."

"I might be, I can't really tell. I'm frightened, Finn, I'm really awfully scared."

"Tell me what to do, tell me where you are."

"I do love you, Finn."

"And I love you as well. I'll get you out of there."

"I don't think so, I don't think you can."

"Don't say that, listen to me, I *will*."

"Finn, something awful's happening, something's happening to me."

"No, this isn't real, this is an illusion, it's magic, is what it is—"

"It's happening. It's happening inside—it's happening now."

"Letitia, stop this, please, this kind of talk won't do us any—"

A moan, a wail, a sad lamentation, a grievous sound that rose into a shriek, into a cry of unbearable pain.

Finn stared in horror, in awesome disbelief as something moved in Letitia, something twisted, something seethed. Something crackled, sizzled, and burst into sight.

Finn shrank back, raised an arm against the blistering heat that surged from his love, not his love at all, but the creature she'd become, a grim apparition that wailed, shouted out his name, stared out at nothing with black and fiery eyes.

And, from this dark, charred cremation, this beauty with slender limbs and ashen hair, burst a nightmare from beyond nature's realm, from a place devoid of light. They spilled from her belly, from the fire that burned within, this foul and hungry blight, this hideous plague, lurching blindly all about.

Finn stood frozen in fright. The terrible horde kept coming, but Letitia Louise began to fade, began to waver out of sight, scarcely a shadow now, scarcely a wisp, as the magic of the horrid machine began to steal away her life . . .

Tears scalded Finn's cheeks as he cursed every dark incantation, every wizard, every witch, every hex and every spell. For magic was his ruination, magic had snatched away the only thing he loved, the being that made him whole, made his life worthwhile. Damned sorcerers and seers, damned—

"*Letitia! Letitia Louise!*"

It struck him then, like a quake, like a bolt that splits a mighty tree.

"The amulet—the amulet, Letitia! Grab it, hold it, squeeze it in your hand, whatever the hell you do with such a thing!"

She was gone though, vanished, nothing left to see.

"Come back," he shouted. "None of it's real, it's magic, it's a spell. Ah, I take that back. The amulet part, that's real, all right? The rest of it's a trick, you don't have to go, you don't have to disappear!"

Nothing.

Nothing but the wheres, nothing but the whens.

A shimmer, then a glow, a flicker, a dim and phantom light. He saw her. She was there, lying quietly, curled in a ball, the way she slept at night.

His heart leaped at the sight. She was still very frail, no more substantial than fireflies winking in the night, but what could you expect? The seer's charm was clearly working well, but these things took a while. He'd wait, give it time, not even try to go to her, to hold her, till then . . .

"I'm afraid this is as good as it gets, craftsman. Bloody rules everywhere, you know."

"What?" Finn started. Sabatino stood just beyond Letitia, a wraith, a phantom himself, better than a Coldie, but not a great deal.

"What do you mean? She's all right now, she'll be just fine."

"She will, Finn, but not with you, I fear. We can't come there, you can't come over here."

"Don't try your tricks on me, I can go anywhere I—"

Not a step, not an inch, no closer than a hair.

Sabatino showed him a wispy smile. "I shall be glad to take care of her, trust me on that. Wherever we are, though I'm not at all certain of that. We're comrades, you know. Brothers in arms."

"No, we're not. Let her go, Sabatino, she doesn't belong to you!"

"No one belongs to anyone, Finn. We are, in the end, whoever we are. Ourselves all alone. Even a liar and a rogue knows that."

"Oh, fine. Words of wisdom from a Nucci. I've heard it all now."

"Sometimes I even surprise myself," Sabatino said.

He bent then, raising Letitia's limp figure in his arms, both of them sheer, gossamer thin, perfectly clear.

"Put her down," Finn demanded. "You can't do this, I won't allow it, you hear?"

"I don't know how it happened, I haven't the foggiest, Finn. But I do have the pleasure of besting you, though I can't take credit, I fear. Oh, if you can, I'd advise you to get out of here. I feel this illusion is rather shaky. I doubt it's going to last."

"Damn you, Sabatino—"

"It could happen, I'll grant you that."

"Get your *hands* off me, right now. I can't feel a thing, but if you touch me, you'll wish you were dead, or possibly alive!"

Sabatino's shade looked startled. Letitia began to pound upon his chest, which did little harm to flesh that wasn't there. Still, he looked annoyed, greatly alarmed.

"Is this how you intend to act? Can I expect behavior like this?"

"You haven't *seen* behavior, you odorous brute. This is just a start."

Sabatino sighed, walked a few steps across nothing, and laid Letitia gently on the ground.

"All right," he said, "I lied. She doesn't truly belong over here. Apparently, for some damned reason, I do."

He backed off, and looked at the two. "Sorry we couldn't have our duel. I was so looking forward to that. You're a miserable person, craftsman, a low-born fellow, no trace of a gentleman about you, nothing proper that I can ferret out . . ."

Perhaps there was more. Finn was sure the fellow could go for quite a while, but he was gone now, not a trace at all.

Finn bent to Letitia to tell her that he loved her, to tell her he was sorry their vacation had not been pleasant so far. Before he could speak, the illusion shattered, and the horrid machine was everywhere, wheezing and chugging, dead Foxers all about.

"You bessst bes comin' with me, getting yourselvesss out of here. Isss bad place to bes . . ."

"Squeen?" Finn glanced up in surprise. "Where have you been? I assumed you'd perished. I was certain everyone was dead."

Squeen William showed him a twisted Vampie smile. "Squeen isss not bes dead, sir. Dead is perssssons in here. Squeen is not stupids, Squeen bes staying outsssside . . ."

Fifty-Two . . .

THE SEA LOOKED GRAND, A BRIGHT, AZURE BLUE
that mirrored the cloudless sky. The ship, a lean square-
rigger, had braved a summer squall the night before. Now
she lay in the calm of the harbor, her sails hung out to dry.
Her name was *Anna Call*, rather catchy, Finn thought, the
sort of thing you'd call a ship as trim and neat as that.

There was not a single Yowlie in her crew and her
captain seemed reasonably sane, or as sane as a captain
might be.

Finn had sent Letitia aboard as quickly as he could, anxious to get her far from that misbegotten shore. Julia was
with her, patched, mended, somewhat out of sorts until
Finn could get her home among his proper tools. Not the
beauty she had been, as far as lizards go, but her temper
and her tongue seemed perfectly intact.

"I regret you've not seen the best of our land in your stay,"
Dr. Nicoretti said. "I fear you'll take a poor impression
back home, and encourage others to stay away."

"With all due respect," Finn told him, "I doubt I'll discuss my trip at all."

"Don't guess I can blame you for that. This has been a most upsetting time for everyone, and you and the Newlie, I suppose, have suffered more than most."

Finn saw no way to respond in a civilized manner, no way at all short of physical assault.

He looked past the doctor, past the wharf itself, empty now, except for a seabird pecking about. The town looked as dismal as ever. Between the sea and the village, there was scarcely anyone around. In a field of dead grass, the Crimson Lancers Volunteers (still with no lances in sight) attempted to form a straight line. Past them, down the dirt road, he imagined he could see a faint smudge, a darkening of the land where the ghastly charred remains of the Nuccis' former home would be.

"I should tell you things before you leave," Dr. Nicoretti said. "Though you haven't been open with me, I see no reason to sink to your level, there's little honor in that. In truth, I did have some interaction with the Foxers. I told you I didn't, but I did."

"I suspected as much," Finn said. "I told you so at the time."

"Well, I did, and I don't apologize, for I did the right thing."

"I'm afraid to ask."

"I merely told them—not long before you came, as a fact—I told them that the Nuccis were responsible for the abduction and murder of many of their kind. Abductions which happened after my sister Ingretta married Calabus and moved into that dreadful house."

"You told them that," Finn said, showing the man a wary look, "and you know that for a fact?"

"Not really, no, but I think it's likely so."

"You *think?*"

"Yes, I surely do. When you think about it, it makes a lot of sense. Ingretta had friends among the Foxers, below her class, of course. When she came into wealth as the bride of Calabus, she often hired Foxers to work around the house. Retainers, gardeners, house maids and such. Calabus and his father couldn't abide the lot. They cut Ingretta off from everyone. They would not allow her to have any friends, servants or not. That included me, her brother, of course."

"And you think the Nuccis killed them. That's why the Foxers took their revenge."

"Oh yes, I'm sure it is."

"This is why they killed the old man and burned his house down."

"I believe it is, yes."

"And why did they wait all these years, Doctor, to get around to that? What took them so long?"

"I can't imagine why."

"I can," Finn said. "They didn't *know* about it till you put the idea in their heads."

"Ridiculous." Nicoretti made a face. "Everyone in town knew the Nuccis and the Foxers were at odds. You'll find a lot of folks think the same as me."

"Rocks and Socks, you think—you believe, but you don't know if any of this is true."

"It very likely is."

"But you don't *know* that. The Nuccis are dead because you *guess* they maybe did the Foxers in. Sometime. Long ago. Or maybe not. And, a great many Foxers are dead now too."

Nicoretti muttered under his breath. "You don't mind asking me a lot, but you won't give anything back. You never said what Calabus was up to down there. I've got a right to know that."

"I don't see you do at all."

"Damn you, boy—"

"Clocks."

"What's that?"

"Clocks. Your brother-in-law was making clocks. Small, delicately crafted clocks. Clocks impossibly intricate and fine. Clocks smaller than a mustard seed, smaller than a gnat. Finally, clocks no larger than a mote, a dot, no larger than a speck. This is the obsession that finally drove him mad—or madder than he might have been before. There came a time when he couldn't even *see* his clocks. He'd breathe and they were gone. Sent him over the edge, poor man."

Nicoretti looked slightly annoyed. "A bunch of little clocks made all that racket up there, sent awesome tremors through the ground?"

"They were little, sure, but there were a hell of a lot of them, I think I mentioned that."

Nicoretti showed Finn an arrogant grin, a sly and cunning old man grin, a grin full of old man guile.

"I'll get a straight answer, boy, but it won't come from you. I don't expect manners from one of your kind. Have a nice trip, Master Finn. And give that pretty a feel for me."

"You'd best quit right there," Finn said, "while you're barely still ahead . . ."

At the end of the wharf where the skiff and the loaders and the other small craft came in, Finn found a Bullie and a cart. On the cart was a most familiar chair. Standing by the cart was Master of Chairs, Dalto Frick.

"You bought a chair," Frick said, "now take it out of here."

"No thank you," Finn said, "I don't need a chair."

"You *bought* a chair, mister. Why'd you buy it if you don't need a chair?"

"It seemed like a good idea at the time. Have a pleasant day, I've got to run now."

"Damn tourist," Frick shouted after Finn. "You don't know the rules here, you don't know the customs of the land!"

"I can't argue with that," Finn said to no one at all, picked up his pace, and hurried to the skiff.

"It's a beautiful evening," Letitia said. "I never imagined I'd be so happy to be on a ship again. Still, I hope I never see another after this."

"You don't feel bad, about missing Antoline Isle?"

"You know better than that," she said, coming close under his arm, resting her head on his chest. "I don't want to go anywhere but home."

Finn breathed in the salt air, squinted at a weary amber sun dropping behind a purple cloud.

"I don't know if I can talk about this," Letitia said, "but if I don't, I'm sure I'll never get a night's sleep again."

"You know about as much as I. There's little more to tell."

"There is, too. I don't recall a thing, except getting lost from you and waking up outside with an awful pain in my head."

"It's just as I told you," Finn said, looking anywhere but in Letitia's eyes. "The Foxers killed Calabus and set the house afire. I doubt we'll ever truly know why. I'll tell you what Nicoretti said, once I've thought about it some. Sabatino didn't make it either. We talked about that."

Letitia shuddered, but not from the pleasant night air.

"I don't know why, but I feel sorry for the man. I don't

think he could help it, being what he was. I think we all maybe have to be what we are, don't you?"

Finn didn't answer. He didn't care to get into such a thing at the time.

"I think I saw that awful old man standing on the roof. I think he held Calabus in his arms. I think they were both on fire. Could that be, Finn?"

"Why, I guess," Finn said, "anything could be . . ."

"Finn, look right at me." She drew away a bit and searched his eyes. "There's more you've got to tell. Don't try and protect me, dear, that doesn't help at all."

Finn let out a breath. "No, I guess it doesn't. Someone else perhaps, but not you. Both of us nearly died in there, but not how you think, Letitia. This is hard to fathom, which is why I didn't want to tell you now. I didn't believe in Calabus' Prophecy Machine. I didn't, but things—happened down there. Sabatino didn't die. He left, but he wasn't exactly dead."

Finn paused, trying to get the words right. "I said this was hard to credit, and it is. Sabatino got caught up in something down there. Something, in that device, that twisted Time inside out. I believe he went into the past, I think he made a great fortune with his knowledge of the future, and returned to Makasar. He built the Nucci house. He married, or got someone with child. That child was Calabus . . ."

"What?" Letitia's eyes went wide. "Finn, you can't mean what I think you mean. You've got the names wrong."

"I do mean it, though, as wondrous as it seems. Sabatino was the Grandfather too, dear. It was he who invented the machine, not his son. Or maybe he *remembered* it somehow, from the past. But if he did, where's the start of the thing, does it have a beginning or not? I don't want to think about that.

"At any rate, I feel he was mad, nearly from the start. I

think it likely that the cruel dilation of Time has an undesirable effect on the mind.

"Did he know what had happened to him? Did he know who he'd been, what he'd become? Perhaps, but I think not for long. I think the shock of falling through the years brought on the madness at once.

"I believe the seer told me true, Letitia, as far as she could know. There was indeed a spell that protected that horrid device. Only, she couldn't understand it wasn't a sorcerer's spell at all. The *spell* was the great distortion of Time itself, an awesome bit of magic for sure, but one we never dreamed of before."

"Finn . . ." Letitia closed her eyes and frowned. "What you say just couldn't be. Sabatino and the old man—his grandfather—they were both *here*. How could—how could two of the same person be in the same place at one time?"

"How can magic be? How can you and I, and everything on earth, possibly exist? I don't pretend to know the logic or the reason, what kind of *rules* Time follows, if it follows any at all. But I *saw* the men together. I made no connection at the time, of course, but, Letitia—they were the same.

"I know this is so, but I can't explain why. I'm a maker of lizards. I'm not a magician, and I don't wish to travel through Time. As a fact, I wholly agree with you. I don't wish to go anywhere at all. Are you coming down, now? You need to get all the rest you can."

"In a while, love. I want to watch the sea. I doubt that I can sleep with all this in my head . . ."

"You told her that, but nothing more, then. I hope she'll be satisfied. Letitia has a curiosity that's most unnerving at times."

"Why wouldn't she?" Finn said. "What could be more awesome than what she knows now?"

He sat in the dimly lit cabin watching an ill-formed lizard perched atop his bunk. He tried not to look too hard, for she knew her condition, and resented any glance at all.

"She remembers nothing, and I pray she never does. I would do most anything to keep that horror from coming to mind again. This is a truth Letitia must never see. I saw it happen with my eyes, or I surely wouldn't credit it myself.

"When Letitia was caught in the grip of Time, it wrenched her back to what she'd been, split every spark, every nit, every cosmic mite that makes us what we are. Shattered her into a horde of those creatures and tossed them to the winds of Time."

"The same winds, I gather, that caught Sabatino as well."

Finn shook his head. "I don't know that. I can't say when or how the myce appeared. But they were there in the house Sabatino built. Did his transition bring them there? I don't suppose they have to wait in the hall, so to speak, until the proper *time*, which isn't even there.

"All I can say is that Sabatino, in his madness, invented, created, conjured up the Prophecy Machine. Because his other self remembered it was there—or because some fixed, rigid rule of the cosmos says it happens, so it does?

"What's clear is he used those poor, primal creatures, used their hunger perhaps, and their fear, to race about their wild and twisting paths, to drive the gears and wheels of that horrid thing, to tap some incredible force that spews out an endless, ceaseless record of the future, the past, every day gone, and all that's to come. One that, doubtless, even a madman cannot understand.

"And that, Julia, is a thing Letitia must never, ever know. I only hope her dreams will treat her kindly, and leave her nights in peace."

"All will be well, I'm sure," said Julia Jessica Slagg. "Letitia is stronger than you think, and wiser, too. She puts up with you, we must consider that."

"Thanks for the encouragement and help. I am greatly relieved now."

"I will be greatly relieved when I'm put together right again. When do you imagine that will be?"

"There are two factors here. One has to do with the time it takes this vessel to wend us home. The second, the greater factor, depends upon a remarkable transition, a breakthrough, a true conversion as it were, a change in attitude. Dwell upon that, if you will . . ."

He watched her awhile before he moved to join her, watched her standing at the rail, the wind pressing strands of ashen hair against her cheek.

While he watched, he thought of many things. He thought about **TAVERN** and **BAR**, he thought about Bowsers and the Dobbin he'd met, and how he wished they'd had a chance to speak.

He thought about the seer, and wished, for an instant, he had seen her in the light, though dreams imagined were often better in the dark. She could never be as lovely as Letitia, he told himself at once, that was surely not the point. But Mycer ladies ever touched his heart.

He wondered if Squeen would find work somewhere, and wished him well. He had to fare better this time. How could he do any worse?

He wondered, then, if Captain Pynch would return to Ulster-East. If they might meet again on Garpenny Street, when the Coldtown shades came about.

One thing he knew and understood well: he didn't need an invention of any sort to tell him where his future lay. His future, just then, turned from the rail and showed him a gentle smile.

"Besides my understanding of love, and what it's all about," he said to himself, "I know mixing spells with a noisome device is a foolish thing at best. I know, from the frightful venture just past, that magic is one thing, and machinery is ever something else . . ."

About the Author

NEAL BARRETT JR.'S NOVELS AND SHORT
stories span the field from mystery/suspense, fan-
tasy, science fiction, and historical to mainstream fiction. He has been nominated for both the Nebula
and Hugo awards. He has received a Western Writ-
ers of America award and the Theodore Sturgeon
Memorial Award.

The Washington Post called his novel, The Here-
after Gang, "one of the great American novels."
His current work includes a collection of short
stories, Perpetuity Blues. His new novel, Interstate
Dreams, received an award from the Texas Institute
of Letters.

The Prophecy Machine will be followed by another novel featuring Finn, the Lizard Maker, also to
be published by Bantam.